Sap & Secrets

The Maplewood Series

Book 1

Daphne Elliot

Melody Publishing, LLC

Published by Melody Publishing, LLC

Editing by Beth Lawton at VB Edits

Cover Design by Jenny Richardson at Classy Creeps

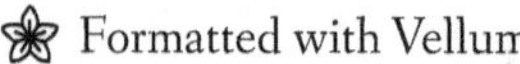 Formatted with Vellum

For the girls who say "I got this" even when they don't - and still figure it out anyway."

Prologue

JASPER

Chaos.

Pure chaos. The intense crush of bodies on the sidewalk made it difficult to even walk through town.

The April air was freezing, but not a soul cared. This was the event the whole town came out for. The Maple Festival. It was the motivation needed to get us all out of our homes after six months of winter, and the festival usually brought with it our first wave of tourists.

America's most charming small town could not survive without those tourist dollars, and since childhood, I'd been conditioned to smile and provide directions for all manner of folks here to visit.

The shopkeepers had been sprucing their places up all week. The daffodils and tulips had just popped out of the ground in the town square, and the massive tents had been set up, the sugar shack tours had been scheduled, and all the artisans had their booths ready to go.

It was the busiest time of year for me. Not only was I needed on the farm to help with tapping trees, changing and cleaning lines, and delivering sap around the clock, but it was all hands on deck at my day job too.

Space heaters plus artisanal alpaca sweaters usually resulted in a few small fires. And out-of-towners would slide off the icy roads. There were emergencies galore. Chief had us working our max number of hours each week. Thankfully, the department was well funded and had a year-round crew in addition to volunteers. But as one of only three licensed paramedics in the vicinity, I'd worked almost nonstop for weeks.

I was bone tired, frozen, and questioning why we cared so much about sticky shit that leaked from trees when the first scream rang out.

If the schedule Mayor Harding had emailed to every citizen of Maplewood was correct, it was time to open the first barrel of syrup. It was technically last year's sap, but it had been boiled and processed for this occasion. My family had been providing the sap for the annual ceremonial barrel for several generations, something my brother Josh took a great deal of pride in.

It was so like him, to care about that stuff.

I was built different. Sure, I enjoyed the farm and trees, and I could appreciate the family legacy, but I didn't possess an ounce of passion for any of it. Maybe it was because I was the youngest child. Or maybe I'd been dropped on my head too many times. But in my thirty years, I'd seen life and death and everything in between, and I'd discovered one universal truth. We were not here for a long time, but for a good time. So I did my damndest to make sure I had a good time.

Obsessing over sap or rainfall or fertilizer nitrogen ratios was not my thing. I needed adrenaline and movement. I needed a purpose. And fighting fires and saving lives gave me just that.

I adjusted the strap on my radio and scanned the crowd. My neck ached the way it always did when I worked festivals and events. I was a firefighter, a paramedic, and a babysitter of the drunk and reckless. My job tonight was to make sure people left here with nothing more than a maple sugar buzz and a slew of happy memories.

Beneath the ache, my senses tingled. My heart picked up speed in response, an instinctual reaction to an invisible danger. Something felt off.

The radio crackled, and Marty, our dispatcher, quickly relayed information regarding the crisis my body had already picked up on. "Code three at the sugar shack."

Nolan, our police chief, took off in a sprint toward the folksy sugar hut from the other side of the town green.

My gut tightened. Shit. This was bad. And not just Betsy Ross breaking in and making a mess bad.

As I wove past festival goers, I ignored shouts and startled looks. The sugar shack was only fifty yards away, its chimney puffing smoke eerily into the night sky.

Twenty feet from the structure, my forward movement was stopped by a strong hand on my bicep.

"Jasper."

I stumbled, my heart lurching, and turned toward the voice. Tony Moretti, the high school football coach and owner of the pizzeria in town, gripped my arm, face red and sucking in air.

"It's an emergency," he said, pointing at his shop. "We called, but dispatch said the crew had already responded to another call."

I shook my head. Shit. The sugar shack. I eyed the small building, my pulse pounding.

Sirens pierced the air, and one of our volunteers pushed through the people crowding around.

Tony tugged my arm, his grip tightening, his expression grave. He was built like a linebacker, but he had the personality of a cuddly puppy. "We've got a medical emergency. Please."

I nodded once. He was right. The chief had already responded to the other call, and I couldn't ignore a medical emergency. So I jogged after him, in the opposite direction of the surging crowd.

Inside the old brick storefront, the noise of the festival was muffled and the smell of oregano and singed mozzarella clung to the air.

The restaurant was mostly empty, though my attention was immediately drawn to the woman curled up on the cracked leather booth, crying.

Evie.

The curvy brunette I'd had my eye on for two years.

She was from New York, but had moved to town to work at Sugar Moon, the syrup conglomerate that was headquartered in town. She generally kept to herself, though I'd spotted her from time to time at yoga, at the farmers' market, and giggling with friends at the Drip Line.

She was buttoned up, never sparing me more than a

polite nod. But today she was pale and sweat soaked, and the raw scream that escaped her was one of pure pain.

"What's wrong with her?" Frankie Dunne demanded, mopping her forehead with a napkin. She was one of the few people Evie socialized with, from what I could tell.

"Give me a minute to assess her." I set my bag on the table and dropped to my knees beside the booth, scanning her, searching for signs that would help me determine the problem.

"Evie," I said, using the gentle tone I always adopted in these situations. "It's Jasper Lawrence, can you hear me?"

She gasped, her voice strained. "Pain. Everywhere. Stomach, back."

Softly grasping her wrist, I checked her pulse. It was racing, her breathing shallow and her skin clammy.

I peered out the windows that lined the front of the restaurant, taking in the chaos, and grabbed for the microphone part of my radio attached to my shoulder. I needed transport, and fast.

"Marty," I said, head turned to one side so the mic would pick up my voice. "This is Lawrence. Need a rig at the pizza shop. Patient in distress. Call it into the hospital. Over."

"Copy," Marty replied. "Body found at the sugar shack. Our unit is over there. I'll call over to Birch Hollow."

Aw, shit. That could take a while.

Evie cried out again, curling her legs up. Like this, I could see the back of her leggings. The black fabric was wet, and fluid was gathering on the seat of the booth.

"It comes in waves," Frankie explained, stroking Evie's hair. "Every few minutes."

With a hand on her calf to get her attention, I asked, "May I examine you?"

Evie nodded, her face screwed up with pain.

I palpated her abdomen, noting how swollen and hard it was. As I was assessing her, her abdominal muscles contracted, and she whimpered, her eyes squeezing shut. After several seconds, they relaxed again.

"This fluid?" I asked.

Frankie glared at me, her brows pulled together severely.

"It just gushed out of me," Evie said. "And there was some blood."

"I need to press down a bit more," I said. "This might hurt." I moved my hands, checking her fundal height. As I suspected, her uterus was distended up to her rib cage.

She was pregnant.

And in hard labor.

My radio crackled. "The rig from Birch Hollow is on the way. Fifteen minutes out."

Thank God. If her screams were any indication, her contractions were still several minutes apart. We had time.

"Evie," I murmured. "You're in labor."

She lurched, lifting her head off the seat. "No," she said, her expression panicked. "Not possible."

I examined her abdomen again. "This is labor," I told her, keeping my tone low. "Comes in waves. I can feel your uterus contracting. Do you feel pressure in your pelvis?"

She nodded. "Yes. So much pressure."

"Okay," I said. "I need to check the baby's position. The ambulance is on its way, but I need a better idea of how much time we have. Can I pull these leggings down?"

She nodded, her eyes welling, her breathing choppy.

My heart clenched. She had to be in so much pain. As gently as I could, I peeled her leggings over her hips, bringing her underwear with them.

When I'd lowered them, I tapped her thigh. "Spread your knees apart for me."

Frankie got up and stood between us and the front of the restaurant and the hordes of people outside. Given her tiny size, it likely wasn't doing much, but I appreciated the protectiveness she displayed for her friend.

A quick look confirmed we still had time. I wasn't an expert at delivering babies, but the head wasn't crowning. That much I remembered from training.

"The good news is that it's not time to push yet."

Her only response was a groan, her eyes still screwed shut.

"Now we're gonna time the length of your contractions and how far apart they are." I helped her pull her pants back up. "And get you to the hospital."

"No," she sobbed, shaking her head. "You're wrong. It can't be. I'm not pregnant. It's food poisoning."

She didn't know.

That thought hit me like a kick to the chest. Damn. No wonder she looked so scared and vulnerable.

Frankie scurried over, holding her phone up. "Ruby's meeting us at the hospital. You've got this."

Evie's sobs continued, her breaths choppy, her head tucked, as if she was trying to hide from reality.

With a fortifying inhale, I took her hand and gave it a soft squeeze. "Eyes on me," I commanded. "You can do this."

"I can't—" She cried out as she was hit with another contraction. I coached her through it, sweat dripping down my back as my radio screamed nonstop. A fatality at the sugar shack. Panicking tourists. A fender bender on Market Street. Chief was calling for backup.

It was utter chaos out there.

But I was here. With her. Fully.

Drowning out the noise, I spoke gently and firmly. "Breathe," I said. "Let the pain roll through you. It will crest and then recede. Like a wave."

We continued like this for several contractions, her eyes fixed on my face, her grip tight on mine as she breathed through the pain.

Eventually, the sirens grew closer, and moments later, the paramedics crew from Birch Hollow barreled in with a stretcher.

As they prepped to move her, I didn't let go. Didn't let my focus shift. She needed me.

Even once she was loaded onto the stretcher, I remained at her side. Frankie stood on the other.

Outside, the festive town green had turned into a war zone, blue lights flashing and crowds of people scattering, some with cell phones out, recording, others crying and shouting.

We loaded her into the ambulance, and while Frankie climbed in with her, the Birch Hollow crew got the fetal monitor set up.

She was good. My job here was done.

I took a step back. I was needed elsewhere. My radio crackled with orders for me to head straight to the sugar shack.

But with the second step, my mind was flooded with questions. And one big one in particular.

"Evie," I said quietly. "Do you need me to call anyone for you?"

She shook her head, her face tearstained.

"The baby's father?" I prodded.

She opened her red-rimmed eyes wide, her whole body trembling.

"You," she gasped. "You're the father."

An explosion went off in my chest, the sound louder than the sirens. Louder than the festival. My ears rang, my vision going hazy.

One of the Birch Hollow guys pushed me back and slammed the doors shut, and a minute later, the ambulance roared off into the night. I was on duty. I'd been ordered to report to another incident. People needed me.

Yet I stood in place on the sidewalk, my chest heaving and my mind spinning.

Caught between two disasters. One unfolding at the sugar shack and one racing off toward the hospital.

My gut lurched as reality began to sink in. After tonight, nothing in Maplewood would ever be the same.

Chapter 1

EVIE

My son. I was holding my son.

He was so tiny. And perfect.

Ten fingers and ten toes. Long eyelashes and tufts of curly black hair.

The nurse commented about it, asking if I'd been suffering from heartburn lately. It was a joke, but little did she know that I had, and I couldn't explain why.

I felt like I'd been hit by a bus and then dropped off a cliff onto a field of cacti, Wile E. Coyote style. But as I looked at him, snuggled peacefully in my arms, a deep warmth bloomed inside me.

"Yesterday, I had no idea you existed," I whispered, my lips brushing the top of his head, "and today, I can't live without you."

I'd never felt stranger than I did now. I was more exhausted and bloodied than I ever imagined possible, yet I was equal parts ecstatic and content.

When I looked at him, all the noise faded away. When I

stroked his tiny fingers, my anxiety eased. And the guilt of not knowing faded. So did the fear and panic consuming me. I was completely unprepared for the biggest responsibility of my life, and no, I didn't have even the slightest clue that I'd become a mother today.

But he was here. And he was perfect. In the end, that's what mattered.

I'd never dared to dream that this was possible. A baby. Motherhood.

Not only because I'd never been in a relationship even remotely serious enough to warrant discussing kids, but because I had been told my body couldn't do it.

Having struggled with PCOS since puberty, I'd come to terms with my infertility. With the knowledge that my body, that had already betrayed me in so many small ways, couldn't handle a challenge this big.

I had no idea what day it was or even the time. The shades in the sterile room were closed, though slivers of sunlight peeked in around them.

To say my life had been turned upside down today—yesterday?—was an understatement. More like it had been thrown into a cement mixer and smashed to bits, then rearranged.

But I had this little guy. And every time I looked at him, the panic briefly subsided.

I hummed the tune of "Ninna Nanna" softly, tears stinging my eyes. How was this even possible?

In the chair in the corner, Ruby was sleeping soundly. She was six months pregnant herself, and she and Frankie had been with me every step of the way, taking shifts and fussing over me constantly. When the baby cried, they'd jump into action, changing diapers and soothing him. They refilled my water before it was empty and had brought me a variety of snacks. Paul, Ruby's husband, had come over several times and tried to persuade her to go home and rest, but she'd fought him off in her usual style.

I'd never had close friends. My sisters were preoccupied with their own lives, my parents couldn't care less, and the various folks who'd floated in and out of my life had been friendly acquaintances at best. But here, in this weird yet charming small town in rural Vermont, I'd found my people. In less than two years, I'd found a place where I could belong. A place where I could make a home for myself, a life for myself.

I looked down at the sweet little face. And now a home for my son.

My son.

The nurses came in to do yet another vitals check, waking the baby and Ruby in the process. They urged me to try nursing again, which was not the intuitive, natural process everyone made it out to be.

"Flatten it," Kate, the lactation consultant instructed. "Like a hamburger. Then shove it into his mouth."

She hovered over me, dressed in yellow scrubs, and manhandled my not at all small breast, brushing my nipple over the baby's little rosebud mouth. In response, he opened up and magically latched around it.

With her pinky, she pulled his bottom lip down. "There. That's a strong latch."

The sucking sensation was strange, but this time, it wasn't painful.

"You know," Ruby said, shuffling to the side of the bed

and stroking my hair. "I've read at least a dozen pregnancy and birth books, and not one of them mentions how challenging nursing is."

"Breastfeeding is a complicated dance where both partners have to learn their steps," Kate explained, giving Ruby a pitying look. "And one partner is exhausted and experiencing raging postpartum hormones, while the other is only a few hours old and not yet strong enough to hold their head up."

"So it's not easy." Ruby deflated. "I feel like I've been lied to, and I haven't even started the third trimester."

I winked at my friend. "This part, where you and Frankie and the nurses do the work for me and I sit here like a cow, is pretty easy."

She rolled her eyes. "Overachiever."

Kate smiled. "We work with every caregiver and baby to find the right fit. Fed is best, whether from breast or bottle. But this little champ is doing pretty well so far."

He suckled, swallowing greedily, his eyes closed.

A wave of elation washed over me. For what felt like the first time in my life, my body was actually doing something right.

"It takes a few days for your supply to fully come in, and I'm here to help. But the most important thing is that you are both healthy."

"Thank you," I said, tears filling my eyes and spilling over. I'd been doing a lot of crying over the past twenty-four hours.

Ruby patted my shoulder. "Don't mind her. Surprise pregnancy and childbirth can really do a number on a person."

Kate smiled. "I'll be back in a couple of hours to check, but you've got this so far."

After several minutes, I burped him, then Ruby helped me get him latched on the other side. I tried to hamburger my own boob, but I wasn't coordinated enough to do it properly while also supporting my baby's fragile neck and head. So Ruby did it for me, and again, my hungry little guy got right in there.

"You're a natural," she murmured.

"No. But I have you, and *you're* a natural. Plus you've spent the last six months reading up on the subject."

She smiled. "I'm glad all my obsessing helps. And I've got you. We're doing this together."

In addition to being my first and closest friend in Maplewood, Ruby owned Stitch and Stone, the local clothing boutique. She was bright and bold and stylish, basically my complete opposite. Tiny, with red hair cut into a bob and a full sleeve of tattoos on her left arm, she exuded confident cool, even while she was heavily pregnant. Her husband Paul was a straitlaced accountant who liked to cut loose by playing bass in one of Maplewood's rock cover bands.

Dressed in a black and white checkered maternity dress paired with an oversized lime green cardigan, she smiled down at me, rubbing her belly. "Raising our little beans together. We both know my son will be the bad influence hellion and yours will be the one to keep him in check."

I wrinkled my nose. "Nah. He's half Paul. That quiet accountant DNA will balance him—"

The door to my room flew open, ending our debate.

"I'm here."

Frankie pushed through the door, a large shopping bag

hanging from one arm and a pizza box in the other. "And I brought pizza."

"It's ten a.m.," Ruby drawled.

"Tony owed me. I'm constantly fixing up that old Alpha Romeo he's so obsessed with. And besides, you gave birth in his shop."

"I gave birth in this hospital," I corrected.

"And he was in early to clean the amniotic fluid off the floor," she countered.

A wave of guilt washed over me. Oh God, I'd surely made an unholy mess.

The thought was cut short, though, when the most amazing smell hit me. I hadn't realized how hungry I was until one of Tony's pizzas was in my vicinity.

"Hospital food sucks," Frankie said. "So I figured you could use this. You need sustenance to make all the milk this kid's gonna drink."

I looked down at the baby, who was slurping away, unbothered, my heart melting as I once again took in his tiny features.

"I stopped by your house. Picked up your shampoo and moisturizer and some decent comfy clothes."

Confusion flitted through me. "I didn't give you my keys."

She smiled. "I found my way in. Don't worry, I locked up when I was finished."

I huffed a laugh. I shouldn't be surprised. Frankie Dunne was terrifying. All five foot two of her. She was wiry and feisty and had won many fights against larger, stronger male opponents. To underestimate her was at one's peril.

She was also one of the most loving, loyal, funny people I'd ever met. Not that she wanted that information to get out.

She had to maintain her reputation as Maplewood's badass mechanic, after all.

She employed only women and was known for fair pricing, efficient service, and treating her employees well.

Despite the April chill, she was wearing her usual tank top, showing off her impressive biceps and a generous collection of ink. My friends were infinitely cooler than I was. Her honey hair was pulled into a ponytail, and she had her coveralls tied around her waist.

"You name him yet?" she asked, handing Ruby a slice of pizza.

Peering down at my son again, I shook my head. "I just need a minute." I stroked his cheek. I'd just met him, and already, I knew exactly who he was. But it seemed weird to make this decision all on my own.

"Do you want to talk about it?" Ruby asked, her expression full of empathy.

"Talk about my fucked-up body and how I didn't know I was pregnant?" My eyes filled with tears again. "I hurt my baby because I was a clueless idiot who didn't see the signs."

"Stop that," Frankie commanded, giving me a stern look. "The doctors said he's perfectly healthy. You did not hurt him."

"You've been obsessively googling every moment you can," Ruby added. "And demanding he be examined by every health care provider in this hospital. I'm pretty sure the X-ray tech even gave him a once over to make you happy."

The tears feel in earnest now. They weren't wrong. I was

paranoid. Terrified that without prenatal vitamins and the proper care, I'd done irreparable damage. But their kindness was just as heart-wrenching.

"You're already a health nut. We know he was well nourished in there."

"And he was eight pounds," Ruby added with a huff.

We'd had this conversation already. But the guilt still wouldn't go away.

I lowered my focus to him again, my tears dripping onto my hospital gown. Thank God I'd been so hung up on my health recently.

I'd felt off. I was exhausted, and I'd gained weight for inexplicable reasons. In general, I struggled to feel like myself.

Now it seemed so obvious. But I'd been to the doctor, and I'd gotten the usual "lose weight, eat healthy foods, and exercise" advice, so I'd done it.

I'd quit drinking, taken up yoga and hiking, and started taking all kinds of vitamins. I'd even started ordering the kale and kiwi smoothie at Bean There, Sipped That instead of my usual chocolate croissant.

And thank God I'd made so many changes. I shuddered at the thought of what could have happened had I not cleaned up my act.

Regardless, the guilt and shame ate at me.

I'd have to work really hard to make it up to this little guy.

Chapter 2

JASPER

I stood outside the closed door, awash with panic, my heart racing. As I adjusted the gift bag in my trembling hand, I forced myself to take a deep breath. It didn't help. I couldn't wrap my head around the events that had brought me to this hospital room.

Frozen to the spot, I willed my legs to move. I was used to running into burning buildings, for God's sake.

But my body stubbornly remained where it was. I was trained for emergencies, not cozy visits with newborns. Danger didn't scare me, risk didn't scare me, but this? This terrified me.

Was this my child?

Could I even be a dad?

I hadn't put any thought into the idea of having kids. I'd only just turned thirty. That meant I had plenty of time to worry about that later. Way later. After I'd figured the rest of my life out.

Except if what Evie said was true, that time was up.

My stomach clenched. I was unsure of the protocol, but I knew I had to knock and go in there.

So I took another cleansing breath.

Three, two, one.

Feeling weaker than I had in years, I raised my hand and gently knocked. When a soft voice called "come in," I eased the door open.

The room was a hell of a lot more cheerful than the ER, which was where I usually ended up. The room was filled with balloons and flowers, and the sun shone in through the open shades, making the space feel cozy.

Evie was propped up on the bed, a tiny bundle in her arms. A blue hat. A boy? A son?

Knees wobbling, I padded closer. She was feeding him, and he was gulping hungrily at her breast. Tiny, fragile, with balled-up little fists.

Evie's dark hair was pulled back and there were shadows under her eyes, but she radiated pure joy.

I zeroed in once again on the tiny miraculous creature snuggled against her. A tidal wave of emotion hit me, dousing me in joy, fear, and awe. Around the edge of his tiny hat, tufts of dark hair spilled out.

"He's—" A sob rose in my throat, but I swallowed it back. "So tiny," I blurted out. "Smaller than a football."

Evie peered up at me, and when her eyes darted to the far side of the room, I followed her gaze. Only then did I realize we weren't alone.

"I guess I should say congrats?" Frankie Dunne sat near the window, her legs draped over the side of the chair. She was wearing a tank top, her colorful tattoos on display. She was a hell of a mechanic and did a lot for the town, but I knew better than to get on her bad side. "Where the hell have you been?"

"On shift." I said curtly. "Dealing with several small and one very large emergencies."

Frankie clicked her tongue in annoyance.

I gave her a tense smile. The last thing I needed right now was an audience.

I turned back to Evie. "Can we, um, speak?" I trained my focus on her face, avoiding looking at the baby now that I realized just how exposed his mother was. Evie had her whole boob out, and the baby was sucking away. She looked like she was made for this. Like it was the most natural thing in the world.

A fierce protective fire I'd never experienced before rose up inside me in their presence.

"I'm not leaving," Frankie practically growled.

"It's okay," Evie said, gently stroking the baby's cheek.

With a sigh, Frankie stood and stared at me. She was five foot nothing, but I knew better than to mess with her.

"I'll be outside. Let me know if you need me to drag his ass out of here." With that, she was gone, closing the door quietly behind her.

For a long moment, Evie and I stared at one another. I was at a loss for what to do or say. She looked equally unsure, and honestly, that was a bit of a comfort. Because maybe I wasn't the only one out of their depth.

"He's beautiful," I said. I didn't have the first clue how to start what was truly the mother of all awkward conversations.

She smiled softly, peering down at the baby. "He is."

"So, um..." My heart rate picked up again, making my

words come out weaker than I'd like. "What you said last night."

She straightened a little, her attention drifting up to me.

My breath caught as our eyes locked. The beauty of this moment hit me like a punch to the gut. If this was really my son, then one day, I'd tell him about the moment I met him. Would I want to have to explain how I interrogated his mother just hours after his birth. Hell no.

"Not that I want to accuse," I said, tripping over my words.

She shook her head. "I'm sorry. My brain is so scrambled right now. I didn't think this was possible. In fact, I was told by multiple doctors that I'd likely battle infertility."

My heart lurched. "So you really didn't know?" I was a paramedic, not a doctor, but I had medical training. It seemed unbelievable that for nine months, she'd carried a baby and yet had no idea she was pregnant until she went into labor.

Anger rose up in me each time I replayed the moment she told me I was the father of her baby. If she'd clued me in during her pregnancy, I would have done everything I could to support her. Sure, I was a good-time kind of guy, but that didn't mean I'd ghost her when shit got real. If I was the dad, then I deserved to know.

"I have PCOS," she said, her voice timid. "I've never had regular cycles. My hormones are a mess, and it's been such a stressful year for me. I felt off and I gained weight, so I went to the doctor. He told me to eat healthier foods and to exercise more. I didn't even consider that this could be possible, and no one ever suggested I take a test. So I followed his directions, and I've been working to be as healthy as I could be."

My stomach twisted itself into a knot. Seriously? I knew women tended to get worse medical care than men. It was a load of shit, but it was reality. But her story was nuts.

"And while it's natural for you to be skeptical," she hedged. "You're the only guy I've been. Um…" Her cheeks turned a soft shade of pink as she trailed off.

My shoulders relaxed a little. This was hard on her too.

But then her words registered, and my heart seized in my chest. "Ever?"

"*No.*" She rolled her eyes. "Recently, like in the last year."

Brows raised, I surveyed her. Why did I find that knowledge so satisfying?

I shook the thought from my head. That was a sentiment to unpack at a later date.

"So I understand if you want a paternity test. But I'm sure he's yours."

I took a deep breath, digesting all this information. The baby was mine. In theory, that should be terrible news. Evie and I hooked up once. Well, multiple times, but only one night. And the morning after. I wasn't anywhere near ready to have kids. Hell, I wasn't even sure I was dad material. But when I focused on Evie and the baby again, a strange sort of calm washed over me.

"Can I hold him?" I blurted out. "When you're done?"

She nodded. "I think he's dozing off again. How about you burp him?"

I took a step back, a bolt of fear zipping through me. "I don't know how to do that."

"You'll figure it out. Watch."

She pulled her hospital gown closed and eased him up, supporting his head. Then she gently patted his upper back until he let out a massive burp.

"Good job," I said under my breath. Damn. The burp was bigger than he was.

"Here, you can take him. Do you know how to hold a newborn?"

I nodded. "Yes." I'd spent time with my nieces and nephews when they were tiny and both my sisters made sure I coould hold a baby. I stepped right up to the bed and gathered him in my arms, supporting his head using the crook of my elbow. Carefully, I walked over to the chair Frankie had vacated and sat down, finally examining him up close.

"You're a natural," she said in a soft tone.

Warmth bloomed in my chest as I drank in the sight of him. If I didn't know how impossible it was, I'd swear my heart grew a size.

This was my child.

My son.

His eyes were heavy, his tiny eyelashes fluttering. And his fingers? Fuck. They were the most precious thing I'd ever seen. He was perfect.

Before I knew it, I was crying.

And I was not a crier. Lawrence men were stoic. We shoved our feelings down and held them there until we forgot they even existed.

But holding this tiny human brought a whole wave of them up. The love I already felt for this person. The responsibility that settled itself on my shoulders. And the most visceral was the burning desire to have my parents back to witness this moment.

My siblings had been blowing up my phone, urging me to demand a DNA test. But in this moment, I knew this child was mine. On some deep, primal level, I sensed it.

I stared at him, my eyes full of tears, praying to every possible god that I wouldn't fuck this up. That I wouldn't let this little person down.

"What's his name?" I asked gently.

"I haven't settled on a name yet. I thought maybe we could choose together? But I really like the name Vincent," she said. "It was my grandfather's name."

I stared at him, I could see it. Vincent. It was classic. It had gravitas. He would wear it well.

"Sounds great."

She blinked at me, like she was stunned that I'd agreed so easily. But the name was perfect. And this woman had done all the work to bring him into the world; why wouldn't I defer to her? "I know your dad passed away..." she said softly.

"His name was James," I replied, back to memorizing every feature of this little miracle.

"Vincent James," she said. "I like it."

I looked up again, my eyes blurry, my cheeks wet. "Me too."

Her lips curled up on one side, her eyes dancing. "Good. But don't get used to me agreeing with you so easily."

A laugh escaped me, startling the baby a little.

I'd forgotten how much I liked her. She was funny and a little sassy. Her eyes had a mischievous twinkle that said *I know I'm smarter than you, but I'm too kind to remind you of that fact.*

"Understood."

We sat in silence as Vincent fell asleep in my arms. Like he felt totally safe and satisfied. I studied the slope of his nose and his little rosebud lips.

When I shifted so I could rest my elbow on the armrest of the chair, I found Evie watching us. "Are you okay?" I asked. I should have asked that the moment I walked in. "After the birth and everything."

"Aside from the fact that I didn't even know I was pregnant, it was a pretty standard birth, according to the doctors. Ruby and Frankie were with me, coaching me."

"I'm sorry I wasn't here," I said. "I got called back to town."

And it really was an all-hands-on-deck kind of situation. There had been multiple car accidents, and a handful of people attending the festival had fainted, causing a myriad of wounds. I'd worked all night, transporting folks and treating major injuries.

But the part of the day that had stuck with me was the moment the medical examiner zipped Will McManus's lifeless body into a body bag and loaded it into the coroner's van. It was so surreal. Things like this did not happen in Maplewood.

"I'm sure you were so confused."

Blinking, I zeroed in on her. "Yeah, I was in shock, I guess, but that's no excuse. If I hadn't been on duty and the day hadn't gotten so out of hand, I would have been here. I promise."

I paused for a moment, trying to figure out how to formulate the question that had been plaguing me. Finally, I cleared my throat. "Um. I thought we were careful?"

I didn't think it, I knew it. I was always careful. My dad had given me the talk about consent and protection at fourteen, and I'd sworn I'd never let him down.

I didn't want to make accusations or come off like an asshole, but I knew how babies were made.

"Me too," she said. "But that night is such a blur."

Huh. That stung a bit. That night was not a blur for me. I remembered every detail clearly. The feel of her body pressed against mine, the way she'd cried out when she came. And the way she'd tasted. My God, I'd spent many lonely nights reliving those memories.

I'd noticed her immediately after she moved to town, but it wasn't until we danced at Ruby's bachelorette party that I decided to make a move. They'd been drinking and dancing, and the two of us flirted wildly. We made out in the parking lot before she took me home. The morning after, I'd tried to get her number, but she'd made it clear she was not interested.

So I backed off.

Yet here we are.

Unsure of how to respond to that comment, I focused on Vincent, who was now asleep in my arms.

At the sound of a sniffle, I looked up, finding Evie crying.

"I'm sorry," she blurted.

Frowning, I straightened in the chair.

"You probably never even wanted kids," she cried. "I swear I had no idea, and now you're here and probably wishing you didn't have to be."

My gut lurched. She was way offside with that assumption. Anger flared inside me, but I closed my eyes and reined it in. What would my dad do? He was the best man I'd ever known.

Even though he wasn't here anymore, I wanted to be a man he could be proud of.

"Evie," I said sharply.

She continued to cry. I held Vincent a little tighter.

"Evie." My voice was louder this time. Luckily I didn't wake the baby.

She froze and looked at me, tears streaming down her cheeks.

"Already, this baby is the best thing to ever happen to me, and I've only known him for ten minutes," I said. "Unexpected isn't bad. Unplanned isn't bad."

She hiccuped, wiping at her tears. "But we're unprepared."

I held her gaze, making sure she was really listening. "I'll adjust. You'll adjust. We will adjust together."

I lived my life on the edge. Taking risks, caring little about the consequences. Rolling with things, avoiding the desire to control outcomes. Yeah, I liked to have a good time and I didn't take things too seriously, but that didn't mean I couldn't when I needed to.

Her lip trembled, her eyes rimmed red. "I know you didn't ask for this."

The fear was clear on her face. She was worried that I didn't want this. That I didn't want him.

Nothing could be farther from the truth. I'd have to do a hell of a lot of work to live up to the man who'd raised me, but with this little guy in my arms, I knew I was ready to try.

"I'm here," I said firmly. "And I'm not going anywhere."

Chapter 3

JASPER

From the hospital, I headed straight home to deal with the fallout of the last twenty-four hours. Still in my uniform and bone tired, I wanted nothing more than to fall into bed. A quick nap before facing my siblings would be incredible.

When I pulled up to the house and found my oldest sister's Volvo in the driveway, I considered climbing onto the roof of the wraparound porch and jimmying my bedroom window open. I let the idea go quickly, though. Jenn would know. Her instincts were spot on. She was twelve years older than me, so she'd been a second mom to me my entire life. She could sniff me out a mile away. She owned the coffee shop, Bean There, Sipped That, with her wife, served on several town committees, and coached the high school ski team.

Resigned to face her, I toed my shoes off in the mudroom and headed toward the kitchen. Josh had renovated a few years ago, and the homey house I'd grown up in had been transformed into an architectural digest spread. He'd left my childhood bedroom alone, per my request, and I had my own bathroom, so while the kitchen was all rustic oak floors, exposed beams, and copper pots hanging from the ceiling, I had my own untouched space upstairs.

Maybe it was weird that I still lived at home, but my brother was a damn good roommate. He didn't charge me rent, which meant I had healthy savings and had set up a good retirement plan by thirty, and the fridge was always stocked.

It was convenient too. I spent as many hours working on the farm as I did on shift most weeks. The trees, the animals, and the limited crops we grew kept us busy. We were working off an endless to-do list. I'd known at an early age that I had no interest in being a full-time farmer, but I'd been tapping trees and feeding chickens since I was three years old.

Josh was the smart one. He'd headed straight to the Ivy League after high school and then to Wall Street. He made a bunch of money, but then something happened—what, he won't say—and he moved back here and took over the farm.

My sister Jess was in the process of converting one of the small barns into a summer home for her family. The designs were nice. I figured I'd so something similar someday.

But now I had Vincent. I gave myself a moment to remember the warmth and weight of him in my arms. I guess someday was now. I had a lot to sort out.

From the sound of things, my siblings were in the kitchen. Again, I considered avoiding them. But when the smell of coffee hit me, I decided to take my chances.

"Finally," Jenn said when I walked in. Her arms were

crossed, her expression stern. "Did your phone die? I've texted you about five hundred times."

Josh dipped his chin and reached for a mug. Silently, he got to work in front of his fancy espresso machine. I had a couple of heavy machinery licenses, and even I couldn't operate that thing, so I left him to it. Josh wasn't a big talker, but I did enough for the both of us, and we'd figured out our flow long ago.

Jenn had three legal pads fanned out like playing cards on the butcher block island, each with scribbles and high-lights bleeding through the pages. She hovered over them and pressed a button.

A second later, Jess's voice filled the kitchen. "What is going on?" she chided. "I've got my candles lit. Josh, have you saged the sap barn yet?"

I smiled. Jess was the best. She was a social worker slash yoga instructor who lived in New York and was, blessedly, a fellow glass-half-full person. Together we balanced out Jenn and Josh.

"It's gonna require a hell of a lot more than sage," Jenn quipped as Josh slid a mug toward me.

I picked it up right away, scorching my tongue, desperate to get caffeine into my blood stream.

"Gabe is on his way." Jenn turned toward me, a hand on her hip. "Now start talking, because the rumors are flying and your cryptic texts have taken years off my life."

Josh propped his elbows on the table and gave me "the look." It was the one my father had invented and perfected, and by some genetic lottery, Josh had inherited it.

"I have a son."

Silence. Even the espresso machine seemed to stop its strangled hissing.

Josh's eyes widened and Jenn gasped. I swore a gray hair even sprouted from her head.

"Oh my *God*," Jess squealed, the sound ear-piercing. "What's his name? Tell me everything."

Jenn clicked her pen twice. "So the rumors are true." Her tone was one of pure disappointment. "Why didn't you tell us you were having a baby?"

My stomach lurched. "He's not a package I ordered from Amazon," I snapped.

Jess giggled, her voice tinny through the phone.

"I mean—" Blowing out a breath, I roughed a hand down my face. "It was a surprise. For everyone. Me. Her. It's messy."

With every word, I deflated, running out of steam, but I didn't stop, afraid that if I did, I wouldn't find the words again.

"His name is Vincent," I said, taking in the shocked expressions on my siblings' faces. "And he's perfect."

"Of course he is," Jess said. "I'm going shopping today. This is so exciting. Is he wearing newborn sizes? Or should I size up?"

Josh leaned on the table, his knuckles braced. "The mother?"

"Evie Marino," I said, as if two words could convey the entire messy story. One night and too much heat followed by nine months of silence and avoidance and an emergency call to the pizzeria where her water had broken.

While a corpse in a vat of sap had upended the town, Vincent had arrived.

"I didn't know you had a girlfriend," Jess said.

Jenn continued to stare at me, the disappointment radiating from her.

I refused to feel bad. While my track record when it came to adulting was not perfect, Vincent *was*.

So I shook my head and sipped my coffee. Normally I spewed every thought that came to me. My brain moved faster than my lips, and I overshared and overexplained.

But I didn't have a clue how to describe this situation. "It's... complicated. But I'm all in."

Josh gave me a solemn nod.

"I was just at the hospital," I said, throwing a thumb over my shoulder. "I'm gonna shower and go back before my shift tonight." With a sigh, I turned toward the stairs, but I turned back again quickly, digging my phone out of my pocket. "Wanna see pictures?"

"*Yes*," Jess screamed, her voice echoing off the exposed beams above us. "Text them to me right now."

Jenn scrolled through the photos silently, but her expression softened a fraction.

The back door banged open, startling all of us, and Gabe strode in. He had on his usual dress shirt with rolled-up sleeves and carried a battered leather bag.

"Crisis meetings," he said, nodding at Josh.

My brother turned back to the espresso machine and silently made our cousin his own cup.

Gabe squeezed Jenn's shoulder and ran a hand through his hair. "All right, family. Facts only. We've got to get ahead of this."

Gabe Harding was our first cousin as well as the mayor of Maplewood. He'd grown up on the farm next to ours, and we'd all been raised together. Already a successful lawyer, he'd run for mayor a few years ago and had been overseeing the town since.

Josh had bought his parents' farm a while back, and shortly after, Uncle Ed and Aunt Suzie moved to Florida to enjoy retirement.

"Jas has a son." Jenn pushed the phone toward Gabe.

He studied the photo, then gave me a genuine smile. "Congrats," he said. "But did I miss something?"

My hackles rose, but before I could set him straight, Josh jumped in.

"It's complicated."

"The mother is Evie Marino," Jenn added.

"And baby Vincent is the cutest," Jess added from the phone.

"Are you in a relationship with the mother?" Gabe picked up his coffee and carefully brought it to his lips.

"Um," I hedged. "No. It was a surprise. For both of us, actually."

He set his mug down and pinched the bridge of his nose. "I mean it, congrats. Babies are great."

My stomach sank. I could feel the "but" coming.

"But now I have to be the guy everybody loves to hate. We need to protect you, the farm, and the baby. Step one." He held up a finger. "Paternity testing. Step two." He added a second finger. "Establish custody paperwork and a parenting plan. Step three." Yup. Third finger. "No statements about the baby to anyone."

My spine went rigid. "No."

He blinked at me. "To which step?"

"All of them." Heat rose up under my collar, anger surging inside me.

I understood his instincts, but there was no way Vincent didn't belong to me.

"I'm not swabbing my kid like he's evidence," I gritted out. "I'm not starting fatherhood with a lab slip."

Jenn closed her eyes and sighed. "Jasper, be reasonable. This is about legal clarity. If you want to be on the birth certificate—"

"I am," I snapped. "I signed it this morning."

Today had been one of the most intense and joyful days of my life, yet all the questioning was making me angry.

"That's great," Gabe said carefully, "But depending on circumstances of conception and notice, there can still be challenges. A test protects you and the child. It protects Evie too."

"You think she's playing him?" Josh growled.

My vision went red. What the fuck?

Gabe took off his glasses and cleaned them on his shirt. "No. That's not what I'm saying. My point is that this family and this farm are already in the middle of a public scandal. I just want to protect everyone."

The room suddenly felt too small. I would not let them weaponize my son, no matter how well-intentioned my cousin was.

"What scandal?" I glared at Gabe. "A murder in Maplewood is a big deal, sure. But can we stop with the catastrophizing?"

They looked at one another, Jenn and Josh wearing matching stoic expressions, Gabe straightening, slipping back into lawyer mode.

"He doesn't know?" Jess's muffled voice was loud in the silent room.

I frowned at my siblings. What were they talking about?

"It was ours," Josh said solemnly. "Will's body was found in one of our barrels of sap. They cracked it open at the sugar house to do the first demonstration, and he was just..." He shook his head. "In there."

My stomach dropped.

Jenn paced to the end of the room and back. "Inventory logs, transport manifests, and a timeline of where we all were. Everything needs to be airtight. If we don't push our own narrative, the rumor mill will do it for us."

"Narrative?" Josh snorted. "The only narrative here is a dead kid."

Gabe let out a weary sigh. "Listen, this is a shitshow for the whole town. The rest of the festival has been canceled. Vendors packed up and the tourists scattered like pigeons. Folks are canceling reservations at the inn, and I'm trying to find out if we've got a murderer on the loose."

He put his head in his hands and groaned.

"Everyone wants a throat to grab, and guess who's stuck his neck out?" He straightened, his face suddenly looking older. "Me, the fucking mayor."

"Aw, fuck," Jenn said. "Everything's on fire."

"Figuratively," I added. I disliked jokes about fire.

How the hell did a body end up in our sap? We'd started tapping in March like we always did. We sugared a small amount ourselves, but most of it was sold to the co-op our grandfather had founded. The co-op set the prices and negotiated on behalf of the farmers. And Josh was on the board.

Most of the stock was sold to Sugar Moon, which had a massive factory on the outskirts of town.

"Have you spoken to Nolan?" Josh asked. "He told me to be available for the next few days, but nothing else."

Gabe shook his head. "He's using that 'ongoing investigation' bullshit."

Nolan Foster, the Maplewood police chief, had been friends with Gabe and Josh since they were kids. They still played in an old man hockey league together every winter. But clearly he wasn't giving anything up, even to his closest friends.

Jess's breath hitched, making the phone line crackle. "Do they know how he died?"

"No." Gabe pressed his lips together. "The state medical examiner's office was here, but it'll be a couple of weeks before we get a full report."

"It's so sad," she said. "He was so young."

"There's no way this happened on the farm," Josh said quietly. "I oversee everything. We loaded those pallets last weekend, and Will signed for them."

"Did he do any work for us this season?" Jess asked.

We hired seasonal workers each year, and Will had helped in the past.

"No. He got a full-time job at the co-op," Josh said. "We hired him to replace Bob last year. He was handling deliveries and managing the storage swarehouse."

"So he was here on the farm for pickup?" Gabe said. "Do you know when exactly? And you've got cameras, right?"

Josh straightened, his muscles going rigid. "We have them, mostly near the main house. But one of them may have caught the truck coming up the road."

"Okay. Get the footage." Gabe drained his coffee and checked his watch. "Here's the plan. Our focus for now is damage control and helping the police do their job. The sooner they lock up the person who did this, the sooner life here can go back to normal."

"Agreed."

"I'm issuing a mayoral statement at noon and have a couple of interviews scheduled for later. This is a terrible tragedy for our town and Will's family. We can't forget that."

My chest ached at the thought of what his family must be going through.

"Jenn and Josh," he continued, "inventory statements and delivery and tracking info. And get a list of everyone who could have touched those pallets."

"I'll see if we can pull footage from the co-op cameras too," Josh said. "We've technically got legal counsel, but I'm not sure how much help he can be here."

"Keep the circle tight," Gabe warned, his expression stony.

"Jasper." He turned to me. "Keep an ear to the ground at work, learn as much as you can from those who responded to the scene."

Jess exhaled over the line. "After this is over, I'm going to buy the baby the tiniest Carhartt overalls, and we'll do cute photos in the barn. Consider yourself warned."

I smiled at the mention of Vincent. Of course he'd need overalls. He'd be a farm boy like me. Or would he? The realization hit me like a brick to the head. He was my son, but he probably wouldn't live with me. At least not right now. He wouldn't get to grow up on this land like we had.

Gabe pocketed his phone and picked up his briefcase.

"We'll get through this," he said firmly. "Just be careful. Things will work out."

He took a step back, but before he turned toward the door, he pointed at me. "And you need a paternity test."

Anger flared in my chest again.

Maybe they didn't believe Evie, but I did. We barely knew each other, but I trusted her. And I'd held that baby. In my bones, I knew he was mine.

Fists clenched, I worked to formulate a reasonable response. Tensions were running high, and despite the way their demands pissed me off, they just wanted to protect me.

"Paperwork is protective," Jenn said. "Tell him, Jess."

"Brian can help," Jess said.

Jess's boyfriend, Brian, specialized in family law in New York but had recently gotten licensed to practice in Vermont too.

"He can talk to you when you're ready."

Gabe clapped me on the shoulder. "In the meantime, I'll draw up some papers. There is no rush, but it's the right thing to do."

My gut churned. Nothing about this felt right.

The only thing that felt right was getting back into my car and driving to the hospital.

After Gabe left, I stepped into the mudroom, needing a moment. The house smelled like woodsmoke and maple, and Josh's and Jenn's voices sawed through the door of the small room while they argued about murder, manifests, and liability.

As if the universe knew I needed an update, my phone lit up in my hand.

I reread the text I'd sent when I got home, then I smiled at Evie's response.

JASPER:

How's Vincent?

EVIE:

He hates his hat and just got hiccups for the first time. It's adorable.

THE KNOT IN MY CHEST EASED A NOTCH. A FEW FEET away, my siblings were still parsing the worst day of the year into bullet points. I didn't want bullet points. I wanted the warm weight of my son against my chest and the noisy world turned down to a whisper.

JASPER:

I'm gonna jump in the shower. I'll be back to visit before my shift.

EVIE:

You don't have to. I'm sure you have places to be.

JASPER:

I do. With you.

I slid my phone into my pocket, strode through the kitchen without looking at my siblings, and headed upstairs to clean up.

The farm could have me later. My son needed me now.

Chapter 4

JASPER

My hair was still damp when I pulled into the hospital parking lot.

The nap didn't happen, but I managed to choke down a couple of scrambled eggs before coming back. For maybe the first time ever, I was dreading work. Tonight I started my next twenty-four-hour shift. That meant twenty-four hours away from Vincent.

I shook off the negativity. At least I could get some quality time in now.

I wedged the vase of flowers into the crook of my arm and headed for the sliding doors. Jenn had helped me with the arrangement, thank God. This early in the season, we didn't have much, but our tulips were beautiful, and she'd added a little greenery she'd cut to make it look good.

As I took the elevator up to the third floor, I focused on breathing. It was time to lock into dad mode.

My knees were back to trembling when I knocked on the door of room 312. But inside, the moment I laid eyes on my son, I cracked into a huge smile. Vincent was sleeping in that weird plastic thing on wheels the hospital provided. That kid needed a real crib. Or was it a bassinet? Hopefully tonight would be a slow night at the station and I'd have time to google all the baby shit we'd need.

Evie looked at me from behind heavy lids, her eyes still ringed in dark circles.

Smiling, I held up the flowers.

Her face barely moved, but she nodded.

When I handed her a brown paper bag from Bean There, Sipped That next and she eyed the croissant inside, her lips finally tipped up.

"And a Vermont-style cold brew," I said, putting the cup on her table. "My sister said you drink it year-round?"

She nodded and reached for the drink. I felt a strange surge of pride, bringing her coffee and breakfast. Silly, yes, but after the events of the last twenty-four hours, it felt good to contribute.

Quietly, I approached Vincent and hovered over him. His tiny body was swaddled in the hospital-issued scratchy blanket, the blue hat in place. He was captivating.

My son. My child. I'll never get over this feeling.

After taking a few pics, I navigated to my sibling group chat. Ignoring the messages related to damage control and the frantic instructions about police investigations, I sent them all. I'd read their messages at the station later. I wouldn't let anything pull me away from this moment. So I pocketed the device and looked back at Vincent.

Forget the farm, forget the firehouse, forget everything else. This little guy is the only thing that matters right now.

"Can I get you anything?" I whispered to Evie. "Tissues? Water? A margarita?"

Her responding smile was stiff. "No, this is great. Thank you."

Unease swirled through me. She wasn't engaging, and if I wasn't careful, I'd be oversharing in a heartbeat, probably driving her nuts while she needed to rest. So I dragged a chair over to the bassinet and sat, focusing on the baby.

"I didn't realize you'd be back so soon," she said after a few minutes of painful silence.

I dipped my chin. "Got a twenty-four-hour shift in a bit, so I wanted to check on you two beforehand."

"We're fine." Her tone was a little sharp. The warmth and vulnerability she showed during our last conversation was nowhere to be found.

"You don't have to stop by all the time," she continued, her fingers laced in her lap. "You've got your job, the farm, your family... and all your late-night activities. Don't add us to your list of responsibilities."

Her words hit me like a knife to the chest. Did she really think I wouldn't be here to help? That I wouldn't take parenting seriously?

My siblings' voices echoed in my head. Comments about paternity tests and custody papers. It all made me want to throw up. They meant well, and they weren't completely wrong, but for now I was too raw and too vulnerable to broach those subjects. All I could manage was to hold back tears when I looked at my son.

Vincent stirred, making cute baby noises, and instantly, the turmoil in my head calmed. None of that would deter me. Neither would Evie's dismissive attitude. I wouldn't let anything dampen the love and joy I already felt for this precious baby.

The world could doubt me, underestimate me. I was used to it. But I knew who I was and what I was capable of.

Between one heartbeat and the next, Vincent's sweet noises turned into sharp cries.

I leaped to my feet, taking in his scrunched-up face, hands hovering over him. That when I was hit with a... let's say *pungent* odor.

"I've got it." Evie swung her legs over the side of the hospital bed.

I held up a hand. "I can handle a diaper."

How such a tiny person could produce such a mess was beyond me. I focused on cleaning him up, talking to him in low tones as I went. I'd changed diapers, so I wasn't totally clueless, but it had been a long time since any of my nieces or nephews were this tiny.

I snapped up his onesie and pulled his left sock up, since it had worked its way down his foot and was barely hanging on. Then I wrapped him loosely in a fresh blanket.

Cuddling him to my chest, I kissed the top of his head. "He's already got my ears. Poor kid."

Rather than a smile, Evie gave me a sharp look.

Okay. That did not land the way I'd intended.

A sinking feeling settled into my gut. I barely knew her. I had no clue what she liked. What made her laugh. Who she was beneath the prickly, intense exterior.

Vincent deserved better.

"We should establish some ground rules," Evie said.

"There's plenty of time for that." I cuddled him close to my chest. "The kid's a day old."

"We need a plan. We're being discharged tomorrow afternoon."

My spine snapped straight, and Vincent let out a tiny whimper. "That's it? They just let you walk out with a baby?" I blurted out.

God, I sounded like an idiot.

Rather than give me another reproachful look, she chuckled. An honest-to-goodness laugh. *Huh.*

"Apparently." She shrugged. "I'm nowhere near prepared, and I have no idea what I'm doing, but they're kicking us out, so I'll have to figure out how to keep him alive."

With every word, her defensiveness faded away. Instead, her tone was full of genuine worry.

As I studied her, an idea came to me. "I'll take care of it," I said firmly. "And I'll take you home tomorrow."

My phone buzzed in my pocket once, twice, then again and again.

Evie cocked a brow, reaching for Vincent. So with a sigh, I gently handed him to her. Immediately, he started to root. God, this kid already had his dad's appetite.

I dug out my phone and frowned down at the screen filled with text notifications from my siblings, Gabe, and Chief Ashburn, my boss. It seemed as though everyone had information about the murder or road closures or the loss of business. It was difficult to fathom. Will McManus, gone. Such a hardworking, eager kid.

It was so fucking unfair.

And in this town? A place that prided itself on small-town values and helping our neighbors? Just the thought that there was danger out there sent a chill down my spine.

I surveyed Evie and Vincent. I couldn't bear the thought of anything happening to them.

Josh needed me to replace lines and manage deliveries. We were limiting the people who came onto our property for now, so we were shorthanded. And I'd probably be picking up extra shifts with the road closures and the townsfolk in a tizzy like they had been for the last couple of days. How did parents find time to work and take care of other responsibilities while their kids existed?

Just the thought of leaving made my chest ache and a wave of guilt sweep through me. But a whole slew of people needed me.

One by one, I responded to messages, tapping the screen quickly, not bothering to double check that I hadn't made typos. I'd hit Send, then quickly move on to the next.

"Looks like you've got a lot to worry about."

I peeked up at Evie, shrugging. "I've got it handled."

She tilted her head. "It's okay. This is a lot. And Vincent and I don't need you here to play house with us."

There it was again. This time I didn't let the blow land the way it had earlier. I was onto her. She went on offense to avoid playing defense.

"I'm a Lawrence," I said cooly. "Emotional defense mechanisms are a family specialty. So I see what you're doing."

She lowered her head, fussing over Vincent, who was happily suckling.

I flexed my fists, trying to quell the storm brewing in my brain. I had so much to learn and so much to do. It was overwhelming, knowing how different everyday life would be now that Vincent was here.

But my biggest worry? How Evie and I were going to make this work.

Obviously the two of us were different. But she was the mother of my child.

She may not believe me now, but I'd make it my mission to prove her wrong. If there was one thing I was good at, it was showing up. And she'd realize sooner or later that I wasn't going anywhere.

I brushed my knuckles along his tiny fist. "See you tomorrow, buddy," I said softly. Then I straightened, meeting Evie's wary eyes.

"Tomorrow," I said. "I'm taking you home."

She inhaled, like she was preparing to argue.

Before she could shoot me down, I said, "I've already got a car seat, so I'm taking you home."

Maybe that wasn't technically true, but I'd send the rookie to Walmart tonight. He could FaceTime me from there, and I'd find the safest model and have it installed and ready by morning.

For a split second, emotion flickered across her face. Or maybe it was surprise. It could have been my imagination, but I swore she even looked a bit impressed.

Good. Because I was just getting started.

Outside in the parking lot, as I strode to my car, my chest ached with equal parts exhaustion and adrenaline. I'd activate the entire Maplewood network, pull every single string I had. If Evie thought she was doing this alone, she was sorely mistaken.

Chapter 5

EVIE

The weirdest part about having a baby is that they just let you take the helpless, fragile little soul home after.

After less than three days in the hospital, Vincent and I were deemed "ready," whatever that meant. The nurses, who had taken care of us around the clock, packed us up, stuck a stack of diapers in the bag Ruby had brought for us, and dispatched me with nothing more than hugs and well wishes.

Vincent was dressed in an adorable sailor outfit Ruby had also picked up. He looked so tiny in his brand-new bucket seat. Jasper had shown up with it, swearing it was top of the line, and announced that he'd already installed one of the bases in his car and had the resident car seat expert at the fire station confirm he'd done it right.

It certainly looked safe, but disquiet swirled through me anyway. I'd quickly tried researching car seats while Vincent slept yesterday, but the sheer amount of information was overwhelming, so this was yet another area in which I wasn't knowledgeable. So much of Vincent's life was left up to chance because I was so unprepared as a mother.

"Ready?" Jasper asked, hitting me with that big, disarming smile.

Despite his size—the man took up the entire doorway— he was eager, almost boyish. The light in his eyes when he looked at Vincent was innocent and pure.

He was tall and muscly, his Maplewood Fire Department T-shirt stretching across his chest.

A normal woman would look at him and think *handsome young hero.*

But I was not a normal woman. I was a hormonal mess who alternated between leaking milk and leaking tears.

So I saw him much differently.

To me, he was this hot, unattainable man who had bought a car seat and had a professional confirm its safety. He was a man I shouldn't trust. He was too handsome. Too charming. And too loud. A man I needed to stay far away from because he, like every man who'd come before, would flake and leave me utterly disappointed. The confusion alone was enough to make me tear up.

"Are you okay?" He rushed to my side and cupped my shoulders like he was prepared to hold me up. "Should I buzz for a nurse?"

I shook my head. "Just tired," I lied.

He ran his big hands down my arms. "Are you sure?"

Why was he being so sweet? I'd been bitchy and dismissive yesterday. He was right when he called me out on the defense mechanism. But I hadn't acknowledged it or apologized. And now here he was, smiling and being annoyingly thoughtful. I was the queen of pushing people away, and this guy seemed immune to my venom.

"I have to take care of him now," I said with a whisper. "And I'm not prepared."

He looked over at Vincent, who was snoozing in his car seat, a binkie in his mouth. Then he turned back to me. "*We* are going to do a great job. Yeah, we're a bit behind, but I'm catching up. I spent most of my shift watching YouTube videos."

"YouTube?"

"Don't knock it. I've learned a lot about parenting already. And my swaddle game is on lock. Just you wait."

I couldn't help but smirk. His easy confidence was disarming, making me feel a tiny bit better.

The *we* should have thrown me. It should have activated my defenses. There was no *we*. I was doing this on my own. He could be around, of course, but I'd ensure he got the message.

I didn't need Jasper complicating my life any further.

But as I looked at him, gorgeous even in the harsh fluorescent hospital lights, I couldn't muster the energy to fight him on this.

I'd missed my house. It wasn't much, but it was mine. Home ownership hadn't been on my to-do list in New York. It wasn't realistic. But shortly after moving here I'd purchased the cutest little bungalow a few blocks from town. For months, I'd spent my free time decorating and fixing the place up. The pastime wasn't great for my social life, but it filled me with joy every time I looked at the floors that I'd refinished or the cheery window boxes I'd installed.

Now I was bringing a boy into my home. Damn. I'd

probably have to tone down the girliness. The fuchsia bathroom, the cat wallpaper, and the purple velvet sofa definitely didn't scream boy mom. Eh. I could figure that out eventually. Thankfully I had a spare bedroom. It was a catch-all, filled with boxes and all kinds of other shit. But at some point, I'd muster up enough energy to clean it out for him.

Vincent started to fuss beside me in the back seat of Jasper's Bronco. God, the kid never stopped eating. As soon as I finished nursing, which took close to a lifetime, he was hungry again. Honestly, I didn't mind. According to the nurses, most babies lost weight after birth, but Vincent was already gaining like a champ. It appeared that he'd inherited my metabolism.

As we navigated through town, I scanned our surroundings, shocked by how many businesses were closed. The town green was still decorated for the Maple Festival, but the vendor booths were empty and the stage in front of town hall looked abandoned.

The town came alive this time of year, to celebrate the rich history of the maple industry. Jasper had mentioned how chaotic things had been, how terrified the locals were. It didn't make sense. A murder? That sort of thing did not happen in this quaint New England town. A town where doors were left unlocked and neighbors still showed up on porches with casseroles. Where a person was more likely to trip over a sugar bucket than stumble across a crime scene.

Breaking news usually involved Basil writing something nasty about the rival cheese shop on his chalkboard sidewalk sign.

We took care of one another. And no one dared get in the way of the lifeblood of this place: tourism.

Other parts of Vermont had been hit hard. Rural communities were shrinking, the mills and factories that once sustained them closing down and being boarded up. Maplewood had stayed strong all these years, luring visitors with postcard-perfect streets, its colorful history, and above all, maple syrup.

"Did they catch the person who did this?" I asked, breaking the silence that had stretched since we left the hospital.

Jasper couldn't have been driving more than fifteen miles per hours, his hands at ten and two as he obsessively watched the road. I appreciated the care he was taking in transporting us.

"Not yet. But it hasn't even been three days."

Huh. Three days? It felt as though I'd lived a lifetime in those sixty something hours.

He turned onto my street and eased into the driveway behind Frankie's truck. Weird. She hadn't mentioned that she'd be here. But Frankie wasn't the type to wait for an invitation.

Ruby's car was here too, along with several others.

"What is going on?" I asked as Jasper put the car in park.

He pointed at the basketball hoop hanging over my garage door. "I didn't see that." He trailed off, the tips of his ears turning red. "Um, last time."

"It was dark." I added, nerves coursing through me as I referenced the night we conceived Vincent.

"Do you play?"

This was an extremely awkward conversation to be having at the moment, but I replied anyway. "Yes. I played through high school." As a tallish girl, everyone always told me I should play. So I did. And it made my mom happy, because she thought I needed to be "more active and burn more calories."

"We should play sometime."

The front door opened, and Ruby waddled toward the car.

"Focus, Jasper," I snapped. "What is going on?"

He chuckled. "You didn't think we'd let you bring Vincent home to an empty house, did you?" With that, he climbed out of the car and offered me his hand.

When I was steady on my feet, he effortlessly unlatched Vincent's bucket seat from the base and lifted it from the car.

Ruby spread her arms wide as she approached. She was wearing a fuchsia shirt paired with a fifties-style circle skirt covered with giraffes wearing sunglasses.

"What did you do?" I asked.

"Nothing you wouldn't do for me." She threw Jasper a wink. "Plus, we had help."

I turned to the man at my side, but he was busy fussing with the sleeping baby in the car seat he was now carrying.

Inside, my tiny house was a blur of activity, the living room overflowing with diapers, clothing, bottles, blankets, some kind of space chair for babies, and a bassinet.

Tears once again threatened, making my nose sting. "This is too much."

"It's not." Ruby turned to face me head-on. "And besides, you know Frankie. She made it easy. All she had to do was terrify everyone into ponying up."

Frankie waved from the kitchen where she was unpacking a box. "This was just delivered. Top-of-the-line video monitor. You can keep your eyes on the little bean round the clock."

My vision went blurry, the tears winning out. "Thank you," I said, a sob catching in my throat.

She walked around the island, pulling me into a fierce hug. "You deserve everything," she said into my ear. "And we're your friends, so we're gonna make sure you get it."

Rather than calm me, the twinkle in her eye put me on high alert. Frankie Dunne was legendary. I had no doubt she'd have the monitor set up, synced to my phone, and probably watering my lawn in ten minutes.

"Sit down and rest, Mama," she said. "We're almost finished."

Jasper had Vincent in his arms, and my little guy was already rooting. Damn, this kid could eat.

I sank into the couch, and out of nowhere, Ruby produced a C-shaped pillow and shoved it into my lap. "For nursing."

Jasper eased Vincent into my arms as I sniffled, trying to control my tears.

"Where did all this stuff come from?"

"The town," Ruby explained. "We made a few runs to the store, and Jasper coordinated with Basil on the nursery project."

"Wait, what?"

"You know Basil," Frankie said. "He had a vision. He and Etienne are almost finished. They're in there now, 'styling'"—she used air quotes—"the shelves."

I giggled. Frankie was not one for style. She and Basil frequently argued at book club about the aesthetics of the waiting room at her auto shop.

"We know Vincent can't sleep in there for a while, but I didn't want you to have to worry about fixing up that room," Jasper said, planting himself on the edge of the couch.

"But it's only been three days. And you've been working."

Standing, he shrugged. "I'll go install the other car seat base in your car while the baby is content." He picked up the bucket seat and set it on the small table by the door. Above it, on a brand-new decorating hook, was what looked like a navy and white stripped diaper bag. That had Ruby all over it.

When the door closed behind him, Frankie shook her head. "I don't think he sleeps." She held up a cord, working to untangle it. "He wanted to make everything perfect. Worked nonstop. And I yelled at him. A lot."

"She did," Ruby added, her lips quirking. "But he's so damn easygoing."

Jasper had vastly exceeded my expectations by showing up with a top-of-the-line car seat fully installed. But this? Working with my friends to welcome us home?

An uncomfortably warm feeling bloomed in my chest, the sensation triggering another round of tears.

I hadn't known a single one of these people two years ago when I moved to town, yet here they were, showing up for me and my baby when my own family didn't seem concerned about rushing to see us.

And Jasper? I barely knew him, but since the minute my water had broken, he'd been showing up.

I didn't deserve all this support.

My parents had a grandchild, and when I'd called each

of them, they'd murmured about driving up eventually. My siblings sent congratulatory texts, but that was it.

Yet Vincent and I were not alone.

That beautiful sentiment only made me sob harder.

Once I'd quelled my emotions again and moved Vincent to my other breast, the scent in the air caught my attention. "What is that smell?"

"Chicken soup. My mom made it," Ruby yelled from the kitchen. "And Etienne baked a fresh loaf of sourdough."

My mouth watered. Etienne's sourdough was the stuff of legends. His starter was twenty years old and named Florence.

"He is so beautiful." Basil removed his horn-rimmed glasses and dabbed at his eyes with the handkerchief Etienne handed him.

"And Vincent is such a nice name," Etienne declared in his strong French accent. "Distinguished."

"Thank you." I smiled at my baby, who was now snoozing in his brand-new swing. "It was my grandfather's name."

As soon as I'd burped Vincent, Ruby had scooped him up, changed his diaper, put him in a fresh onesie, and gotten him set up with his binkie and a blanket covering his lower half.

Basil produced a bowl of soup and a piece of bread the size of my head, scolding me about fueling my body.

I sniffled as I took the bowl from him. "You guys are spoiling me."

"Nah," Frankie said. "We're just taking care of our friend and her stupidly adorable baby."

Jasper lingered in the kitchen, loading the dishwasher and breaking down cardboard boxes.

Emotions overwhelmed me once more as I watched him. I had a child. With a man I barely knew. And I'd have to figure that out. In this ridiculous hormonal postpartum state.

"We made a schedule," Ruby declared. "We've got meal deliveries set up, and we're all taking shifts so we can help clean and hold Vincent so you can shower and nap." She tapped at her phone screen.

"I've set up calendar alerts as well. We've got you covered."

Jasper walked into the living room, his eyes filled with uncertainty and maybe a little hurt. "Should I send you my schedule at the firehouse? I typically work twenty-four on and twenty-four off, but I can shift to twelves if that works better. Chief owes me after all the overtime I've been putting lately."

Ruby smiled at him. "Sure. You have my number? Text it to me." She eyed me, then stood. "Let's clean up and give them some privacy."

Frankie, Basil, and Etienne jumped up and immediately started collecting bowls.

"I'll change Vincent," I said. Ruby had just done it, but I was desperate to escape this awkwardness. There was no plan here. No playbook. It was bad enough I had to figure out how to take care of a newborn, but with Jasper around?

I was being unfair, but it took all I had to hold it together as I clutched Vincent to my chest and shuffled down the hall. I'd wallpapered it with bright green stripes to make it feel roomier, but it was still pretty dark. I passed my room, heading for the spare room, discovering after a moment that Jasper followed.

Nerves skittered through me as he padded on socked feet behind me. He was Vincent's father, but the fear of being away from my child gripped me tightly. This baby needed me. And the last thing I wanted was to hand him over to another person and walk away. But that was how this worked, right?

I swallowed past the lump in my throat. Not today. We'd figure it out later.

I pushed open the door to the spare room and immediately sucked in a sharp breath.

The cramped space had been transformed. The bottom three feet or so of the walls were covered in dark green beadboard with an ornate chair rail. The top half had been painted, the scene depicting mountains and trees in pastel shades of green and blue.

A beautiful oak crib stood on one side of the room, framed prints hung on the wall, and the shelves were full of children's books.

The matching oak changing table was stocked with perfectly arranged diapers and wipes.

Tears filled my eyes again. This was too much.

"Do you like it?" Jasper asked quietly from the doorway.

I nodded, biting my lip to keep the sobs inside. This wasn't who I was. I was organized. Strategic. I planned my life with precision.

And now I was fumbling to change a diaper while Jasper watched.

Jesus. Get it together, Evie.

"Do you want me to help?" he asked as he moved closer.

"No." The single word came out more clipped than I'd intended, and a rush of guilt hit me. I inhaled and let the air back out slowly. "Sorry," I said. "I've got it."

I surveyed him, searching for words. I wanted him around, for Vincent, but I also needed to figure out how to take care of him on my own. I ached for space. I didn't need help. I'd been crushing it as a one-woman show for almost thirty-five years.

I rubbed circles over Vincent's back. He was so precious. I wanted to clutch him to my chest and never let anyone close, not even Jasper. Especially not Jasper. He meant well, standing there with his broad shoulders filling the room, offering his time to us like it was the easiest thing in the world.

But I knew men like him. He'd show up until he didn't. Men broke promises, leaving the people they supposedly cared about holding the pieces. I'd named Vincent after the only man I'd ever trusted. After my grandfather, every other man I'd met had disappointed me in one way or another. So I'd built a life on my own, and I wouldn't change that now.

"I brought that from the farm." Jasper nodded at the corner of the room.

My heart stuttered. The rocking chair was solid, made of thick, dark wood, the back carved ornately.

"My dad built it for my mom when she was pregnant with my oldest sister. And she used it for each one of us. He carved our names and birthdays on the back."

He turned the chair around and ran his large hand down the back of it.

Sure enough, Jennifer, Jessica, Joshua, and Jasper were all carved into the wood, along with dates.

"And my sisters rocked their babies in this chair too."

Elijah was carved next, with a birth date much more recent. According to this, he was a teenager. Then there was Isaac, Katherine, and Margaret.

The breath left my lungs. For a moment I was speechless. When I could finally breathe again, I said, "And you brought this for me?"

"Yes. Only if you want it." He rubbed a hand through his hair, making it stand up. "I wanted Vincent to have a little part of my parents. Since he won't get to meet them."

My heart ached. My parents, both very much alive and healthy, had already proved that they had little interest in my baby. But this loving, sweet gesture damn near cracked my heart in half.

"Do you want to rock him first?" I asked gently.

His face softened and his eyes went misty. Nodding, he eased into the chair. As I moved closer, he looked up at me with a look of pure gratitude. I handed him Vincent, who was swaddled and happily sucking on his binkie.

Jasper settled in quickly and began to rock him, closing his teary eyes and murmuring to our child.

"And Nana Louise was an artist," he said. "She could paint and draw and sculpt. She struggled during the long Vermont winters, so your grandpa built a small barn just for her. She would go in there and make art and play music and dance. She would have loved you so much."

I turned away. Watching him rock our child, his large frame making Vincent look even smaller, and hearing the heartbreak in his voice was too much.

Too beautiful and too overwhelming.

For several minutes, I silently poked around the room,

taking in the details while distracting myself from my emotions.

Eventually Jasper laid Vincent in his crib and stepped toward the door.

Just as he reached for the knob, I quietly cleared my throat. This situation required delicacy and strategy, neither of which my mind was capable of in this moment. But I had to get this off my chest.

"I don't want to keep him from you," I whispered. "You're his father and you have every right to be here."

"And I will be," he said, his green eyes flashing with determination.

I took a deep breath and steeled my nerves. "I need a coparent," I said matter-of-factly. It was necessary if I wanted to muscle all my complicated feelings into something workable. "Not a man who wants to play house when it's convenient. I can't create a life for my child while waiting to see if you show up." The words tasted bitter in my mouth, but I forced them out anyway.

His eyes flickered again, this time with hurt, disappointment, and maybe a little shame. But then he nodded. Slow and silent. He didn't argue. He didn't fight.

"Okay," he said, his tone resigned. "Then I'll get out of your hair. And I'll check with Ruby. Find out when I'm needed next." He licked his lips and searched my face like he wanted to say more, like maybe he wanted to prove me wrong. Instead, he let the silence stretch out for an uncomfortable few seconds. Then he turned and walked out of the room.

Immediately, I wanted to call him back, to undo what I'd just done, to take back the words. But the fear of finding myself one day needing a man I couldn't rely on kept me frozen in place. We had plenty of time to work out what our lives would look like as coparents, but for this moment, I needed to protect myself and Vincent.

It was better this way.

Even if I felt as though I'd slammed the door on something I wasn't ready to lose.

Chapter 6

JASPER

It felt like I'd just left this place, and here I was, ready for another shift. For a small town, Maplewood was not sleepy. Calls came in all day and night, every day of the week. Most were minor, but they were frequent enough to keep us on the move. The firehouse was a handsome stone building next to City Hall on the town green. It was old, loud, and questionably maintained, but we made do.

I rubbed my eyes. I'd gotten up extra early to drive into town today to pick up coffee and a treat for Evie.

She had not looked particularly happy to see me when she'd opened the door, but between the cold brew and the croissant, she softened. Even let me hold Vincent for a few minutes while she took a shower. It wasn't much, but it was progress.

As I stepped inside, I was greeted by the distinct and familiar smell of a fire station. Rubber and disinfectant, with a hint of exhaust. Since most of our time was spent cleaning, organizing, and maintaining our gear, the smell of the cleaner had seeped into the walls.

It was comforting and a bit nauseating all at once.

I plastered on a big smile, masking the stress weighing me down. My nervous system still hadn't recovered from the events of the past few days. My entire world had changed, my life upended.

"It's Daddy Jasper." Martin slapped me on the back as I walked into the kitchen. "And late as usual."

Frowning, I turned toward the large clock on the wall. Damn. I was one minute late, but everyone always gave me shit.

Magnus, our rookie, gave me a nod as he filled a mug with coffee. He'd earned my respect by helping me buy baby gear, and he'd done a damn good job putting the stroller together.

The kitchen was usually pretty quiet in the morning, but today, the adrenaline was palpable, like they'd just gotten back from a call.

I cleared my throat and stepped up to the coffee pot. "Busy night?"

Chris slid up beside me, reaching for the sugar. "Nah. Dead. Everything is weird now, you know." He raised a bushy eyebrow.

My stomach sank. The murder. The thing the whole town was simultaneously talking about and *not* talking about.

I gave him a nod and headed for the table.

He, Martin, and Chief Ashburn had responded to the scene. Thankfully I had only witnessed the aftermath after getting Evie loaded into the ambulance.

"Still can't believe you're a dad," he said, easing into the chair beside me. "Kid got all ten fingers and ten toes?"

Head bowed over my coffee, I nodded.

"I believe it?" Martin added. "I'm shocked it took this long for Lawrence to have an oopsie baby. You should probably check every other small town in Vermont, make sure he's the only one."

Rage bubbled up inside me, the sensation strange. I'd never let the ribbing the crew dished out bother me before. But this was different. I hated the idea of Evie being associated with all my past flings. Like she was just another girl. Because she was so much more.

A desire to protect Evie and Vincent flared inside me. They were family now.

"Should we take bets on when another one will turn up?" Magnus added eagerly.

Chris and Martin stopped and stared at him. "Fuck you, Rookie."

I smirked. My crew could talk shit about me, but we all upheld certain lines. Letting the rookie join in was one of them. At least some things were still sacred.

"His name is Vincent." I unlocked my phone screen and slid the device to the middle of the table.

All three of the guys leaned in.

"Cute baby."

"Hope he gets his brains from his mom."

Before I could protest, Chief Ashburn came out of her office, her favorite glittery pink coffee mug in hand.

"I heard the news," she said. "Show me photos."

The chief was tall with streaks of silver cutting through her dark braid. In her late forties, she carried herself with the kind of authority that made even the loudest guy in the room shut the hell up. I'd seen her drag a full-grown man out of a burning barn with a dislocated shoulder. Nothing rattled this woman.

We were midway through my Vincent slideshow when the alarm rang. In seconds, we were up and moving, going through the motions and procedures we'd practiced over and over again. Our team was small, and we were vastly different people, but when that alarm rang, we operated in perfect sync.

As we rattled down the narrow Maplewood streets, siren wailing, I checked my SCBA straps. Beside me, Magnus fumbled with his gear. Chris navigated the rig with precision while Chief communicated with dispatch.

"Chimney fire."

Those two words instantly slowed my heart rate. After the Maple Fest incident, it was easy to assume the worst, but this was a common occurrence. A lot of folks in the area had wood stoves and fireplaces, and it was still chilly out.

"Damn chimneys," Martin grumbled. "When will people learn they require proper maintenance?"

"Don't complain," Chris chastised. "After what we saw over the weekend? I'd gladly rescue kittens from trees every day for the next ten years."

Magnus, always eager to get in on the gossip, leaned forward. "Did you hear the FBI is here? They're inter- viewing people and sniffing around."

My gut twisted. That was news to me. Looked like I needed to talk to Josh and Jenn. Aside from a quick visit from Nolan, we'd heard nothing. Which made sense. There was no way our family farm was involved in any of this.

I adjusted my helmet, tightening my jaw. All I wanted to do was hold Vincent and tune out the rest of the world. The idea that there was a murderer running around the town where my child slept had all my protective instincts flaring to life.

Chris turned down Pine Street and hit the brakes. The engine squealed to a stop at the curb, the headlights bouncing off the white clapboard house.

A steady stream of smoke pulsed from the chimney, but there were no sparks.

I inhaled a calming breath. Okay, this wouldn't be too bad.

"Walters and Polanski," Chief barked. "You're on the roof. Check on the residents and ready the chimney kit. Lawrence and Rookie, you're the attack team. Get the camera."

When she released us, we hopped out of the truck.

I turned to Magnus, game face on. "Get your mask on and stay on my shoulder." He was mine to babysit today.

While we geared up, Chief did a three-sixty eval of the property and Martin checked on the residents.

The Glovers were an elderly couple who'd lived here my entire life. They had to be pushing ninety by now. Mr. Glover walked with a cane these days, but when I was a kid, he'd worked at the post office, and he'd always given us lollipops when we came in with my mom. Their kids had moved out of town years ago, and though they sometimes struggled on their own, their neighbors watched out for them.

When Martin approached where they were huddled up on the sidewalk holding their tiny dog, asking if anyone was injured, they waved him off. Once Chris had positioned the ladder and the chief gave us the okay to enter the structure, I headed for the front door with Magnus behind me. The living room was smoky, but not the worst I'd seen.

As Magnus fumbled the thermal imaging camera, I snatched it from him and quickly swept the walls.

"No heat extension," I relayed to the team.

Magnus dropped the salvage tarp in front of the hearth and spread it out as I continued to scan. With every moment that passed, I breathed a little easier. It looked like it was small and easily contained.

"Ready for the bomb drop?" Chris asked.

With a gloved hand on his shoulder, I pulled Magnus back from the tarp. The last thing I needed was him getting hit with debris.

"Focus, rookie."

The chains rattled down the chimney, followed by the whoosh of the weighted brush that came after the drop of the chemical retardant.

Burning creosote clattered into the fireplace, hissing against the embers as the retardant did its job.

With practiced efficiency, I shoveled the debris onto the tarp, waiting for it to extinguish.

"You're so calm," Magnus remarked, shoveling right along with me.

"Done this many times," I replied. "So many folks up here rely on wood to heat their houses, but burning it creates creosote, and when it builds up in chimneys, this is what happens."

Once we'd gotten the debris taken care of and the embers had all been snuffed out, Martin and Chris came in with brooms, and the four of us got the mess cleaned up. The smell was strong, but that would dissipate over the next few days.

"Do you have a place to stay?" Chief asked the Glovers as we were packing up.

"We'll be fine," Mr. Glover insisted, keeping his head high. "We'll bundle up and keep the windows open."

I shuddered. Hell no. Temps still dropped into the thirties at night this time of year, and after Will's death, I'd caution anyone against sleeping with their house wide open like that.

Chief glanced over at me, dipping her chin, and with a return nod, I jogged to the rig and picked up my phone.

After a few minutes and a quick text exchange, I wandered back over to where the Glovers were shivering together on the sidewalk. "I've got the perfect place to set you three up," I said, nodding at their little dog. "The cabin on the farm is empty right now, but Josh wants to rent it out during tourist season. How about you stay a few nights, then let us know what you think? You'd be doing us a big favor, and you'd have a place to stay."

Mrs. Glover squeezed my hand. "You are such a good boy," she said kindly. "And you look so much like your father."

My heart clenched like it always did when people mentioned the resemblance.

"But," she said, her eyes glassy, "we can't afford that."

"No charge." I squeezed her hand in return. "The farm is so busy this time of year. We haven't had the opportunity to really assess whether the cabin is acceptable for guests. And we rarely get homecooked meals with the way we're always working. We'd be grateful if you'd make your famous beef bourguignon in payment for your stay. How about that?"

Her face lit up. "It was my grandmother's recipe. She was born in France, you know. Ooh, Carl. We'll need to stop at the market today so I can pick up the ingredients."

While we finished cleanup and inspected the rest of the house, I texted Josh, letting him know that the Glovers were on board and to expect them soon.

As we headed back to the station, smoke clinging to our skin and gear, the mood shifted, adrenaline waning and silly chatter taking over.

"Clean work," Chief said proudly. "Lawrence, you ran that interior perfectly."

"Thanks," I replied, surveying the Green Mountains in the distance.

"Don't stroke his ego too much," Chris teased, his eyes on the road. "He's already got a baby and a murder mystery to star in."

While the rest of the crew laughed, I shot a dirty look at the back of his head. Asshole.

"Seriously," Magnus said, his face full of twenty-year-old innocence. "Why would anyone kill a person in Maplewood? We're America's most charming small town. Nothing bad happens here."

"Charm doesn't mean safe," Martin said. "Could have happened anywhere. Wasn't it your farm Jasper?"

I grumbled unintelligibly in response. No way was I going to offer up details to anyone.

"Maple syrup, the FBI, a body, a secret baby." Chris hooted. "Those Lawrences have all kinds of secrets."

A growl rolled out of me. Dammit. My family had

always been held in high esteem. How the hell did we end up wrapped up in this bullshit? And on top of that, Evie and Vincent were getting pulled into this harmful gossip. And that's where I drew the line. My skin itched, not from the smoke or the fine mist of chemical retardant, but from the rumors that were no doubt being mentioned in places other than this rig.

"Can it, Polanski," the chief snapped before I could lay into Chris. "The Lawrences are not the Corleones of Vermont. This unfortunate situation is just that. It's a tragedy, Will's death, and not a topic to be chattering about."

Lips pressed together, I gave her a nod of thanks.

"Our job is to counteract the shitty things that befall our town," she reminded him. "To help and assist and serve. Don't forget that."

Chastened, Chris nodded, his focus never leaving the road ahead of us.

The cab had just fallen silent when Martin perked up, waving his phone in the air. "My brother-in-law will be out at the Glovers' on Monday to do a full clean and repair the damage."

Good. The best way to prevent these fires was annual cleaning and inspections of the old brick chimneys, but the upkeep could be expensive, and many people, especially elderly couples on fixed incomes like the Glovers, couldn't afford it.

"We can set up the positive pressure fans tomorrow," he added.

"Did you really offer them a place to stay?" Magnus asked, brows pinched in confusion.

"We serve the public," Chief said, turning in her seat to

look at him. "Putting out the fire is only a small part of that service. Up here, we have to rely on each other."

"So Jasper finds them a place to stay, and Chris's brother-in-law fixes the chimneys?"

We'd had several people stay in the cabin over the past few months. Josh, who could not exist without a project to keep him busy during his downtime, had renovated it last year. At the time, Jess had planned to move back, bringing her two daughters with her. Instead, she reconnected with her college sweetheart and stayed in New York. Rather than use the cabin, they'd decided to convert one of the old barns into a summer house for their family.

Josh had mentioned renting the place out several times, but he'd yet to get around to it. So it was the perfect solution for the Glovers.

"In this case, yes." Chief nodded. "The Glovers are elderly, and they have no family left in town. It's the least we can do."

As we rumbled back to the firehouse, Mrs. Glover's comment replayed in my head. She'd said that I looked like my dad.

Sighing, I closed my eyes and tried to picture his face. It had been close to fifteen years since we lost him. The ache to see him, to talk to him and introduce him to Vincent, hit me hard. He'd know what to say to encourage me, to make me feel capable. He'd make me believe that I had a shot in hell of living up to him. That I could be the kind of father he was.

I opened my eyes and studied the road ahead. The only way to honor my father was to keep showing up. For this town, for my family, and for Vincent.

Chapter 7

EVIE

At the sound of a knock on the door, I popped up from where I must have fallen asleep on the couch. *What time is it?*

I stumbled to the door, and when I pulled it open, I was blinded by bright sunlight. *Okay, I think it's morning.*

"Can I help you?"

The gangly teenager on the porch looked both terrified and a bit bored, if it was possible.

"Delivery," he said, tossing his head so his floppy brown hair revealed one blue eye.

He held out a brown paper bag with a familiar logo and a cup.

"Cold brew, Vermont style," he mumbled. "And a pesto egg sandwich."

My stomach rumbled. I couldn't remember the last time I'd eaten a meal.

"I didn't order delivery."

"Good," he said. "Because we don't deliver." He had already turned and was walking back toward the sidewalk.

"You can thank my Uncle Jasper," he hollered, raising one hand as he walked down the street.

I stared at the coffee in my hand, already feeling more awake. As if the caffeine could leach through the plastic cup, straight into my pores.

Jasper. He was working. Did he really have his nephew deliver coffee to me? I shook my head, both delighted and annoyed. It was just so… Jasper.

I was sitting at the kitchen counter, savoring the last few bites of my sandwich, when the doorbell rang again. Jesus. What was with this town and early mornings?

"Good morning!" Ruby trilled, wearing a big smile.

Frankie trailed behind her, her usual scowl in place.

"It's a beautiful spring day," my effervescent friend said. "Let's go for a walk."

I assessed my friends, then peeked around them. Sure enough, the air was brisk, and the day looked pleasant. Apparently, spring was in full effect in Vermont. Huh. I swore it was just winter.

Then again, I hadn't left the house in…

I peered around at the laundry and the baby gear strewn all over the living room. A week? Maybe two? A month? It was hard to tell.

Frankie pushed into the house and went straight for the laundry pile. Ruby followed her in and ushered me to the bathroom, where she turned on the shower.

"Ruby," I whined, following her out into the hall. "I can't go for a walk. Vincent will be ready to eat again in like an hour. I can't leave the house."

"Why not? You've got the fancy stroller," Frankie said, her arms full of towels. "And the little meatball is already month old."

As if on cue, Vincent cooed from the swing in the living room.

It was true. My baby had arrived a month ago. It had been the longest yet shortest month of my life. He'd aced every checkup, was sleeping for up to four hours a night, and was rocking his tummy time every day.

Was this how the rest of parenthood would be? An endless blur with some moments slowing to a crawl while others passed by in a flash?

"You need a pick-me-up," Ruby said, smiling brightly. "I'll rock Vincent while you shower. Then we can all get some fresh air together."

She was annoying perky and rocking expertly applied winged eyeliner. Makeup. One of many things that had once been a daily part of my life but now felt like ancient history.

"Look at this gorgeous boy," she cooed, lifting Vincent out of the baby swing that looked like a lunar lander. "It's only been two days, and you've already grown bigger and stronger."

She cradled him to her chest, her whole being lit up. "Go. Cleanse yourself. We're good."

"But." I scanned the room, which was much cleaner than it had been only minutes ago. The washer was going, and Frankie was now pulling the vacuum out of the hall closet.

"Go," she growled.

With a nod, I went. How could I turn down the chance to shower in peace? As I assessed myself in the mirror, I realized I couldn't remember the last time I washed my hair. A week ago, maybe?

In addition to being the most perfect baby to ever exist, my son had the unique ability to bend the space time continuum. How was it that he was already a month old? It felt like I'd only just held him for the first time.

After a luxuriously long shower—it was ten minutes, but that was twice as long as any shower I'd taken in weeks—I discovered a clean outfit laid out on my freshly made bed.

Damn, Frankie worked fast.

The moment I was dressed in the leggings, nursing tank, and denim shirt, I began to feel like an actual human being.

As I shuffled back to the bathroom, I took a second to check in on the situation in the living room. Frankie was in the kitchen now, scrubbing down the kitchen countertops, and Ruby stood in front of the couch, gently swaying with Vincent in her arms.

The sight, blessedly, caused a decent amount of my anxiety to drain away.

In the bathroom, I dried my hair and slapped on a thick layer of moisturizer and even a little mascara.

When I was finished, I found Vincent dressed in a new outfit, probably courtesy of Ruby, and a magically clean house.

"You guys are machines," I said, taking the place in.

Frankie stretched, letting out a yawn. "I wanted to hit the baseboards too, but I'm not myself today. I was up late installing security cameras at Basil's store." She rolled her eyes. "He's extra paranoid after what happened at the Maple Festival."

She snagged the throw blanket from where it was bunched on one end of the couch and quickly folded it.

"His rivalry with Lola is a bit unhinged," she teased, "but she's not going to murder him over a little gouda."

I giggled. Basil owned Curd Your Enthusiasm, an artisanal cheese shop. He took great pride in his locally sourced delicacies and had cultivated a never-ending and ruthless rivalry with Lola Prentice, who had opened her own shop, Cheddar Off Dead, across the street.

Feeling more awake than I had in I didn't know how long, I reached for my son. "I'll top him off before we go."

Ruby buried her face in his neck and blew a raspberry, then handed him over. "I'll pack the diaper bag."

"I've already given the stroller a tune-up," Frankie said. "The suspension was a bit off."

I bit back a laugh. Damn, my friends were the best.

"Let's move out," Ruby said when I finished feeding Vincent. "A walk and a little sunlight will do you good. We can run errands and grab lunch, and while we're out, you can speak to humans."

I huffed. "I speak to you guys."

And Jasper. Though I didn't say it out loud. He texted constantly to check on Vincent, and every time he stopped by to visit, he tried his best to chat with me. I couldn't deny him time with his son, but his presence unnerved me. It undercut my confidence as a mother. I should be enough for Vincent. I didn't need help.

I buckled my little guy in his stroller, adjusted his hat so it shaded his face, and pulled the canopy over him. Then we set off.

I'd bought my house because of the proximity to town

and the neighborhood's homey feel. This kind of community was one I'd never had back in New York, and every day, I fell more in love with it.

We took our time walking around the town green, taking in the spring flowers and the festive historical signage that had recently been added. The downtown area looked like it belonged in a snow globe. The streets were lined with wide brick sidewalks and flanked by maple trees strung with twinkle lights that stayed up all year, glowing like fireflies at dusk. And the storefronts boasted sturdy brick façades and historic charm.

Every couple of minutes, someone would stop to coo at Vincent. Ned Shaw, the postman, leaned out of his truck to wave, and Stacy, the florist, had the door to the shop propped open so the scent of fresh-cut lilacs drifted into the street. Maplewood was gorgeous, but it wasn't just the cobblestone sidewalks or the revolutionary war cannon on the town green that made the town so memorable. It was this intangible charm. This place had its own rhythm. The people here prized history but openly embraced quirks. Gossip ran faster than the river that poured over Lover's Leap Falls, but so did kindness and concern.

From the warring cheese shops to the cramped bookstore and the old-fashioned apothecary, I never tired of exploring this place. The waves, smiles, and greetings from people who seemed genuinely happy to see me out and about didn't hurt either.

New England was bursting with charming towns, but the feelings one experienced in Maplewood were what brought the tourists back year after year. And what made it such a magical place to live.

Across the street, the large door of the fire station was open, and the big red engine sat inside, polished so it gleamed, a piece of town pride for all to admire. Inside, a couple of men bustled around, dressed in their navy blue MFD T-shirts.

Was Jasper on duty today? My heart flipped at the thought.

I touched my clean hair and fought back a cringe. Because when he'd dropped by yesterday to see Vincent, I hadn't looked nearly as presentable.

Oh well. I pushed the thought away. Why did I even care?

"Coffee first." Frankie led us down Maple Street, heading toward Bean There, Sipped That.

I waited outside with Vincent in his stroller. The place was packed, and this thing was as big as a mid-sized SUV. And, as a perk, staying outside meant I could avoid bumping into Jenn Lawrence, the owner and Jasper's oldest sister. She was a lovely person, but this situation was too awkward to tackle at the present moment. Plus, I'd already had my coffee courtesy of Jasper and a surly teenager.

"Look how handsome you are," I cooed to Vincent as I tucked his blanket around him. He was happily riding around, seeming to enjoy the fresh air and sunshine. God, this kid was already a Vermonter.

I was admiring the windows of Basil's cheese shop when, like a demon summoned from hell, Bitsy Bramble appeared before me on the sidewalk, dressed in a sweater and pearls as always. She'd probably been lying in wait in a sewer grate somewhere like a pearl-clutching Pennywise.

"Well, if it isn't Maplewood's newest resident," she

trilled, peering at Vincent in his stroller like a critic at an art gallery opening.

She studied him and then gave me a disapproving glare. "He does look like a Lawrence."

My hackles rose. Was she questioning the paternity of my son? She shouldn't even know anything about us. I'd never actually spoken to the woman, but the small-town gossip mill had surely been at work.

Bitsy was of an indeterminate mature age. She was spry in a way that suggested youth, but her gray bob, lined face, and permanent judgmental scowl suggested she'd soon be a resident of the local nursing home. She was the unchallenged don of the Maple Street Mafia, the group of elderly ladies who ran this town and most of the small businesses on Maple Street.

I should have known better than to wander into their territory so soon.

"Between us," she said, her eyes glittering, "Jasper Lawrence is not known for his... follow-through. Wild as a march hare, that boy." She tsked. "He drove his father's tractor right through Mrs. Manning's hedge. Just yesterday, Olive Foster and I were talking about—"

Jaw clenching, I pulled my shoulders back. "He's a present and wonderful father."

"Of course, of course," she murmured. "Those Lawrence men settle down eventually. Well, sometimes. Just don't get your hopes up, dear. They may be tall and handsome, but reliable?" She tossed her hands up.

My grip tightened on the handle of the stroller. If I wasn't concerned about hurting Vincent, I'd ram her with it. Roll right over the toes of her orthotic sneakers. Thanks to

Frankie's all terrain tires, this thing could do some real damage.

"Bitsy," Ruby snapped. She was holding open the door for Frankie, who was juggling coffee cups and paper bags.

"Don't you have a committee meeting to run?" Ruby asked, hands on her hips, belly protruding.

"Or a spell to cast?" Frankie added with a sneer.

Bitsy straightened up, adjusting her purse on her arm. "I have been appallingly busy. With what happened at the Maple Festival"—her gray eyebrows shot up, one hand fiddling with her pearls—"this down is a powder keg. Got to keep on top of things. Dig into what really happened."

I blinked at her, a puff of air escaping me. This little old lady thought she was going to solve a murder? I supposed if anyone could, it would be Bitsy.

"I won't keep you," she said, peering down at Vincent again. "I'll just let the ladies at the historical society know that this little bundle of joy has arrived. Have a blessed day." With that, she swanned off, leaving behind a cloud of floral perfume and a rock settling in my gut.

I watched her retreating purple form, my pulse still thudding in my ears. Not because of the confrontation with the town busybody, but because of what had slipped out of my mouth.

He's a present and wonderful father.

The phrase had escaped me, hot and fierce, without my permission.

Jasper really was a good dad.

He really was present. He showed up as often as I would let him, attended to every diaper disaster he could, and carried Vincent around like he was made of spun glass.

I hadn't expected Bitsy to take a swing at him, but my instincts kicked in, and I was ready to swing back even harder. It was unsettling. But he was my son's father. And I would not let Vincent grow up in a town where people talked shit about his dad.

"Harpy in pearls," Ruby said.

"Demon in cashmere." Frankie handed me a paper bag and took over stroller duties. "Pan au Chocolat," she explained as I peeked in the bag, practically drooling over the heavenly concoction. "You deserve it."

Chapter 8

JASPER

One more hour, and I could head over to see Evie and Vincent. Thankfully today's shift had been easy. Just one slip-and-fall and now, a brush fire. The reported fire was on Old Mill Road. It was a common occurrence this time of year. Smoke had been seen near the ridge, a possible lightning strike, or, more likely, some careless campers.

Martin pulled the engine up behind the police cruiser, and we swung into action, checking in with Nolan, who was running point on the scene. As I approached, Nolan's face fell.

Instead of a blaze near the tree line, we found a hundred pounds of fur and attitude.

"Motherfucker," Nolan grumbled.

"Grab an extinguisher," I said to Martin, focus on Betsy Ross, who was sitting next to a smoldering campfire like she'd clocked in for a shift.

Smoke curled lazily from a trashcan lying on its side.

She'd probably knocked it over, and its contents had caught the embers of the dying campfire.

"Dispatch, this is engine one," I said. "We've located the source of smoke. No active fire. Just some embers and a misbehaving bear."

The line crackled. "A bear?"

"Affirmative. Betsy herself, one eye and all. Appears to be in good health and halfway through a family-size bag of marshmallows."

Nolan approached, looking older and wearier than ever. "She's tagged. The university tracks her. She's probably broadcasting to some grad student who thinks she's foraging naturally."

Betsy looked up with her single golden eye, marshmallow smeared across her muzzle like shaving cream, and gave Nolan what I could only interpret as a slow blink of disdain.

"Just give me a reason to shoot you," he muttered. His dislike of the bear was legendary.

Amusement rolled through me. She loved fucking with him.

Slowly, Betsy got to her feet and waddled toward the woods. On her way, she picked up the top of the supposedly bear-proof trash can and flung it in our direction.

For a second, I thought Nolan might draw his service weapon and shoot it.

When Betsy was out of sight, Chris extinguished the flames and we cleaned up the trash.

"Fucking bear," Nolan grumbled. "I should make a rug out of her."

"That bear has a hundred thousand followers on Instagram," I reminded him. "Her life's worth more than yours."

With a shake of his head, he headed back to his cruiser. "And don't I know it."

———

I CLIMBED OUT OF THE CAR, THEN DUCKED BACK IN, gathering the coffee and food and the box of diapers under my arm. Then, freshly showered, fed, and caffeinated, I headed for the front door. As I eased my way up the steps, I couldn't help but smile up at the sky. I was enjoying the earlier sunrise and the long-awaited first rush of spring.

I'd worked two shifts in a row, so I'd been missing my little guy terribly. During my last visit, Evie had hustled me out after thirty minutes or so. While it was clear she didn't want me here, Vincent shared my DNA, and I wasn't going anywhere.

Slowly, I was wearing her down. She still kept me at arm's length, but every time I came by, she treated me a little less like a visitor and more like Vincent's dad.

Gabe had reminded me several times that I had rights. Every time I saw him, he'd mention filing paperwork. He was just waiting for my approval. But that seemed like overkill. I hated confrontation. And when she was this tired and overwhelmed, shoving a stack of legal papers in her face would be a dick move.

We were still adjusting to being parents to a newborn. Why introduce legal proceedings now? I'd learned over the last few weeks that Evie needed to feel in control. So I'd let her adjust and get comfortable in her new role as a mother. Then we'd work the situation out together.

As I knocked, coffee balanced precariously and box of diapers slipping from under my arm, Vincent fussed on the other side of the door.

Evie appeared a moment later, wearing an old T-shirt stained with spit-up. Her normally neat hair was a mess, and the look on her face was one of pure exhaustion.

With a sigh, she stepped back and let me in.

The sink was full of dishes, the laundry was piled up everywhere, and the air smelled like a diaper pail.

Vincent, who was propped up on his mom's shoulder, was red-faced, his little fists clenched tight.

"I just fed him," she breathed, her body deflating. "I don't know what's wrong."

I put down the box of diapers and held out the coffee. "Vermont-style cold brew." I'd made sure that Evie got her favorite drink every morning. If I couldn't deliver it, Elijah, my nephew did. He was usually with his moms at the coffee shop every morning before school. Slipping him a few extra bucks to make sure Evie was taken care of was a no-brainer.

I placed a small paper bag on the cluttered coffee table, then straightened. "Pesto mozzarella egg sandwich."

As she looked from me to the bag, eyes wide, I picked up a burp cloth from what looked like a clean pile of laundry and threw it over my shoulder.

"Here." I reached for Vincent. "Let me take him so you can caffeinate and eat."

She took a step back, her expression one of alarm. "I've got it," she snapped. "You don't need to drop in with treats, thinking you can fix everything. That's not—" Her voice cracked and tears spilled down her cheeks. "I'm just so tired, and he's always crying."

Stomach clenching in sympathy, I squeezed her shoulder. "Evie, it's okay." I ducked, catching her eye, hoping she could see that I only wanted to make things easier for her.

Eventually she nodded, and I scooped Vincent out of her arms.

"Take a minute," I told her, picking up the sandwich and shoving it at her. "Sit down and eat something."

As she shuffled across the room, I got Vincent over my shoulder, massaging his back and dancing around the room like he preferred. He was angry, poor little guy, and according to Evie, he'd just finished eating and was in a fresh diaper.

"He keeps spitting his binky out," she said from the kitchen island, where she sipped her coffee, her eyes closed.

With even breaths, knowing if I got worked up that would only upset him more, I continued dancing around the room. While I bounced and rocked and shushed him, I flipped through the tips I'd learned from the newborn videos I still watched regularly.

When the one the group of dads I follow had talked about recently came to me, I laid him down on his back on the couch and cycled his legs like he was riding a tiny bike. Around and around. Up and down, back and forth, I gently moved his chubby little legs.

At first he cried louder, but remembering the encouragement the guys in the video gave, I continued. And after a moment, Vincent ripped one of the loudest farts I'd ever heard. And I spent most of my days in a firehouse.

I was grinning down at him, half stunned, when Evie

broke into laughter. It quickly turned hysterical, and I started to laugh too.

Vincent stopped crying and watched me with interest.

"Wow. Respect, son," I said, my eyes blurred from happy tears.

When I offered him his binky and cradled him in my arms, getting comfortable on the couch, he settled quickly.

Evie walked over, still giggling. "What the hell came out of him? He only weighs eleven pounds."

I shook my head. "Something unholy."

Her smile dropped, her shoulders sinking. "You make it look easy," she said softly. "How did you learn that trick, with the legs?"

I patted Vincent's back. "One of those baby YouTube videos. Since they don't move around a lot yet, gas gets trapped in their tummies. Cycling the legs helps get it out."

Impressed with myself, I sat a little straighter and gave her a smile. "Eat your breakfast. I've got him."

Rather than a high five to celebrate this parenting win, I was met with a quivering lip.

And then she was sinking onto the couch next to me, her body convulsing with sobs.

"I can't do this." Her shoulders shook, her words garbled. "I'm a bad mom. I'm a bad person. I fucked this all up from the start."

"Evie." I shifted Vincent to my other side so I could take her hand. "That's not true. You're doing great."

"Yeah," she huffed. "Great for the dumbass who didn't even know she was pregnant. Vincent deserves better."

As she cried, face buried in her hands, I plucked a clean washcloth from the pile of laundry beside me and handed it to her. Jenn had warned me about crashing postpartum hormones, and since Vincent was now a month old, this seemed to be right on schedule.

I put my free arm around her and squeezed, wishing I knew how to convince her of how incredible she was. First-time parenthood was hard as hell, even for the people who planned for it. She was making the best of it, and it was okay to ask for help.

Not knowing how to formulate an argument she'd buy, I just hugged her to my side.

Finally, when her breathing slowed, I said, "You're an amazing mother, and I'm the lucky bastard who gets a front-row seat to watch you shine."

The thought that this woman doubted herself ate at me. She was so capable, so resilient. Her entire life had changed in a few short weeks, and here she was, rolling with it all remarkably well.

"I'm stumbling," she admitted.

"And I'm happy to stumble right alongside you," I assured her. "Between the two of us, we will figure it out. And we've got the whole town if we need them."

She shook her head violently. "I don't want to lean on anyone. If it doesn't last, it'll only make things harder." She let out a shuddering breath. "And nothing lasts."

That comment hit me square in the chest. I wasn't going anywhere, and I'd told her that. But telling her again right now wouldn't help. So I tucked the information away, saving it for another time. If I wanted to stay in her and Vincent's lives. Then I would have to prove that I was all in using small, steady actions that wouldn't scare her off or push her away.

She hiccuped. "My life is a disaster."

"You know," I nudged her gently, "maybe this was meant to happen."

She glowered at me, dabbing at her tears with the washcloth.

"You are a type-A overachiever boss-bitch planner," I said, like she didn't already know that.

She nodded, clearly comforted by my accurate appraisal. "Maybe this was the surprise you needed."

She scoffed, the sound a little watery. "You think I ended up pregnant on accident and remained clueless about it until my water broke in a pizza parlor because the universe didn't want me overthinking and obsessing for nine months?"

I tamped down on a smile. She was annoyed, but at least mad was better than sobbing and beating herself up.

"And us," I said. "We would have argued the entire pregnancy."

"Yes." She slumped. "Because you would have annoyed me by bringing me snacks and gifts and insisting on coming to all the doctor's appointments."

"Yup," I quipped. "I would have been at every single one, with snacks."

She shook her head, though one corner of her mouth quirked up. "You are the worst. I would have hated you and pushed you away and told you I could do everything on my own."

"Really?" I gasped, feigning surprise.

For that, I got a light punch in the arm.

My body lit up with the contact she initiated. I was the kind of person who gave and received touch casually. It was natural to me. But Evie, so far, had been very selective about it. So her touch made me feel special, even if it had been violent.

Because violence from Evie Marino was preferable to nothing.

She dried her eyes for good, then took Vincent from me. When my hands were free, I jumped up, determined to make myself useful before I said something stupid and made her cry again. According to Jenn, the best thing I could do was be useful. So I unloaded the dishwasher, then refilled it with the stacks of plates and bowls in the sink. I'd tackle the laundry next.

After I'd cleaned off the island and started folding the load of clean clothes, Evie put Vincent in his baby swing and padded over, the color already back in her cheeks.

"How do you do it?" she asked quietly, picking up her coffee.

I folded the tiniest pair of pants and started a pile for Vincent's things. "Do what?"

"Be so positive all the time. Smile so much. Make the best of things."

I shrugged easily. All my life, I'd gotten questions like this, so the answer came quickly. "I was born like this."

"Bullshit. Try again." She folded her arms over her chest, the movement drawing my eye to the pink nursing bra visible through her old white T-shirt. "Give yourself some credit, Jasper. You had to have done work to get to this point. Don't deny it."

The fire in her eyes made my stomach clench. This was the Evie I was used to. Passionate and opinionated. Damn, good coffee really could work miracles.

"I was young when my dad died," I explained. "Heart

attack when I was in high school. He'd had his first heart attack a few years before that, but he rallied. For a while, life was great. Things went well and I relaxed, but then one day, he was gone."

A soft breath escaped her. "I'm so sorry."

"My mom spoiled me rotten. I'm the baby of the family, so it was my birthright. We were close, so losing her broke me inside. She's been gone for three years, but I wake up every morning aching to talk to her."

The moment turned really heavy really quickly. But at the same time, I appreciated the question. This was the first time Evie had really been curious about me. And I wanted her to know me, just like I wanted to know her. In therapy, I'd learned that achieving connections was worth the vulnerability, so I rolled with it.

"We have no idea how much time we have," I continued. "Every day is another opportunity for joy and fun and all the good stuff. So I try to remember that and choose the good stuff. The smiles and delicious coffee and laughing at baby farts."

She regarded me for a minute, sipping her coffee, a hint of warmth in her eyes, though it died quickly. "I wish I could feel that way. My brain is wired for worst-case scenario every day."

"The bad stuff?" I said. "It's unavoidable. Grief and loss and sadness. They sneak up on you. Taxes and storms and flat tires are all part of life whether you like it or not. But joy." I took a step toward her, holding her dark gaze. "You've got to choose joy. It's not just out there to stumble onto. You've got to actively seek it."

If I let my mind spin, it'd be brimming with doom and

gloom. Future custody disputes, worries about my financial future now that I had a child, the murderer on the loose in our small town.

There was so much fear, so much to lose. Enough to swallow me whole. So I had to stay focused on the good.

"You're full of life lessons today," she said, her lighter tone a little forced. "Baby gas mitigation and now philosophy? You are a pretty good inspirational speaker."

With a wink, I tipped an invisible cap. "Happy to indoctrinate you into the church of Jasper anytime."

She threw a onesie at me, her cheeks turning pink. "And you just made it weird."

"It's okay." I kept folding, my smile growing wider. "People have told me I give off handsome cult leader vibes."

Chapter 9

EVIE

Eyes squeezed shut, hand on Vincent's back, I ran through the mile-long to do list in my head.

With a breath out, I kissed the top of my sweet boy's head. This little guy had really thrown a live grenade into my life. Work was chaotic, since I hadn't planned on taking maternity leave. I hadn't technically returned to work, and my team had stepped in to help, but there were always fires waiting for me to put out. As director of marketing at Sugar Moon Syrup, I coordinated all corporate communications and worked with research and development to review all claims and labeling language, all while keeping legal off my back.

The environmental audit we were waist-deep in right now required a lot of careful messaging and emails, especially to our investors, meaning the entire company had been working nonstop.

As I opened my laptop, I prayed Vincent would snooze so I could at least go through my inbox. My three-month maternity leave was almost half over, yet I could still barely manage showering most days or keeping the house stocked with groceries. How the hell was I going to survive once I went back to work?

Closing my eyes, I forced a deep breath. For now, my top priority was time with Vincent. I could tackle everything else later.

Jasper would be proud of that mentality. Not that I'd mention any of this to him. He'd been so patient and kind, even when I was a raging bitch and pushed him away. Yes, I should let him help more, allow him to parent more. But the thought of letting go of Vincent for even a minute filled me with dread.

Before I could spiral again, a car pulled into the driveway, its tires crunching on the loose asphalt.

I popped up and peered out the window. Jasper was out front, stepping out of a truck that said *Lawrence Farm* on the side rather than his usual green Bronco.

Why was he here? He'd texted earlier, saying he was off work, but I'd told him we were fine and not to come by until tomorrow.

As irritation stirred to life inside me, I draped a blanket around Vincent and tucked it into the sides of the baby sling. Then I shoved my feet into my shoes and stomped outside.

Jasper was unloading a large item from the bed of the truck. He set it on the ground and went back for another.

Was that... a sleeping bag?

"What are you doing?" I asked, my voice harsher than it should have been.

"Good evening, Evie." He broke into a charming grin. "And Vincent."

He was wearing a blue T-shirt without a damn coat, when any sane person would be zipped up in a down parka right now.

I gritted my teeth at the sight of him. Why did he have to be all muscular and tattooed? It was annoying.

"You didn't answer my question."

"I'm camping," he replied, his ever-present smile making my stomach warm. Damn him.

"Camping?"

"Yes. This." He pointed at the rectangular item in a black zippered case he'd set on the driveway. "Is a tent."

"Where are you camping?"

"I was thinking the lawn." He put his hands on his hips, eyes bright. "If it's okay with you."

Confusion swirled in my head. "Why in God's name are you camping here?"

"Because I want to be close by for you and Vincent."

"Close by, like on my lawn?" What was his problem? This was ridiculous.

He shrugged. "It's only trespassing if you don't give me permission. So if you want me to move to the sidewalk, I can."

I closed my eyes and pinched the bridge of my nose, searching for the logic in his words. I came up empty.

"No," I said. It was the easiest answer. "Why do you want to sleep on my lawn? It's freezing out."

He scanned the yard, an almost dopey look on his face, like he hadn't noticed the temperature. "Eh, it's May. I'm good."

I blew out a loud breath. "Are you some kind of survivalist?"

He shook his head, his messy hair falling into his face. "Nah. I'm more of a softcore outdoorsman."

"Softcore?" What the hell did that mean?

"Yup. I like my creature comforts, like tents and sleeping bags and warm mugs of hot cocoa around a campfire."

Huh. That sounded pretty good, actually. Not that I would admit it.

"I still don't understand why you're here."

"I'm here because I want to be close. To participate. To help." He yanked a backpack out of the bed of his truck and set it at his feet. "I respect you and what you're doing, and I don't want to pressure you. Promise. But I can't help but feel like I can be of use here. Vincent is my son, and I want to experience this phase of his life too."

My heart sank. I couldn't argue with him. He was entitled to see Vincent, and I understood the pull to be with him at all times.

"It's okay that you don't like having me in your house. But the farm is twenty minutes away. Response time is important."

Now the guilt kicked in. Shit. Of course he didn't think I liked having him in the house. Because honestly, I didn't. I couldn't handle the proximity.

I sighed. His reasoning made sense. He was a firefighter and paramedic, it was natural for him to be concerned about response time.

"So I'll be here. Unless I'm working. If you need me, just yell."

I adjusted the blanket covering Vincent, pulling it up a little higher. The air was cool and crisp, a pretty great spring night, actually.

Sure, the farm wasn't all that close, but this seemed like overkill. But I was too weary to protest.

"I couldn't sleep there," he said softly, his shoulders drooping. "I kept worrying that you two would need me. This way, I can be close by, so if you think of something, just crack a window and call my name. I'm a light sleeper, so I'll be fine."

My chest panged. It was both sweet and ridiculous.

"I won't push you. I swear. Our situation is..." He paused. "Unique. So it calls for a unique solution. And I told you, I'm in this 100 percent."

His words held weight. They were maybe the most serious he'd ever spoken to me.

Legally he was entitled to time with his son. But the thought of being away from Vincent for even ten minutes caused panic to course through me.

At some point we'd need lawyers. A parenting plan and schedule. But for now, I couldn't go there. Not when he was so little and helpless. I'd fought so hard to successfully breastfeed, to decipher his cries and meet his needs. I didn't want to stop now. I wouldn't say anything about our situation was easy, but it was getting less impossible.

He was growing and gaining weight and sleeping a bit longer. The thought of Jasper taking him off to the farm made me sick. Not because Jasper couldn't care for him, but because he needed me. And I needed him too.

"I just want to be close," Jasper said, eyes pleading. "Things are scary right now."

He was referring to the murder. I'd been out of the loop, but Ruby had told me that his family farm was being searched and that they still hadn't caught anyone.

"And I need this," he pleaded. "I need to protect you and Vincent. I need to provide, in my own weird way."

His words hit me square in the chest. Dammit. It was time to face reality. I could put up walls and ice him out all day long, but there was no getting rid of Jasper Lawrence. He was on his own parenting journey, and it was wrong of me to get in his way.

"Fine," I said. "But please set up your campsite in the backyard." The last thing I needed was the Maple Street Mafia coming by on one of their morning power walks and finding Jasper in a tent on the front lawn.

"Got it." He swung his backpack onto his back and hefted the tent and sleeping bag up, then headed around the house.

Vincent was stirring, and pressed this close to my chest, my body was reacting naturally. I'd have to feed him again soon.

But I was hit with another wave of determination, so I followed Jasper in hopes that I could talk him out of his plan this time. "This isn't bizarre to you?"

"Nah." He dropped the bags and found a flat patch of grass. "It actually make sense. We're short-staffed, the budget's been slashed, and I work a lot. Now that we're into May, I'm not needed at the farm as much. My time is better spent here."

I sighed. "But you're sleeping on the ground."

"I've got an inflatable sleeping pad. It's great."

I shook my head, equal parts annoyed and impressed by his attitude toward primitive conditions. I could only sleep when equipped with a sound machine, an eye mask, and a fancy pillow.

"I want to be close without invading your home, so this is an easy solution. I was living in my childhood bedroom anyway. About time I got my own place."

"Your own place?" I scoffed. Unbelievable. "It's a tent."

He waggled his brows. "This thing is top of the line, with two rooms. It's swanky."

With a roll of my eyes, I turned toward the house. Fine. If he wanted to sleep on the ground and freeze his ass off, who was I to argue? "I'm going to go feed Vincent."

Inside, I settled into the rocking chair in his room and got Vincent latched. Six weeks in, and this kid was a pro. Maybe it hadn't been easy, but it was incredible, the way my body could feed and sustain him.

As I rocked, I picked up my phone and debated calling my friends. This entire situation was ridiculous.

But zipping in behind that thought was another one. This one unexpected. Maybe Jasper was serious. Maybe he would be a great dad and prove the gossipy old bags wrong.

Eyes squeeze shut, I quickly extinguished the idea. I couldn't let myself get hopeful that he'd step up.

He was a virtual stranger, a playboy, and, if the town rumor mill was to be believed, not the most reliable guy.

But he was Vincent's dad. There was no changing that.

Motherhood had been unexpected, but the minute he was in my arms, the biological instinct kicked in. The internet had been a much-needed resource, but I'd begun to realize that my intuition could be trusted when it came to my son. My body responded to his cries. I'd learned to distinguish between the different types too. And more often than not, I found myself waking up a minute before he did, even in the dead of the night.

This was my reality now. And though I felt mentally unprepared, physically, I was built for this.

But navigating this coexistence with Jasper? I had no clue.

We'd had a fun night all those months ago, but then we'd avoided one another. He was a hot playboy and I was me.

But now this relative stranger was my child's father. A man I'd be tied to forever and someone with whom I had to get along.

So I'd let him sleep on the lawn if that's what he wanted. Maybe he'd get uncomfortable after a few days and go home. Or maybe he'd be useful.

After I burped Vincent and got him latched to my other breast, I texted my friends rather than calling.

EVIE:

He's here.

RUBY:

?

EVIE:

Jasper. He brought a tent. He's gonna camp on my lawn.

RUBY:

Did he bring a boom box too?

FRANKIE:

Should I get my shotgun?

EVIE:

What are you talking about?

RUBY:

> Looks like we've got the selection prepared for our next movie night. But why the lawn?

FRANKIE:

> I can shoot at him. Or just scare him off if you prefer. Ignore Ruby. This is not Say Anything, this is more of a Red Dawn situation.

EVIE:

> He says he wants to be close to us.

RUBY:

> You can't say that stuff to me. I'm forty-three months pregnant.

I giggled. Ruby had entered what she called the eternal whale phase of pregnancy, where day after day, her thoughts solely revolved around getting the baby out.

EVIE:

> How do I make him leave?

FRANKIE:

> I'll tow his ass out.

> Or maybe see how this plays out? Let's say his intentions are good. How bad would it be if he left you alone for the most part but provided an extra set of hands when you needed them?

RUBY:

> Large, strong, capable hands. Probably a bit callused from all the manual labor.

FRANKIE:

Gross.

RUBY:

I can't help it. Pregnancy makes me horny.
This baby is killing me, and I've got
months to go.

FRANKIE:

Maybe make staying there uncomfortable
for him. That might encourage him to
leave.

RUBY:

Yeah, send him out to fetch things and call
him in for the blowout diapers.

FRANKIE:

Make him mow the lawn.

EVIE:

I'm not making him do yardwork.

RUBY:

You should. Maybe the gods will smile
upon you and he'll take his shirt off while
he does it.

FRANKIE:

It's forty degrees out.

RUBY:

Just let me live. You've got a hot guy
camped out on your lawn and at your beck
and call. Accept this gift from the universe
and focus on one of the other million
things you have on your plate.

FRANKIE:

Or I'll get the shotgun, just let me know.

JEEZ, MY FRIENDS WERE NO HELP. IT WAS EITHER SEX OR violence with those two, and I needed to be clear-headed about this.

I wiped Vincent's mouth, shoved my boob back into my tank top, and put him on my shoulder so I could coax a burp out of him. Silently, I walked the house, patting and rubbing his back and maybe spying on Jasper in the backyard.

Luckily, there was just enough space to peek through the curtains without moving them. And outside, the flood lights were on, bathing him in a hazy glow.

He worked diligently, expertly setting the poles and the straps until the tent was fully assembled. It felt almost pornographic. The precision. The attention he gave it. How carefully he worked.

That may have been what surprised me most about Jasper. He was competent. He did things efficiently and he completed tasks.

If he was changing a diaper or doing laundry for Vincent, he did it. All of it.

That was a quality I'd rarely encountered before, and certainly not with my dad or any of my stepdads.

It was... unnerving.

He unfolded a small chair, turned on a large lantern, and went inside the tent. I'd never camped before. I'd never done anything outdoorsy, really.

Maybe it was strange that I'd fallen so hard for Vermont, but the scenery had captivated me instantly.

As a city kid with parents who didn't give a shit, I'd missed out on so many experiences. When I'd come up here with friends for a weekend and hiked for the first time, it was an almost religious experience. Fresh air, mountains, dense forests.

I fell head over heels in love.

I rubbed Vincent's back, contentment settling in my chest. His childhood would be far different. He'd get to grow up here, spend time outdoors. Jasper would probably take him camping and teach him to fish.

That made me strangely happy.

In fact, as I changed my little guy, put him in his sleep sack, and sang him his favorite Italian lullaby, that peace and contentment only grew.

This kid was going to be okay. His parents were clueless, sure, but after watching Jasper pitch that tent, it was hard not to think that we might just have a chance.

Chapter 10

EVIE

The No Book Club was extra rowdy tonight.

We typically met in the tasting room at Etienne's wine shop or in a small private space at the Drip Line, Frankie's mom's bar. But tonight, my friends had come to me. I both appreciated the thoughtfulness and hated it. Hosting meant I'd spent most of the afternoon cleaning up, but also that I could put Vincent to bed and hang out with my friends for a bit.

Sure, he'd need one more feeding before I went to sleep, but that wasn't an issue. I didn't want to brag, but this kid was already a champion sleeper. He was doing five-to-six-hour stretches once he got his top off around midnight.

Naturally, every guest showed up with wine, food, or presents for Vincent.

"I had to buy this," Ruby gushed, showing me the tiny green sweatsuit she'd picked up. "And look at these sneakers!"

They were positively adorable. Even if he'd probably

outgrow them in a hot minute. The kid was getting bigger every day.

The doctor was amazed by his weight gain. He got that from me, that's for sure.

While we usually had more members, tonight, it was just the core group.

"You will die when you eat this Brie!" Basil declared as he set a delicious-looking salad on the countertop.

Wow. A salad should not look that pretty. Were those pomegranate seeds? His cooking and access to great cheese made him an MVP friend.

Ruby set up her portable Bluetooth speaker and turned on music, and within minutes, I was starting to feel like an actual adult again. For better or worse, these were my people.

When I'd picked up and moved to small-town Vermont, my friends and family thought I'd lost my mind.

I'd spent so many years being overworked and depressed. And so much time questioning who I was and what I was doing. Feeling bad for myself as I scrolled through the wedding announcements and photos and gender reveal parties all my high school and college friends posted.

I wallowed. For a long-ass time.

Eventually, though, I realized I had a freedom none of them had. So I changed my mindset.

So many people dreamed of blowing up their lives and taking off. Going somewhere new, starting fresh.

And I was one of the lucky few who could actually do it.

My therapist told me to list the things that made me feel happy and put them in a journal.

During that exercise, the tiny town in Vermont I'd visited

with friends came to me. We were here for my friend Liz's bachelorette weekend. We'd stayed at the most gorgeous inn and spa and spent our days hiking and sipping maple lattes.

On that trip, I'd felt like myself for the first time in years.

So I called my sister Giovanna, one of New York's most successful and ruthless headhunters, and told her to find a job for me in Vermont.

My older sister, while not big on empathy or quality time, delivered in a big way. And within a few months, I was packing up and heading north.

Marketing for the financial services industry was a hell of a lot different from maple syrup, but numbers were numbers, and this job made me feel more empowered and creative every day.

Not long after I'd moved into my little bungalow, I saw a flier for the No Book Club in the coffee shop, and it piqued my interest. Joining a book club was the exact kind of thing the new small-town, relaxed Evie would do.

Once upon a time, it had actually been a book club, but the members had vastly different tastes, making it difficult to choose books, so the group descended into chaos. Eventually, they revamped, and now we read any book we want and then show up.

Or we didn't. There was no rule stating that a member must read a book to attend. Which was great for moments like this, because I didn't even have time to shower, let alone read.

Our get-togethers consisted mainly of eating snacks and gossiping, with a side of random activities. Like the time Dr. Chao, I mean Liz, convinced us to go line dancing in Birch Hollow.

Last fall, Frankie had talked us into driving down to Springfield for a monster truck rally. It was an experience, for sure.

It took some time, but once I was settled here, I began to discover myself and make the most incredible friends.

As we chatted and ate and admired the adorable baby clothes, I was filled with warmth and contentment.

"Are we going to talk about your handsome squatter?" Etienne asked, gazing out the back window to where Jasper's tent was set up. "Didn't realize you were living together."

My stomach lurched. "We're not."

"She lets him sleep in the yard, like a dog," Frankie said. "Best place for him."

Basil rolled his eyes with a huff. Frankie's anti-man stance was nothing new.

"He wants to be close by to help out," I said. Yes, it was weird, but in a way, it kind of made sense. "He works twenty-four-hour shifts, so he wants to get as much time with Vincent as he can."

Basil nodded, though his expression was skeptical. He was clearly not buying what I was selling. "Where is he now?"

"At the farm. He works there with his brother doing..." My voice trailed off. What did he do there? Honestly, aside from tapping the trees and collecting sap, I didn't have the first clue.

I knew a lot about maple syrup. It came with the job description. But I didn't know much about how we got the sap or how the land and trees were cultivated.

The Lawrence farm was big. I knew that. And they had several employees. Jasper had mentioned that his brother had bought the adjacent farm from their aunt and uncle when they were ready to retire.

"You haven't been?" he asked, one brow cocked. "It's not that far."

I shook my head. "I've been holed up here with Vincent, and Jasper always comes to us."

Damn, out loud, that sounded shitty. The farm was part of Jasper's identity, and I'd never taken Vincent there. Jasper hadn't really even pushed me to introduce him to his family.

It occurred to me, as I surveyed his little campsite, that he was making all the effort.

My heart sank. Wow. When had I turned into such a selfish person?

"Seriously? You could be out there watching that man throw hay bales and chop wood, and you've elected not to?" Ruby practically shouted. "You need your head examined."

Basil clapped and let out a whoop of agreement.

"Ignore the horned-up pregnant woman," Frankie said with a dismissive wave. "Her taste is questionable."

Ruby's taste was spot-on. Jasper was objectively attractive. The shoulders, the tattoos, the round eyes and sharp jawline. There was a reason I'd taken him home last year.

But his muscles weren't what I dreamed about when my head finally hit the pillow at night. Night after night, my subconscious would conjure images of him cradling Vincent or attempting to teach him about *The Lord of the Rings*, despite this kid only now wobbly lifting his own head.

Or snapshots of his big, callused hands moving gently.

Which led to thoughts about how rough they could be.

And then I'd blush and give up the ghost.

Okay, I had a tiny crush on the man. So what? He

brought me coffee and treats and soothed my screaming baby. Anyone in my situation would feel the same.

"You're gonna marry him," Basil declared, his chin lifted smugly.

Frankie gagged. "Ew, gross. I hope not. You can do better."

After I'd been filled in on town gossip, we talked a little about the various books everyone had read and stuffed ourselves with yummy food. Basil and Etienne said their goodbyes close to midnight, and once they were gone, I got Vincent up to change his diaper and feed him. With any luck, once I topped him off, he'd sleep well and I could rest.

Frankie and Ruby were cleaning up the kitchen when I carried him to the couch, but the second he was latched, they pounced.

"We waited until the guys left," Ruby said. "But it's been almost two months, and we still don't have details. So spill."

"Yeah, we need to know how this"—Frankie nodded at the baby—"happened and if it's in danger of happening again. We gotta protect you."

"Or encourage you," Ruby said with a wink.

Frankie crossed her arms and gave me a stern look. "Start talking, girlie."

I looked down at Vincent, who was sleepily nursing, and my body relaxed. It did this at every feeding. Like, subconsciously, I was always afraid something would go wrong and he'd go hungry.

Oxytocin, the love hormone, flooded my veins as I fed him. I blame that for how easily I gave in to the inquisition of my friends.

"I'm surprised you're not giving me a polygraph," I joked.

"Polygraphs are for amateurs," Frankie huffed. "You know I can get the truth out of you."

I stuck my tongue out at her. "Fine."

That night all those months ago had been hot and sticky. We'd been drinking and dancing, and my heart was full. Ruby was getting married, and I was surrounded by friends. It was the kind of experience I'd been chasing when I moved to Maplewood.

"At your bachelorette party," I started. "We were all dancing."

Ruby reeled back. "How did I miss this?"

"You'd already gone home to Paul," Frankie explained. "The rest of us went over to Timberline. They had live music that night."

The Timberline Brewery, located on the outskirts of town, had a massive party barn that hosted events most weekends. The band that night had played folksy, bluegrass versions of eighties hits, and I'd stayed on the dance floor for hours.

"I was having a good time. We were dancing, and I just felt this desire. I wanted him. You know?"

Ruby whistled, her eyes glimmering. Frankie, on the other hand, scowled.

Desire wasn't something I'd had a lot of experience with. Yes, I'd been attracted to men from time to time, and that kind of sensation, in my experience, had always grown from those feelings.

But with Jasper, I'd barely known him, yet I'd wanted him. And it felt so liberating.

I licked my lips. "I'd written him off as a player."

"He is a player," Frankie replied

"But I was celebrating, and I wanted to be a little wild for once. I never let loose. I'm always following a plan, but that night, I wanted to explore something different. When I moved here, I cut ties with a lot of toxic people, and since then, I've been trying to figure out who I am." My cheeks heated. "And having a hot guy all over me while this kind of desire that I'd only ever read about in books had taken over? I got swept up."

"And you didn't use protection?" Frankie tried to conceal the judgment in her tone, but it bled through anyway.

Ruby elbowed her.

"We did," I said. "The first time."

"There was more than one time?" Ruby's smile grew.

I shrugged, my face flaming now, my whole body a little too warm, actually. There had definitely been more than one time. We laughed and fooled around and didn't sleep. It was sexy and fun, and while the memories were hazy, my body remembered enough to torture me about it regularly.

"I'm going to need a number, please," Ruby insisted, rubbing her hands together. "And I don't mean a ballpark figure."

I cringed, sinking a little deeper into the cushions. "Three? I think."

"You fucked him three times in one night?" Frankie knocked her water bottle over, sending it rolling across the living room floor.

"Frankie," Ruby admonished. "Please don't break anything,"

"That's not a one-night stand. That's a fling," my rough

around the edges friend nearly shouted. "That's a fucking sex marathon."

It had been, and it was incredible.

I couldn't help the smile that spread across my face. I'd be lying if I said I hadn't thought about it a few times in the months since.

"Look at her face. She's still dickmatized."

I nearly choked on my tongue. "I am not." Careful not to jostle Vincent, I shifted in my seat.

The night was amazing, yes. It was wild, and I'd walked away with fun memories, but that was it. It wasn't meant to be more than that. If anything, I was a little embarrassed by my actions afterward. I was normally controlled and strategic, but those senses were nowhere to be found.

"So you didn't want a repeat? After three times, I can't believe you didn't go back for more. And he is right back there." Ruby waved a hand, wildly gesturing to the backyard.

I shook my head violently. Nope that was not happening. "God no. We both went back to our lives."

"But this is a small town."

My chest ached the smallest bit, but I ignored the sensation. "Not that small. It wasn't that hard to avoid each other. We weren't friends. Didn't run with the same groups. We barely knew one another, and while I do see him around from time to time, my life is busy. I just kind of blocked it all out. We're cordial and pleasant, and that's that."

Ruby stared at me, open mouthed, rubbing her belly.

"Basil's right," she said after a lengthy pause. "You guys are gonna get married. This is fate."

Frankie rolled her eyes. "Let's get you home, preggo. Your hormones are making you hallucinate."

"No," she argued.

The single sharp word startled Vincent, and he popped off my boob. Taking advantage of the moment, I brought him up to my shoulder and patted his back.

"Think about it," Ruby went on. "Evie has PCOS. Was always told she couldn't get pregnant." She holds up one finger. "She had this insane, sexy connection with Jasper, a guy she's seen around town, and they have a magical night together." She holds up another finger. "Then they accidentally conceive the most perfect baby ever. And her one-night stand turns into a devoted dad who's now sleeping on the ground to protect his child and his child's mother."

She fanned herself.

"They're gonna get close, bond over the baby, and boom. Married. He'll probably knock her up again because, apparently, he's got a magic peen that can go all night long." She threw her hands up. "These are facts."

Frankie stood, holding out a hand to our ridiculous friend. "I'm driving you home. I'm worried scripting this Hallmark movie is going to send you into preterm labor."

"Fine, fine," she said with a wave of a hand. "But the evidence doesn't lie. Buckle up, Evie."

The girls left, and within minutes, Vincent was down for the night. I confirmed that the doors were locked, brushed my teeth, and climbed into bed.

As I lay staring at the ceiling, though, Ruby's words replayed in my head. Like Frankie said, it had to be romantic hallucination.

But part of me wondered: Was she right? Was there a connection here? If so, was it as strong as it had been that night. And could I survive it?

Chapter 11

❦

JASPER

This kid was a genius. Nothing would convince me otherwise. His tummy time game was elite. Already, he had the neck strength of a bear.

I was so damn proud of him.

We lay together on the play mat while I used his favorite giraffe, this weird-ass French rubber thing that he loved to eat, to keep him entertained.

I beatboxed, really going for it, making all kinds of weird sounds while the giraffe—Sophie, apparently—and the Very Hungry Caterpillar engaged in a dance battle.

It was our thing. Vincent and I hung out while Evie showered and drank the coffee I brought her or checked her work email, and I acted like a fool. Vincent seemed to enjoy it.

It was my contribution.

Evie did 100 percent of the feeding, but being a silly source of entertainment? I'd claimed that job. And I took it very seriously. Clowning with an infant was not easy.

"Look at the caterpillar." I used my best sports announcer voice. "He's doing the worm. Cross species dance moves."

I moved the caterpillar across the playmat as I rapped about eating leaves. It was utter nonsense, but Vincent was enraptured.

And then it happened.

He giggled.

He'd been smiling for several weeks now, but I'd never heard him laugh.

My heart leaped, and my chest nearly exploded with joy.

I moved the caterpillar again and rapped a little more, and again, he laughed. A full belly laugh, kicking his legs like a little swimmer.

For a second, I only stared at him in shock. But when I got my wits about me, I jumped up.

"Evie." I spun in a circle, looking for my phone. I had to get this on video. "Evie," I called again as I opened the camera app.

The bathroom door flew open, and Evie darted toward us.

"What's wrong? Is he okay?"

She was dripping wet, a yellow towel wrapped loosely around her, her chest heaving with panicked breaths.

My vision tunneled, and every muscle in my body locked up. Her long hair was plastered to her shoulders, water running in rivulets, only to be absorbed by the towel. Her lips were pink and plump. More so than usual.

And the towel hid almost nothing.

I was in the presence of a goddess. The lush, sexy body

that had enraptured me one wild night and had haunted me since was nearly within reach. Memory after memory hit me. The feel of her under me. The soft gasps and the cry she let out when I pushed inside her.

"Jasper." Her tone was sharp, pulling me out of my haze. "What's wrong?"

I inhaled sharply, only now realizing I hadn't been breathing.

I looked at Vincent and then at her again.

"He laughed," I said, holding up my phone. "I was doing dumb stuff and he laughed. A real laugh."

Her face lit up, her dark eyes warm. "Really? Vincent, you're laughing? Do it again," she said to me. "I can't believe I missed it."

As much as I didn't want to look away from her and miss a second of the excitement in her face, I kneeled and picked up Sophie the Giraffe, making her twerk as I rapped badly about the Very Hungry Caterpillar eating all the leaves off the tree.

It took a minute, but he did it again. It started with a tiny rumble but quickly turned into a full laugh.

Evie sat next to me, that towel hiding very little, and wiped a tear from her eye. "Oh my God. It's amazing. He's amazing. The baby book said three to four months."

Filled with pride, I grinned at her. "Ahead of schedule. He's a genius. Obviously."

Nodding, she tickled his foot, causing him to kick and giggle. "We're not supposed to say that out loud," she chided me playfully.

"Yes, but it's undeniable. He's the smartest and most

handsome baby ever." I leaned down and blew a raspberry on his stomach. "You get all that from your mom. I take no credit. But I'm so proud of you, bud."

Evie beamed at me, her attention making my stomach do backflips. I'd gotten them both to smile today, and that sent me soaring to a level of joy I'd never experienced before.

The sheer satisfaction of making my son laugh? Of making Evie look at me like I was some kind of hero? This was a type of high that couldn't be replicated.

"I'm gonna get dressed," she said, standing and awkwardly arranging her towel. "Then we need to get this on video."

I used every ounce of self-control I had to keep my eyes on my son.

"Vincent," she cooed. "Your dad is so silly."

My heart expanded even further. *Dad.* The title made my think of my own dad and how much fun he'd be having right now. How he'd obsess about every milestone and take blurry photos with the phone camera he never bothered learning how to use properly.

This was why I was here. This was why I slept in a tent in the backyard. Because I couldn't bear the idea of missing these moments with either of them.

Our origin story was not typical, but with every day that passed, that mattered less to me. Because like it or not, the three of us were a family.

I'd been blessed. I didn't deserve Evie or Vincent, but someone out there was looking out for me. I looked out the window toward the blue sky and said a silent thank you to my mom and dad. They'd taught me to be patient and warned me against my impulsive nature. And now I finally understood. Some things were worth waiting for. Some things were worth hard work and sacrifice. And I hoped I could make them proud.

Chapter 12

EVIE

Tonight, the full cast of characters from No Book Club met at the Drip Line, the only bar in town. Frankie had organized this gathering, urging us all to read *The Housemaid*, even if there were no rules stating we had to. I hadn't read it, but if I knew Frankie, it was heavy on murder and men behaving badly.

Dottie, who had owned the bar for years, was Frankie's mom and had closed the place down so we could eat, drink, gossip, and blow off steam at the dart boards. Oh, and maybe talk a little about books.

Frankie was behind the bar, helping out. If the lore was to be believed, she had been pulling pints and kicking out drunks by the time she was in kindergarten. She loved her mom, who'd raised her and her siblings on her own, but referred to her childhood spent here as her villain origin story.

By Maplewood standards, the Drip Line was a dive. By

any other measure, it was a charming tavern with wood-paneled walls and funky light fixtures. The kind of place with sloping wood floors, deep booths, and the tap list written on an artsy chalkboard sign that hadn't been updated in two years.

The menu consisted of foods that were either deep-fried or involved maple syrup. Or both. And Vermont's finest craft beers were served right alongside PBR.

Despite No Book Club nights being my favorites, I was out of sorts. Jasper had insisted I get out of the house and spend time with friends, so I'd furiously pumped for days and left him with a full page of information for caring for Vincent. And he was at my house, texting me constant updates.

Being here, I felt like I was missing a limb. I had not been separated from Vincent since he was born almost three months ago.

But I agreed with Jasper. Getting out for a bit would do me good. So I breathed deeply and headed toward the gathered group.

"She made it!" Ruby cheered from the long wooden table. Her husband Paul was seated next to her, his arm draped over her shoulders. They were so damn cute together.

Frankie waved from the bar. "The woman, the myth, the milk machine. Need a beer?"

With a small smile, I shook my head. I wanted to nurse Vincent as soon as I got home rather than having to pump and dump.

Despite how little sleep I was getting these days, I was

feeling pretty good. I had managed to squeeze myself into an older pair of jeans, and I'd put on a soft, oversized sweater that fell off one shoulder, exposing the strap of my non-nursing bra.

"Thank you," I said, tipping an invisible cap to her. "What a dignified title."

She stuck her tongue out at me.

I made my way through the bar, greeting the people milling about. Basil and Etienne were at the bar with a tasting flight of artisanal ciders, and Tony was halfway through a plate of maple wings.

When he saw me, he hit me with a big smile. He was a hulking mountain of a man with deep dimples and salt-and-pepper hair.

"How's my pizza mama?" He pulled me in for an almost suffocating hug. "When is my little pizza baby gonna come visit me?"

"I'll bring him in this week," I promised. "He loves going for walks through town."

His smile grew even bigger, if possible. "When he's ready for a job, he's gonna come work for me. The pizzeria is his birthplace, after all."

Not quite. Thankfully. God, if I hadn't made it to the hospital before he was born, I'd never live it down. And Vincent wouldn't be working anytime soon, but I warmed at the thought of my sweet boy growing up here, in a town where he was known and valued.

Nora Hatch, the town's elegant and slightly witchy pharmacist, put her arm around me. "You are glowing. Come sit and show us all the baby photos."

At the table, Jimmy Dandridge was chatting about his Revolutionary War reenactment group, and Nina, Frankie's little sister, was bent over her phone, typing furiously. She was twenty-three and by far the most stylish citizen of Maplewood. Tonight, she was wearing massively oversized wide-leg pants and a cropped vest, and she had half a dozen thin necklaces artfully layered around her neck.

"The rest of the world has brunch spots with DJs and bottomless mimosas. And stores that stay open past six," she whined. "And here I am, still stuck in Maplewood, Vermont, where you can't get dinner from a restaurant if you're not into early-bird specials."

Ruby patted her head. "And the rest of the world has higher crime rates, more expensive rent, and bad coffee. Count your blessings. You're the youngest small-business owner in town. Be proud of that."

Nina's lips twitched in a small smile. Last year, she'd opened a nail salon in the space next to Frankie's garage. She'd even brought on a few employees. There was no argument that she was the authority on nails, lashes, and eyebrows in town.

I looked down at my own hands and made a mental note to ask if she could fit me into her packed schedule.

Callie slid into a seat with an annoyed sigh. "Sorry I'm late. The twins glued my car keys to the toilet again." She was principal of the local school and mother to the notorious Mayhew-Beauregard twins, who caused havoc wherever they went. She had long bright red hair and was soft-spoken in that sweet kindergarten teacher kind of way.

Chuckling, Nora reached into her massive tote bag.

"Here." She slid a jar across the table. "Vitamin blend for relaxation. May calm them down. Or keep it for yourself."

Callie held up the bottle, studying the label. "Does it work on husbands too?"

While the group around me chattered and caught up, I slipped my phone out of my purse.

Sure enough, I had another text from Jasper.

It was a photo of him in the rocking chair with a sleeping Vincent in his arms.

JASPER:

He's milk drunk. Chugged that whole bottle, burped, and passed out.

MY HEART FLOATED A LITTLE IN MY CHEST. VINCENT was so cubby and drooly now. As a newborn, he'd been tiny and precious. Now he had thigh rolls and could make silly faces. Time really did go by so fast for parents of young children.

EVIE:

The whole bottle? Is there more in the fridge? Should I come home?

JASPER:

We've got three more bottles. Relax, Mama. Have fun and talk about your murder books.

I put the phone down, smiling to myself. Mama. I liked when he called me that. I had no idea why, but it was affectionate and kind of sexy at the same time. Was that possible?

Clearly I needed to get out more.

Following his instructions, I rejoined the conversation, discovering that the group had skipped right over the murder book and gone straight to discussing the real-life murder that had rocked our town.

"Are you sure we should be talking about this?" Callie peered around the empty bar. "It feels wrong."

"Will deserves justice," Nora argued.

The group erupted with overlapping theories and stories.

I looked from person to person as people speculated, sadness and frustration coursing through me. I hadn't known Will, but I'd met his mother a few times and couldn't help but imagine her pain. And the violence? In our town? I couldn't—

"They say he was dating someone who worked at Sugar Moon."

That caught my attention. If it were true, it was news to me. I didn't know everyone, but I knew most of my fellow employees.

I scanned through a mental list of folks he could have been involved with.

"He was recently hired on there too. To make deliveries." Also news to me.

"I wouldn't be surprised if Louisa was involved," Nora sneered. "That woman is corrupt."

Marty shook his head and sighed. "My mom can't stand her. She thinks she's better than everyone."

"Guys," I said, uncomfortable with the way they were badmouthing my boss. Louisa Meyers, who owned Sugar Moon, could be prickly and difficult, but to be branded a villain in town? That didn't seem warranted.

"She could have hurt Will," Frankie muttered. "I wouldn't put it past her."

I glared at my friend. "How many times have you actually spoken to her? Let's put the pitchforks down."

"Didn't Will date a girl from Birch Hollow when he was in high school?" Tony asked.

Nora cocked a brow. "Have you been eavesdropping from the pizza counter again?"

"It's called listening with intention," Tony snapped back, his head held high.

Frankie stood over us, two plates of appetizers in her hands. "Evie is right. We shouldn't be spreading rumors. His family is grieving."

Relief hit me. She may not have liked Louisa, but at least she had sympathy for Will's loved ones.

It had been months since he was found dead, and there still hadn't been an arrest. I didn't understand why the police hadn't done anything.

Nina, who was sitting at the end of the table Snapchatting or whatever the youths did these days, looked up. "It's not just a rumor," she told her sister. "And according to Caleb, he and Will had been arguing about it."

Frankie went rigid, a small gasp escaping her.

Caleb was their brother, who I gathered had been in and out of town over the years, but had been back and working here recently.

"Were they friends?" Ruby asked.

Nina nodded. "Yeah, for a long time. Will helped Caleb a lot when he..." She trailed off.

We all knew what she was talking about. Even me, the relative newcomer. Caleb's struggles with mental health had been alluded to over the years, but I'd never asked Frankie about it directly.

Right now, my friend was glaring at her sister. "Drop it," she barked. With that, she turned around and headed back to the bar.

For a moment, the rest of us sat in awkward silence.

Marty eventually cleared his throat, cutting the tension. "He came to the diner," he said softly.

He was a quiet guy, though once he warmed up to a person, his wicked sense of humor came out. He ran the diner with his mom, Clem, and mostly kept to himself. But Tony had talked him into coming to book club a while back, so he'd show up once in a while, drink a single beer, and go home.

Every eye was on him now, and in response to the attention, his cheeks went pink. "The day he died," he continued, "he came to the diner. Sat at the counter and drank coffee. Said something about how 'it would all blow up soon.' I had no idea what he was talking about, and we were slammed, so I nodded and kept working."

Ruby slapped a hand to the table and sat up straight. "Oh my God, Marty. You can't just sit on that kind of info."

"I told Nolan after Will's body was found," he said, frowning. "Who would've expected a syrup vat tragedy?"

Behind the bar, Frankie growled. She hated Police Chief Nolan Graham passionately. I'd never gotten the full story, but she never missed an opportunity to question his ability to keep this town safe.

"Course he can't solve the one murder this town's ever seen." Her words were muttered, but they traveled to us clearly in the empty space.

"It may be out of his hands," Callie said. "Rumor is the FBI visited the Lawrence farm."

My stomach lurched. Jasper's farm? The FBI? He hadn't mentioned it, but God, he must be stressed.

Nora crossed her arms. "Something's been up with Sugar Moon lately. They keep expanding that north lot and applying for zoning variances."

"And our deliveries have been delayed on and off for months." Marty added.

My instinct was to jump in and defend. We were the largest employer in town and gave back to this town and its people. In fact, I oversaw many of the charitable initiatives, including the science scholarships for kids from the local high school.

There was no way the organization could be involved, and this kind of speculation could be harmful to their reputation and business.

When I went back to work next week, I'd nip it all in the bud. Clearly there were topics that needed better messaging.

As the conversation flowed to the book I hadn't bothered to read and the need to bring tourists back for the summer, my thoughts drifted to Vincent.

Without a second thought, I checked my phone again. The screen was free of notifications.

EVIE:

Update?

JASPER:

He just smiled in his sleep. Cutest fucking thing ever.

. . .

My heart warmed as I pictured Jasper at home, one of his big hands steady on Vincent's back, relishing the steady rise and fall of his baby breathing.

"You're glowing," Callie said, shaking a wing in my direction.

"And it's not the alcohol," Nora added. "She's drinking water."

"Hormones and exhaustion," I said, tucking my phone away.

"Or her baby daddy," Ruby teased, raising her eyebrows.

Every head snapped in my direction, the scrutiny causing heat to creep up my chest and neck and into my face.

Thankfully Callie got distracted quickly and hollered for Dottie, taking the spotlight off me. "Can I get another beer? If I don't relax, I may ship the twins off to military school."

The group broke into a round of laughter.

Tony was the loudest, his voice bouncing off the paneled walls. "You say that every week."

"Don't threaten us with a good time," Basil added.

Her response was a single middle finger.

I chuckled at that, thankful they had moved on from questioning my growing affection for Jasper.

"This is self-care," Callie said, lifting her glass in one hand and a maple-glazed pretzel in the other.

"I can make you a serum for that," Nora said, pushing her jeweled glasses up her nose.

"Of course you can, witch queen. But first you promised me stretch mark cream," Ruby shouted.

"I got you," Nora said, pulling out her phone to make note of requests.

Tony mentioned his concern about the lack of tourists this spring, and the conversation turned again. Tourism was the lifeblood of this town. It sustained the local economy and provided jobs and opportunities for our young people.

"I don't mind the break from the douchebags in Teslas who drive up for one jar of syrup and a sense of authenticity."

"Yeah, but douchebags in Teslas keep the lights on in my store," he said. "So let's dial it up, get even more authentic. We can't let this tragedy drive everyone away."

"Birch Hollow is celebrating our struggle," Ruby growled. "They are going all out for Fourth of July, think they can beat us this year."

A hush fell over the table. Birch Hollow was twenty miles north of Maplewood, a pretty town with a river and covered bridges and cobblestone streets. And the citizens there were our nemeses. They had been trying to steal our Most Charming Small Town in America title for years, but they had yet to succeed.

"Have we considered that Birch Hollow might be behind this?" Etienne asked, his brows pulled low. "They have the most to gain from Maplewood's downfall."

That question set everyone off. There was nothing this town loved more than shitting on Birch Hollow.

I sincerely doubted that a group of small-town Vermont hippies would kill someone to get a leg up in a competition, but this crowd would not be deterred.

Regardless, I soaked it all in. The wacky ideas to attract tourists, the wild conspiracies about our rival town, and the gentle ribbing and support flowing around this table. The sensation that took over was one of comfort, of belonging. I'd never experienced this until I moved to Maplewood. Not in college or previous jobs. Not even at home with my family.

But here, in this weird-ass town, I belonged. Whether or not that was a good thing remained to be seen, but for now, I'd enjoy it.

Chapter 15

JASPER

The Maplewood PD lobby smelled like burnt coffee and rubber. The large corkboard on the wall was covered with overlapping flyers asking about missing pets, notifying us about last year's church bake sale, and reminding us that Jim offered chainsaw sharpening.

"Lawrence." Nolan dipped his chin. "Thanks for coming in."

I'd known Nolan Foster Junior my whole life. He'd played hockey with Josh growing up, and he and his parents were often present for our family's Sunday dinners.

His dad had been chief of police for my entire childhood. Nolan Senior was a tall, broad guy with a thick mustache who walked the line between stern and kind perfectly. I'd never met anyone who took as much pride in this town and its history.

Foster's mom, Kitty, had been a teller at the Maplewood bank. She'd helped me open my first savings account the summer my dad started paying me for farm work, and she sang in the church choir.

Sadly, both Foster Senior and Kitty were killed in a car crash on icy mountain roads about ten years ago.

The entire town mourned their loss.

But no one more than Nolan. He'd gone from fun-loving prankster to grumpy lawman in the blink of an eye. He and Josh were still friends, and I had a lot of respect for the guy, but as firefighters, we usually left the police to their own devices, really only interacting when business called for it.

A platter of delicious-looking cookies sat on a large table in the dispatch area. A piece of paper had been folded in half and propped up like a tent beside it with *Compliments of Olive Foster. Do not share with my grandson. He's a narc* written on it.

With a hum, I confirmed that Nolan wasn't looking and snuck a snickerdoodle from the platter.

Once I'd shoved the whole thing into my mouth, I followed him into a cramped office that smelled like it had once held cleaning supplies. The place was barely big enough for his desk, along with two wobbly chairs, and a coffee mug filled with pencils that looked like they'd been chewed by beavers.

In the flickering fluorescent light, Nolan looked haunted. His face gaunt and pale.

"I've got to run through these questions with you." With a weighted sigh, he dropped into his chair. "Obviously you know we're investigating the death of Will McManus."

My gut twisted as I settled into one of the uncomfortable chairs across from him. "You said I wasn't a suspect."

"You're not," he said, his focus fixed on the notebook in

front of him. "Chief Ashburn sent over the schedule. You were on shift at the firehouse. In fact, it looks like you did a forty-eight-hour shift for the Maple Festival."

I roughed a hand through my hair. "We're short staffed."

He huffed. "Aren't we all." He hit the button on the voice recorder and a red light flashed, then he said, "Tell me more about your work on the farm."

Elbows on the armrests, I laced my fingers in front of me. "I help out part time. Josh tells me what to do and I do it. Mostly, I check lines. I can change tubing and repair leaks quickly, so he likes to take advantage of that. When I'm working, I usually walk the property and check the tubing, especially when we have a surge of sap flow."

He looked up at me from beneath his brows. "And that's dependent on the weather?"

"Yes. Sap flow occurs when daytime temps reach forty degrees. The combination of warmer days and below freezing nights is what makes the sap run. It's different every year."

"And Will McManus?"

"I'm so sorry he's dead." My heart ached in earnest and heat burned at the backs of my eyes. "He was a good kid. Worked for us off and on for years. Usually as seasonal help. He always seemed eager to learn more."

I'd had little interaction with him over the years, though it didn't take more than a few minutes to realize that he was a hard worker. From what I'd heard, he'd taken a job at Sugar Moon this year, making deliveries, doing pickups, and swinging by to check yield. That sort of thing.

"Can you remember the last time you saw him?"

I scratched my chin. My stubble was beginning to turn

into a beard. Damn. Chief Ashburn would have my ass if I didn't shave soon. "Probably a few days before he died. Maple syrup is shelf stable for years, but the sap is perishable. During the season, we have to collect it every day. Since we sell to Sugar Moon and they boil and process, their delivery guys were at our farm daily."

"And Will was one of the delivery guys?"

"Yes. I saw him on and off. It's hard to say. April was busy because of that March snowstorm. Delayed the sap season, and so we were late this year. Filled a lot of barrels. Will came by with the Sugar Moon truck for a pickup, and we got it all loaded. Murph and Tom, the guys who work for Josh, see him more than I do. Sorry I can't be much help."

He shook his head, scribbling notes in his pad. "You're helping more than you realize. You've got insight into how all the maple stuff works. You're close to it."

I grunted. "Not that close. If you want all the nitty gritty, ask Josh. He's the science guy."

"I have," Nolan said, still scribbling. "What do you think happened?" He finally looked up at me fully.

Confusion hit me. Why would he ask me that? I was a firefighter, not law enforcement. I didn't care about the why or the how. My concern was getting everyone out alive.

"I thought this wasn't an interrogation." I leaned back and crossed my arms over my chest.

"It isn't." He mirrored my posture. "It's me being curious about whether your reputation is deserved."

My lips twitched. "Which reputation? Smartass or idiot who can fix anything but himself?"

Nolan barked out a laugh. "Thanks. I needed that."

Reality settled back in quickly, the mood turning somber

again. As I looked at the paper filled with chicken scratch, I thought about Will. "He wasn't sneaky or secretive. But he was young. Maybe he trusted the wrong person," I guessed. "If he went out to meet someone late at night, it had to be because he trusted them."

"And," I continued, "if it happened where you think it did. Then that person knew those back roads. The ones past the old logging cut. No cameras, no motion lights, no houses for miles. You can kill your engine at the bend and roll down the hill if you really wanted to be quiet."

Nolan put the pen down and rolled his shoulders a few times. "Thank you. You wouldn't believe the crap I've got to dig through to get insights like that."

"Try me."

"The tip line is a shit show. Half the town's lost its mind."

A low laugh rumbled out of me. "Only half?"

"Yesterday, someone called, claiming that Will's ghost was haunting the sugarhouse. Turned out to be an opossum wearing a maple bucket like a helmet." He fought back a smile. "Then I got Mrs. Goodwin calling twice a day to tell me her neighbor's Yorkie can 'smell guilt.'"

"Maybe you should borrow it. See if it'll pick up a trail."

"Don't tempt me." He hung his head. "I've got half a mind to deputize the mutt. Can't be worse than Bob Pearson's midnight patrols."

"On his four-wheeler? He comes by the firehouse."

"Yup, with floodlights the size of hubcaps. He cruises Main Street like it's a warzone."

It was annoying as hell when we were trying to sleep at the station. "Can't you arrest him?"

"I've tried, but he always hauls ass to his own property and then gives me the finger."

None of this was funny, but I couldn't help but chuckle at the absurdity.

"People are scared," I said when I got myself under control. "They want answers. This town, it's not violent."

He shot me a scathing look. "Don't you think I want answers too? Unfortunately they don't grow on trees."

"In this town, everything else does."

Snorting, he rubbed his hand over his face. "You always were a smartass."

"Is that why you called me down here?"

"I called because you notice things." He tapped the pad. "And you're smarter than you look."

"Aw, shucks." I gave him a dopey grin. "Thanks."

He leaned back and closed his eyes, letting out a sigh. "Before you go," he said. "Anything else unusual at the farm? Deliveries? Visitors? Contracts?"

He should be asking Josh. My brother monitored everything with precision. I did my job and let him worry about the details. "Just tourists taking selfies and almost getting hit by farm machinery. Do you think our farm's involved?"

"Doubtful, but I've got to look at this from every angle. Sugar Moon's watching this like a hawk. If they pull contracts, your family won't be the only ones feeling the hit. Out-of-towners are canceling reservations at the inn. If I don't get this figured out, we could lose our leaf peepers in the fall. Basil only sold two wheels of Brie on Tuesday. In June."

I angled forward. "Damn. That is a crime scene." People crossed state lines for that Brie.

"He filed a police report," Nolan deadpanned. "Incident: fromage felony."

I snorted, appreciating the moment of levity, but before long, we were somber again. The economic impacts of this were real and impossible to ignore.

"I'm scraping this together, and the town is rioting. I'm down two officers, and the selection board wants updates in PowerPoint, which should be illegal. The tip line rings like it's auditioning for a talent show. And every interview somehow includes citizens monologuing grievances dating back to 1998."

"Sure you don't want to borrow Mrs. Goodwin's neighbor's dog to help you sniff out the guilty party?" I teased.

"How's the baby?" he asked, not even bothering to acknowledge the joke.

I didn't mind. I'd take any opportunity to brag about my son, so I pulled out my phone and navigated to the photo app.

"He's loud, hilarious, and perfect."

"And how's his mother?"

My heart clenched. Just as perfect. Struggling but crushing it.

I cleared my throat. "She's good. Tired. Going back to work. Sugar Moon is panicking because of all of this." I gestured around. "But she's amazing."

When he responded with a quirked brow, I regretted opening my big mouth.

"Okay, then." He stood and offered me his hand. "If you hear anything, and I mean anything, come straight to me. Not to Gabe, not to your brother. Right here."

I nodded.

"And please don't do anything stupid."

"Define stupid."

He leveled with a weary look. "Be careful."

As I stepped into the reception area, Olive was arranging more freshly baked cookies on the table.

"Take some, sweetheart," she said, pinching my cheek.

Her smile turned into a scowl when Nolan appeared behind me. I had no idea what he'd done to get on her bad side, but Olive had a knack for finding trouble.

On my way out, I paused at the corkboard, noting the handwritten note that said *Justice for Will* but with one glance back at Nolan, I headed out.

It was a warm, sunny afternoon, and Main Street was busy, though nowhere near as crowded as it should have been.

Ahead, Nora came out of the apothecary hauling a crate of lavender, and Etienne was wiping down his outdoor tables and opening the umbrellas.

This was my town. I had devoted my adult life to protecting it. But more and more, I worried there was no coming back from this.

Chapter 14

JASPER

By the time we pulled up to the Maplewood Farmers' Market, I already knew it wasn't a real emergency. The radio dispatch had said *Possible medical—female down, unknown cause.*

But there were no crowds screaming, no frantic waving. Just the usual Saturday chaos: the scent of kettle corn, a banjo on the busker stage, and someone shouting about dairy ethics. Two cheese stalls faced off in the center aisle like rival gangs in matching gingham.

On one side: Curd Your Enthusiasm, manned by Basil Pelletier—neat hair, smug smile, and an apron ironed within an inch of its life.

Across the way: Cheddar Off Dead, where Lola Prentice was holding a cheese knife like she was ready to throw it.

And between them, dramatically sprawled on the pavement in a faint worthy of daytime television, lay Olive Foster—second in command of the Maple Street Mafia—fanning herself with a coupon flyer.

"Good Lord." I stepped out of the ambulance and nodded to Chris, who grabbed the equipment bag. "Not another cheese war."

"Think we need the stretcher?" he asked.

I shook my head. "Gimme a minute."

Bitsy Bramble rushed toward us, wringing her hands. "We were *this close* to another 2019 incident, Jasper. I told Olive to faint before the wheels started rolling again."

"Wheel—"

"She means actual wheels of cheese." Marigold Shaw approached on her mobility scooter, only stopping when the front wheel hit my boot. "You remember." She raised her heavily painted-on eyebrows.

I nodded. Everyone knew about the 2017 incident. It was still spoken about in hushed tones. The police department held an annual moment of silence in remembrance at their department cookout every summer.

I keyed my radio. "Dispatch, this is medic two. We're on scene at the farmers' market. No active emergency. Appears to be a fainting spell. I'll update shortly."

"Copy that, medic two," came the dry reply.

I crouched beside Olive. "Olive, can you hear me?"

Her eyelids fluttered open like she was auditioning for community theater. "Oh, heavens. My heart simply couldn't handle the tension. Basil accused Lola of *temperature tampering.*"

"I didn't accuse; I *observed,*" Basil said, arms crossed. "Her cooler's been unplugged since nine a.m."

Lola slammed down her cheese knife. "Because *someone* tripped the extension cord running under *his* fancy Brie display."

"Okay," I said, checking Olive's vitals just to look busy. "Pulse steady, respiration normal, dramatic flair elevated."

Chris nodded, spreading his arms out to keep the onlookers back.

Lola jabbed a finger toward Basil's stall. "He *deliberately* tilted his canopy so the sun melted my cheddar samples first. That's predatory behavior."

Basil sniffed. "Your 'cheddar' is more orange than a road cone, Lola. It deserves to melt."

"Say that again, you pasteurized peacock—"

"Enough!" I shouted, kneeling beside Olive, who cracked one eye open.

"Oh, heavens." She sighed, limp as overcooked spaghetti. "I saw tempers rising and my blood sugar fell in solidarity."

"You're fine," I told her gently. "But maybe stay out of the line of dairy fire next time."

Bitsy leaned in conspiratorially. "She's faking, of course. Classic de-escalation strategy. It's why she's in charge of church bake sales."

Meanwhile, Marigold had started spritzing Olive's face using a sample bottle of Maple Mist toner from the skincare booth next door. "For hydration," she declared.

Satisfied she wasn't about to keel over, I stood and gave my report. "Dispatch, patient stable. No transport needed. We'll clear the scene."

I helped Olive up, got her a folding chair and a cold glass of lemonade, and tried to wrap my head around this latest lunacy. Once we had taken her vitals, established that she had not suffered any serious medical event, and was, in fact, in perfect health, we packed up.

"Please don't tell my grandson," Olive pleaded. "He's

angry with me because we got a little rowdy while watching *The Golden Bachelor* this week. I'll get another lecture about misuse of community resources." She rolled her eyes. I would, in fact, be telling Nolan. He'd cut a deal with Chief Ashburn a few years ago to keep tabs on his wild grandma, who was a known quantity to every first responder in town.

As I turned toward the rig, Lola called out, "Wait. You have to try my smoked maple cheddar. It's the taste of Vermont in a bite. Aged six years."

Basil snorted. "Please. Jasper and Evie are my close friends." He glared at her. "I respect this man too much to expose him to your subpar curds."

Bitsy shoved a toothpick stuck in a cube of Lola's cheddar into my hand before Basil could object. "Just one bite, Jasper. Be diplomatic."

I sighed, chewing as every set of eyes watched me like I was judging the Olympics. "It's... good."

Basil scoffed. "Good? Try this triple-cream Brie and then tell me if that's *good*." He slid over a wedge the size of my fist.

Before I knew it, I had three samples in my hands, and Sally Murphy was snapping photos for the town Facebook page which she would surely caption *First Responder Chooses Sides in Cheese War II*.

I swallowed and wiped my mouth. "All right, all right. Official verdict—cheese is amazing. You are both excellent at what you do. Now please go back to your businesses and resume your days."

Olive, now sitting upright and sipping lemonade like a queen, beamed. "See? Peace through dairy diplomacy."

As I headed back toward the rig, it was hard not to notice

that the farmers' market seemed less busy than usual. The line of kids for balloon animals was short and the bakery hadn't even sold out of cinnamon rolls yet.

"Don't worry, dear," Bitsy said. "We can keep the peace from here on out. Sometimes you've just got to get dramatic to make sure no punches are thrown."

As we pulled away, I glanced in the rearview mirror. I couldn't wait to tell Evie about this latest ridiculousness. Just thinking about her made me grin. Even as I wrote up the incident report for the unhinged bullshit that went down at the farmer's market, my mood couldn't be dampened.

***

As I stepped inside, I was engulfed in the scents of coffee and baby lotion. The combination was familiar and cozy, if not a little chaotic.

Immediately, I was stunned stupid by the view.

Evie sat on the couch, laptop perched on the coffee table, wearing a purple blouse and makeup. With earbuds in place, she spoke assertively, her focus fixed on the computer's built-in camera. Next to the laptop was a half-empty cup of coffee and a stack of files and pens. She talked quickly, her hand grazing a binder filled with color-coded tabs.

She looked brighter and more energized than I'd seen her since that night a year ago. It was hard not to stare.

That familiar rock settled in my stomach. The want that hit me when she was near.

I'd never experienced this with anyone else. I was a simple guy; if I wanted something, I either went for it or got distracted by the next shiny thing and moved on. But this ache was endless. Every night I slept out in my tent, chest tight, knowing she was so close and yet so far away.

Dad, I'd think, staring up at the highest point of my tent, *I feel this. This feels right. I want things I've never wanted before.*

He wouldn't respond, but I'd close my eyes and pretend he was there, telling me the story of how he and my mom met.

I'd grown up in a house filled with love and chaos. But mostly love. Most days, my dad would pick wildflowers for my mom and present them with a flourish when he came in for dinner. And Mom fussed over him, always so proud of him and of us.

Our time here was limited. They'd proven that, so I'd done my best to have fun and stay away from all the hard, heavy stuff.

But I was drawn to all of Evie. The fun parts and the parts that brought up my fears.

The smiles and the sass, but also the hurt and the pain.

I wanted more. I wanted everything.

Instead, I'd settle for the small scraps she'd give me.

Because Evie had made one thing clear. She did not want more.

I waved at her, and she gave me a nod, then used her foot to rock Vincent in his play chair without missing a beat.

I propped myself up against the doorframe, taking my time unzipping my hoodie so I could watch her. The calm authority in her voice was magnetic.

"Let's be clear," she chirped. "If Costmart isn't satisfied with the transparency statement, then we need to dig deeper internally. The integrity of our product is our brand. End of story."

The confident statement was followed by an incredulous laugh, as if the person behind the other screen had pushed back.

"No," she said. "We're not fucking around with labeling and supplementation. If we're using something new, then I need the full composition data before we print another label. I don't care what Evergreen provides. We verify and compile our own data."

She turned away and made a silly face at Vincent. She was multitasking like it was a competitive sport.

"No, Dave." Her tone was firmer. "I had a baby. I didn't lose my ability to spot PR landmines. And this is one. So get me the data, and we'll update. But I'm taking your word for it. Please."

When she scoffed, I cheered internally. I had no idea who Dave was, but he was getting a verbal ass-kicking.

After she ended the meeting, she quickly lowered the laptop screen, then jumped up and scooped Vincent into her arms, peppering his little face with kisses.

As he squirmed, I noticed a Post-it stuck to his butt. The words *Q4 targets* were written on it.

My heart clenched. Evie looked exhausted but unstoppable. Like a woman who'd been running on fumes for months and still refused to fail.

Her steely resolve was admirable, but it only made me feel like I should be doing more for her.

I wandered closer and peeled the Post-it off his butt.

"You sounded like a boss," I said proudly.

She passed Vincent to me, eyes brighter than they had

been recently. "I like it," she said. "Being back, doing something I'm good at. And the place is a mess without me."

She said that last part with an eye roll, like she was annoyed, though the way her lips tipped up told me she was secretly pleased.

"Of course they are." I blew a raspberry into Vincent's tummy. "Mama is the smartest. And she absolutely handed Dave his ass." I lowered my little guy and cradled him to my chest. "Who is Dave?"

She was standing in front of the mirror by the front door, putting her hair up into a ponytail. "The procurement lead. We're midway through an environmental audit, and there are label concerns. So I asked for the BGX data files, but they're archived for internal use only. And that's bullshit. We can't legally claim sustainability and maintain organic certification without—"

"Why does that sound familiar?" I asked. "BGX?"

She waved a hand. "It's a tree supplement thing. The farmers are using it. Totally legal, but we have to know what's in our product so we can be transparent about it, and it's Dave's job to make sure that happens."

I'd have to ask Josh if he'd heard of it. We used a variety of management methods on our trees, including supplementation when necessary. But he was the science guy. I just did the labor.

She picked up her coffee and took a sip, immediately wincing. She must have finished the cold brew I sent Elijah over with this morning. Before I could offer to warm it up for her, Vincent fussed in my arms.

"I know, buddy," she cooed. "It's past lunchtime. Let me get changed, and then you can eat."

She strode down the hall, using one thumb to tap at her phone screen while she used her other hand to unbutton her blouse.

Damn. It hit me then. The weight of the expectations she was carrying. She was navigating motherhood while kicking ass at her job. She'd mentioned once that her family was unsupportive, and I certainly hadn't seen them in town to help. That meant she was doing everything but the few things I forced her to let me help with. Because this woman would rather walk through fire than ask for help.

When she returned and took Vincent out of my arms, I held her gaze. "You don't have to do everything yourself."

She let out a dry laugh, patting Vincent's back. "Course I do. That's the only way it gets done."

Chapter 15

EVIE

My hands shook as I tapped on the name in my contact list.

"Evie?" The low voice washed over me, but it didn't settle my fears. "Is everything okay?"

"No," I said, my voice reedy. "Vincent has a fever. He's burning up and won't stop crying."

The phone clicked, and seconds later, he was lightly tapping at the back door, like he'd sprinted from the tent without hesitation.

Vincent wailed as I unlocked the door and pulled it open.

Immediately, Jasper took him from my arms and cradled him, making soothing shushing sounds. He was barefoot and wearing shorts and an old T-shirt. His hair was stuck to one side of his head like he'd been sleeping when I called.

Right away, having him here, I felt a bit better.

"Little guy," Jasper crooned. "I'm sorry you're not feeling good."

"What do we do?" I asked, my thoughts spiraling. "Should we take him to the ER?"

"No. Let's assess him first. See if we can figure out what's going on."

My heart thundered in my ears. "What about Dr. Chao?"

"It's one a.m. The office is closed," he said, frowning. "But maybe she uses an after-hours answering service."

"He's in pain," I cried. "We've got to do something."

He rubbed circles on Vincent's back, swaying from side to side. "Take a breath. I'm a paramedic, remember? Let me get my bag from my car."

Carefully, he transferred our little guy back into my arms. Then he darted out the front door, still barefoot, and returned with his medical kit in a matter of seconds.

First he scanned Vincent's forehead with his fancy thermometer. "One hundred point one"

My heart sank. My poor baby.

"His temperature would have to be above 100.7 to be considered a fever," Jasper explained. "So this is a good thing. Let me check his lungs."

It was comforting, knowing that Vincent's dad had a decent amount of medical knowledge and was here to help. It was tempting to ask him if he'd consider going to medical school just so he could handle this kind of situation again in the future, but I'd probably sound out of my mind if I did.

He took out a stethoscope and instructed me to turn Vincent around so his back was to my chest. Then he listened to his breathing, the most serious expression I'd ever seen from him on his face.

"Chest is clear."

He took out another tool with a light on the end and looked in Vincent's ears. This made him scream even louder and thrash in my arms.

"Ooh, this ear is very angry." He took him from me again and shuffled to the couch. "Shh. It's okay, bud." With careful movements, he laid Vincent on his back on the couch, then pressed lightly on his tummy and moved his legs and arms. "Nice and soft. Good job, bud," he cooed.

"He definitely has an ear infection. Probably from a virus. He'll be okay for the night. We can take him in first thing in the morning. Get him some antibiotics."

My stomach rolled. A virus? "Who exposed him to germs?" I growled.

Jasper gave me a sympathetic smile. "Germs are everywhere. It's okay. Let's call the twenty-four-hour medical line and ask about the appropriate dosage of children's Tylenol."

We had to leave a message with the answering service and wait for a return call, but within minutes, Sheri, one of the nurse practitioners, called and spoke to Jasper, instructing him on the correct dosage of medicine and suggested we bring Vincent in tomorrow.

Jasper was so calm and cool. And I was... the opposite. A sweating, hysterical mess.

"I'm sorry," I said, my whole body tense. "Seeing him in pain. It makes it impossible to think straight."

"Of course it does," he soothed. "It's biological. You're his mom. The connection between you is primal. It's okay to be shaken up. But we can manage this."

After we gave Vincent the Tylenol, he changed the little guy and walked around the room, once again rubbing circles on his back.

In a matter of minutes, Vincent's cries turned into sniffles. God, this man was far more capable than I gave him credit for.

As I sank into the couch, I was hit by a wave of shame. Feeling helpless like this brought back so many painful memories from my childhood and even my early adult years. Of the moments I failed or couldn't fix things for myself or others.

Of the times my father berated me.

Calling me a loser. Telling me how much I embarrassed him.

For the most part, I kept these memories locked away in the back of my mind, but once in a while, they popped up and played on a loop in my head.

"Are you okay?" Jasper asked as he continued swaying Vincent, even though he'd quieted and gone to sleep. "You're crying."

Shit. Really? How messed up was it that I'd been so caught up in yelling at myself that I hadn't even realized tears were streaming down my damn face?

"I'm so sorry." I waved him off. "It's stupid."

"Nothing is stupid," he murmured, eyes locked on me. "You can tell me. Let me put him down. I'll be right back."

He returned a few minutes later and sat next to me on the couch, setting the baby monitor on the table in front of us.

"You're pale and sweating," he said, bringing the back of his hand to my forehead. "Are you feeling sick too?"

"No. No." I shook my head, ducking to hide the tears in my eyes. "I'm just happy Vincent is okay. And..." I heaved out a breath. "I'm happy you're here."

"You can talk to me," he said, angling closer and meeting my eye. "We're friends."

Friends.

I both loved and hated the term.

When Vincent was born, I prayed that someday Jasper and I could be friends. That we could respect and care for one another as coparents.

Now, though, the word felt hollow.

Both too much and not enough at the same time.

"Sometimes, when I'm tired or overwhelmed, old memories surface," I explained.

"What kind of memories?"

"Small things. Snapshots," I said. "They play in my head like a movie. Times when I screwed up. Fell short. Memories of the things my dad used to say to me."

He scooted closer. "What do you mean?"

I shook my head. There was no way I'd dive into that with him. The last thing I needed was Jasper thinking I was a complete basket case.

He cupped my shoulders, his large hands warm and soothing. "Look at me."

Reluctantly, I obeyed. The compassion bleeding for him only made it harder to hold back tears.

"Vincent is okay. But you're clearly not. You faded away for a minute, and when you came back, you were shaking and crying. Please let me in."

I took in his warm eyes, his easy smile. He wouldn't understand. And I didn't want to sound like that girl.

The broken girl

The self-conscious girl.

I'd worked hard to leave her behind. To grow into a

version of myself that could manage all the challenges life threw at me. Yet here I was, breaking down when my baby had a fever.

"It's okay." He pulled me into his arms, folding me against his warm, broad chest. "Just try to breathe."

"My family," I said, the words escaping me without my permission. "Growing up..."

"It's okay. I'm not judging. I want to help."

"My dad. He's not a kind person. He'd pick one of us girls, mostly me, to use as his scapegoat."

"Why?"

"I don't know why he did it, but he would berate me for being chubby. He'd police what I ate for dinner, rail against me when I did anything wrong. Or when I didn't get an A on every test. He'd yell at me after basketball games. It didn't matter what I'd done right. He'd always remind me of the ways I should have done better."

The warmth of his arms made me feel safe in a way I didn't think I ever had.

So the words continued to pour out of me. "It didn't matter. None of us were safe. After he came home from work, we'd sit at the dinner table and wait to see who he'd target that day. Sometimes it was my mom. But she'd usually throw one of us under the bus to divert his attention."

My body trembled as I spoke, but Jasper just held me tighter, keeping me grounded. "If his steak was overcooked, she'd pivot and tell him I'd forgotten my violin at school or that I'd gotten a math problem wrong. Then he'd turn on me."

He let out a long breath. "That sounds horrible."

"It was normal to us. I didn't realize it wasn't until I was an adult. Most of the time I'm fine, but sometimes, when I fall short, the memories and shame come back. Thoughts I banished decades ago resurface, and suddenly I feel inadequate and unlovable."

As he squeezed me tighter, I realized his T-shirt was damp with my tears. "None of that was your fault," he said firmly. "You were perfect. You are perfect. Kids make mistakes and screw up. Parents should not weaponize childhood against their own children."

The tears wouldn't stop, so I closed my eyes and rested my head on his chest.

"That's abuse." His words were low but firm.

I bristled, shaking my head.

"Evie," he said, tipping my chin up with two fingers. "That is abuse. And what you're experiencing? This is PTSD."

My chest tightened painfully. No. Not possible. These emotions were overly dramatic. Silly, even. I hadn't been to war. My dad had never hit me.

He stroked my hair, and rather than pull away, I gave him more of my weight. The gesture was intimate and protective and deeply comforting.

"No. Negative thoughts just took over and ran amok," I explained. "Sometimes I get pulled into this vortex in my mind. Memories crash and overlap, taking over my thoughts, and then my body joins in, like I'm eight again and being screamed at on the way home from my father's boss's pool party in the Hamptons because, according to him, I looked like a whale in my purple swimsuit. I was fat and it embarrassed him, and he was so sure that would hurt his career."

Jasper's body went rigid. "What the fuck? How could he do that?"

I swallowed past the lump in my throat. "When I came home for Christmas after my first semester of college, he called me a loser at dinner, in front of my grandparents and cousins, because I'd gotten a B in philosophy. Went on and on about how I was wasting his money drinking beer and eating pizza instead of studying.

"No matter what I did, I was wrong. When I failed my driving test because I couldn't parallel park, got a poor grade on a hard test, or dropped a glass in the kitchen, it always came back to my body."

He tucked my head against his chest, his warm palm cupping my jaw, and I let myself breathe in the scent of him.

"The way you're shaking... This trauma lives in your nervous system, and something about tonight brought it all back. Maybe because you were tired and overwhelmed..." He trailed off, stroking my hair.

All my life, my parents had made sure I understood that I was inferior. I was fat and stupid and I wasn't beautiful like my sisters and my mother.

I was an embarrassment. I reflected poorly on my family.

It was my original sin. If I'd been thin and beautiful, my childhood would have been so different.

"I'm so sorry," he whispered into my hair. "You are beautiful and smart and capable. You are a wonderful mother to our son. And those people have no place in your life here."

"I went no contact two years ago." I sighed. "Sometimes I text with my older sister, and I did text my parents when Vincent was born, but that's it."

He hummed. "I'm proud of you."

A strange mixture of doubt and hope swirled inside me. No one had ever said that to me before, especially in regard to cutting off my shitty family.

"What is wrong with me?" It was time to defuse the emotional intensity of this moment. "Vincent has an ear infection, and I'm sitting here making it all about me."

"It is about you," he whispered. "You're Vincent's mom. And he deserves the best mom. A mom who is loved and supported and healed. So I'm here. To listen whenever you need me to."

"You give great hugs," I blurted awkwardly.

He broke into a smile, like that was the best compliment he'd ever received.

But he was great at so many other things too.

I blushed just thinking about all the ways he took care of us. About his confidence and charisma.

"How do you do it?" I asked. "Remain calm. Be so damn optimistic?"

"Calm is relative," he murmured. "And I've been trained to handle emergencies without letting my nerves get to me, so I can't take credit for that."

"No, I don't believe it." I flattened a hand on his chest and pulled back. "This is who you are. This isn't about training."

"Nope." He shook his head. "I panic just as much as the next person. But I'm good at compartmentalizing so I can focus on what needs doing. It's a skill that's been drilled into me for almost a decade."

I huffed. "Deny it all you want, but I think your ability to problem-solve and the way you make everyone feel safe are your superpowers."

Removing my hand from his warm, solid chest, I sat back on the couch. The moment was getting too intimate for my comfort. Now that I'd gathered my wits, my skin prickled at the thought of how much I'd exposed myself to him.

"What's wrong?"

I pushed my hair behind my ears, conscious of how gross I must look. God, couldn't I at least look cute during my emotional breakdown?

"I just spilled my secrets." I avoided his eye. "So I'm feeling a bit exposed."

"Okay, then I'll tell you a secret."

I sat up straighter, crossing my arms, hoping the move would help me put a little more emotional distance between us.

"I love rom-coms," he said quietly.

I scoffed.

"Growing up," he continued, "my mom and I had a tradition. Sunday night was movie night. We'd settle in before the week started and watch rom-coms and eat popcorn. My siblings were all grown up or busy, and Dad played poker with his buddies once a week."

I was hit with a pang of sadness, knowing that I'd never meet these people. That Vincent wouldn't know his grandparents.

"*Notting Hill, You've Got Mail, Serendipity*, all the classics." His lips ticked up on one side. "I liked happy endings. I liked the simplicity of knowing with certainty that the characters were on the right path and making the right choices. Sadly, life doesn't always turn out like that."

"Trust me, I get it," I said. "But the fantasy of the rom-com is nice."

"I was convinced it wasn't real." He lowered his gaze to his lap. "That *hit you like a lightning bolt* kind of love."

"It's not real," I corrected.

He shook his head. "You're wrong. When I held Vincent for the first time in the hospital? It hit me just like that. And it was crystal clear that I was in the right place at the right time with the right people. Doing exactly what I was destined to do." A sigh escaped him. "Be a dad. The stars had aligned to give me my shot at happiness. That's when the movies finally made sense."

The sentiment hit me hard, my eyes welling with tears again. Goddamn Jasper and the sweet things he said. His love for Vincent made him even more attractive to me. And there was only so much an exhausted new mom could take.

Chapter 16

EVIE

"Relax." Ruby eyed me as she sipped the cucumber water. "Jasper's got the baby."

"Yes," Frankie added from the cold plunge pool. "He's basically auditioning for hot dad of the year today. Just let him do his thing."

I sipped my own cucumber water and rolled my eyes. "I don't think I *can* relax."

Ruby glowered at me. "It's your birthday, and you've been through a lot. Today is about girl time and hanging out."

"Maybe I should text Jasper. Check on Vincent."

Frankie sat up in the cold plunge pool. How she managed to survive in there for so long was a wonder. "No phones allowed," she barked. "They said they had to be locked away."

With a smirk, I reached into my cleavage. "I'm not leaving my phone."

"Did you seriously stash an entire iPhone in your tits?" Frankie asked, though she suddenly wore an impressed look.

I nodded and tapped out a quick text to Jasper.

He responded immediately with a photo of a happy-looking Vincent gumming on his dad's tattooed arm.

Okay, fine. They were okay. For now.

"That's some impressive acreage," she said, cupping her own small breasts over her bikini top.

Ruby, who was sitting on the edge of the hot tub, dangling her legs in the water, kicked, splashing me. Even though she couldn't fully enjoy the experience while pregnant, she'd pestered me to get in there and relax. The place was lovely. The lounge was dimly lit, with soft music playing, and in here, with the large whirlpool and cold plunge, we had an incredible view of the Green Mountains. Not to mention access to fluffy white towels and a variety of expensive lotions.

This should have been a birthday dream. Instead, I couldn't shake the feeling that I should be with Vincent. Jasper had taken care of him plenty of times, but never for more than a few hours. This was a whole day. And while my heart was full of gratitude for my friends, who'd coordinated with him for a special birthday surprise, I was uneasy.

"I just don't want to do anything wrong." I set my phone on a low table nearby and lowered myself into the hot water. As I settled, I let out a sigh. Shit, this felt amazing.

Frankie pulled herself out of the cold plunge tub, then rolled her shoulders and shook out her chin-length hair. "You're doing everything right. When I first met you, I thought you were uptight."

"Hey." I splashed her.

She stuck her tongue out at me. "But I've watched you adapt," she went on. "To this town, to your new job, and now to being a mom. You were this big deal city girl in heels, and now look at you." She waved an arm, gesturing to me. "You're a real Vermonter."

Ruby nodded, her lips pressed together. "You've grown, kid. You're more mature."

"And a shit ton weirder," Frankie teased.

"Life has taken some turns." Ruby's smile was affectionate. "But you're not screwing up. Honestly, I'd say you're killing it."

Frankie nodded sharply. "Agreed."

The heat behind my eyes was back, the tears threatening to once again escape. Damn. Would the postpartum emotions ever level out?

Before they took over, thankfully, our wellness concierge, Shea, appeared, holding a clipboard. "It's time for your citrus espresso detox."

I'd been to the Thistle Inn a couple of times since I'd moved to Vermont. Once for brunch and a second time for a company event last summer. It was fancy.

New England fancy. Which is not the same as New York fancy.

The facility was in a massive white clapboard mansion, with green shutters and wide porches adorned with baskets of colorful flowers and climbing ivy. The staff dressed in cheery green uniforms, and vintage chandeliers lit the grand lobby, which was filled with overstuffed wingback chairs and shelves lined with impressive looking books.

There were flowers on just about every surface—lavender, wild lupine, and daisies—creating a serene, old money elegance.

Shea led us down the path to a converted barn with arched windows. The view was breathtaking. Every time I looked somewhere new, all I found was beauty.

"We have you booked for the full day of pampering," Shea said. "You have a private lounge, access to our amenities, and a full schedule of treatments. The chef is preparing some nibbles for you now, and we have multiple hydration options."

Frankie smirked. With the cut-off tee she'd thrown on over her bikini and colorful tattoos, she looked extremely out of place, but she kept her head high, not the least bit bothered.

Especially once Shea mentioned reiki. For several minutes after, Frankie asked all sorts of questions.

"We use Vermont ingredients in our treatments where we can," Shea explained. "We have maple sugar scrubs, local honey facials, and herbal soaks with wild chamomile collected on site."

After we stripped out of our swimsuits and slid into the fluffiest of robes, Shea led us to a sunlit conservatory with wicker lounge chairs. I zoned out while she directed us to the various amenities, too busy taking in the wide expanse of green lawn that led to thick forest and wild mountains.

Close to the mansion, the shrubs and flowers were meticulously maintained and geometrically arranged, but farther out, the landscape got more and more wild. It was what I loved about this area. Maplewood was a quaint, charming town filled with every comfort, but just outside city limits? Pure wilderness. Bears and moose and mountains and waterfalls. Thick forests and the kind of isolation I'd never had the chance to experience in the city.

For the next couple of hours, I was subjected to a detox scrub, a massage, and something called "sound healing" that made me doze off. All of which effectively forced most of the stress out of my body.

The girls and I were enjoying lunch on the terrace in our fluffy robes when Ruby squeaked and pointed across the rolling lawn. "Is that Jasper?"

Frankie lowered her sunglasses, her brows arched. "Jesus H. Christ. That is unfair."

I followed their line of sight, and my stomach flipped over itself.

Jasper.

He was strolling around the ornate gardens with Vincent strapped to his chest in the baby carrier, bouncing and pointing out flowers and butterflies while our son smiled and kicked. The man was clad in worn jeans and T-shirt, as usual, but the aviators cranked the hotness factor up a couple of notches.

Damn.

"Look at him," Ruby hissed. "The tattoos. The broad shoulders. And the gentle dad moves. It's like Mister Rogers and Tom Hardy wrapped up in one sexy package."

"Mister Rogers?" Frankie cackled. "You're into Mister Rogers?"

Ruby harrumphed. "I find nontoxic masculinity very attractive. Get some therapy. You'll understand."

"I guess that explains why Paul wears so many cardigans," Frankie teased.

Ruby gave her the middle finger. I was too busy staring at the man still strolling around the grounds to respond.

"Are those tourists taking photos of him?" Ruby asked, a hand shading her eyes. "He's officially a tourist attraction. Maybe we should make a calendar. We could sell it in my store. It'd sell out in days."

"I may have just ovulated," Frankie admitted. "And I'm pretty sure those parts of me are dead. Good thing Ruby's already pregnant."

Hit with a sudden wave of jealousy, I snagged my phone from the pocket of my robe.

EVIE:

> Are you and Vincent enjoying the gardens?

JASPER:

> I didn't mean to disturb you, but you seemed worried about being so far away from him.

> I figured I'd bring him closer. But we can leave. This day is about you, mama.

My heart melted a little. I was enjoying myself, but knowing Vincent was close by chiseled away at my stress even more.

EVIE:

> Is he hungry? I was just about to pump.

JASPER:

> He's my son. He's always hungry

EVIE:

> Meet me in the spa lobby. I'll feed him before my reiki session.

I stood, tightening the belt on my robe. "I'm going to check on Vincent and nurse him."

Frankie tossed her head back and barked a laugh. "*Sure.* Check on Vincent." She turned to a delighted Ruby. "I think that's code for 'ogle the hot dad some more.'"

I pinned her with a look, though heat crept up my neck. "I'm not ogling."

"Tell that to your face," Ruby chirped. "It's bright red."

Frankie raised her mimosa. "I hate men, but if I had to hate one a bit less, it would be Jasper. He is a walking thirst trap with those sunglasses and the baby carrier."

I left the lounge, annoyed with my friends but more so with myself and my traitorous stomach, which was flipping at the thought of seeing my child's father.

Jasper and Vincent were settled on a plush loveseat when I stepped into in the small lounge area where Shea had led us to earlier. Jasper had his long legs stretched out, and he was holding Vincent so he hovered over him and making silly faces.

My breath hitched at the sight, and my heart thudded strangely when I realized that rather than fussy or distressed, Vincent was completely delighted.

As if he could sense my attention, Jasper shifted and zeroed in on me quickly. Then that damn smile—the slow, lazy one that made him look like he was holding on to a fun secret—spread across his face.

Shaking off the thought, I strode over and took Vincent and quickly situated myself on the chair beside Jasper's.

The infuriatingly gorgeous man leaned over and produced the diaper bag, then pulled out my trusty nursing cover.

I spied the inside of the bag, confused. I'd never seen it look like that.

"Did you clean and organize that?" I asked, marveling. It looked like the kind I'd see on Instagram and glower at when I scrolled late at night. The ones posted by moms who had the most perfectly organized homes, cars, and diaper bags.

He smirked. "Yes. Preparedness is kind of my thing. On the rigs, every tool must be in the right place. There's no time to hesitate during an emergency. And not having a binkie within reach definitely qualifies as an emergency."

Once Vincent was latched, my body did its thing and relaxed. "Thank you."

He put his hands behind his head and reclined. "No problem. Just admit you missed us."

I averted my eyes and gently stroked Vincent's head. "I missed my sweet baby."

"Ouch," Jasper said, putting a hand over his heart. "Ice cold. But I'll take what I can get."

He shifted, the motion pulling his shirt taut across his chest.

My gaze slipped before I could stop it, tracing the lines of ink down his arms, and heat quickly curled low in my belly.

When I forced myself to look up again, he was watching me, wearing a smug grin.

Shit. Busted.

"Today is about you, Evie. You deserve a break. And I'm happy to hang nearby if it helps you feel more relaxed." His tone was so sweet and sincere. For one dizzying second, I debated sitting next to him, letting him put his arm around Vincent and me. But just as quickly, I banished the idea. No way could I let my guard down like that. So I focused on burping Vincent, not caring when he drooled all over my robe.

We sat silently as I switched sides, soaking up as many baby snuggles as I could. But before long, Vincent turned away, finished with his meal.

Reluctantly, I handed him back to his dad. "I should go. Frankie might drown in the mud bath without me."

"Have fun." He cradled our little guy in those inked, muscular arms as the baby's eyes grew heavy. "He'll be out for a while."

"I'll see you back at the house." With that, I turned sharply and headed back to my friends. I needed to exit this situation before I said something stupid. Because as I'd eyed him holding our son, a heavy realization had hit me. I had missed him too.

Chapter 17

JASPER

A wave of energy hit me as I headed to Evie's from the station, eager to see her and my boy. My siblings and my cousin, and even the guys at the station, gave me a lot of shit about this arrangement, but I was happy, and the last thing I wanted was less time with my son.

Vincent might be asleep, but that just meant I had an excuse to hang with Evie.

It was hard not to think about her, especially during long shifts. Her body haunted me. Memories of our night together, while hazy from the maple whiskey shots, were burned into my brain. Her curves, her confidence, her passion.

She'd ruined me.

I couldn't even look at other women. I had no desire to text any of my hookups or even flirt with tourists at the Drip Line. The thought of bringing her cold brew and seeing that sleepy smile got me up in the morning.

I wanted to talk to her, make her laugh and smile.

And more. There was no denying that. My hands ached to touch her. To tug on that thick hair until her neck was exposed. I wanted to run my teeth down her earlobe and feel her shiver in my arms.

For now, though, I'd settle for any time she was willing to give me.

I knocked softly, knowing Vincent should be asleep, and she answered quickly, her eyes tired but her lips tipped up in a small smile.

"I brought you a late birthday present," I said. "Heads up." Gently, I tossed it to her.

She caught it easily, her eyes widening. "You got this for me?"

"Yeah. I noticed you didn't have a ball, and I know how much you like pink. You've got to teach Vincent to play someday. Show him your moves. He's damn lucky to have such a badass mama."

She looked down at her feet. "I have no moves anymore."

"Bullshit," I said. "Grab your shoes."

She scrutinized me for a long moment, then flicked on the exterior lights. A few minutes later, she stepped out, wearing sneakers and a hoodie, and tossed the ball to me.

I dribbled up the driveway and shot. The ball bounced off the rim before falling through the net.

Lunging, I snagged it before it could bounce away. "Come on. Your turn." I stepped in front of her and eased the baby monitor from around her neck, where it hung on a string, breathing in the scent of her.

"See." I pointed at the screen, where Vincent was asleep in his crib, binkie in place.

The war raging in her head, the push and pull, was impossible to ignore. Every time we were alone, this happened. Like she was afraid to let her guard down around me. Like she didn't want to risk having fun with me.

"Come on. A little shoot around," I said, dribbling between my legs. "What's the worst that could happen?"

"I could get pregnant again," she deadpanned.

I laughed, my chest loosening.

But hell if the idea of impregnating her again, on purpose, didn't make my blood heat. That was a reaction I'd have to unpack later.

With a jut of my chin, I passed her the ball. She shot from the grass, making the move look easy.

"Damn."

She cocked a brow. "I told you I was good."

"Noted."

We passed and dribbled, each taking shots. And yeah, she was good. I was a lot taller, but she shot so well it didn't matter. Out here like this, she was different. More confident and open.

So I took a chance.

"How are you feeling?" I shot and missed, then had to chase the ball onto the front lawn.

She checked the monitor, then set it on the hood of my car. "I'm okay. It's weird. I'm excited to go back to work but terrified of leaving Vincent."

She shifted on her feet, as if debating whether to keep talking.

I gave her a minute. I'd learned with my sisters that sometimes the best thing I could do was be quiet.

"I've only been a mom for three months, but it already

feels like my entire being has shifted." She sighed. "It's hard to remember my life before Vincent. But at the same time, I miss that version of myself. You know?"

The tightness returned to my chest. "I feel the same way."

"You do?"

"Not the mom stuff, obviously, but it's hard to remember my life before Vincent." I raked a hand through my hair. "That version of me is fading away. I don't want the same things anymore. I don't think I even like the same things."

She tipped her head and studied me. "I didn't expect you to say that."

Wincing, I shrugged. "Sorry."

She waved off the apology. "No, I'm impressed. I thought it was just me. I feel like I exist on a totally different plane of reality. And honestly, part of me is excited to go back to the office. I miss it. And they've been so flexible and kind, giving me a part-time schedule and plenty of work-from-home hours."

"But?"

"But can I still do my job?" she asked, her brows knitted. "Will I be good at it? Does professional Evie still exist?"

I took a step closer, wanting to touch her, to comfort her.

But I didn't know the rules here. Did any even exist? Or was I just stumbling along without a playbook?

Taking a chance, I reached out and brushed her shoulder. "You're going to be great. I saw you in that virtual meeting the other day. I was blown away by how articulate you were. You were locked in, even while rocking Vincent with your foot. If you can multitask like that, I doubt there's much you can't do."

She sank her teeth into bit her bottom lip. A tell, I'd recently learned, when I surprised her. Before I could process my small victory, she stole the ball from my hands and dribbled toward the net.

"One on one," she declared, doing a perfect layup. "Clear it at the big crack over there."

With a smile, she passed me the ball. She enjoyed this. Competition.

That was one thing we had in common.

"First to ten," she said.

I stood in the spot she'd pointed out, grinning. "I'm not going to hold back."

"I'd hate you if you did." She spread her arms wide to defend me, her eyes fiery.

Boundaries established, I inbounded. Right away, she crossed me, throwing an arm out and hitting me in the chest.

A laugh bubbled out of me. "Aggressive."

"It's my house," she said, effortlessly going for another layup.

"So you play prison rules?" I asked. Damn, it felt good to spar with her.

"Wouldn't you like to know." She winked, then shot a three from the edge of the driveway, sinking it easily.

From there, she only continued to dominate. I'd had no idea how distracting she'd be while playing.

When she shoved her ass into me while dribbling around me.

When her tits brushed my arm while she defended me.

What I thought would be a friendly way to blow off steam was winding me up in ways I hadn't anticipated.

"How'd you learn to shoot like that?" I asked when I got control of the ball again.

"My dad," she said, her face flushed from exertion. "He's an asshole, but I was the tallest of his three daughters, so we spent every weekend in the driveway. He really wanted a son."

"He's lucky to have you," I said, trying to fake her out.

Naturally, she could read me. With far too much ease, she stole the ball and cleared it to the crack.

Shit, I was going to embarrass myself.

"He'd disagree," she said. "My parents have been divorced a long time, and they're both remarried. They do not, on principle, agree on anything, except that I'm a disappointment."

I came to an abrupt halt, frowning at her, remembering all the painful stories she'd shared the other night. These people were monsters, and I'd love nothing more than to tell them that.

"You could never be a disappointment. I know parental scars run deep, but I want you to hear me right now."

She froze and we stared at each other for a moment.

"You are magnificent," I said. "Beautiful and brilliant and so fucking capable. Maybe you've made some mistakes along the way, just like the rest of us, but you are so far from a disappointment."

She blinked at me, the outdoor lights casting part of her face in shadow. "I... Um." She pushed her hair behind her ears. "Thank you?"

"You're welcome," I said firmly.

I resumed dribbling, and she came at me hard. "It took a long time—plus a lot of therapy and a move to rural Vermont

—to convince myself that their opinions were bullshit, but yeah." She gestured to her body. "My mom has always been horrified by my size and my inability to find a suitable husband. And my dad? He took issue with my size too, plus, in his mind, I wasn't smart enough or good enough at sports to deserve his attention. I was nothing more than the ordinary middle child."

My brain struggled to process all the information she was sharing and figure out how to respond in a way that wouldn't shut her down. Evie was usually a tightly closed book. But she was talking. To me. Again.

The other night had not been a fluke or hormones. We were building trust.

Fucking patience. It was so goddamn annoying but usually did the trick. I mentally gave my dad a high-five.

Finally, I held her gaze and said, "Nothing about you is ordinary."

Then I went for a jump shot. The ball bounced off the rim several times before finally going through the net.

"Seven-two." She snagged the ball. "And you don't have to say that."

My stomach twisted at the uncertainty in her tone. "But it's the truth."

A huff escaped her. "I don't want your pity."

I stole the ball from her hands and stood directly in front of her.

In the dim light of the driveway, her face glowed. She looked more beautiful than ever.

"I don't pity you," I gritted out. "I respect you. There's a big fucking difference."

She looked up at me, those dark eyes searching for a lie, her chest rising and falling rapidly.

I stepped even closer, the move making her tilt her head back. She was tall, but she only came up to my chin.

Her lips parted slightly, as if she was surprised by how close we were.

We weren't touching, but we were close enough that I could feel the heat radiating from her body.

It was delicious, this feeling of being close to her, but not close enough.

I wasn't sure there was a such thing as close enough.

"Jasper," she said, her voice a whisper.

I ran my thumb along her jaw and tipped her chin up. "You are incredible," I said, zeroing in on her mouth.

That mouth.

God, it haunted me.

I needed it more than I needed to breathe.

I had to taste her. Had to feel her lips on mine.

The world fell away as I angled in. Her eyes widened, but she didn't pull away as I pressed my mouth to hers in a gentle kiss.

The baby monitor crackled, and a heartbeat later, Vincent cried out.

We sprung apart, both darting for the video monitor on the hood of my car.

In a matter of seconds, Vincent was screaming bloody murder.

She clutched the device to her chest and peered up at me, still breathing hard, her face flushed. "I gotta go."

Then she was gone, jogging toward the house without looking back.

Leaving me holding a pink basketball and wondering what the hell had just happened.

Chapter 18

JASPER

With a roll of my shoulders, I walked toward the large barn. The path to the patio was lit up by string lights, but rather than follow them, I headed straight to the entrance, where a chalkboard sign: *Summer Ale First Pull—7 p.m.*

The high ceiling was made of cedar beams, and copper tanks gleamed in the back of the space. A massive bar stretched along one side, lined with dozens of taps and gleaming glassware.

Unsurprisingly, the place was packed. Tapping the first keg of a new brew usually drew a crowd.

The bar hummed with chatter and a light seasoning of tension. Clusters of service industry folks gathered together. A few off-duty firefighters ribbed one another. One table was full of teachers. Even a few tourists were here, posing for selfies near the taxidermied moose head.

And, of course, the Maple Street Mafia had set up at two high tops near the front of the room.

I gave them a solicitous wave, pleased with myself when Olive Foster gave me a small smile. Bitsy Bramble glared, and Dot, Marigold, and Sally didn't even acknowledge me. They were too preoccupied with the tasting flights lined up in front of them.

Nate's face lit up when he saw me. My cousin was a science nerd turned technical brewmaster. He'd opened this place a few years ago with Chief Ashburn's little brother Reed. The two of them made quite a team. They'd put a lot of work into making this place a success.

So I'd come tonight to support them, even though my thoughts were elsewhere. My muscle memory said grab a pint, find some friends, flirt with girls. But my brain was fully fixated on Vincent, who was probably enjoying a bath right now.

This used to be my place. I'd eat a pretzel, chase it with a pint or two of good beer, and talk to people. Listen to music. Unwind.

The louder and more chaotic a place, the easier it was for me to relax.

But that had all changed recently. Tonight, the chaos made me agitated and uneasy.

"Hey, Jas." A small, warm hand landed on my bicep.

On instinct, I shuddered and spun around. "Brynne." I gave her a tight smile.

She pulled me in for a hug that felt all wrong. "Haven't seen you in ages," she said, her tone flirtatious. She sipped her beer and raised a pierced eyebrow in challenge.

Brynne was an old friend, and yes, we'd hooked up off and on for years. She was pretty, fun, and a champion skier turned instructor who spent most summers partying and rock climbing.

"Been busy," I said. "I'm a dad now." With that statement, I stepped back, putting some distance between us.

The playful smile on her face fell, like she was registering the words I wasn't saying out loud. "I heard. That's so great. Congratulations."

Before I could respond, Reed stood on top of a barrel and shouted, garnering the attention of all the patrons.

"All right, Maplewood. Y'all know the drill. One clean strike, minimal foam. Let's pretend to be civilized."

"Safety glasses on," Nate cautioned from where he stood beside the barrel, along with Reed's wife, Faith.

I used the distraction as a chance to get some distance from Brynne and wandered toward my cousin.

As I approached, I offered him my hand. "You finally dialed the summer ale?"

He nodded, adjusting his safety glasses. "Took me weeks. I was trying to achieve a drier finish."

Reed gave him a playful punch, then pressed a kiss to his wife's cheek. "Leave it to Nate to try to create an emotionally unavailable beer."

He hefted the mallet in his hand, then held it up. Those of us standing near took a big a step back. "Tip your bartenders," he shouted.

The crowd erupted in cheers, then began a countdown.

Reed's strike was clean, causing white foam to spurt out around the tap Faith was holding in place.

The cheers started up again, the sound deafening.

After adjusting the tap, Nate filled two glasses. Then he and Reed posed in front of the keg for photos.

We all lined up for a taste, the scent of hops and lemon soon filling the air. I accepted a glass from Nate, and immediately, the hint of lemon brought an image of Evie to mind. The scent was reminiscent of how Evie's hair had smelled when we were so close the other night.

That thought came with an echo of the delicious anticipation of almost kissing her.

I was tempted to text her a photo and ask her how Vincent was doing, but I resisted. We'd made so much progress recently, and the last thing I needed was to scare her off. She had opened up to me and shared her fears, and every day, she allowed me to play a bigger role in Vincent's life.

Life would be easy if I slid back into my old lifestyle. Became that guy again. Loud laughter, bar tabs, groggy mornings. It took work to hold steady, to earn trust dirty diaper by dirty diaper.

I reached for that guy, like I did occasionally, trying to connect that version of myself, but day by day, he faded farther away.

So I resolved to sip my beer and enjoy the evening.

Minutes later, Gabe pushed his way through the crowd, a tense smile on his face.

His sleeves were rolled up and he was putting off that "I run off four hours of sleep and Italian espresso" vibe, his hair shaggier than usual, his five-o'-clock shadow approaching unruly stubble, and his normally bright eyes dull.

He gave Nate a big hug and a genuine smile. "Proud of you brother."

The two of them posed for a photo with their parents, my Aunt Suzie and Uncle Ed, who'd come to town for a visit. Then Gabe downed a sample glass in one gulp.

"Mister Mayor," one of Maple Street Mafia ladies calls out.

The smile he wore now was the professional one. The one that helped him keep the townsfolk happy, though it slipped when he caught sight of the empties piled up on the table in front of them.

Oh no. The last thing we needed was a repeat of last year's Oktoberfest.

"We need to talk," Gabe said to me.

Before I responded, Opal appeared with a tray of what looked like sliders.

She was the executive chef at Thistle & Boar, the fancy restaurant at the inn, and a tiny ball of culinary energy who'd earned a Michelin star early in her career, then decided to make Maplewood her home. Each time Nate and Reed launched a new beer, she'd set up a pop-up and serve the most incredible food.

My mouth watered as I got a look at the food on her tray.

"Charred corn and brown butter lobster sliders?" she asked.

"Bless you, Opal." Gabe took two and immediately shoved one into his mouth whole.

"The glaze has some bite," she said as I plucked one from the tray a little less violently.

"So do you," I teased.

She gave me a warm smile. "I always liked you. Now," she said, her expression going serious, "make sure this one eats. We can't have him fainting in the middle of his big press conference tomorrow."

Press conference? I eyed my cousin, searching for an explanation. Damn, I was out of loop.

But before Gabe stopped chewing, a whole crowd descended.

"Mayor," Tony said, weaving his hulking form through the crowd. "I'm down 30 percent week over week. If this month tanks, I'll be tossing dough in the dark."

Tony was joined by Marty, who ran the diner alongside his mother. Mac, who owned the ice cream shop, appeared next, and then Nora, our pharmacist.

"Bus tours have been canceled," Marty added. "Apparently people don't want murder syrup with their pancakes."

"Caroline and Linda had a wedding cancellation next month," Nora said, pushing her jeweled glasses up her nose. "The father of the bride asked if our river was contaminated. What on earth is happening?"

Gabe slipped into his mayor mask, his demeanor completely calm, and held his hands up. "I hear you. This is a difficult situation for everyone. And we're coordinating with the state. I've requested additional investigative support and—"

"Coordinating doesn't pay the bills," Bitsy snapped. She'd left her friends and pushed her way into our group. Now, hands on her hips, clad in all purple, she scowled. "Or hire seasonal staff. You need to fix this, Gabriel. The entire town is terrified, what with a murderer running around."

Several people milling around nearby moved closer, a crowd gathering around us.

Gabe's jaw ticked, signaling that he was at the end of his rope.

"What's that?" I pushed up on my toes and peered at Nate, who was on the other side of the bar, a concerned look on his face. "Sorry, guys," I said, pulling Gabe by the arm.

"Nate needs us in the kitchen. Busy night. Family's gotta chip in."

Quickly, we pushed through the crowd to the kitchen, but I didn't stop until we hit the keg room.

"You okay?" I asked my cousin. "That was intense."

Gabe, shoulders slumped, shook his head.

"What do you need?"

When he looked up at me, it was like he'd aged a decade. The weight of carrying this town was getting to him. "I need an arrest," he said softly. "I need to be able to tell the citizens of this town that they are safe. I need Nolan to get some rest, and I need him to not kill himself trying to find this murderer. And I need to get through Founder's Day without a recall petition."

I blinked, the weight of his words settling in. He took his role so seriously and sacrificed so much for this town, yet so many seemed close to turning on him.

"Actually." He sighed. "You can do one thing for me."

"Anything."

"Call Brian. File the paperwork."

I reeled back. The words were like a physical blow. "You called Brian?"

My sister's fiancé Brian was a big deal family law attorney. He'd recently passed the Vermont bar so their family could spend summers here. I liked the guy a lot, but professionally, he was an absolute shark. He'd gone above and beyond for Jess and my nieces, and he'd even managed to fuck over her shitty ex-husband in the process.

"He's the best," Gabe said. "And together we can get you through this."

Anger stirred to life in my gut. "There's nothing to get through."

He closed his eyes and exhaled. "Dude, the kid's three months old."

"My son *Vincent* is three months old," I gritted out, my hands balled into fists. "And his mother and I are doing great."

Gabe crossed his arms, giving me a big brother look that dripped with condescension.

I loved the guy, but we'd never been close. He'd mostly stuck with Josh growing up, while Nate and I had always been buddies. Like us, there were four of them, and our parents discovered early on that the easiest way to deal with all of us was to put us together and send us off into the woods to entertain ourselves.

"You need to get serious."

"I am extremely serious," I said, that anger winding its way to my chest. "I'm serious about being Vincent's father."

"Of course you are." He dragged a hand down his face. "But you can't just ignore the legal side of this."

"Why not?" I loved to ignore unpleasant things, I'd gotten pretty damn good at it over the years.

He frowned, his brows pulled low. "Because this could go very badly for you. And there's a lot at stake."

I wished I hadn't left my beer at the bar. Maybe the cool ale would calm the rage rising up inside me. Of course there was a lot at stake. Vincent was a human being, a child who needed love and care and braces and summer camp. The responsibility was enormous; I didn't need to be reminded of that.

"Legally and financially," he said.

"I'll do whatever is right for Vincent."

Gabe buried his face in his hands. "Okay, no. Don't say that."

I bristled. "Why not? It's the truth."

"Because we need to be strategic."

"I'm not going to battle against Evie." My gut sank at just the thought. "She's the mother of my child. We get along, we coparent."

I took a step back, not trusting myself not to take a swing at him. I never got mad, and I certainly never yelled, but my desire to defend Evie and Vincent was stronger than my desire to people please.

"Coparent?" he laughed. "You sleep in the backyard like a dog, Jas. You have no set visitation or custody schedule. You've never even taken the kid to the farm."

"Because all the baby stuff is at her house, and she's nursing."

"Dude." He huffed. "I love you. We're family. And I'm impressed with how much you've grown these last few months. Your love for this child; we all see it and we all respect it. You're becoming more and more like your dad every day."

I let out the air I was holding in my lungs. Because damn, that was not what I was expecting.

"But," he hedged, "you can't just close your eyes and ignore the hard stuff. The complications. The challenges. This..." Lips pressed together, he exhaled. "This situation. Is not in your favor. Have your siblings even met the baby?"

No. Because I'd kept my distance. I'd been respectful, letting Evie make all the decisions. I'd put myself in a position to support her. It felt like the right decision.

My entire being deflated. "So what do you propose I do?"

"Get a paternity test. Then we kindly and civilly negotiate a custody agreement and parenting plan." He straightened a little, the professional in him returning. "Child support, college planning. All the things Vincent needs to thrive. Brian has everything ready to go."

I bobbed my head, trying to reconcile all of this. The thought of bringing in lawyers and paperwork made me feel sick. Evie and I got along, we had fun. I loved being close by. She didn't treat me like a dog; she was navigating a tough situation the best she could. Just like I was.

We'd been caught by surprise, and we'd done our best.

"Please just let us draw up papers. A petition, the basics. You have rights. You have assets. I love you, and I just want to protect you and Vincent."

Hands on my hips, I dipped my chin. Maybe he was right. Gabe and Brian were a hell of a lot smarter than I was, and I trusted them. At some point, Evie and I would have to make choices.

The door to the taproom opened, and Nate stepped in. "The IPA's already kicked. I blame the mafia ladies. They're thirsty tonight." Without slowing, he skirted around us and got to work changing the keg. "Gabe, you should get out there. Nolan just walked in."

Back out in the bar, we found Nolan standing under the twinkle lights, his uniform crisp and his eyes rimmed with fatigue. If Gabe looked tired, Nolan looked as if rest had filed a restraining order against him.

As he walked through the tasting room toward us, the

cheers and the clinking of glassware quieted, folks pivoting and whispering at his presence.

Gabe held out a hand. "Evening, Nolan."

Nate appeared a moment later with a glass of water with a lemon slice, Nolan's usual order when on duty.

With a nod, Nolan took the water and scanned the room. He only stopped when he landed on the members of the Maple Street Mafia, who were drinking and carousing without a care in the world.

Sally thrust her hand into the air, causing her drink to slosh over the tasting glass. "This one tastes like a lemon got into a fistfight with a pine cone."

"I enjoy the aftertaste of regret," Marigold added. "Reminds me of my first husband."

Nolan headed their way, but not without encountering several people peppering him with questions.

"Is it true about the kayakers?"

"I heard it's a government conspiracy."

Donny Sullivan, unsurprisingly inebriated, stumbled up to the chief. "Any news, or are you just here to chauffer the bingo bus?" he slurred.

When Nolan's jaw ticked in response, I stepped in, putting my body between them. "Let's get you a water, Don." With a hand on his shoulder, I guided him back. Then, using my calm firefighter voice, I said, "He's working, you're drinking. Give the man some space."

Don scoffed. "Who asked you, Maplewood hero?"

The urge to throw him over the bar hit me hard, but that would solve nothing, and this town had enough problems already. "No one asked me," I said, keeping my tone even. "I'm volunteering. Now sit down, drink a glass of water, and call for a ride home." I steered him toward the bar, where Nate gave me a nod of gratitude.

"Evening ladies," Nolan said to the table of chattering senior citizens. "Nana." He eyed the stack of small glasses in front of Olive. "How many flights did you order?"

"A girl's gotta stay hydrated, sweetie."

"That's IPA, not Fiji Water, Nana."

Her friends burst into laughter.

Olive, on the other hand, gave him a bored look. "Arrest me, then, grandson."

"Public intoxication statutes are not suggestions," Nolan said to the assembled ladies. "Now who needs a ride home?"

Suddenly sheepish, they peered around at one another.

"Okay, I guess all of you, then."

"We're having fun," Olive said, picking up her purse. "And you're ruining it."

Nolan crossed his arms and looked down at his beloved nana, who couldn't have weighed more than one hundred pounds soaking wet. "Olive Foster, if you don't hand me your tiny glass and let me escort you and your friends to my car, I will book you for drunk and disorderly. And if you even think about using the crochet hook in your purse, I'll slap on a weapons charge."

With a glare, she gathered her things, and slowly, the ladies filed out. "Fine." She patted Nolan's bearded cheek as she passed him. "But I get shotgun. And no pot roast for you tomorrow."

It was not the first time he'd driven his grandmother home after a wild night. Though this might have been the first time the entire town was here gossiping and slinging insults at him while he did it.

"Solve the murder," a man yelled from the crowd.

"Yeah," another agreed. "Stop babysitting and do your damn job."

I left my glass on the bar and headed out after Nolan. I'd had enough of the mayhem for one night.

"Jasper," Opal called before I stepped outside.

I turned, finding her scurrying over with two to-go boxes in her hands.

"One for Evie, because I like her more than you."

Smirking, I took the offerings.

"And the other is for Nolan. I'm worried he's not eating."

Outside, the ladies were now needling Nolan because his police car was too clean.

With a shake of my head, I strode over and gave him one of the to-go boxes.

Then I headed for my car. Halfway there, my phone vibrated in my pocket, and when I pulled it out and found a text from Evie, my heart swelled.

EVIE:

Vincent hiccuped himself to sleep. The house is so quiet.

JASPER:

I'm on my way. Opal gave me a lobster roll for you.

EVIE:

Yummy.

JASPER:

Save me a slice of quiet. I could use it.

I started my car, and for a moment, I sat in the lot, letting my mind wander. Imagining opening Evie's door without knocking and rushing in to give her a kiss.

If only. In reality, I'd politely knock, hand her the to-go box, ask to use the bathroom to brush my teeth, and then head back out to my tent.

I needed to knock.

I needed to wait.

Because we were making progress, and I would earn every step.

Chapter 19

JASPER

Humming quietly, Evie loaded the dishwasher. She had shoved me aside when I started, insisting she didn't want my help.

Sure, I'd made dinner, but it was boxed mac and cheese. Hardly fine dining. The woman had been more grateful than I expected for such a simple gesture. Shit, now I'd wished I'd put in more effort. My siblings could all cook, but I'd managed to weasel my way out of kitchen duty growing up. It was one of the perks of being mom's favorite. Unfortunately, that also meant I missed out on learning all her recipes.

While Evie worked, I busied myself wiping down the countertops. The kitchen was small but filled with charm. A set of shelves near the coffee pot displayed several mugs, and the scalloped curtains over the windows let just enough light in during the day. The framed pressed flowers that hung on the wall were cute, if not a tiny bit crooked.

It wasn't showy, and it wasn't perfect, but it was hers.

Little by little, Evie was peeling back the curtain and giving me a peek at her inner life. And like the obsessed man I was, I relished every detail, filing them all away in my mind. The efficient way she moved around this space. The little sigh of relief she made when Vincent latched. The way she played with her hair when she was lost in thought.

After turning on the dishwasher, Evie popped up on her toes and pushed down on the open window with a grunt.

"Ugh." She steadied herself and did it again, pushing it harder with the heel of her hand.

"Stuck?" I asked.

She shook her head. "I've got it." This time she gripped the sill hard and pulled with everything she had.

It didn't budge.

"You okay over there She-Hulk?" I asked, setting the dish rag next to the sink.

She glared at me over her shoulder. "This stupid window always sticks when the temperature changes. It's fine."

I stepped back and propped a hip against the counter. I could fix the issue easily, but I knew better than to step in. This woman had pushed me to a level of patience I never knew I could possess. These days, I was approaching monk-like status. When I had more free time, maybe I'd start giving Zen life advice on TikTok.

She pushed again, the muscles in her jaw clenching.

Worried she was going to pull a muscle, I finally sidled over. "Evie." At her side, I gently nudged her over.

The glare was back, along with a large sigh.

I wiggled the pane, thinking I could jimmy the lock and lift the window, and lifted up, hoping that if I pulled the frame gently, I could ease the stick, but this fucker was stuck good.

After a couple of tries and using damn near all my strength, it finally released, and I slid it into place and latched it.

"Fucking figures," she growled.

"Wood's swollen." I stepped back, schooling my expression when really, I wanted to grin maniacally. She was adorable when she was frustrated. "I'll sand the sill down tomorrow. There's moisture stuck in the groove. Easy fix."

"I can fix it." She stepped in front of the sink again, her arms crossed like she was trying to box me out.

With a nod, I put my hands on the counter beside her, bracing myself, and peered out the window to the darkened backyard.

"I bought this house because I wanted something I could manage," she said, turning and surveying the yard too. "Something small that I'd never have to share."

I put my hand over hers. "You've done a great job. You've put a lot of love and work into this place."

"I've tried." She deflated. "But like everything else in my life, it never feels like it's enough. This stupid window, the bathroom fan that whistles, the creaky front stairs, the damn bushes that need to be trimmed all the time."

The frustration in her voice cut me up. How could this woman think she wasn't enough? She was so much more than enough. She was everything.

"You're busy," I murmured. "Busy being awesome at your job and busy being an awesome mom. The bushes and the creaky steps? Small potatoes in the grand scheme. And I can help."

She nodded once, her body loosening beside me. The muscles in her jaw were no longer tense like they'd been when she said she was never enough. Like this stupid window was a symbol for the other parts of her she hadn't had time to fix.

But tonight, she'd let me help.

As we stood silently, both still looking out the window, I couldn't help but think how idiotic I was to assume that showing up meant flowers, fancy dates, gifts, or back rubs. The Instagrammable type of effort. Cliched shit.

In reality, this was showing up. It didn't have to be loud or flashy. And I was beginning to realize this may just be my superpower.

And Evie was finally letting me use it.

"I wanted to ask you something," I said. "Feel free to say no."

She dropped her arms to her sides, which felt like a gesture of cooperation.

"You've mentioned a few times that you wish you had a fireplace. That you enjoy sitting by a fire to relax."

She nodded.

"What if I built a fire pit out back? With a small patio?"

Her eyes widened. "You can do that?"

"Yeah. Josh and I built a massive one at the farm. And we'll do another at Jess's house when it's finished."

Maybe her family wasn't the type to build and create things. Maybe they hired people to mow the lawn or fix the roof, but I was a farm kid. We used good old Yankee ingenuity and elbow grease to get things done.

"That's too much."

Lips pressed together, I shook my head. "I've already

drawn up some sketches to show you, but I don't want to intrude."

She blinked and searched my face, a line forming between her brows, as if she was looking for an ulterior motive. She was too smart and guarded to just say yes to all my outrageous plans.

"Sitting around a fire is one of life's great pleasures," I explained. "My dad taught me to build a fire and nurture it and keep it going." Heat prickled at the backs of my eyes, but I continued on. "I'd like to teach my son like he taught me."

My son.

I desperately wanted to share these things with him. Take long hikes and talk about life. Teach him about tapping trees and keeping bears off the property.

But Evie had gone eerily silent.

My stomach pitched. Shit. I'd probably offended her.

I cupped the back of my neck and squeezed. "I know it's silly. If you hate the idea—"

"I don't hate it," she blurted out. "I've always wanted a patio, and a fire pit would be wonderful."

"Great, then I'll work on it."

She twirled the end of her ponytail like she always did when something was bothering her. "I just." She closed her eyes, as if searching for the right words. "I don't want to take advantage of your generosity. I could wait. Hire someone eventually."

"I want to."

She frowned at me, confusion swimming in her eyes.

Damn, this woman was just not getting it.

"Evie. If I didn't want to, I wouldn't have offered. I'm a

simple guy. I want to be here. I want to help you out. I want to be Vincent's dad."

She opened her mouth as if to respond, but I went on before she could, my head full of steam.

"In my world, this is what dads do." I gripped the edge of the countertop on either side of me. "They fix problems, they provide when they can, and they help out. This isn't just your house."

Her brows rose, and a concerned look flashed across her face.

"It's our son's home," I said softly before she could get the wrong idea. "And that means something to me. I may not live here, but I'm damn sure going to provide the best possible home for him. You are so capable, so if I can mow the grass or fix a window or even build a patio to take a little of the load off you, then I'm happy to do it."

For a long moment she only stared. My nerves made me restless, but I didn't move. I'd probably said too much. I'd probably tipped my hand. We'd been tiptoeing around this arrangement for months. And so far, ignoring it had worked. But at some point, we had to face the facts that we had a baby together but weren't a couple.

I'd respected every one of her boundaries since day one, but this was a silly place to draw a line, so tonight, I'd push a little.

My mom used to say I wore my heart on my sleeve. For years I thought that was a bad thing, a curse to battle against. I worked hard to be detached and indifferent.

Maybe it was because I was sleeping on the ground. Maybe I was too damn tired to wage that war any longer.

Because the urge to be myself with Evie and Vincent, to let them see who I was, had taken over. Maybe I didn't have much to offer, but this was one area in which I could contribute.

"I'm not going away," I said softly, grasping her hand.

The touch sent a surge of energy through me, giving me the strength to stand straighter and step closer.

Her eyes widened, and her chest rose as she inhaled deeply.

"This is who I am," I said with a squeeze of her hand. "You've heard a lot of bullshit rumors about me, but they aren't true. I want Vincent to know me. I want to teach him and guide him to grow into a man who can be authentic and strong and vulnerable. But in order to do that, I need to be here, contributing. Coparenting or whatever you want to call it."

She lowered her head a fraction, breaking eye contact. "I know."

Realizing that my passionate plea had been a little too loud, I forced a calming breath. "I'm doing it," I said, my voice lower. "I've given you time and space and support. He's my son too. He's never even met my family. Never been out to the farm."

She reeled back like she had been punched.

My gut dropped. Shit. But still, Gabe's words echoed in my ears.

"This is bigger than a window, Evie. I've earned the right to fully participate in Vincent's life."

"You have," she admitted, her lip trembling. "And I'm sorry. He should go to the farm, meet the family. I think it would be lovely."

The tightness in my chest eased. I had not expected that reaction.

"I want those things for him too." She shook her head, tears cresting her lashes. "You have been a great dad. And you're right. I've treated you like shit."

I deflated. Fuck. I was a total dick.

"No, that's not true," I said, panic rising in my chest. "I'm sorry if I made you feel that way."

"Don't be sorry. You've done nothing wrong." She covered her face, her shoulders shaking.

I pulled her into my arms and held her tight. Dammit. What the hell was I thinking harassing the exhausted new mom like this?

"You're a good man," she said into my now damp shirt. "And I hate that we're fighting about..." She sniffled. "About home repairs. What a dumb thing for me to get territorial about."

She pulled back and looked up at me. Even like this, face tearstained, her beauty hit me straight in the solar plexus. Every time I was close to her, every time I got to touch her, I was overwhelmed with this intense need to be even closer.

"I've been dismissive and downright nasty to you," she whispered.

I handed her a paper towel. She used it to dab at her eyes, then blew her nose with it. It was adorable.

"I'm a bitch," she said, fresh tears falling. "I push you away, and you just keep coming back. Do you know how infuriating that is?"

A mix of frustration and affection churned inside me at that comment.

"I just want you to be another shitty man. Another person who lets me down so I can write you off and then smugly control everything. But you." She poked me hard in the chest. She'd gone from tears to rage in the blink of an eye. "You just keep being decent and helpful. You want to build a patio, for fuck's sake." She threw her arms up. "Do you know how much easier it would be for me if you were a deadbeat?"

My breath caught. "What? How would that be easier?"

"You don't have enough childhood trauma to under-stand." She poked me in the chest again. "So I appreciate you and what you're doing, but give me a minute to catch up, okay? You can't just show up here day in and day out, being all decent and helpful and handsome and expect me to be okay with it."

"Um... what? Why not? and *handsome*?" Ego stroked, I grinned down at her.

She only glowered back and turned away, pacing the small room. "So yes, you can do stuff around the house," she said, "I actually appreciate it. I just need to process. My default setting is icy bitch. But you just have this way of, ugh. I don't know." She squeezed her eyes shut. "Of defrosting me and catching me off guard."

My heart lifted, though I had to hold back a chuckle. This conversation had gone in directions I could never have predicted. But I got the sense I needed to quit while I was ahead. Evie didn't need me, but she was willing to put her own baggage aside and let me be here anyway.

I'd take the offering gladly. And I'd take this moment and tuck it away to think about later. Tonight, I'd made a tiny bit of progress. She didn't know it yet, but I didn't want to be anywhere but here. Even when she was yelling and crying, I wanted to be with her and Vincent.

And I couldn't imagine that desire ever fading.

Chapter 20

EVIE

"Get in here," I yelled from the back door. The man was being a stubborn ass.

It was one thing to sleep outside when it was cold. But in an absolute downpour? Hell no. Once the thunder started, I expected him to show up at the back door, but he remained hunkered down in that tent. Up here in the mountains, the weather could get extreme quickly, and even though it was only June, the stifling summer humidity had already begun. So I pulled my raincoat around me and trudged into the backyard.

"Jasper." I was an asshole. Night after night, I climbed under the blankets in my warm, cozy house, and he was outside.

With a storm like this, it would be downright cruel not to invite him in.

Inside, the lantern was on, and his shadow moved over the tent wall. Then he unzipped the flap a few inches and peeked out.

"Come inside," I yelled over the rain, gesturing with one arm.

He disappeared, and then the flap was fully unzipped and he was hopping out, barefoot.

And shirtless.

Oof.

He sprinted into the house wearing only mesh athletic shorts, but he pulled up short at the door.

"You sure you want me inside?" he asked.

Holy hell. As he stood before me, water droplets slowly rolled down his chest. And it was a chest, that was for sure. Wide and muscular and a bit hairy.

I blinked several times, chiding myself for my lack of control, and pointed into the house. "Hold on. I'll get you a towel."

With a smirk, he held the door open for me.

I scurried to the linen closet and returned quickly with a fluffy mint green towel.

When he took it, I should have walked away. That's what a normal person would have done. Instead, I watched as he toweled off, making sure each inch of tan, muscular skin was dry.

"Thank you," he said. "But if you'd rather have me out there, that's okay. The tent's technically waterproof."

"You're not staying out there in a storm." At this point, between my crying in his arms, our bonding over Vincent, and the argument we'd gotten into where he forced me to accept more help, any pretense had been dismantled. This man had seen me at my absolute lowest. I wasn't going to let him get soaked.

He nodded, giving me a grateful smile. "I won't get in your way."

"Oh my God." I wanted to scream. I wanted to slap myself. "You're not in my way."

Was I really that bitchy. That intractable?

This guy, who had done nothing but show up every minute of every day, would rather sleep on my lawn than inconvenience me, even a little.

Fuck, I'd turned into my mother.

That was a chilling thought.

Over and over, I'd replayed our argument the other night. It had been eating at me. I'd been in survival mode for so long that I hadn't even realized how badly I'd been treating Jasper. He wasn't a deadbeat baby daddy. Not even close.

Hit with the overwhelming need to apologize, I took a step toward him. "Jas—"

A gurgling cry echoed down the hall, startling me.

I pinched the bridge of my nose. "Oh shit, I woke him up."

"I got it." With his signature lopsided grin, he bounded toward the nursery.

He came out a few minutes later, Vincent cuddled to his chest, happily sucking on his binkie.

"He just needed a fresh diaper. Right, little dude?"

This was not fair.

He was shirtless.

Holding my baby.

In my living room.

And I was wearing stained sweatpants, and my hair was stringy and dirty.

The universe was punishing me. And I deserved it. After a week like this one, I had no energy left to bother with a shower or clean clothes. I'd worked from home while caring for Vincent, I'd done the grocery shopping, and I'd visited the daycare where he'd start part time next week. I'd overdone it, and now I was paying for it.

"I should shower." I patted the messy bun on the top of my head. It might have looked cute three days ago, but it had almost calcified at this point.

"Can't shower during a lightning storm," he said.

A hint of annoyance flitted through me. While that was very logical, I hated it.

"Safety is kind of my thing, remember?"

Sighing, I searched his face. Underneath that little bit of frustration, I was dumbstruck. Because despite my gremlin-like appearance and demeanor, he was once again being kind and helpful.

"I'm gonna rock this guy and see if I can get him back to sleep," he said, making a silly face at Vincent.

I cringed. "Do you want a shirt."

"Sure." He lifted one shoulder. "But I don't want to stretch anything out."

I surveyed his taut, toned body, then peered down at my own lumpy, dumpy one. "I'm sure I can find something."

In my closet, I snagged an oversized NYU T-shirt from a hanger. Then I ran a brush through my hair and slapped on a thick layer of deodorant.

A few minutes after I'd returned to the living room, he emerged with the baby monitor, smiling happily.

"I can't believe how big he is now," he marveled. "It was like yesterday he could practically fit in my hand."

"Eighty-fifth percentile," I bragged, my heart lifting.

He chuckled. "I'm convinced he's a genius."

"Of course he is."

"The way he makes eye contact and listens to me when I talk to him about how to tap a maple tree." Jasper shook his head. "He gets it. Sometimes I feel like we should tell someone, but I like keeping our super baby genius to ourselves."

"Me too." I laughed.

He crouched and plucked two baby toys from the floor. "He must get it from you. I'm dumb as a box of rocks."

My stomach twisted at the seriousness in that comment. That was absurd. "No you're not."

He looked up at me, his expression sweet and trusting, like always. "Nah. But it's okay. School was never really my thing. Josh is the super smart one. Brilliant even. But me?" He lifted one shoulder and dropped the toys in the basket where they belonged. "I could never sit still long enough. I wanted to be in the mountains or jumping into a cold pond. Not doing calculus."

"Nothing wrong with that," I said. "You're a paramedic. Work like that takes real brain power."

"Eh. Maybe. I had to study like hell. Took all the prep courses, Jenn and Josh quizzed me constantly, and because I already worked for the fire department, I got to shadow a few folks."

"Don't talk down about yourself," I chastised. "Vincent will hear that, and we can't allow it. You're his hero."

He laughed.

"I mean it," I urged. "You're his dad, and his face lights up when you're here."

Jasper smiled. "He's four months old, Evie."

I crossed my arms, head tilted. "I'm his mom. I can decode all his looks and cries and giggles. Yet he is obsessed with you. It's annoying."

"Okay, mama bear. I believe you." Once he'd gathered up the rest of the toys and put them into the basket, he stood to his full height, smoothing down his shorts. "What if I got him a tiny hatchet? So we could be twinsies."

I scoffed. "Absolutely not."

He took a step toward me, his eyes dancing. "Pretty please?"

"Not on your life, Lawrence. No weapons. He can't even roll over yet."

"He will soon. Baby genius and all. He'll be tapping trees and climbing mountains next week. You're raising a Vermont boy, so you better watch out. We're kind of feral."

The way he said that last part made my insides heat. Especially when he was sitting in front of me shirtless, that thin line of hair that trailed down his stomach and disappearing into his shorts, distracting me.

"Here," I threw the T-shirt at him, then shuffled to the kitchen to hide the way my face burned. God, what was wrong with me?

I hated being wrong. Despised it.

But I couldn't deny any longer just how wrong I'd been about this man. I'd written him off as a fuck boy. A hot guy I let myself have a single night of fun with.

Yet every day, he showed me that he was so much more. It had taken me this long to appreciate it all, but along with the appreciation came a good deal of confusion. About how I felt about him. About the way he looked at me.

"Want some dinner?" I asked, desperate to move on.

"Sure."

I busied myself in the kitchen, making turkey sandwiches. Basil had dropped off fresh bread and Brie, so I could get fancy.

Jasper continued picking up the living room, folding the pile of laundry on one end of the couch and digging a binkie out of the cushions. He had put on my NYU shirt, and each time he lifted his arms, it rode up to reveal his abs.

Not that I noticed or anything.

While we ate in the living room, he filled me in on all the personalities at the fire station, including Keanu, the cat they had adopted who liked to sleep in the coiled-up hoses.

By the warmth in his voice, it was clear he enjoyed his work and loved this town.

"Make it make sense," I said, waving an Oreo at him. We'd raided my secret snack stash and were sitting on the couch, waiting for Vincent to wake for his late-night feeding. "It seems so dumb to me. They killed themselves."

I could not for the life of me figure out why everyone in this town was obsessed with a couple of dumbass teenagers who'd lived here centuries ago.

"Because though they were on opposing sides of the war, they couldn't live without one another. And they probably would have been killed anyway."

"Flinging oneself off the top of a waterfall at nineteen years old is the definition of dumb."

"Wow," he huffed. "Didn't figure you for such a romantic."

With a slow blink, I gave him an unimpressed look.

"True love? It's worth dying for." To punctuate the sentence, he shoved an entire Oreo into his mouth.

"Nope." I shook my head. "That's where you're wrong. Love is about living. Fighting and surviving and making it work."

Though my tone was sharp, he grinned at me.

Somehow, we'd managed to inch closer together on the couch. Unintentionally, of course. But I couldn't help but angle myself toward him as I argued.

"Why is this town so obsessed?"

He blinked, genuinely surprised by the question. "With Nathaniel and Cora? First, the Revolutionary War is kind of a big deal around here."

"Okay."

"No, really. It's not like Mass or Connecticut. Vermont was its own country for years before joining the United States. that's why we were the fourteenth state, despite the rest of New England being most of the first."

He dove deeper into the story, clearly relishing the opportunity to teach me something.

"And everyone knows the Green Mountain boys, an independent militia, helped win the war."

I cocked a brow. "Oh, really?"

"Yes. That's the thing about Vermont. We're weird. We do our own thing. We don't handle authority well. The state's history is filled with stories about people who went against the grain. So Cora and Nathaniel mean a lot to us. Her father would have killed him first, and when she was discovered to be a spy, she would have been done for too. So they took the leap."

"And they were never found?"

"Nope. Never. They got to be together forever. And we got our waterfall legend."

"Dumbasses," I muttered.

"Romantics," he countered, his voice low and his green eyes dark.

My heart thudded heavily under his scrutiny, my skin prickling with awareness.

When had he slung his arm along the back of the couch? At what point did our thighs begin touching?

I opened my mouth, wanting to break the tension, but no words came out.

Instead, the air crackled around us.

Finally, feeling a bit dizzy, I forced myself to speak. "I don't think love should hurt that much."

He leaned forward, his eyes locked on mine. "Sometimes it's supposed to."

This close, I could feel the heat of his breath on my skin. The urge to reach out and touch his face, run my fingers over the ridge of his jaw, feel his warmth was all-consuming.

Could I? Should I?

One of us moved. Him? Me? I couldn't be sure. Either way, we were pulled together like magnets with opposing poles.

Our lips met in an impulsive kiss. Half defiant and half surrender.

Not slow. Hard and fast and open-mouthed. We jumped right into the deep end of the ocean without a life preserver.

Messy and frantic, lips and tongues and teeth. Not smooth, not gentle.

This was Jasper. No polished edges, no holding back, just pure energy and enthusiasm. I wanted to get closer, so much closer. He slid his hands down to my ass, gripping tightly. I clung to his too short T-shirt like I was ready to claw it off his body.

I was mindless. Absorbed in Jasper. In his mouth, his hands, the scent of him everywhere. It was natural, falling into this, into him. Turning my brain off when he was touching me.

He shifted, the movement causing his hardness to brush against my stomach.

An alarm went off in my brain then. This could go way too far too fast. And I couldn't do that again. Losing control once was enough.

As I pulled back, his grip tightened on my hips.

God, what I wouldn't give to throw caution to the wind. But the heaviness in my breasts reminded me that I had responsibilities now.

"Sorry." I pushed against his chest. "I've got to feed Vincent."

Releasing me, he looked away. "Of course. Right. I'll just... um. I'll sleep on the couch."

Heart racing, I debated just jumping him. But only for a second before I thought better of it.

"Okay, great. Blankets are in the hall closet." I got to my feet and dashed toward the nursery on shaking legs, my thoughts consumed by that kiss.

Chapter 21

EVIE

Pulse pounding, I smoothed down my skirt. This was nerve racking.

Ruby had come by and supplied an outfit for this occasion. She'd also played with Vincent while I did my hair and makeup. Though I did have to help her up off the floor.

"I'm ready to pop," she whined. "I've been eating all the spicy food. Why can't I just go into spontaneous labor like you did? Should I go get a pizza?"

"You're almost there," I said. "Enjoy sleeping."

"I can't. My little ninja likes to kick me in the kidneys while I sleep."

On the playmat, Vincent rocked back and forth, determined to roll over. His persistence was impressive, and I loved how he scrunched up his face in concentration when he was learning a new skill.

"You're gorgeous," she said, cradling her belly. "Look at your waist. I miss my waist."

A light laugh escaped me. "Thank you for helping today."

She looked down at my little guy in his Oxford shirt and cuffed jeans. Another outfit she'd brought over. "I wanted you both to look great when you meet the family for the first time. These people could be your in-laws."

My heart lurched. "Stop. It's not like that."

She patted my cheek. "Sure thing, gorgeous—" With a harsh breath in, she winced.

"Are you okay?"

She shook her head, her brows pinched. "All good. Fucking Braxton-Hicks. I'm fine. Go have fun. You look hot as hell."

The ride to the farm was scenic and beautiful. A typical early summer day in Vermont. After being holed up in my house for months, it felt good to breathe in the fresh air. I blasted Lake Paige's newest album as Vincent and I drove up the winding road toward Lawrence Farm.

When the place came into view, it took my breath away.

Giant red barn, pretty white farmhouse, flowers lining the long driveway, rolling hills and dense maple forest. Exactly as Jasper had described it.

I'd visited several farms in the area for work, doing PR and business relations stuff, but none had been this beautiful. As I rolled toward the house at a snail's pace, a giant dog trotted alongside my car, wagging its tail.

I parked in front of the house, and before I could even get out, Jasper was opening the door for me.

"You made it." The joy radiating from him was so genuine it knocked me back. He'd been working, so I hadn't seen him since the day before yesterday. Since the morning after we shared that soul scorching kiss.

Though kiss was a conservative term. Since I did end up in his lap, I'd probably categorize it as a make-out session.

We'd awkwardly danced around it the next morning before he left for work. Yes, we needed to talk, but I couldn't bring myself to force this conversation. Not until after this visit, at least.

He scratched the dog's ears, head tilted up to look at me. "This is Wayne. He looks like a killer horse, but he's harmless."

The dog sat and thumped its stumpy tail on the dirt, waiting eagerly for attention, so I bent down and gave him a scratch.

"I'll grab Vincent." Jasper practically bounced around me to the back door of my car. "I'm so happy you're here. Can I give you a tour?"

"Sure." I leaned into the car and grabbed the wine Etienne had explicitly instructed me to bring, along with a loaf of lemon blueberry sourdough Basil had baked.

With Vincent's bucket seat in the crook of his elbow, Jasper strode across the grass, talking about trees and chickens, as excited as a little boy on Christmas morning.

"Look," he said to our son, pointing. "There's an eagle's nest in that tree. The mating pair have been there since I was a kid. My mom named them Lucy and Desi. And here are the chickens," he said, eyes bright.

The property was enormous, with several outbuildings in the distance. He pointed out tractors, equipment, a barn filled with sap barrels, and trees connected by a complex web of tubes and steel tanks.

There were fruit trees and a vegetable garden. Even a massive tire swing. Every detail was idyllic and calming.

As we wandered back to the house, admiring the views and the breeze, he grasped my wrist, stopping me, his face earnest.

"You know how I told you this was just a casual family dinner?"

I nodded. He'd said his sister Jenn and her wife organized family dinners on Sundays.

"So when everyone heard you were coming..." He trailed off, his attention darting to the side. "They wanted to come too."

A hint of nervousness stirred in my chest, but I gave him a smile. "Okay."

"So we've got kind of a full house in there." He winced. "I'm sorry. I don't want to overwhelm you. My family is just." Head bent, he cuffed the back of his neck. "Kind of intense. Especially about babies and kids."

His embarrassment was adorable.

"We're fine," I said, determined to believe that myself.

I wanted to be social and bubbly and fun. I wanted Jasper's family to embrace Vincent. But these things didn't come naturally to me. Maybe it was the resting bitch face or maybe it was because I was a New Yorker. Either way, I rarely hit it off with people during our first encounter. Ruby called me a "slow burn."

"Vincent is social," I said. "He loves his walks through town and smiles at everyone." Maplewood had expanded my horizons. I had to remember that. I hung out in groups pretty often, in fact. This would be no different.

He reached down and squeezed my hand. "Thank you. Let's get in there."

He brought us in through the mudroom and led us into the main part of the house, smiling widely.

The home was gorgeous and not at all what I'd expected. It was newly renovated, with pristine wide plank oak floors. All the accents were neutral and soft, giving the place a calming vibe.

"I've got a Pack 'n' Play upstairs for Vincent," Jasper said over his shoulder as he led me deeper into the house.

A Pack 'n' Play? I hadn't even considered needing one. Dammit. That single thought brought with it a wave of panic.

What must these people think of me?

At best I was an irresponsible dumbass who hadn't realized she was pregnant. At worst, I was a conniving, calculating bitch who'd trapped their brother. Neither impression was flattering. Chest tightening, I considered how long I had to stay before I could use Vincent as an excuse to run away.

The kitchen was bustling, the sounds of cooking and chatter floating toward us as we made our way over.

Jenn Lawrence was here. I recognized her since I'd frequented her coffee shop for the last two years. Although most of our interactions had been limited to professional greetings from her and ordering and paying from me, she embraced me warmly.

Josh, who was chopping carrots, nodded. I didn't see him often. He was a bear of a man, with dark hair and a full beard, though the resemblance to his brother was obvious. He was a thicker, more serious version of Jasper.

A petite blond woman had already approached and was

kneeling in front of Vincent's car seat, cooing. "Oh my God, he's gorgeous. Girls, get in here and meet your cousin."

She tipped her head back, smiling radiantly, and made eye contact. "I'm Jess. Older sister."

"And I'm Brian," a man with auburn hair said. He had a short beard, and the sleeves of his dress shirt had been rolled to the elbows.

"My aunt and uncle are out back, manning the grill," Jasper said. "C'mon. I'll take you to meet them."

He set the car seat on the floor, and Jess quickly scooped Vincent up, exclaiming how handsome he was.

With a hand on my back, Jasper led me toward the doors that opened onto an expansive back deck. Before we escaped, I turned back, worrying my lip, and checked on Vincent.

"He's fine," Jasper urged.

He was right. My little guy was already grinning widely at his aunt.

So I let Jasper lead me through what looked like a magazine spread.

"Two men live here? That's it?" I asked, marveling at the window treatments, throw pillows, and framed black and white photos on the walls.

"It's all Josh," he whispered. "He's got impeccable taste. And likes to stay busy, so he's always working on a project. Running two farms and day trading apparently doesn't keep him busy enough."

We skirted around the large sofa, our shoes tapping against the wood floors.

"Pretty sure he's trying to create some kind of middle-aged dad life for himself, except without a wife and kids." He shrugged. "I let him do his thing."

The back deck was set up with a rustic set of furniture, and the view of the forest was awe-inspiring. An older man stood in front of the grill with tongs while a woman walked around with a pitcher of lemonade, filling the glasses of kids who were busy playing cornhole in the grass.

"This is Aunt Suzie and Uncle Ed," Jasper said proudly, "And I think you know my cousin Gabe."

I eyed the younger man in the group, recognition taking over. "The mayor?"

Gabe jumped out of his chair and offered his hand, his sparkling white smile on display. Gabe Harding was well-liked in Maplewood, and he was handsome. But that was about all I knew about him.

"Great to see you," he said. "My mom and dad are so excited to meet you and baby Vincent."

The older woman, Suzie, wrapped me in a hug. "You are gorgeous. Jasper, you were right." As she pulled back, she winked at him.

Cheeks going pink, he quickly turned toward his uncle, focusing on the grill.

"Hope you don't mind," Suzie said, tucking her arm in mine, the gesture maternal and comforting and also strange, at least to me. "We invited ourselves along. Since my brother and sister-in-law aren't here anymore..." She looked briefly at the sky. "We do our best to take care of these kids. we've got four of our own, but no grandkids yet." Her eyes lit up and she patted my arm. "Ooh, the kids. Let me introduce you."

She led me down toward the grass. Two lanky teen boys

were playing with two slightly smaller girls, the four of them arguing over the rules of the game.

"This is Elijah and Isaac. They're Jenn and Mel's," she said. The older, taller one I recognized as my surly morning coffee delivery guy. He gave me a cool nod and his younger brother shook my hand like he was running for office.

"And this is Kit."

The older girl with a serious face and glasses gave me a tight smile. "We're excited to see Vincent. We've got extensive baby experience. Don't worry, we know what to do," she assured me.

"And I'm Greta," the smaller one said with a big wave.

Warmth bloomed inside me in response to this family dynamic, and I let my shoulders drop. This wouldn't be too bad. I could do this.

"They belong to Jess," Suzie explained.

"We're from New York," Greta said proudly. "But our summer house is right over there." She pointed at what looked like a small barn in the distance. "I have my own goats now."

Breathing in the fresh air, I took in the scene in front of me. Extended family, kids playing in the grass, the comfortable house. It was nice.

And it tracked. Of course Jasper had grown up surrounded by people who were genuinely kind.

My family members would run screaming from this place. And a slight discomfort rolled through me with each hug. But it was nice. It was normal. Unlike my own childhood.

We ate dinner on the deck, and while the kids regaled us with stories from summer camp, jobs, and sports teams, the adults fussed over Vincent. He loved the attention, giving gummy smiles to anyone and everyone.

"Your home is gorgeous," I said to Josh. "I can't believe you did this work yourself."

"I had help," he said, his tone low. "And it keeps me busy."

"The kitchen is incredible." I sighed, peering through the doors into the house. "I'm not much of a cook, but even I'm jealous."

Jenn nodded. "That giant farmhouse sink is epic."

"The copper pots were my idea," Mel chimed in.

Josh hovered over his plate, shoulders rounded like he was uncomfortable with the attention. "Trust me. The kitchen needed a lot of work. I had to take out walls just to get the burnt maple syrup smell out."

The table erupted in laughter, but I was confused.

"When Jas was ten, he tried to make breakfast in bed for Mom on Mother's Day," Josh explained, his lips twitching. "Jenn and Jess were off at college, and I was out working with my dad."

His sisters giggled.

"Jasper made pancakes. Then he decided to heat up the syrup on the stove."

"I wanted to be classy," Jasper added, his tone a little defensive. "But it started to burn, so I took the pot off the stove—"

"And put it on top of the newspaper." Josh took over. "It caught fire and melted part of the Formica countertop. The drywall smelled like burnt maple syrup for years after that."

Everyone was laughing now, including me.

"Jasper's first fire," Jess said, ruffling his hair.

"I put it out," he said. "Even back then, I had good reflexes."

Jenn picked up her glass of water. "Mom was so mad."

"Not that mad," Josh argued. "She never got mad at Jas. He was her favorite."

A flash of sadness passed over Jasper's face. He made no secret of how much he missed his mom.

While I hadn't spoken to mine in a year.

Heart aching, I looked down at Vincent, who was now snoozing in my arms, and vowed I'd always be there for him. That he would be number one in my life forever.

"Have you told her about the time you stole the tractor? And took out a beehive?" Jenn asked.

"That's how we found out Jasper's not allergic to bee stings," Jess deadpanned.

"I was seven. Not my fault the clutch stuck."

We laughed for hours on the deck, eating pie and sharing stories. As the evening went on, my nerves eased, and I found myself having a genuinely good time. They all knew so much about one another. There were inside jokes and old stories and so much warmth. I was a stranger, an outsider, but every person here made Vincent and me feel included.

Jasper was so lucky to have these wonderful people in his life, and I couldn't help but hope that Vincent and I could stick around.

Chapter 22

EVIE

Singing along with Lake Paige's newest single, I bounced around the living room, cleaning up.

It was surprising, how good I felt. I'd been so anxious about meeting Jasper's family. I'd stressed for hours, preparing explanations for the unknown pregnancy, my decision to breastfeed, and any other slightly controversial parenting topic I could think of.

As it turned out, I hadn't needed to prep a defense. No one asked me intrusive questions or judged my choices.

I'd let myself relax around strangers and even had a good time.

It was eye-opening, really. To step into Jasper's childhood home, to listen to stories about his parents and watch as his siblings ribbed him playfully.

It hit me in the middle of dinner, just how grateful I was that he was Vincent's dad. That his loud, messy family also belonged to Vincent.

Because my family? My stomach soured even thinking

about them. Neither my narcissist mother, who'd been through three husbands so far, or my alcoholic father had much love for me, and the feeling was mutual. The last thing I wanted was Vincent exposed to that type of emotional pain. I'd come to Vermont for a fresh start. Maplewood was my safe little bubble. And I'd work my ass off to give my son a safe, nurturing childhood.

I peered out the back window at Jasper's tent. He was in there, as always. The man hadn't once complained.

God, I was a terrible person.

Why had I been so uptight about having him here? More and more, it felt like he belonged in my home, here with Vincent and me. But I couldn't very well invite him in and give him a room now. Where would he even sleep? The house was a two-bedroom, and Vincent had been sleeping in his crib in his own room for a couple of months already.

The stars twinkled above, reminding me that it was a nice night.

Maybe I should go out and talk to him. Thank him again for today.

I ran my fingers over my lips, reliving our kiss.

It had been a mistake. Yet I couldn't stop thinking about it.

The pull toward him was undeniable. While I was exceptionally good at resisting these types of urges, tonight was different. After the day we'd had, I couldn't stop myself from slipping my feet into my shoes and heading for the back door, monitor and phone in hand.

Just as I was unlocking the dead bolt, my phone buzzed.

With a step back, I dug it out, and when Ruby's name flashed on the screen, I answered quickly.

"*Fuck*," she screamed on the other end.

My pulse quickened and my mind spun. Was she hurt?

"It's happening," she grunted into the phone. "Motherfucker, this hurts."

"You're in labor?" Panic took over, causing me to ask dumb, obvious questions.

"Yes."

There was shuffling, then Paul said, "We're on our way to the hospital."

"I'll be there." Without a second of hesitation, I jogged to my room to take off my PJs. "And I've got the playlist and the essential oils."

"Thank you," he said while Ruby moaned in the background.

I tugged on a pair of sweats, tossed my laptop into a tote bag, then collected the clean pieces of my breast pump from the kitchen.

When I approached the tent, the flap was open, and Jasper was splayed out on top of his sleeping bag, shirtless, reading a book.

My stomach clenched at the sight. Shit, that was hot. And why wasn't he ever wearing a shirt? It wasn't that warm out.

"Ruby," I huffed, tossing him the baby monitor. "It's time."

He hopped up in one smooth movement, his expression calm. "Okay, I got Vincent. Is there milk in the freezer?"

I nodded. "And I packed my pump. When do you have to be at work?"

"Tomorrow night."

He stepped in close and kissed my cheek, his lips warm in the cool night air. "Proud of you."

As I drove to the hospital, I replayed that moment over and over, then found myself examining the ease with which we communicated and the affection he so openly gave me.

It wasn't passionate. It was a friendly, fond kiss. Nothing like what had happened a few nights ago.

We were friends.

Nothing more. The kiss had just happened. Exactly like he said it would.

That bastard had worn me down and earned my trust.

So why did I hate how it felt?

"About fucking time," Ruby roared when I walked into the hospital room. "Five more minutes, and I was going to name this kid after you out of spite. Paul's been playing that hippie shit."

Paul gave me a sheepish look, his body sagging with exhaustion.

"I'm only four centimeters," she raged, standing in the middle of the room, dressed in a hospital gown. "Four fucking centimeters. That's like a thumbnail. How the hell am I getting this watermelon out?"

With a deep breath in, I slapped on a calm mask and stepped up beside her, squeezing her hand. "Ruby Stone, look at me."

She obeyed, her hair sticking to her face.

"You are a warrior woman," I reminded her. "This is

primitive shit. Your ancestors used to squat in fields and give birth. You will do this and it will be fucking magical."

"It hurts so fucking bad," she growled. "Why did the book say intense period cramps? This is more like I'm being ripped apart from the inside by a rabid raccoon with a grudge."

"Just breathe, babe," Paul said from across the room.

With faster movements than should be possible, Ruby picked up the large rubber birthing ball at her side and chucked it at him. "You tell me to just breathe again and I'll make sure you never draw another breath."

Paul, to his credit, took it like a champ, only smiling lovingly at his wife. "You're doing so great."

When she looked back at me, her anger had been replaced with fear. The look brought me back to Vincent's birth, when our roles were reversed.

"Let's get the playlist going and get fucking focused," I said. "This is the hard part, but you're a bad bitch. You do not quit."

Once I'd connected to her Bluetooth speaker, I cued up the Swedish death metal she had requested.

As a nurse scurried in, wearing a confused frown, Ruby yelled, "Track three. The one with the screaming. It helps me focus."

The nurse adjusted the fetal monitor and smiled at Ruby. "Are you sure you wouldn't like something calmer?"

I flinched. This woman did not understand what kind of bear she was poking. "I'm sorry. Is there a Spotify playlist titled Screaming Into the Void While Pushing a Human Being Out Of Your Vag?" Ruby asked in a demonic voice. "Yeah, I didn't think so. I'm good."

Bristling, the nurse gave her a tense smile and headed for the door. "I'll get more ice chips."

As she stepped out, Frankie arrived, wearing a tank top and her coveralls tied at the waist. She had oil smeared on her cheek, and her wild hair was pulled back into a knot on top of her head.

"I'm here," she said. "Great song."

"Paul doesn't like it," Ruby grumbled. "I know you wanted whale songs, honey," she said to him, her tone softening just a little. "But I want Wolves of the Apocalypse—"

She doubled over, moaning.

With a hand on her back, I spoke calming words to her.

"I've got this." Frankie approached Paul, who physically stiffened in her presence. I couldn't blame him. Who wouldn't be afraid of my badass friend?

"Paul," she said, puffing up. "She's birthing your child, and you have an awkwardly large head. There is no fucking compromise."

When all he did was nod, wide-eyed, Frankie smiled and turned back to us, rubbing her hands together.

"You bitches ready? Let's have another baby."

The nurse returned with a cup of ice chips, noting that they had several deliveries and informing us that the doctor would be in shortly.

Soon, we discovered that it helped if we scratched her back while she screamed to the music through each contraction and threw anything she could get her hands on at Paul.

Paul, to his credit, was proving to be extremely good-natured and supportive.

"Don't come back without an epidural," Frankie shouted

at the nurse, her voice barely audible over the death metal and Ruby's screeching.

"The anesthesiologist is on her way," she said. Again. She'd told us that the last time she came in. And the time before that.

And Ruby was running out of steam.

The smell of antiseptic and the beeping of the fetal monitor brought with it flashes of my own labor. The fear that had overtaken me that day prickled inside me again. The hiss of the oxygen line reminded me of the numbness and terror I'd felt.

I'd had Ruby's and Frankie's hands to squeeze, but I'd still felt so alone. Initially, I'd assumed it was my punishment for not knowing I was pregnant. For not seeing the signs. For being so detached from my body that I had no idea I'd been creating a human life for the better part of a year.

But as Paul sat on the bed, his forehead pressed to Ruby's, whispering words of love, there was no room in my heart for envy. Instead, a strange peace enshrouded me.

I'd survived. Not just labor and delivery, but the shock and the fear. And Vincent was thriving. I'd figured it out with no preparation or planning.

Maybe I'd already done the hard part. Maybe I could let this go and focus on what came next.

Maybe it was time I stopped punishing myself for my sins.

"PAUL," RUBY CRIED AS SHE CRADLED THE TINY BABY IN her arms. As I looked on, I thought about Vincent. The feeling when he was placed in my arms for the first time. So tiny and small, so fragile.

Frankie and I stepped out, giving Ruby and Paul privacy as they cried happy tears and admired their healthy baby.

I'd really only known Paul as Ruby's straitlaced accountant husband, but today, I'd seen a different side of him. He was so tender, so demonstrative and affectionate. I could see how Ruby had fallen in love with him.

And that made me think about Jasper. His quiet presence. The way he kept showing up, day after day, even when I snapped at him or pushed him away.

He was devoted to Vincent.

"He's also devoted to you." Frankie handed me a Diet Coke from the vending machine.

"He's a great dad."

"It goes further than that. Think about it." She held up a finger. "He's entitled to time with Vincent on his own, but has he ever pushed for it? Or does he show up to support you, to help you, and to make you feel comfortable?"

Heart clenching, I opened my mouth to respond, but no words came out.

"Vincent is a baby," she went on. "He doesn't care where he's sleeping and shitting. It could be at the farm or it could be at your house. But Jasper's sleeping in your backyard."

I dipped my chin. "Yes. He wants to be close by. What are you trying to say?"

"He brings coffee, fixes things around the house."

"His nephew usually delivers the coffee," I countered.

Frankie clasped her hands and looked up at the ceiling. "Dear God." After a huff, she leveled me with a look. "Think, Evie. Who is he really supporting here?"

The truth I'd been denying came barreling over me. She was right. Jasper did way more than necessary. He went above and beyond. For me. But...

"Since when are you the voice of emotional clarity?"

"I'm feeling sentimental, okay?" she groused. "Don't hold it against me. I operate under the general assumption that all men are shit and disappointments. But once in a while, I'm pleasantly surprised. Take Paul, for instance. He stepped up. Even when she was throwing things at him."

A laugh bubbled out of me. She wasn't wrong. Ruby had been throwing ice chips at Paul's face while he coached her, and he was completely undeterred by the random acts of violence.

"Your baby daddy is one of the good ones," Frankie muttered. "And trust me, it's very difficult to say those words."

He really was. But if Frankie of all people could see it? Damn.

"Also," she said. "He's extremely easy on the eyes."

I slumped back in my chair. "Oh, I'm aware. Did you know he hangs out in his tent and reads books while shirtless?"

She made the sign of the cross. "The man reads? Hot damn. Ooh." She snapped up straight, the move so abrupt that Diet Coke sloshed out of her can and onto her jeans. "I have an idea. We could start an Instagram account where all we post is pictures of hot men reading. You know, like the ones that are full of images of hot men holding puppies. Boom. Millionaires."

Giggling, we clinked our Diet Coke cans together.

Throughout the morning and into the afternoon, several

people showed up to visit. Bitsy and Marigold with a massive basket of baked goods and a baby blanket, Nora with home-made nipple cream, and Basil and Etienne with a wardrobe of designer baby clothes and an assortment of cheeses. If I knew Maplewood, the town would turn this waiting room into a massive potluck celebration.

On the way home, a surge of energy ran through me. For months, I'd begrudgingly accepted Jasper as a coparent. Tolerated his presence and worked damn hard to maintain distance. But he was so much more than just a coparent.

When Ruby had gripped Paul's hand like it was the only thing keeping her tethered to the earth during those last minutes, something in my chest twisted.

I wanted that. Partnership, understanding, the complete certainty that I wasn't alone in the difficult moments.

A partner who showed up, not because he had to, but because he wanted to. Frankie was right. Jasper wasn't just helping with Vincent; he'd been quietly supporting me too.

He showed up, over and over again. He held me when I broke down. He built me up and hyped me up when life was daunting.

I'd spent my life believing that I'd never find my person, and I'd resigned myself to being alone. Yet for weeks, my person had been sleeping in my backyard.

Chapter 23

JASPER

When Evie walked through the door, I was struck stupid. Her hair was in a messy ponytail and the skin beneath her eyes was bruised with exhaustion. She was wearing old sweats and a worn-out tee, yet she looked alive and joyful. And damn, was she beautiful.

"Jasper," she said, her voice breathy, as she strode straight over to me. "I—"

I set the onesie I'd just folded on the counter in front of me and studied her, at a loss for what to do or say, and the air between us sparked and crackled.

She stared back, her eyes searching my face for several heartbeats. And then she launched herself at me.

As her lips landed on mine, shock and delight erupted inside me. She kissed me fiercely, and I responded just as intensely, gripping her hips, my body humming with satisfaction.

With a gasp, she pulled back, though she left her arms draped over my shoulders. "Sorry. I just needed to do that."

I blinked, wondering if I'd dozed off on the couch and this was just a dream. "Don't apologize."

Dark eyes flashing, she pressed herself against me and captured my mouth.

I staggered back until I hit the kitchen counter. This dominance was such a fucking turn-on. Though I couldn't help but push back a bit, grabbing her ass so hard she let out a squeak. Goddamn, she was soft and warm, and she smelled incredible.

A gurgling noise snapped us out of the moment, and Evie pulled back.

"Vincent." She zeroed in on our little guy, who was happily batting at the hanging toys on his playmat. "Oh my God."

She rushed over and swept him up, peppering his face with kisses.

"Mommy missed you, baby. I got to meet your new best friend today. You two are going to get into so much trouble together."

Kiss-drunk and confused, I stayed where I was, using the counter to steady myself. While I was still reeling, I couldn't deny how damn lucky I felt.

Evie took Vincent to his room, murmuring about needing to feed him, and when they were out of sight, I staggered to the couch and buried my head in my hands. What was that? And how was I supposed to keep doing this back-and-forth bullshit? This dance of desire?

Because to her, that may have been just an impulsive kiss, but to me it was so much more. I was already struggling to keep my emotional and physical distance with so much time together. The intimacy of caring for a baby with her only added a layer to my respect and affection for her.

Some nights I tossed and turned, my head filled with fantasies of coming home to her after a long shift. Stripping her down and fucking her all night long. Losing myself in her softness until she cried out my name.

I'd tried to bury these feelings. I'd even considered calling one of my casual hookups in hopes that a quick fuck would get this out of my system.

But my dick and my heart only wanted Evie. Those curves, those dark eyes, her stubbornness and determination and all that sass.

I was lost in my self-torture when she padded back into the room.

"Jasper," she said. "I can explain."

I jackknifed to my feet, digging deep for the courage to stand up for myself.

"I can't do this," I rasped, despite how much the words hurt to say. "I don't want to be toyed with. My feelings are real. So is my attraction. I can respect that you're not in the same place, but—"

"Jas." She grasped my hand and pulled me onto the couch so we were sitting side by side, her eyes locked on mine. "We are in the same place. Or a similar place, at least. I'm so screwed up that I don't know how to talk about the stuff that makes me feel vulnerable, so who the hell knows. But I kissed you today because when I walked in and saw you, I just... couldn't *not* kiss you. The pull toward you, it's too strong. You are so much more than I ever expected. I can't stop myself from wanting you."

There comes a time in a man's life when he has to make a hard choice. And this was mine. A stronger man. A more emotionally mature man, would sit here with her and talk all this out. Make my feelings clear.

But I was not that man.

I stood, her hand still in mine. "Is Vincent napping?"

"Yes. He should be out for at least an hour."

"Great." I pulled her to her feet, bent over, and slung her over my shoulder. Then I quietly jogged toward her bedroom.

Every hint of hesitation dissolved the moment I placed her on the bed and she pulled me on top of her, her hands pressed to my cheeks, her mouth on mine again. I could live here, on this new plane of existence, with Evie writhing beneath me while I ravaged her mouth.

In seconds, her hands had found their way to the button of my jeans.

Before she could undo it, I grasped her wrists. "Not yet," I growled, gently kissing her jawline.

She rolled her hips against me. "But we don't have much time."

"No," I said, surprised by my dominant tone. "I've waited so long. I've been so patient." I pinned her hands on either side of her head. "Be a good girl and let me enjoy it."

She nodded mutely, her muscles relaxing. So I released my hold on her and sat back, dragging her shirt over her head. For a moment, I stayed there, enjoying the view. Those breasts, barely constrained by the nursing bra, were enough to make me come in my pants on sight.

Fingers hooked in the waistband of her pants, I eyed her. "Is this okay?"

She nodded quickly, arching against me. "Please."

In one quick move, I tore her sweatpants down. Then I kissed every inch of her, from her ears to her knees. Though I avoided the places she wanted me most, driving her need higher and enjoying the sighs and gasps she let out as I discovered new spots.

"Spread," I commanded.

Without hesitation, she did, the wet spot on her cotton panties calling to me like a siren song. I breathed her in, eyes closed, her scent making me impossibly hard.

"Please," she whimpered as I nipped at the sensitive flesh of her inner thigh.

I shook my head. I was a man starved, and with this feast spread out before me, I'd savor every bite.

But before I could calculate my next move, she took control and flipped me onto my back. Straddling me, she brought her chest to mine, fire flashing in her eyes.

My vision blurred. This goddess might just end me tonight.

"Get naked. Now." She pushed up and slid back, then got to work with the button of my pants. "And if you listen, I'll take my bra off."

She did not have to tell me twice. Heaving myself up, I grasped her hips and slid her to the mattress beside me. While I scrambled to get my shirt, jeans, and boxers off, she watched me, toying with the straps of her bra.

Finally naked, I dove back onto the bed, getting situated a moment before she tossed her bra across the room. She straddled me, trapping my hard cock between us, leaving it leaking and screaming for attention.

I ignored the sensation. I had work to do first.

There were not enough nerve endings in my hands to fully register the exquisite softness of her breasts. They were bigger than I remembered, her nipples a shade darker too. I reveled in the weight of them. Kissing and squeezing and licking with abandon.

I could lose myself here. Time had no meaning. Evie was all that existed.

I was lost in my ministrations when she reached between us and gripped my length. As she lifted up on her knees and lined the tip up with her entrance, then lowered herself onto me, black spots danced in my vision.

"*Yes*," I hissed, head pressed back into the pillow. "Take it. Take anything you want, mama."

She moaned and huffed out a breath, slowly working me deeper. "So full," she gritted out.

The visual alone was enough to make me come, but I staved off the need to fuck into her and let her take what she wanted.

"That's it," I coached. "You're doing so well. So gorgeous and so needy. That's it. Go slow."

She rolled her hips, sinking lower, her eyes on mine, her expression mirroring how I felt. We were both in shock. This was really happening.

"I need to move." She whimpered, working her hips again.

With both hands, I clutched her ass hard, spreading her wide to help, and she bottomed out. Fuck. I thought I'd been turned on in the past, but I'd never been as enthralled as I was while Evie hovered over me, riding my cock, gasping and moaning, those glorious tits bouncing, begging to be grabbed and bitten.

My spine tingled, my impending orgasm threatening to end this too soon. "Fuck." Eyes squeezed shut, I inhaled deeply, gathering my wits. I had to focus. This needed to last.

But I was still barreling toward finishing too quickly. I'd endured months of foreplay, spending time with her, smelling her, touching her. My body was not going to listen to reason.

"I need you to come," I growled. "I won't last much longer."

With a wicked smile, she cupped her breasts, teasing and caressing.

"That's not helping," I gritted out.

Moaning, she threw her head back. As she continued massaging her breasts, a drop of milk leaked from one nipple, then another.

I lunged up and licked her clean with a groan.

In response, her walls clenched around me. "Oh my God," she said. "That was embarrassing. But also hot."

It was hot. Hotter than I could handle. Lying back again, I found her clit and applied pressure with my thumb, and when her channel tightened further, I silently rejoiced. "How's that, mama?"

She rewarded me with a long sigh.

"Good girl. Keep going," I directed. "Ride me. I want to watch you come like this."

Teeth gritted, staving off my release, I focused on the rhythm. I let her set the pace and rubbed gentle circles on her clit. Her breathing picked up, her breasts heaving, and more milk leaked from her nipples.

I couldn't help myself. I needed more. So I lapped at one, then the other.

"*Ah.* Jasper," she shouted, clenching around me. My girl enjoyed nipple play. The realization felt like winning the lottery.

"That's it," I encouraged. "Show me. Show me how beautiful you are when you come."

On command, she shook and shuddered, squeezing the life out of me, making my control crumble.

"Yes," she cried, grinding against my pubic bone. Every part of her trembled as she gave in and let go.

As she spasmed around me, I lost my battle and followed her into the abyss. My cock strained and twitched inside her, making me nearly black out from pleasure.

She collapsed on top of me, panting and sweating.

I wrapped my arms around her until our pulses slowed and our hearts pounded in time.

"That was..." She trailed off dreamily.

I rolled so she was pinned beneath me. "Fucking spectacular." I eased out of her, taking a moment to relish the sight of her gorgeous pussy, pink and stretched and full of me.

As I headed to the bathroom to get her a washcloth, I couldn't help but smile.

Tonight had been my every dream come true.

Chapter 24

EVIE

We lay tangled up in my bed, burrowed under a pile of blankets, scrolling through the photos of Ruby, Paul, and Brooks in my camera roll.

"He's beautiful," I whispered. "Eight pounds. He looks so tiny. I barely remember Vincent being so small."

He chuckled. "He's a meatball now. I swear he's bigger every day."

"The kid never stops eating."

Still naked, still recovering from what we'd just experienced, I couldn't muster the energy to freak out or get anxious. Jasper made me feel safe, so my usual defense mechanisms had gone into hiding.

"Not that I'm complaining," he murmured into my neck. "But what happened at the hospital? You came back... different."

Sighing, I surveyed the ceiling, taking a moment to collect my thoughts. I was not at my most articulate after our romp.

"I had this moment," I hedged, struggling to put into words the sensation, "where I realized just how much time I'd spent feeling guilty and punishing myself. Thinking I was a terrible mom and an irresponsible parent."

"Evie—"

I held up a hand. "Wait. And after today, after being there with Ruby like she was with me, it hit me that childbirth *is* unpredictable and wild. All the preparation and planning in the world would not have allowed me to control any of it. And Vincent is here now. And I'm doing it. Being a mom."

He kissed my shoulder tenderly. "You're not just doing it. You're crushing it."

My chest pinched. "Thank you. And you could have made coparenting difficult. You could have made it painful. But you've been patient and kind and you keep showing up."

"It's nothing."

"No it's not nothing. Quite the opposite." I sat up, heat building behind my eyes. "I treated you terribly. But suddenly, it's like the postpartum hormonal haze has lifted and I can see so clearly how terrible I've been. I can think again."

He searched my face, his own expression full of questions.

"It was so shocking," I said. "And the pressure of taking care of a newborn was intense. I was angry at you. Not for any specific reason, but because you were a man."

Head cocked, he frowned. "Sorry?"

"I've been let down many times. And while I've survived time and again, my protective instincts kicked in and I built walls. I assumed you'd let Vincent down. But now that I know you, understand the man you are, I realize that will never happen."

For the space of a couple of heartbeats, he was silent, like he was letting my words sink in.

When he spoke, his voice was full of emotion. "I'm sorry you've been hurt and let down so many times in your life," he said. "If you ever want to talk about it, I'm always willing to listen."

My heart swelled. This man always knew exactly the right thing to say.

"And I'm *here*. In any capacity you want me."

The words were an opening, a soft launch of a complex conversation I wasn't remotely ready for. So I pivoted to more apologies.

"I was so shitty to you for so long. And you're not just one of the good ones." I licked my lips and dug deep for the courage to say this next part. "I think you might be the best one."

The way the slow smile lit up his face made my stomach flip. He was beautiful.

With a grunt, he wrapped me in a bear hug. He covered my neck and shoulders with kisses, his stubble tickling my sensitive flesh and pulling ridiculous giggles from me.

It was strange, how light I felt. Usually after sex, I was hit with a heavy dose of anxiety and embarrassment. Followed by the desire to cover up and get out. Never had I craved giggles and cuddles and kisses.

Yet here I was. Was this what I'd been missing all along?

My cheeks hurt from smiling, and Jasper's laugh was caught in his throat, a low, husky sound I'd never tire of.

As the afternoon light filtered through the curtains in

lazy stipes, I closed my eyes and enjoyed the strong warmth of his body and the feel of his lips against my skin.

For a brief moment, life was simple. Nothing but skin and warmth and affection. No ghosts. No guilt. Just Jasper.

The moment was spoiled, though, when my brain caught up.

We hadn't used protection. We'd fallen into bed without talking. We had Vincent to worry about.

What if I'd made a terrible mistake?

"You look stressed all of a sudden," Jasper said, nuzzling my neck. "Start talking."

He pulled back, the corners of his mouth softening into understanding, or worse, maybe. Because the look was almost one of hope.

I couldn't promise him anything. Not when I was still piecing myself back together and learning how to be a mother. Not when a whole little person depended on me to make good choices. Responsible choices.

"We didn't use protection," I said.

"I thought you couldn't get pregnant while breastfeeding." He kissed one breast, then the other, unconcerned.

"I'm not sure that's 100 percent reliable," I replied, heat already curling in my belly again. "Fuck, what if I get pregnant again?"

Jasper lifted his head, a massive grin on his face. "That would be awesome."

My stomach plummeted.

"Sorry." He winced. "But if that's not what you want..." His expression turned sheepish.

"I just had a surprise baby," I said, pushing off his chest, putting a little distance between us.

"Do you want more kids?" he asked as he flopped onto his back.

This was a way bigger conversation than I was ready to have. "No idea. I never thought I'd be able to have a baby. Doctors told me I'd be infertile. And Vincent is such a miracle. It feels greedy to want more. What about you?"

He shrugged. "Vincent is amazing. For now, I'm thrilled just to wake up every day and be his dad. And I want to do it right," he said, his tone taking on a more serious quality. "Do a good job. If more kids arrive in the future, I'll be thrilled, but I'm content for now."

Dammit. Why did this man have to be so perfect? And why did he have to look so sweet and earnest all the time?

I sat up and pulled the sheet up over my chest. This pillow talk was getting too intimate too fast. Every alarm in my brain was screaming at me to flee the scene of this sexy crime.

"We should probably not..." I swallowed past the lump in my throat. "Um, make this a thing."

He frowned at me. "A thing?"

The confusion in his voice broke me. The furrow of his brow and how his hand stilled against the mattress like he wasn't sure if he should touch me again made my heart ache.

"I just mean." My throat tightened. "We got caught up. It was good."

"You're mispronouncing amazing," he said, forcing a cocky grin that fell a little flat.

"Amazing," I corrected. "But it's all complicated."

He was quiet for a moment, studying me. "You're allowed to want something good, Evie," he eventually said, his tone careful. "You know that, right? You're allowed to want support, love, and orgasms. You deserve it all."

That nearly undid me. I nodded, unable to look at him. "I know." That was a lie. I didn't really think I could have those things, but it seemed best to agree. "But I can't afford to get this wrong."

He exhaled slowly, his eyes shuttering, like he was retreating. Not out of anger, but out of respect.

That only made it worse.

"It's not that I don't want to," I hedged.

He tipped my chin up and brought his face close to mine. "We can take it slow. I'd never rush you. But I'm not going anywhere." The words were resolute. "And I won't force you. If you want me, you know where to find me."

With that, he stood and gathered his clothes. As I watched him dress, my chest ached with the emptiness left behind.

"I need to get ready for my shift anyway."

The moment he stepped into the hall, the tears began to fall.

Because for a few moments, I'd believed I could have it all: safety, love, laughter, and warmth. But that was a lie. Life had taught me differently. Except now all I could think about was how good it had felt to stop fighting the need to push this man away.

Chapter 25

EVIE

I loved my office. It was just as girly and cute as my house, except for the fluorescent lights and drop tile ceiling. Since coming back, I'd added a few framed photos of Vincent. I was proud of myself for my restraint, because my camera roll had thousands at this point.

With a sigh, I dropped my pump bag. While I was grateful to my employer for how accommodating they had been, they'd missed the mark when it came to the space they had reserved for me to pump in. It was an old storage closet with no windows, a pull chain light, and a thick metal door that stuck terribly. I'd ordered a small refrigerator for my office to store the milk. It wasn't perfect, but it worked for now.

But I supposed this was one more part of working motherhood. Making compromises, juggling all the things.

Despite the challenges, I was damn happy to be back.

Sugar Moon Syrup was one of the largest manufacturers and distributors of maple syrup in the US. And we didn't create vats full of brown corn syrup. Ours was the good stuff. Organic, no fillers, straight from the trees of Vermont.

We sold our Sugar Moon syrup at a few local spots, but our bread and butter was Costmart. The biggest wholesale store in the US.

We supplied their in-house high-end maple syrup brand, packaged it, labeled it, and then shipped it all over the world.

I knew very little about how the syrup was actually made. We had an entire factory staff and machinists, scientists, and engineers for that. While the production was fascinating and the bottling machines alone were worth millions of dollars, that was not my domain.

I ran the marketing department. My rag tag team included three other employees. My job sat at the intersection of science, sales, and storytelling. We took the work of chemists, production managers, and farmers and translated it into a clean, wholesome brand that raked in millions of dollars every year. And we did it well. Our tasks included keeping Costmart happy, analyzing all the data, and allocating a budget to ensure we were positioning our brand and product well in the market. All while maintaining the company values. Farm to table transparency, organic production, and Vermont authenticity.

It was a far cry from the marketing and PR I'd done for a hedge fund in New York. The financial industry was soul-crushing, and although my excel spreadsheets could make even the strongest Wall Street bro weep, this job was far more fun.

But I couldn't help but worry about the bottom line. One

of our employees had just been murdered, and we'd been questioned about supply quality. Then, on top of that, I'd just taken an unexpected three-month maternity leave.

Gerry, who had been filling in for me, tipped his coffee mug at me. "How do you do this job? People are so demanding, and they expect us to have all the answers all the time."

"Of course they do. We're the smartest department," Marci chirped.

The twenty-four-year-old social media director spun in her ergonomic chair. "Boss, you are glowing. Did you buy the new glazing milk from Rhode?"

I nodded. For someone who was not only blessed with youth, but with plenty of collagen, Marci was deeply committed to skin care. Not that I was complaining. I bought everything she recommended, and she'd never steered me wrong.

Being in the office energized me. I'd had a shit morning. Vincent hadn't even cried when I'd dropped him off at daycare. If anything, he was happy to be there.

And that was like a dagger to the heart.

While I wanted my baby happy and healthy, I couldn't help but wish he'd miss me. God, I was such a mess.

"Louisa was looking for you," Gerry told me. "Wants to talk about brand audits at noon."

I let out a sigh. There went my easy morning. Louisa Meyers, the CEO of Sugar Moon, had been awarded the company in her divorce from her much older ex-husband who worked in private equity. He'd kept the penthouse and the Hamptons place, and she'd gotten the Vermont estate and one of the companies from his portfolio to keep her busy.

But Louisa, a former Miss USA turned socialite, had

surprised everyone when, rather than being a hands-off busi-ness owner, she dove into the company headfirst. She was savvy. An expert negotiator. And she was the kind of leader who wasn't afraid to go out into the woods and get her hands dirty.

The company had flourished under her leadership, growing year over year and beating out more established manufacturers for big contracts. But all of that determination meant she was intense. She was very results-oriented and very focused on the bottom line.

So I needed to have my shit together by noon. If I knew Louisa, she already had dozens of questions prepared and would not be impressed by my hurried attempts to catch up on the developments that had unfolded over the last few months.

With a fresh cup of coffee in hand, I headed into my office. Quarterly brand audits were the bane of my existence on a good day, but having been out of the loop meant I was playing catchup.

My laptop fan hummed as I scrolled through supplier verification reports for our Pure Maple Plus campaign. Ingredient specs weren't my favorite, since my background was *not* in science, so I took notes as I pored over them, trying to make out what was going on. We planned to roll out a new sustainability line this fall, complete with glossy photos of smiling farmers and copy about "climate resilience" and "eco-friendly growth solutions."

My focus caught on a new term buried halfway down the lab report. BGX-9. A sap growth accelerator? I frowned. We had strict contracts with our suppliers regarding agricul-tural products, and I didn't remember seeing it before.

I opened up last quarter's audit summaries and scanned them. They'd been in draft when I had Vincent, so I hadn't finalized them.

The top of the document read *internal review*. Huh. That was PR code for not cleared for general consumption. Weird.

As I perused our shared drive, I found a folder labeled *yield enhancement initiative*. I clicked on it, finding various subfolders inside. It was mostly R&D stuff. All things I didn't work on here. There were also several labels and statements from Evergreen. They produced fertilizers, pesticides, and other products to farmers, though we only used them for equipment.

When I double-clicked on the compliance folder, finding it empty, I leaned back and rubbed my temples. It was probably nothing. These R&D eggheads always filed things improperly. They loved to rename chemical compounds and conveniently forget to tell marketing about it.

Sighing, I snagged a stack of Post-its and scribbled *ask QA to confirm BGX-9 status before finalizing labels*. I couldn't fall down a chemistry rabbit hole right now. Not when I had a meeting in less than an hour that I was nowhere near prepared for and I needed to pump. So I'd let the compliance and oversight teams deal with the chemistry bullshit.

Grabbing my bag, water bottle, and phone, I headed toward my sad pumping closet. The setup was the worst part. The cleaning and sanitizing of all the components, hooking everything up, wrangling my heavy, aching boobs into the weird pump bra thing. But once I got it all going, it wasn't so bad.

Mostly I scrolled through photos of Vincent on my phone. Photos that more recently included Jasper.

EVIE:

How's it going?

He sent back a selfie of the two of them on the tummy time mat. Jasper was making a silly face and Vincent was giggling. He was rolling a little now. It was so cute but also terrifying. Jasper's hair was sticking up in every direction, and he was wearing one of his many MFD T-shirts. I thought about stealing one on a daily basis but always chickened out.

JASPER:

Having a good time. May go for a walk in a bit. It's nice out.

EVIE:

A whole lot nicer than this closet I'm pumping in, that's for sure.

JASPER:

Good job, mama. This kid just crushed six ounces.

I sighed. Vincent's appetite was endless. A part of me was desperate for him to start solids so I didn't have to spend so much time in pumping purgatory, but the other part of me, the emotional part, got choked up at the thought. Was this the paradox of parenthood?

My phone buzzed with an email from Louisa, and I checked the time. Shit, I had nine minutes to get out of here, clean and store the pump parts and milk, and get to my meeting. I packed up, then unlocked the door and pulled it hard.

It didn't budge.

Fucking door always stuck. I put my bag and water bottle down, digging in with my feet, and pulling hard with both hands. Only then did the damn thing open.

Evie: Headed to meeting. Give him a kiss for me.

Jasper: What about me? Do I get a kiss?

Evie: Undecided.

Chapter 26

JASPER

The smell of maple and cinnamon hung in the air as I wandered into the kitchen.

Over the last couple of months, I'd noticed that Evie would throw herself into a project when she was stressed or something was bothering her.

After my run, I had peeled my sweat-soaked T-shirt off outside, then come in to refill my water bottle.

I still wasn't exactly sure what was going on, but staying away was impossible.

Crossing my arms, I leaned against the counter, watching her scoop dough with surgical precision.

"Smell delicious," I said. "Is it just me, or do you bake when you're trying to avoid something?"

She pinned me with a delicious glare. "They're for Ruby. And is it just me, or do you seem to lurk when you want something but are too chickenshit to ask?"

Her sass had my athletic shorts tightening. God, this woman drove me wild in the best ways.

"Guess we both have bad habits." Shrugging, I pushed off the counter and took a step toward her.

She slid the cookie tray into the oven and turned around, crossing her arms over her chest. Fuck, the sight of her, tank top with no bra, hair down and wild, made me desperate to touch her.

"You're awfully smug for the guy whose big romantic moment was ruined by a coffee table."

Oh shit. "I'd forgotten about that." I ran my hand through my hair, searching for the courage to dive into this conversation. We'd been tiptoeing around this for months. That night last year.

The night that changed everything.

"I limped around like an old man for days. That shit left a bruise." I eyed my now heeled shin. "Was it placed there strategically, so I'd end up injured? Or was it just a poor interior design choice?"

Her mouth twitched. "You're the only man I've ever known who could bruise himself mid-kiss and act like it was the inanimate object's fault."

I held up my hands. "In my defense, I was ambushed by the hottest women I'd ever seen, so I was distracted."

Her eyes flared with heat, despite her schooled expression.

"And that damn table came out of nowhere."

My leg could have been severed, and it would not have kept me from kissing Evie. The morning after, it hurt like a bitch, but it was so worth it.

"You were drunk."

"Tipsy," I corrected. "You, on the other hand."

"Don't even start, Lawrence."

I arched a brow. "Oh, I'm starting. You dragged me onto the dance floor during that ridiculous Bon Jovi cover, said you needed to dance. And by dancing, you meant endangering the lives of everyone around us."

She clamped her mouth shut to keep from laughing. "That's right. You stepped on my feet several times."

"Don't remember you caring." I lifted my chin. "In fact, you were laughing and smiling like you were having the time of your life."

Her energy shifted then, the humor softening, like a breeze quieting. "I can't believe we're talking about that night."

"We should talk about it." I took another step closer and cupped her cheek. "We can't just forget about it."

"The night that rearranged my life? All the cells in my body and my entire universe?" She huffed. "No chance I'll ever forget that." Chin tucked, she wrung her hands, but she eventually looked back up at me. "It was so out of character for me," she said quietly. "That night. You. I don't do things like that. I don't... let go."

My heart stumbled over itself. "Maybe you didn't lose control. Maybe you chose me that night."

"No. It wasn't like that," she rushed out. "It was silly, drunken antics."

"Nope." I wouldn't let her dismiss what we shared. If we were talking about this, then we were *talking* about it. "You think it was random? That I'd never noticed you before that night?" I took a step back, heat prickling up my spine. "For months, you were this calm in the middle of the noise.

Always poised and serious and trying so damn hard not to be seen. Made me want to look even harder."

"You n-noticed me?" The raw vulnerability on her face made me wish I could go back in time and kick the asses of everyone who'd ever made her feel worthless.

"The first time I saw you was in line at Bean There, Sipped That," I said. "Two years ago, I think. You were wearing this black skirt suit and sky-high heels with red soles. You looked professional yet also sexy and badass."

A pink flush creeped into her cheeks.

"You should have looked out of place," I continued. "But you fit right in. Your confidence and your energy were so damn attractive. You seemed to know who you were."

"While waiting in line for caffeine?" she gasped.

Her confidence that day had drawn me in. And every day after. She marched into the equivalent of an L.L.Bean store in her red-heeled shoes and just kicked ass.

Eventually, I heard the typical town gossip about the newcomer. The new VP of marketing at Sugar Moon. The woman from New York who had all the bright ideas and was knocking everyone dead.

The woman who immediately befriended Frankie Dunne, a Maplewood citizen who hated everyone.

The woman who made this town a tiny bit brighter every day.

She'd bought a craftsman on Spruce Lane and on the occasions that I'd driven by, she always seemed to be out planting flowers, painting a fence, or hanging Christmas lights.

"You seemed untouchable," I told her. "Beautiful and accomplished. The kind of woman I knew existed in this world but was sure I couldn't have. And so I let you live your life. Smiled politely when we crossed paths, knowing that you were destined for better. But that one night? I couldn't help myself."

The way she danced, the way she looked in that dress? I just had to talk to her.

When I was a kid, my dad had given me a talk about using my powers for good and not evil. Most of the time, I did. I swear, but once in a while, I would pop a dimple and drop a sexy smirk to get what I wanted.

And I wanted Evie. Her chest rose and fell rapidly, though she quickly narrowed her eyes on me.

"You sure remember a lot for a guy who didn't even text the next day."

Wincing, I rubbed the back of my neck. "You told me several times that night that you weren't looking for anything. In fact, if I recall, you said it to me mid-blow job ..."

Her cheeks flushed quickly, the sight so damn satisfying.

But again, she recovered quickly. "I didn't want anything messy."

"And I was nothing but messy back then." I admitted. "I thought I was doing what you wanted, following your instructions. I felt lucky to have gotten even that little bit of time with you."

"You're still messy," she said, inching closer.

"Maybe. But I'm trying to clean myself up," I promised. "Become the type of man you'd give a second chance."

The oven timer beeped loudly, breaking the spell, and Evie blinked rapidly and busied herself donning oven mitts and opening the oven.

"I meant what I said," she whispered, still facing the

oven. "That night wasn't me. It was like I was being pulled toward you and I couldn't stop it." She set the cookie sheet on the top of the stove, and when she freed her hands from the oven mitts, they were shaking.

I swallowed hard, my gut tightening. "Then maybe it wasn't a mistake. Maybe it was the one time in your life where you followed your heart and did what you wanted rather than what was expected of you."

She turned quickly, eyes bright. "And look how that turned out."

I eyed the baby monitor on the counter and crossed my arms over my chest again. "It turned out perfectly."

I was an easygoing guy. I didn't push for much, but I wasn't going to let her off the hook. This was the most I'd gotten out of this woman in a year. So I'd keep pushing until she could be honest with me and herself.

"Can you at least put a shirt on?" she snapped. "It's hard to argue with you with all those muscles on display."

I smirked, my chest expanding. "These aren't even my best," I teased. "If you want a distraction I'll turn around and give you an eyeful of my best asset." Spinning, I shook my ass at her.

She giggled, the sound lighting me up inside.

With another spin back, I said, "I never skip leg day."

She looked down at her own thick, delicious thighs. "Apparently I don't skip leg day either."

"Oh, I know." I stalked toward her and backed her into the countertop, caging her in. "My girl is strong as hell. And it'd be my absolute privilege to wear those thighs as earmuffs tonight."

The scent of warm sugar filled the air as we stood, focus

fixed on one another, the world narrowing down to just the space between us.

Finally, she exhaled. "You're trouble, Jasper Lawrence."

I leaned in, ghosting my lips over the shell of her ear, relishing the way the contact made her shudder. "You say it like it's a bad thing, Evangelina Marino."

She gasped at the sound of her name on my lips.

But I kept going, gently pressing my mouth to her neck. "You say it like trouble isn't exactly your type."

She tilted her head to the side, giving me more access. "It wasn't. Until I met you."

Chapter 27

EVIE

Anxiety coursed through me, making me doubt him. Trying to convince me that he was doing this because of Vincent. That I was a consolation prize. A convenient fuck.

But the heat in his gaze and reverential way he touched me banished those thoughts.

He hooked his hands under my hips and picked me up. The way he manhandled me as he set me on the kitchen counter made me wild for him.

I cupped his face, kissing him, and in return, he dug his fingertips into my thighs.

"God." He sighed. "I love kissing you. I love these lips."

His kiss was both hard and soft and a little messy, his hands anchoring me to the granite. As he coaxed my mouth open, he stepped closer, his body crowding me, protecting me, and wrapping me in his masculine scent.

He moved lower, kissing my jaw, my neck, and my collarbones. With one hand tangled in his hair, I used the other to palm his erection.

A little roughly, he grasped my wrist. "No. Last time I let you take charge."

"But—"

"I need to take my time and do all the things I've been dreaming about," he rasped into my ear. "If you rush me or rob me of this chance, I'll have to tie you to that bed."

Oh, fuck me.

Jasper was easygoing. Calm yet energetic with plenty of goofy humor.

But sex-crazed bossy Jasper? Barking orders at me and threatening to tie me up? Be still my vulva.

He kissed up my thighs, gently teasing them apart. My shorts provided little resistance, and soon he was yanking them to the side and nuzzling my damp panties. "Fuck, you smell so good. And you're already so damn wet for me."

His fingers traveled under the seam, ghosting my sensitive skin, the touch making me shake with anticipation.

"Are you going to be a good girl and let me eat?" Head between my thighs, he looked up at me. The visual made my pulse race. Eyes burning and bare chest gleaming with a sheen of sweat. It was pornographic.

I wanted it. Him. Never had I considered myself a sexual person. In fact, I routinely went years without sex. I got horny as much as the next girl, but the sensation was nothing my fingers or my pocket rocket couldn't take care of.

For years, I rolled my eyes at friends who waxed poetic about their sex lives. Orgasms were great and all, but they weren't worth unraveling my life over. It was nice when it happened, but when it didn't, I was perfectly fine.

Until Jasper. Until that pulse between my legs became impossible to ignore. The need, the ache for him to touch me.

The certainty that I would combust without him. The desire to feel him on me and inside me. To give him access to every single part of me.

"You can do anything you want to me," I said, my voice huskier, more desperate than I expected.

He scooped me up and walked out of the kitchen with ease. Damn, what was it with this man and hauling me around?

Grunting like a caveman, he kicked open my bedroom door. Then he deposited me on the bed and rubbed his hands together. "Mama, I've been dreaming about the way you taste. Please, can I taste you?"

I lay back, lifting my hips, giving him silent permission to remove my shorts. In one quick move, he yanked them and my panties down. Then he was on his knees and pushing my thighs wide open. All self-consciousness fled my mind when raw need flashed in his eyes.

The first brush of his tongue made my hips buck off the bed. He nibbled and teased, driving my need higher, making my legs tremble. Only when I was babbling incoherently did he start to eat. There was no other way to describe it.

Moans and licks and groans and bites. Fingers and teeth and lips and tongue. I clutched at his hair to steady myself.

It was dizzying. Not just because it felt good, but because he was enjoying it so much. This wasn't a chore for him; it was a delight.

In a matter of minutes, I detonated, screaming and shaking and levitating as he worked, never stopping, never slowing. One orgasm flowed into another until my vision was nearly black and my lungs were burning from lack of oxygen. Finally, I collapsed on the bed, unable to feel my toes.

As the tension drained from my body, I searched for the words to tell him that what he'd done was world-altering.

Before I could come up with a coherent sentence, he was wrapping me in his arms and kissing my shoulder, making me feel completely cocooned and protected.

"Jas—"

"Shh. Just enjoy it. When you're ready, I'll go again."

He shifted me onto my side and curled himself around me. His hard cock dug into the flesh of my ass, but rather than grind it against me or make a move for more, he buried his face in my hair and whispered in my ear about how sexy and perfect I was. How pretty I looked when I came. How, next time, he wanted me to sit on his face.

I began to drift, the warmth of his large body lulling me into a state of pure bliss. I'd never been much of a cuddler, but with him, it didn't feel compulsory or forced. It felt necessary, like the perfect extension of what we'd just done.

"I want to do that every day for the rest of my life," he said as my eyes fluttered closed.

And my post-orgasmic, cozy, blissed-out brain thought *same.*

Chapter 28

EVIE

Halfway to Ruby's house, I was regretting my decision to walk. Though it was only four blocks from my little craftsman, it was hot and sticky out today. My hair was going to be an epic pile of frizz by the time I arrived, and I worried that Vincent would overheat in his stroller.

Ruby and Paul's house was a traditional brick colonial on the outside, and a chaotic wonderland on the inside. Vintage furniture, plants hanging from the ceiling, a gallery wall of family photos interspersed with abstract art, and several murals Ruby had painted over the years.

Paul greeted me with a kiss and parked the stroller in the garage while I carried Vincent inside, along with the cookies I'd baked.

On the couch, Frankie sat with Brooks, her soft expression as she looked down at him unfamiliar. Ruby was seated in a reclining chair, rocking a messy bun and a lime green silk kimono. Nina sat on the floor in front of her, a mini pedicure station set up, and was busy painting Ruby's toes lemon yellow.

"Evie," Ruby cheered. "I'm so happy to see you. Sorry the place is such a mess."

It was not a mess. Not by any standard. This woman had a week-old baby, yet there wasn't a pile of laundry in sight. No burp cloths draped over the furniture. And she was getting a pedicure.

A mini flare of jealous lit me up inside me, but I quickly extinguished it.

"Hold still," Nina chastised, flipping her pink tipped hair over her shoulder.

Shoulders slumping, I looked down at my own raggedly cuticles. I was way past due.

"Don't worry, I'll get you next," Nina said without even turning around. "But no fucking baby pink. Either you let me have fun or enjoy your hangnails of shame."

I spread out a blanket and laid Vincent on it, along with a squishy toy, and agreed. At this point, I'd take what I could get.

When Stella, Ruby's younger sister, arrived shortly after me, we settled in for girl time.

Paul made himself useful, fetching coffee and changing diapers but otherwise remaining scarce.

"He's a good one." Stella gave her sister's hand a squeeze.

Ruby looked so serene, so at peace, now cradling a sleeping Brooks in her arms.

Meanwhile, Frankie was on the floor with Vincent, using a wooden toy car to explain combustion engines. He drooled and happily stared at her while she lectured him.

"Evie, is it true?" Stella asked. "That there are lawyers

crawling all over Sugar Moon? That Louisa Meyers is armoring up?"

Frowning, I shook my head. "No more lawyers than usual." We had a small legal team and routinely worked with outside counsel on bigger issues. None of that had changed recently.

"Tony said that teams of New York lawyers are involved. The big guns, he called them."

"That woman terrifies me," Ruby said. "She could probably curdle milk with a glare."

Frankie rolled over and propped herself up on an elbow. "Didn't she buy up several of the bankrupted farms when prices tanked two years ago? Greed is a powerful motive."

"No." Paul handed me a fresh mug of coffee, then set a glass of water with a lemon slice on the end table next to his wife. Yes, a lemon slice. Paul was truly a peach of a man. "That agrochem place did," he said. "Evergreen, I think? They were the vultures. Some of my clients sold to them."

As a CPA, Paul did a lot of work for the farm community here, but more than that, he advocated on their behalf. His family owned a massive estate with a lot of farmland, but neither he nor his sister Rowan seemed interested in taking over the family business.

"Either way, she's an ice queen," Nina said. "Saw her at Bean There, Sipped That the other day. Full cashmere armor in eighty-degree weather."

"She probably sweats diamonds," Frankie jabbed. "You think she's ever touched flannel?"

"She ordered tea," Nina reported. "Hot tea in July. All the other customers had cold drinks, and she frowned like we'd failed a test."

"She's gorgeous," Ruby said. "But she gives off that main character in a psychological thriller vibe."

Unease rolling through me, I shifted, focusing on my coffee. I didn't want to gossip about my boss, even if she hadn't made herself a lot of friends in town.

"She's intense and precise," I said, feeling the need to defend her. "She's not cold, and she's incredibly smart." Louisa had been nothing but kind to me, and she'd been so generous when I unexpectedly had Vincent. Since I'd returned to work, she'd been nothing but complimentary of my work.

"Let's not villainize her because she's not likable," Frankie said, coming to my rescue. "She's a woman kicking ass. People are automatically going to hate her for it."

"True," Nina chimed in. "But you have to admit, in a Hallmark movie, she's the big city businesswoman trying to shut down the small-town family business."

"Fair," Stella said. "But those are the more interesting characters anyway."

Frankie lifted her mug. "Truth."

"Do you really think she was involved with Will?" Stella asked.

That stopped me in my tracks, making my heart thud heavily. There was no way. First of all, she had to be fifteen years older than him, and second, she was way too professional and focused on success to have a relationship with an employee.

"Apparently they were close. Rumor is that he was messing around with someone at Sugar Moon."

Frankie tsked. "That's harmful gossip."

"Sure, but she's been everywhere since he died. I've seen

her downtown almost every day," Nina said. "And she's been visiting the farmers and asking questions. Plus all those meetings with the police."

"Yes," I said, unable to keep from sticking up for her. "Because her company is going through a scandal. I would know. Since it's my responsibility to deal with it."

"Paul plays Dungeons & Dragons with some of the science guys," Ruby said. "According to them, there have been several diverted tankers in the past few months. Shipment issues, quality control errors. They could be hiding something."

Every head turned my way, like they were all waiting for me to give them more information. But I refused to add fuel to this fire.

"Louisa isn't hiding anything. She's acting in the best interest of her company and her employees and suppliers," I explained diplomatically. "I've seen her at her best and at her worst. The steel behind her calm. The weariness of late-night strategy calls. She's an incredible businesswoman."

As if they'd picked up on my unease, they gave me nods and murmured half-hearted agreements, then changed the subject.

Thank God. Though even as the conversation moved on, a knot of worry formed in my stomach.

This situation had continued to spiral out of control, and the wild gossip wouldn't stop until someone was arrested and the town felt safe again.

"Sales are way down," Ruby explained. "Stella's doing a great job running the store on her summer break, but we usually do big numbers for the Fourth of July."

"Same," Nina said, mixing eyebrow tint in what looked

like a baby food bowl. "I expanded my hours, hoping for more walk-ins in the summer. We even invested in expensive massaging pedicure chairs."

"The inn has vacancies and Opal had to discount her summer tasting menu," Frankie added. "Which is pure sacrilege. That woman is a culinary genius."

"Maplewood doesn't feel the way it used to," Stella added. "Maybe that's the problem. People feel unsafe, and they're turning on one another. And don't get me started on the cheese wars. They've become unhinged."

Discussing cheese in mixed company was a challenge, because the loyalty of the citizens of Maplewood was pretty evenly split. Neither cheese shop owner was a saint, either. Basil was a dear friend, but he was no angel and hadn't even bothered to try to defuse the conflict.

"I feel like we're careening toward another incident," Frankie added.

The women around the room all sucked in harsh breaths. From the stories I'd heard, the town had barely recovered from the Cheddar Incident of 2019. The mayor had had to mediate, and Nolan, our police chief, still walked away when it was mentioned.

Both shops found themselves banned from farmers' market participation for a year, which in Maplewood was the equivalent of a death row sentence.

Petty town rivalries or not, I felt it too. The hush in the air, the fear, the constant anxiety that the tourists wouldn't come back. Not to mention Will's tragic death. He really was a good kid with a bright future.

The conversation fizzled out while we all grappled with this reality.

Vincent, bless him, blew a raspberry and broke the silence. When Frankie tickled his belly in response, he descended into a fit of giggles, his chubby cheeks wobbling.

"Oh my God, he is the happiest baby," Ruby trilled. "He must get it from his mama."

Frankie pinned me with a look. "Or his hot firefighter dad."

I surveyed Vincent, ignoring Frankie's scrutiny. Damn, she was like a dog with a very tasty bone.

"You know, now that Frankie mentions it," Ruby said, "you are sort of glowing."

"And it's not from her new moisturizer," Nina deadpanned. "She caught feels. Not collagen."

"Yeah. She's got a whole drunk Disney princess look going on." Frankie sat up and shifted so she faced me directly. "She's definitely getting some."

Face lit up, Ruby clapped. "Now this is what I need to hear. Start talking."

Cheeks flaming, I contemplated tucking Vincent under my arm and sprinting to the front door. But knowing they'd only hound me again the next time I saw them, I sighed, letting my body deflate, and gave them a tidbit of the information they were looking for. "We're exploring things."

Stella squealed. "OMG. You two have such a cute story."

"You don't have to settle for him just because he's your baby daddy," Frankie said.

That chafed a bit. In fact, I'd fought my feelings for him for that exact reason. Not that I'd opened up to her about it. And she'd been the one at the hospital who first suggested it.

"He always shows up," I told them, fiddling with Vincent's giraffe toy. "He fixes things before I ask and makes

Vincent laugh until he hiccups. And when he looks at me." Head ducked, I searched for the right words and hoped like hell I wouldn't sound like a lovesick teenager. "I feel safe. Like I can breathe."

The room had gone completely silent, and as I shifted, uncomfortable with the way every eye was on me, Ruby reached over and squeezed my hand. "Babe, I'm happy for you. We all see it," she assured me. "How devoted he is to you and Vincent. How much he's changed."

I picked up my mug, hiding a smile behind it, my heart full.

Frankie, surprisingly, kept her commentary to herself. The rest of the girls seemed generally pleased and not at all surprised that Jasper and I were together. Granted, we hadn't defined our relationship, but he was sleeping in my bed and we spent all our nonworking time together. I was the one who'd asked to take it slow, but as I sat in Ruby's living room, I found myself yearning to slap a label on this very unorthodox situation.

Luckily, the girls moved on quickly, Ruby lamenting that Brooks would only fall asleep to yacht rock while Nina shuffled over, ready to do my brows.

My heart was full. Being part of this sisterhood was more than I could ask for. Throw in my perfect, amazing baby and the incredible man waiting for me at home, and for the first time in a long time, the ache in my chest wasn't loneliness. It was hope. Terrifying, beautiful hope.

Chapter 29

JASPER

The July heat was already settling in for the day. The air smelled like pine and smoke, and though it was only seven, Josh was moving like he'd been up and working for hours.

As I climbed out of my car, he approached, Wayne trailing behind him. He was wearing a hat and sunglasses, making it hard to read his expression, but a sense of urgency radiated from him.

"Didn't know you knew how to set an alarm that went off before eight a.m.," he said.

The sarcastic ass had texted me last night to be here at seven, so here I was.

"Good to know you're still incapable of saying thank you," I replied.

He clapped me on the shoulder and strode off toward the barn. In July and August, our work consisted mostly of maintenance. We harvested our sap in March and April and followed that up with plantings. Now it was time to check, sanitize, and recheck all our equipment and remove any brush or branches that could get in the way. Access to the tree stands was essential, and the work of clearing was never really done.

These were some of my least favorite tasks, but they were necessary.

Josh had the ATVs ready to go, with a wagon full of tools hitched to one.

As we hauled brush and hiked the lanes between the trees, I filled him in on Vincent's newfound ability to roll over and the silly sounds he made. And I chuckled as I told him about the awful face he made when he tried mashed avocado for the first time.

We'd been doing this kind of work since we were old enough to walk, picking up branches, pruning, and inspecting.

Waving at a fly buzzing near my head, I caught sight of a damaged line, so I collected the tools I needed and hiked down the slope. In an operation as big as ours, faulty tubing could cause major problems.

"What happened?" Josh called down. "Don't make it worse."

"Pretty sure the squirrels already handled that. But they didn't finish the job. It'll be an easy fix."

Josh squinted at me. "Guess they've got your work ethic."

Asshole. I gave him the finger, then replaced the cracked fitting.

Having cleared this sector, we hauled brush and branches back to the pile near the barn where we would chip some of them for mulch and cut the larger ones for firewood.

Inside the barn, we took a breather, the two of us going for our water bottles.

"You never mentioned that you hooked up with Evie," he said as he recapped his water.

That was hardly out of the ordinary. We'd never discussed hookups. "It was a one-night stand," I said sheepishly.

Josh loved to give me shit for having a good time just like I teased him for being a grumpy old man.

"Why didn't you use protection?"

I was the baby of the family. The goofy, fun one. The one who received calls when moods needed to be lightened. All my life, no one had ever taken me seriously. Honestly, I'd never minded. Until now. I wasn't that guy anymore, and I wouldn't take this dismissive, demeaning shit.

"My son is four months old," I said. "It's a little redundant to discuss the lack of birth control now, don't you think? And while the circumstances of his conception weren't ideal, I refuse to feel shame or guilt for bringing Vincent into this world."

Josh stared at me, his features still shadowed beneath his hat.

I pulled myself up to my full height. I was an inch taller than him, but he had at least forty pounds on me. He'd always been stockier, and farm work had made him freakishly strong.

After a long minute, he nodded. "Understood. So what's your endgame? Gabe said he and Brian drew up papers for you. When will you get the testing done?"

I bristled. This was the last thing I wanted to talk about.

My brother was haunted and had been for a long time.

The lasting effects from whatever had caused it popped up here and there, despite the way he tried to hide them. To this day, he'd never opened up about what had made him leave New York, his fiancée, his condo, and his big deal job.

Selfishly, I was glad he'd come home. While he lived in the city, we never saw him, and the farm would not have survived if he hadn't been here. He did so much for Mom, and she passed peacefully because she knew our family's legacy was taken care of.

I'd always given him space, let him do his thing. He'd start another obsessive project, and I'd keep my mouth shut. He'd buy a new piece of equipment for the farm and force me to spend twenty hours on a training course so I could use it. I said nothing.

But my own tiny family is where I drew the line.

"I've always given you space. Respect," I said firmly. "You have your secrets and I've never pushed you. So I'm asking for reciprocity."

He shifted, crossing his arms over his chest, but he didn't respond.

"This is my life, my child. And I'm leading with love and support. For Vincent and for his mother."

"Of course you are," he said, dropping his hands to his sides. "You're a good man, Jasper, and you've changed."

I wiped my sweaty forehead on my T-shirt. "Was I really that bad before?"

He shook his head. "Nah, but I didn't expect you to stick. With Vincent. You've got roots now. You're a father. Dad would have loved to see it. But I don't want you to be taken advantage of."

My gut sank. "I get that, but it doesn't feel right to lawyer up and fight. Life is short. We have no idea how much time we have. I'd much rather take advantage of every minute I get with Vincent than fight with his mom."

"But he's your child."

"Yes. And Evie is his mother. He's an infant and she's nursing."

"We could make space for him here. I could convert Jess's old room into a nursery."

Josh and his desire for more projects. He was sincere, his voice strained, the deep desire to help bubbling up inside him. One day, maybe he'd realize that burying himself in work was not healing him.

"Thank you," I said calmly. "But his home is Evie's house. And I'm content to be there."

"But you're not really there, are you? You're sleeping in a tent. You're on the outside, dropping in when you're allowed."

How could I explain it? How I felt when I was with Evie and Vincent. It felt right. My life was complete. It was instinctual, the knowledge that it was where I needed to be. And I'd gotten there by being patient. Sleeping in a tent, demonstrating my commitment day in and day out.

Maybe my reasoning wouldn't pass Josh's standards for logic, but I just knew it in my bones.

"I'm in love with her," I said.

He staggered back a step, his jaw dropping. Then he did the most un-Josh-like thing ever. He dragged himself over to a hay bale and sat.

Wayne, his massive dog, circled once, then again, before curling up on the dirt floor. He was Josh's constant companion, seeming to read his moods and share his preference for silence and hard work. Typically, he remained at Josh's side, though he'd run off to chase squirrels every once in a while.

"I guess hell froze over," he croaked

I laughed to defuse some of the tension that had built between us.

"Nah." I shrugged. "They changed me. Vincent and Evie."

"I can see it."

"I used to think that love was adrenaline," I told him. "Now I know it's the quiet things. Changing diapers at two in the morning, bringing her coffee, fixing a window because it sticks. Things that I thought were boring before now fuel me, they motivate me to do better and be better."

My words hung in the air. This was one of the qualities I admired about Josh. He never tried to fill the silence.

"She's perfectly capable on her own," I admitted. "But she wants me around. Beneath her careful control, she's full of warmth and wit. And she has a heart that's braver than she knows. Being with her feels like being home."

Josh scratched at his thick beard. "Shit. You sound like Dad when he talked about Mom."

I dipped my chin. "That's how I know it's real."

He stood up, and Wayne and I followed. Apparently the break was over. Time to head back to the sugarbush. As we walked, I rambled about Evie and Vincent. Josh let me. Getting all my thoughts out was a relief. And it made this new normal I'd found feel more real. We could be a family. We could be together. It was possible.

We fixed several dozen lines and had to get the chainsaw out to deal with a dead tree all before lunch. Once that was finished, Josh opened a cooler and handed me a sandwich.

Then the two of us sat under the canopy of green leaves, enjoying the rare breeze.

"There's still time for you too," I said.

He hated the topic, but all the honesty lately had gotten me a bit addicted. It was freeing to talk things out, to own my feelings. With any luck, I could teach my brother a thing or two. He was the reigning champion of the repression Olympics.

"Nah." He huffed. "I'm good. Had my shot. Didn't work out. Decided the farm was a safer bet for me."

He went back to eating his turkey sandwich, as though his answer was even remotely acceptable.

"Dude, you're thirty-five not ninety-five. You're smart and successful. And a lot of women dig the beard, flannel, and grunting thing."

He glared at me. "Not so simple."

"Really?" I cocked a brow. "Try me. I may seem simple, but my situation is complicated. Yet I'm at least trying."

For a long moment, he looked out at the trees, as if hoping they could explain why his romantic life was so dismal.

"Allie had a baby," he finally said. "A daughter."

My stomach sank. Shit. Allie was his ex-fiancée. The one he left abruptly when he moved home. He'd told us it was over and that we were never to speak her name again. But it had been a good three years since then.

"I'm sorry, dude," I said lamely. "It sucks when an ex moves on."

"No. You don't understand. She got pregnant when we were engaged. While we were planning our wedding. That's why we postponed."

Squinting, I assessed him, finding him wearing his typical stoic expression. "Okay. So..."

He took his hat off and ran his hands through his hair. And as if he could sense his owner's discomfort, Wayne got up and rested his head on Josh's knee.

"I thought the baby was mine," he said softly. "I was thrilled. Read the books, bought all the stuff. All while she drifted farther apart.

"After her first ultrasound appointment, when we could see the baby, hear its heartbeat, Allie broke down. Told me she had been having an affair with her boss and that the baby was his."

The admission knocked all the air out of my lungs. Josh had always worshipped our father. Wanting to be just like him, settling down with the love of his life and having a houseful of kids. He was a wonderful uncle to Jenn's and Jess's kids and led school field trips around the farm, teaching students about maple sugaring.

"It almost killed me," he rasped. "That the woman I loved had cheated and then had led me to believe she was carrying my baby."

"But it could have been."

"That's what I thought. Hoped, really. So we did testing." He hung his head. "It wasn't mine."

I swallowed past the lump in my throat. "So that's why you left."

He looked up at me, tears in his eyes. "I wish it was that easy. I had a breakdown first. Blew up my career, my life, my finances. But this place." He scanned the trees. "It saved me, gave me a purpose. Helping Mom, helping Uncle Ed and Aunt Suzie out so they could finally retire, it was what I was meant to do. This land and this farm mean so much to our family and this town. Spending my life here is a privilege."

I nodded, even as I choked on the guilt and sadness pummeling me. "I agree," I said softly when I found my voice. "But it's okay to want more too."

He shook his head and uncapped his water and took a swig. "I'm good. This place and Wayne are all I need."

With a huff, he stood and started to clean up.

"Should we work on the west side next?" I asked as I did the same.

"Not today. I've got to go over to the cabin and fix a few things."

"Did you finally list it on Airbnb?"

Josh had put months of work into an old cabin on the property, transforming it into a bright and comfortable home for Jess and her daughters. They'd planned on moving here last summer, and he'd put in a ton of effort to make the place perfect for them.

But plans changed. Jess met Brian, and her oldest, Kit, was accepted into a prestigious music school in New York, so they decided to stay. They spent summers here, but rather than take over the cabin, they were converting Mom's old barn into their dream house.

So the cabin mostly sat empty. Aside from the odd guest now and again, like the Glovers.

"No. But Callie's been hounding me. Apparently the school hired a woman from out of town for the upcoming school year, and she's looking for a house to rent starting next month."

"All the way out here?"

"Yeah. Sounds like she's got kids, so she wants room for

them to play outside rather than trying to cram into an apartment in town."

Lips pressed together, I nodded. "Sounds like a good deal for the both of you."

Josh stretched. "Not really. I still don't love the idea of having tenants. But Callie is insistent. And the other night, I was at the brewery, and Faith started in on me. According to her, the school is desperate to fill this spot. They really need her to take the job."

"I wouldn't cross them." I chuckled. "You know teachers. They are ruthless and organized."

"True. And the last thing I need is the Maple Street Mafia joining forces with them and making my life hell."

I grinned. Fearing a cabal of Patagonia-clad old ladies was the stuff of pure Vermont small-town life.

"Can I help?"

"Nah, go back to Evie and Vincent. Enjoy your time with them."

I coiled the tubing and put the tools away, then got my ATV packed. "Didn't think I'd ever hear you say you were proud of me," I teased.

Head down, Josh packed up his own tools. "Didn't say I was, dumbass. Just said Dad would be." He sighed, and under his breath, he added, "But yeah, I am proud of you."

A lightness grew in my chest. "Guess we're both growing."

"Suppose so. Now don't let it go to your head."

I headed back to the barn and got my things put away quickly, eager to get back to Evie. I had to work tonight, but a couple hours with her and Vincent would do me some good.

When I'd woken up in her bed this morning, my world had felt completely right.

As I exited the barn, I was hit with a whiff of my own sweat, so I headed for the house, figuring I'd grab a shower and clean clothes before driving back into town.

I was approaching the door to the mudroom when a familiar red Jeep rolled up and parked, and my cousin hopped out.

"Hey, Gabe."

He was dressed in his customary slacks and dress shirt with the sleeves rolled up. It was hotter than Hades out, yet he looked totally cool.

Maybe it was a skill he'd learned in law school, because after a morning outside, my T-shirt had liquefied against my skin.

"Glad you're here." He gave me a big white smile. "Got those papers we discussed. Though Brian did a lot of the work, since I've been dealing with town stuff."

Confused, I stepped toward him. "Papers?"

"Yeah, I've been driving around with them for days. Just haven't had time to drop them by. Figured I'd eventually run into you."

He held out a dark brown stretchy folder.

"There are petitions in there." He nodded at the file. "Some printouts regarding Vermont law and paternal rights. Child support guidelines. And the request for a paternity test."

The folder suddenly felt like a cinderblock, its weight too much to carry.

"I don't need this," I said, pushing it toward him.

Rather than take it, he ran his hands through his hair. "I have a call with the governor in an hour. I don't have time to discuss this again. Read through it. Think about it. You don't have to do anything right now. But promise you'll read everything."

The stress etched into the lines on his face was hard to miss. My cousin was overwhelmed. Shit. With the murder still unsolved, of course he had more important things to worry about. And he and Brian had done all this free legal work for me.

"Of course," I said, tucking it under my arm. "I'll read through it, but I'm not ready to make any decisions yet."

He clapped me on the shoulder. "Great. Text me with questions. I gotta find Josh."

He took off at a light jog toward the main barn, leaving me in the dusty driveway, confused and frustrated.

I ambled over to my car and tucked the folder under the passenger side visor. I'd read through it tomorrow during my downtime at work. I also had more important things to do right now, mainly visiting my girl and my son.

Chapter 30

EVIE

"Are you sure you can take the time off?"

"Of course."

The sight of Jasper packing unlocked a whole new kink for me. The diaper bag was prepped for blowouts and every other potential natural disaster. The items in the trunk of my car were neatly arranged, and every weather possibility had been accounted for.

I'd also caught him ironing my clothes while I was on a Zoom call in the living room. "You iron?"

"Yes." He dipped his chin. "My uniforms have to be ironed. Why?"

"It's hot."

"Yes, Evie," he teased. "Irons use heat to press out wrinkles."

I stuck my tongue out. "No. I mean the action. You ironing? It's sexy."

Jasper drove, as cautious as ever with our precious cargo

loaded in the back seat, while I prepped my notes for the roundtable I was attending in New York. I spent most of the trip researching the other attendees and generally freaking out. I used to do this thing all the time. The hedge fund I used to work for employed few women, so I was always trotted out in the name of so-called equality. Assholes.

I'd agreed to this trip months ago, before Vincent was born. It had seemed like a great opportunity at the time. Now, I'd rather cuddle up with Vincent and Jasper and shut the world out. With all that had been going on at work, taking two days off was a luxury I wasn't sure I could afford.

But Jasper had jumped at the chance to help out with Vincent so I could keep him close by. And it was an honor to be invited to this kind of thing, to network with peers. And selfishly, I need the validation that I hadn't thrown my career away when I moved to Vermont. That what I did had value and relevance in the broader world.

So we set off with way more gear than we could ever need and the snacks Jasper had packed for us.

For a baby who didn't ride in the car much, Vincent was pretty happy. I'd ordered a mirror toy that hung from the top of his car seat recently, and he seemed to really enjoy it, kicking and squealing every few minutes.

As we sang along to Jasper's playlist, his hand on my thigh, I found even navigating the city's ridiculous traffic to be less stressful.

"I did something," I admitted to Jasper as he was putting the Pack 'n' Play together in the hotel room. "I texted my sister."

He looked up, his face a mask of concern. "Are you okay? Did she respond?"

The simple questions hit me in the solar plexus. Because even as this big, strong man kneeled on the floor, trying to make sense of the instructions that had come with the Pack 'n' Play, he was more than happy to spare time to worry about my emotional state. I was living in a dream. I had to be.

But I'd told him more about my fucked-up family than I'd shared with even Ruby or Frankie. And he'd listened intently, never interrupting. And he hadn't even tried to fix it for me. But putting my hurt into words was a blessing. His family was a damn Norman Rockwell painting, but somehow, he didn't judge me or pity me for my dysfunctional one.

"She lives in the city." I sighed. "And I don't know. I just thought maybe she'd want to see Vincent."

"What did she say?"

I yanked my phone from my pocket and eyed the screen, trying to quiet my racing heart. "She said she'd come to the hotel to see us after the conference."

He stood up and wrapped me in a hug. "If this is what you want, then I support you 100 percent. If you change your mind at the last minute, that's fine too. We can hide in an alley if we need to."

His eyes crinkled as he teased. God, he was gorgeous.

I couldn't not kiss him. So I pulled him down, and he was more than happy to oblige.

Our son was not so easygoing a moment later when he fussed and shifted in his car seat and promptly screamed at me to be fed.

Jasper was right. I didn't have to see my sister. She and I had a tense relationship. Mainly because I'd stopped speaking to my abusive parents and she was still deeply enmeshed with them. She was the consummate daddy's girl, the golden child. All our lives, she'd managed to escape his wrath. Giovanna could do no wrong.

To this day, she defended him, so when I stopped speaking to my father, I lost her by default.

Jasper was right. I could always cancel if it felt wrong. I was the one who'd had the baby. He was the perfect built-in excuse to get out of things I didn't want to do.

For now, though, I had to put that out of my mind. It was time to put on my big girl pants, which were finally starting to button again, and be professional Evie.

Did I even belong here anymore? That thought had run through my mind more than once. I'd spent thirty years of my life in this city, yet it felt so foreign. So wrong. Too loud, too busy, just too much.

The sky was barely visible between skyscrapers. And had the sidewalks always been this crowded?

At the Women in Marketing Conference, Jasper kept Vincent strapped to his chest and hung out with me while I waited to be introduced for the panel I was speaking on. He was distractingly handsome, something that just about every other attendee appreciated if the looks they were giving him were any indication.

"Look at Mommy," he said to Vincent, cupping his head tenderly. "She's so pretty and smart. We're so proud of her, aren't we?"

The noise in the bustling lobby echoed off the sleek marble floors, making it nearly impossible to have a conversation, and women in suits furiously tapping out emails on their phones, stood everywhere I looked.

I gave Jasper a sassy look, but deep down, my heart was melting. Both dressed in blue today, it hit me. How much

Vincent looked like his father. The green eyes and the arched brows, the single dimple.

For months, all I'd seen in my son was myself. My dark hair and the shape of my lips. But he was half Jasper. Obviously, but emotionally, I supposed I hadn't processed that.

"You could run this whole thing, you know that?" Jasper shuffled closer and kissed my forehead, being sure not to squish our little guy between us.

I was still getting used to how casual his affection was. How he touched and kissed and hugged in the most natural way. How generous he was with his smiles and his laughter. How perfectly his body comforted me.

He had been true to his word and had not pressured me or asked for any definition. We were floating along in a sea of orgasms and baby giggles and forehead kisses. Strangely, other than that blip of desire for a label at girls' night, the unknown hadn't prompted anxiety attacks, and every day, I felt more comfortable with him.

"Please." I rolled my eyes. "I could not. I'm just hoping I don't have spit-up on my blazer and can speak coherently for an hour."

"If you do find spit-up, then think of it as a badge of honor." He winked at me. "And don't talk negatively about yourself. You've got this. We're your cheerleaders."

He raised Vincent's little arms in a mock cheer, and the two of them smiled, their matching dimples on display.

"Evangelina Marino." An impeccably dressed woman in her fifties wielding a clipboard scanned the space.

I waved at her, pressed a kiss to Vincent's head, then took a step back.

Jasper grasped my arm before I could walk away. "Do I get one too?"

Lips twitching, I moved in again. I kissed him chastely, but as I did, his hand traveled down, giving my ass a firm squeeze.

"Knock 'em dead."

Chapter 31

JASPER

From the moment I first saw her, I'd known that Evie was smart. But watching her captivate hundreds of people and speak so eloquently was an experience. And not just for me. All over the room, people scribbled notes furiously, their eyes bouncing from their notebooks to her and back again.

My chest expanded with pride as she was recognized and celebrated for her talents.

After the roundtable, one person after another rushed up to her with questions and to introduce themselves.

The woman struggled to accept all the compliments, but she handled every conversation with grace.

The old Jasper may have felt insecure. May have compared his small list of accomplishments to what Evie had done with her life and fallen woefully short. But the day Vincent was born, that mentality disappeared. I was more than happy to be here watching her. Helping her. Cheering for her alongside our son.

I was consumed by peace. Because this was what I was supposed to do. Who I was supposed to be. It had taken a long time to get here, but I'd found myself. And I wouldn't let go.

Once the room cleared out, we headed to the restaurant just off the lobby. The place was mostly empty at the moment, so we settled in one of the large booths, Vincent still in my arms, gnawing on his Sophie toy and exploring the leather of the booth seating with his tiny fingers.

The glow radiating from Evie earlier had dimmed. In fact, she seemed dimmer in general.

Heart aching for her, I squeezed her hand. "You okay?"

She nodded, but rather than respond, she stood and peered toward the restaurant's entrance.

I turned, following her line of sight, and found an elegant woman walking our way. She looked like a runway model, tall and willowy and holding a massive designer purse.

"Evie." She opened her arms and hugged Evie warmly.

"I'm Giovanna," she said as she stepped back and looked at me. "And this gorgeous bug must be baby Vincent. Grandpa would have loved his namesake."

She and Evie sat on the other side of the booth, side by side, and chatted.

The family resemblance was strong. Both had dark hair, pouty lips, and expressive dark eyes.

But where Evie was soft, vibrant, and lively, Giovanna was hard, cold, and impassive.

As time went on, Evie's posture relaxed, like she was

feeling more comfortable. She missed her sister, so I was thankful she hadn't chosen to bail on this visit.

Giovanna hadn't asked to hold Vincent, and though they'd both seemed to settle well into the conversation, there was still this standoffish distance between them.

It was so foreign to me. My own family was overwhelming and effusive. Especially my sisters. But even Josh had recently shocked me with his openness.

After about ten minutes, the air in the restaurant changed. There was a drop in pressure. A cold shift I couldn't explain. The room suddenly felt wrong, and all my first responder instincts kicked in.

Holding Vincent to my chest protectively, I scanned our surroundings. Quickly, I zeroed in on a newcomer.

The man was in his early sixties, tall and heavyset, with a graying combover and a very fancy watch that he checked as he walked our way. He had that performative kind of authority.

I didn't need an introduction. I knew.

"Two of my daughters in one place," he said, his tone harsh. "What a happy coincidence."

Every muscle in Evie's body clenched, and Vincent began to fuss in my arms, like he could sense his mama's distress.

Quickly, I found a binkie and rocked my little guy against my chest, making soothing shushing sounds.

All the color drained from Giovanna's face as she turned and gave her father a fake smile. "Hi, Dad. We were just catching up."

"You shouldn't be here," Evie said softly.

"Nonsense." He pulled up a chair, making himself at

home at the end of our table. "Why wouldn't a father be able to visit his daughter?"

The smile he directed at her was wrong. Full of practiced warmth, with edges as sharp as glass. His eyes roamed over Evie, then Vincent, and then me.

"You finally convinced someone to settle for you, I see. Congratulations."

The words landed heavily, like a blow to the gut. My instincts only grew stronger, my blood running hot and my brain screaming at me to pick this motherfucker up and throw him out of here.

I'd fought fires and rescued people from floods and car accidents. Helped men who were cornered and desperate and scared. I could read danger. But this was an entirely different kind of danger. Psychological rather than physical. This man killed with words and enjoyed it.

"You couldn't even tell me my grandson was visiting New York," he said. "Giovanna had to be the one to fill me in. Really, Evangelina." He gave her a disdainful look. "You never had any sense of propriety or gratitude."

At the same moment Evie flinched, my jaw locked tight. It took all my strength not to jump up and tell this guy that he wasn't allowed to speak to her like that. But I waited, sensing not just fear in Evie. This other emotion was stronger, fiercer, as it rose up inside her.

"You don't get to do this anymore," she said calmly, her head held high.

He scoffed. "There it is. The dramatics. You've always been good at making yourself a victim, haven't you?" He shook his head. "If you would have listened to me, done what

I told you, you wouldn't have ended up with a bastard child like this."

Evie was shaking, her eyes flashing with rage. Still, I waited, giving her a chance to stand up for herself. Knowing it was in her to do it.

"For years, I took your abuse.," she finally said. "Believed you when you told me I was the problem. I beat myself up for every misstep and every failure. Eventually, though, I realized that you're nothing but an abusive little man who destroys others to make himself feel good."

Pride unfurled in my chest. Her rage, her clear controlled anger, was long overdue. Now, though, strength radiated from her body.

The bastard's mouth curled in a humorless smile. "Abuse? It's called fatherly love," he spat. "All I wanted was for you to be your best. To actually amount to something, you ungrateful brat. And after all I did for you, all I paid for, you're still nothing more than a disappointment."

As much as I loved watching Evie stand up for herself, I had reached my breaking point. Slowly, I stood and passed Vincent to his mother. Then I crossed my arms. He was a big guy, but I would absolutely destroy him if he made one more nasty comment.

"You're done here. Leave," I said in a low voice.

He tilted his head up, assessing me with a sneer. "Who the hell are you to tell me what to do?"

"The man who won't let you speak to her like that ever again." My tone was dark and dangerous and unfamiliar. But my control had begun to slip.

The old man's eyes flickered with what might be fear, but it died quickly. Standing, he loomed over her. "You'll regret this. Shutting me out, having your goon threaten me. If you do this, I won't be around to bail you out, and we both know you're too soft and stupid to make it on your own."

Evie's reply was soft but steady, her dark eyes full of fire. "I've already made it on my own, Dad. I survived. Not because of you but in spite of you. Now please go, and I'd appreciate it if you never spoke to my family again."

My heart twisted. She was rewriting the story in real time, unwilling to hide behind her shame. It was beautiful, watching her stand on her own and protect our son. Hell, protect me too.

My family.

The words bounced around in my skull, and in this moment, I fell even harder for her.

He opened his mouth like he was going to argue. Instead, shoulders dropping, he shook his head and turned away. "Come on, Giovanna," he said as he strode toward the exit.

Giovanna scooted toward the end of the booth, her expression full of pain.

"You don't have to go," Evie murmured.

Giovanna gave her a small smile. "I love you." With that, she gathered her purse and headed out after their father.

I unclenched my hands and exhaled, long and slow. Then I turned to Evie, who clutched Vincent to her chest, her eyes glassy and her chest heaving.

Quickly, I rounded the table and took Giovanna's spot. Then I held the two of them tightly, willing their heartbeats to anchor me to the ground.

"He doesn't get to scare me anymore," she said eventually.

I rested my chin on the top of her head, relishing the

smell of her shampoo and the warmth of Vincent's little body between us. "No," I said. "He never will." She was strong enough to handle him on her own, but if there ever came a time when she wasn't, I'd ensure that fucker would never get near them again.

Vincent began to fuss, probably ready to be fed, and the noise of the hotel lobby seeped back in, bringing us back to the present.

As we got in the elevator to head back to our room, my entire being shifted. This time, it wasn't those protective instincts flaring up. No, this sensation was quieter and deeper.

I had always known I'd do anything to *keep* them safe.

But now I had a new goal: to be the *place* where they were always safe.

Chapter 32

EVIE

Jasper led me up to the hotel suite, his arm around me protectively.

Emotionally drained, all I could do as I fed Vincent was stare blankly at the wall.

Even my baby boy's giggles couldn't lift the fog.

When I'd finished nursing him, Jasper laid out the tummy time mat, then took him from me and played with him until he rubbed at his eyes, signaling that he was sleepy. Picking up on the cue on his own, Jasper changed him for bed, then sang to him while rubbing his back in the Pack 'n' Play.

With any luck, he'd sleep in this strange place. At four months old, he slept for good stretches of time most nights.

My little guy was growing so fast.

The thought brought with it a wave of emotion, causing tears to leak from my eyes without permission. It was all happening so fast. Everything had changed. And nothing would ever be the same again.

"Come on," Jasper said, suddenly standing in front of me. "You've been staring at that wall since we got here. Time for a bath."

He helped me to my feet and led me to the large bathroom where the freestanding tub was filled with steaming water and the air smelled like jasmine.

Slowly, he turned me around and unzipped my dress. "Just get in the water. It will help."

I nodded, helpless, and let him gather my hair and sloppily secure it in a claw clip.

It was sweet, how much he cared. But I was too numb to appreciate it.

My muscles screamed as I lowered myself into the tub. I felt like I'd climbed Everest.

The tears kept coming, bringing with them all the built-up anger and shame that had been gnawing at me since the moment I'd seen my father.

"I'll order cheeseburgers and find a rom-com to watch. Sound good? This is our first trip as a family. We can't let toxic assholes ruin it." Jasper plucked my clothes off the floor, pulled out his phone, and tapped at the screen until classical music began to play. Then he left the bathroom.

Damn my father for ruining such an incredible day. I'd networked and met some of my heroes, and dozens of young women had asked me questions about my career. After months and months of second-guessing my decision to leave my job in New York, I was starting to take pride in my new position. I was building something special at Sugar Moon, and it was about time I owned it.

But my father had the uncanny ability to dissolve my self-confidence with nothing more than a look. Add in his tone and the way he'd looked at Vincent, and I was sick.

Then Jasper had to witness it all. God, it was gross.

My fingers had wrinkled by the time Jasper returned and sat on the closed toilet.

"I'm proud of you," he said. "Breaking generational cycles is hard, but you're doing it."

My chest felt hollow. "I think my desire to protect Vincent is stronger than the conditioning or the shitty feelings my father evokes."

"Exactly. I'm so proud of you."

He leaned over the edge of the tub, nuzzling my neck. The man was maybe the most beautiful thing I'd ever seen. The smile, the dimple, the muscles, and the arms covered in ink.

The emotion that stirred inside me as his warmth soaked into me was more than lust. It was longing. To touch him. And need. To feel him and possess him and be part of him.

I looked up at him, surveying the stubble on his jaw, the glimmer in his eye, and couldn't stop the words from tumbling out of my mouth. "I love you."

His body went stiff, his eyes widening.

"I love you," I said again. It was too early for this kind of declaration, but I didn't care. The words would not stay in my mouth, and I was too exhausted to fight them.

Without a word, he pulled me out of the tub. He toweled off every inch of my skin with care and then wrapped me in the fluffiest of robes.

As he tied the belt around my waist, his head bowed, I cupped his cheek.

"Jasper," I whispered, my heart pounding.

He looked up at me, his eyes shining with tears.

Exhaling, I brought my other hand to his face too. Then I kissed him, desperate to ground myself to this moment.

Before I could get totally lost in him, I pulled back and searched his face. "Are you okay?"

He ran his hands through his hair. "Yes. I'm just in shock and can't really think right now."

"Do you want me to say it again?"

With his lip caught between his teeth, he nodded. The action was so damn sexy that I was tempted to drop to my knees right there on the bathroom floor.

Instead, I untied my robe slowly and let it fall to the tile. "I love you, Jasper."

Heat and affection flooded me as he drank me in, his expression one of desire and respect and something bigger. Something that looked a lot like love.

"Now take me to bed."

Without hesitation, he scooped me up. The bedroom was dark as he deposited me on the fluffy bed, Vincent's sound machine turned up.

"Can you be quiet?" he asked, his fingers traveling down to my thighs.

Before I could answer, he stole my breath by stroking my clit with his thumb.

I arched up, already more than ready for him.

"Fuck, you're soaked."

As he slipped one finger inside me, I grabbed a pillow and covered my face. It was necessary, with the way I was already struggling to keep from moaning.

"I bet you could come like this." He nipped at my inner thigh.

I removed the pillow and nodded, weaving the fingers of one hand through his hair.

"Is that what you want, mama? You want to come?"

Rather than beg, I gave him a deadpan look that I hoped he read as "no shit."

With a deep chuckle, he slipped a second finger inside me. "Hmm," he said, sliding them out again, leaving me empty and desperate. "I'm not sure I'm going to let you."

"Let me?"

He stood and shucked his shirt, pants, and boxers. All the while, I watched, drinking in the hard lines of his body.

"Good girl," he said, palming his cock. "I love the way you look at me. Makes me believe that what I feel isn't one-sided. The need. The lust. The longing."

A low moan escaped me before I could stop it. It sure as hell was not one-sided.

"Look at you," he murmured as he climbed back onto the bed. "Laid out for me. I'm so fucking lucky."

He kissed his way up my torso, lavishing each of my breasts with attention.

I dug my nails into the muscles of his back, desperate to have him closer and nearly moaning again when his erection pressed against my thigh.

I needed him. I was an empty, needy mess, and the only remedy for that was to have him. To give in to the craving that had overtaken me. Only then would I feel complete.

"Please," I gasped. "I need you inside me."

He pulled back. "Okay," he whispered. "Let me get a—"

"Bare," I hissed out. "I need you bare. We're both

healthy." We'd been using condoms since that first time, but I hated it. He was Vincent's father. I was in love with him. I wanted all of him.

It was reckless. Exclusive breastfeeding was not foolproof birth control. But I couldn't find it in me to care. Being with Jasper was all that mattered. This was bigger than me and my anxieties.

"Please."

He bit down on one nipple, pulling a gasp from me, then lapped at it, easing the sting.

"You are all my fantasies come to life." He pinned my arms above my head.

"All your fantasies?" I rolled my hips, reveling in the weight of him on top of me.

He entered me slowly, then took his time setting a rhythm, his eyes closed like he was savoring the delicious friction. "Almost. Because I wish I'd been able to see you pregnant."

"Why?" I may not have known I was pregnant, but I'd felt like shit during those months, and I hadn't looked much better. I'd taken millions of vitamins and done yoga endlessly, thinking my body was falling apart.

He sped up, bottoming out inside me, causing the heat in my core to burn hotter. "The thought of you, your belly rounded and carrying my child? Fuck, Evie, it makes me so hard."

A thrill zipped through me at the admission.

"God, I'd love to walk around town, showing you off. So the whole world knew that you were well-fucked and taken care of. And I'd love taking you home just as much. So I could fuck you and care for you and satisfy every need you had."

My legs shook and I squirmed, more turned on than I'd ever been.

"You like that don't you?" he murmured against my lips. "Tell me, Evie. Tell me what turns you on."

Eyes closed, I tilted my head back. "You coming inside me."

He pushed one of my knees up, hitting me at a new angle, even deeper and harder than before, and I gasped, my vision going spotty. With him, I was consumed by a sensation I'd never wanted before. But now I didn't think I could survive without it.

Total trust. In him.

"Fuck, this won't last if you keep talking like that," he gritted out.

His heat and his words and the sound of his body against mine drove me higher, making it difficult to stay quiet.

A moan slipped free, but he quickly clamped his hand over my mouth. That move only served to make me more desperate.

"That's it," he encouraged. "You're so close. Come around my cock, Evie. I want to watch you take every inch of me as I fill you up."

When he locked eyes with me, I only soared higher, my muscles contracting, the tension coiling around me tighter.

Bracing myself, I clutched him to my chest. His bulk pinned me to the bed as he fucked into me hard and deep.

As I let go, spiraling into oblivion, I held tight to the words he whispered in my ear. "I love you. I love you. I love you."

Chapter 33

JASPER

Evie didn't let go of my hand the entire ride back to Vermont. The trip was more than five hours, with a stop in Springfield for a bathroom break, snacks, and a diaper change. Her fingers were cold, but her grip was like iron. Like she was anchoring herself to me.

We didn't speak much, and here and there she teared up, but when I'd peer over to check on her, she just squeezed my hand, her jaw set and determined.

By the time we hit highway 89, she was ready to talk. "I can't believe I said all that stuff," she whispered.

"You needed to. It was all true."

She sat quietly for a few minutes more, letting the sound of Fleetwood Mac fill the car.

"I think I realized something."

I looked over at her.

"I'm not scared of him anymore. It's a strange feeling. He holds no power over my life or my decisions. His anger doesn't hurt like it used to."

My stomach ached. How could someone be blessed with a daughter like Evie and not understand how incredible she was? My own parents would have been obsessed with her, I knew that in my bones.

"I'm proud of you. You're evolving."

"Hardly."

"Nope." I squeezed her hand. "And I'm lucky I get to be here while you do it."

A shaky laugh escaped her, soft and a bit disbelieving. "You know what's wild? When I first met you, I thought you were so ..." Her voice trailed off as she looked out the window. "Wild. Reckless. Immature."

I scoffed. "Hey. I resent that." My mouth pulled into a grin I couldn't fight. "I prefer heroic, charming, and handsome."

She nudged my shoulder and stuck her tongue out at me. Her teasing was a balm, her voice lighter than it had been in days. Hell, maybe since I'd met her.

"Let me rephrase for you. The first time you saw me, you fell a little bit in love with my rakish good looks, my bulging biceps, and my heroism."

She chuckled. "It took me a while to notice you, actually."

My face fell. Wow, that was a blow to my ego.

"No, you need to understand. I don't notice men. Especially the good-looking ones. At an early age, I learned that they have no interest in me, so I conditioned myself to have no interest in them."

I brought her knuckles to my lips and pressed a kiss to them. "I hate to break it to you, but men notice you."

She shook her head. "Not like that. Trust me, I've had

enough rejection. But I'd seen you here and there. Usually flirting, dancing, and hanging all over a pretty girl."

Oh great. Now my face was burning.

"I avoided you. Flirty guys are trouble."

I grinned. "I will neither confirm nor deny that one."

"So I assumed you were a hot fuck boy and forgot you existed."

Wow, that one hit me like an arrow straight to the chest. "Damn. You really know how to wound a man."

She patted my arm and smiled. "But at Ruby's bachelorette party, something shifted."

My heart lifted a little. Now we were getting somewhere. The vision of her in the dark room, swaying slowly to the music had been burned into my brain. The curl of her hair, the flare of her hips, the mischief in those dark eyes.

"When we talked, I felt things. When you pulled me into your arms to dance, it felt inevitable. And when you smiled at me." She closed her eyes and bit her lip. "I damn near melted."

I chuckled. This conversation had taken an excellent turn. We'd gone back to her place after, and I'd slowly peeled her clothes off, then propped her up on the counter so I could devour her.

Fuck, my jeans got tight just thinking about it.

"And what do you think now?" I asked. "Still a menace?"

She contemplated my question as we drove through town.

By the time I pulled into the driveway, she still hadn't answered.

"I think," she said as we gathered our things from the trunk, "that you are steady. And brave."

I smiled, securing Vincent's bucket seat in the crook of my elbow.

"And somehow exactly what I needed when I didn't even know I needed anything."

I opened my mouth to respond and then shut it. I had no words.

So I tilted her chin up and kissed her instead.

She wrapped her free arm around my waist. "Vincent chose well," she said into my chest.

Pain and joy and hope twisted together in my gut. "He's smarter than both of us."

"He is," she murmured. "And he loves you so much."

I swallowed hard. Every instinct inside me screamed to wrap her up, promise her I'd never let anything or anyone hurt her or Vincent again. But she didn't need promises, she needed the truth.

We carried our stuff inside, and while we got Vincent settled on his playmat, I searched for the right words. "You know." I stared at the carpet so I didn't lose my nerve. "After my parents died, I just..." My voice cracked. "I told myself I'd never have what they had. That I could never live up to them."

She sighed. "Jasper."

"I mean it. I thought I was better off as the good-time guy. The fun guy. I could be useful. Work hard. Throw myself into burning buildings because it's easier than thinking about what I lost."

She sank down next to me on the floor, wrapping her arms around me.

"You deserve everything. You are everything. To Vincent

and to me. You believe in us. Hell, you believed in me, even when I was pushing you away."

"I will always believe in you. And I'll work my ass off to be worthy of you. When you stood up to your father? You were so strong. I just—" My throat tightened. "I realized then that we're a family. You, me, and Vincent. It's us against the world."

She was crying now, happy tears as she kissed me softly. "I believe in you too," she said as her kisses turned urgent. "And I believe in us."

We kissed and kissed, clinging to one another tightly.

"I can't believe I have to go to work," I hissed, cupping her chin.

"It's going to be a long twenty-four hours." She climbed into my lap.

"But then we've got the Founder's Festival this weekend," I said. "And I'm off for two days."

I kissed her again, enjoying the tease, going slow. For so long, I'd been desperate to soak up every minute I got with this woman, never knowing when they'd run out. Now, I knew I had time. There was so much to look forward to.

"How long until you have to be at work?" she asked.

I checked my watch. "One hour."

She broke into a grin. "Good. Give me five minutes."

She picked up Vincent and Sophie the Giraffe, then hustled toward the nursery.

When she returned, she was pulling her shirt over her head.

My heart skipped a beat. "What—"

She put her fingers to her lips, then sank to her knees. "He's in his crib. We have a few minutes."

"But—" I protested, though all rational thought left me when she was half naked and this close.

"I'm not going to see you for twenty-four hours," she said, her fingers at my fly. "I need to make the most of this time."

With quick, precise movements, she pulled my aching cock out, and when she kissed the tip, my knees buckled.

I had an active imagination and had spent the better part of a year obsessing about this. Her smell, her taste, the way she glared at me when I annoyed her.

But nothing my brain could imagine came close to the sight of her on her knees for me. To the desire in those hooded dark eyes as she opened those plush pink lips and took me to the back of her throat.

I groaned, swaying a little. Fuck. *Get it together, man.* The sight of her was already awe-inspiring, but add the feel of her mouth and hands, and I was close to blacking out in seconds.

She trailed her fingers down my abs, her focus locked on my face.

Gripping me hard, she ran her tongue up my shaft.

I raked my hands through her hair and inhaled sharply.

"You like?" The playfulness in her tone gave me all kinds of dirty ideas.

"I love," I said. "But I want a turn to play."

She shook her head. "I'm in charge right now."

Before I could protest, she took me to the back of her throat again.

Head dropped back, I groaned. "You're always in charge, mama. I'm just here to do what you tell me."

She released me with a pop and smiled. "Good. Now fuck my mouth."

I damn near collapsed, but I would not disappoint my girl. If there was one thing I was good at, it was following orders.

"Anything for you," I gritted out as she worked me over. There was no more teasing, no hesitation. Just the hottest and most intense blow job of my life.

"Fuck, Evie. Your mouth." My legs shook and every muscle in my body clenched.

When she looked up at me again, that was it. The eye contact did me in. There was no going back. There was no making this last. I was powerless when it came to this woman. I'd give her anything and everything. Always.

Chapter 34

EVIE

It was hot and sticky, but Vincent was enthralled by the sights and sounds of the Founder's Festival. The event, part small-town fair, part historical reenactment, and part wild summer party, was set up on the village green and down Main Street.

It was our town's largest summer event, typically filled with tourists and locals alike. Mainly because of the historical bent. The Revolutionary War reenactors were in their glory, the elementary school was putting on the annual summer production of *Love Never Falls*, directed by Bitsy Bramble, and the vendors were selling Cora and Nathaniel–themed merch, including mugs, signature cocktails, and dish towels.

The smell of maple kettle corn and fried dough permeated the air as kids ran wild, faces painted and hopped up on maple candy and snow cones.

"My nieces are here somewhere," Jasper said, "They really want to take Vincent on the carousel."

Hand in hand, we walked toward the gazebo, where the band was warming up.

"And Opal's doing a pop-up with Nate and Reed," he went on. "Told them I'd stop by and say hello."

The line of tourists waiting to take selfies in front of the Welcome to Maplewood sign was promising. The preceding weeks had been full of hand-wringing and stress about tourism revenue, but this place was packed.

My heart warmed as I took Jasper in. Vincent was once again strapped to his chest, and the man wouldn't even let me carry the diaper backpack. As he waved and smiled at everyone we passed, one muscled, tattooed arm wrapped around our son, he was the picture-perfect dad. And when he stopped to speak to people, gently swaying to keep Vincent happy, I nearly melted.

He was gorgeous and so damn sweet. Always.

Going out like this, at an event catered to families, would have alarmed me even a month ago. Now it felt right. Comforting. This was our community. Vincent would grow up coming to the festival summer after summer.

I'd been fighting this. The domestic ease. The pull of Jasper's steadiness. But surrounded by laughter, music and sunshine, the last vestiges of that urge faded.

Just inside the beer tent, Frankie waved at us, so we pivoted and headed that way. Basil and Etienne were there too, along with Gabe, who looked particularly mayorly in his wayfarers, and Josh, who immediately jumped up to greet us.

"Evie," he teased, "I can't believe you got my little brother to trade in his turnout gear for a diaper bag."

Jasper stuck his tongue out. "I'm on shift later, so we're soaking up all the fun now. I'll get a couple of lemonades," he said, kissing my forehead. With practiced ease, he unclipped the baby carrier and passed Vincent to me. "Wait here." With that, he wandered off, Josh at his side.

I sank into an empty seat, and as I sighed, thankful for the shade, I found Frankie, Basil, and Etienne staring at me.

"He did it," Basil said. "The firefighter made a move."

My face burned.

"We need details. But"—he looked at his watch—"we've got to get back to our booth. Break's over. Tonight. Bonfire. You're gonna tell us everything."

I crossed my arms. "Only if you promise not to make it weird."

He scoffed. "Darling, you know me better than that. Gotta go. The Brie does not sell itself," he declared, looping his arm through his husband's and wandering toward their booth.

No more than twenty feet from us, Louisa stood. She was impeccably dressed in white linen and heels that managed to not sink into the grass while she chatted with Simon Hatch, who ran the chamber of commerce.

"What is she doing here?" Nora sneered as she plopped down next to me.

"Sugar Moon is a major sponsor of this event," I explained, trying to keep the irritation from my voice.

I felt for Louisa. Maplewood had adopted me the moment I'd moved here. No matter how hard I tried, I hadn't been able to escape the warm embrace of this town. Louisa had not been so lucky.

"Maybe she's trying to look innocent," Frankie scoffed.

Standing, I shot her a glare.

Wincing, she mouthed, "Sorry."

With a shake of my head, I wandered toward my boss.

Although she looked out of place among the sticky-fingered kids and men in beer logo tees, Louisa's face lit up when she saw me. "Evie," she said as I approached, her tone measured but friendly. "I didn't expect to find you amid the chaos."

I bounced Vincent on my hip. "Baby's first festival."

"He's beautiful," she gushed, squeezing his little foot. "Congratulations." Her face softened as she took him in, the cool detachment gone.

She took a step to the side, closer to another table, and picked up a paper plate weighed down by a hunk of powdered sugar–covered fried dough. The kind that left greasy fingerprints on everything it touched. "Don't tell anyone," she teased, "but I've waited all year for this."

"You eat fried dough?" The question came out a little too loud and a little too disbelieving.

"Once a year," she replied dryly. "I consider it character building."

I chuckled. "I think that makes you an honorary local."

She shook her head. "Hardly. But it's a beautiful day to indulge. Enjoy the festival."

At her parting words, I headed back toward our table. Jasper had returned with lemonades and the group was talking about the events planned for the day.

"The Maple Street Mafia is in charge of the dunk tank this year," Nora explained, "I took a photo of the posted schedule." She slid her phone across the table, and Frankie jumped to her feet.

"Gotta go." She reached into the pocket of her jean

shorts and pulled out a wad of cash. "I've been waiting for this moment."

As she stalked off, Nora shook her head. "I hope she doesn't get arrested."

We followed along, Jasper joining us, to enjoy the show over at the dunk tank. The elderly ladies had taken this from an afterthought to the highlight of the Founder's Festival, and all the money raised went toward funding after-school programs. They had filed a motion at a town meeting last winter to include it in the Maple Festival, but the hypothermia risk was too high in April around here.

Every major town figure took a turn, and as we approached we discovered why Frankie was so excited.

Sitting on the platform, in full uniform and a pair of aviator sunglasses that were frankly a little too sexy, was Police Chief Nolan Foster.

Jasper squeezed my hand as Frankie rolled her shoulders, a dangerous glint in her eye.

"Does she have a good arm?" he asked.

"She has a good everything when hurting Nolan is involved," Nora said, navigating to her phone's camera so she could capture this on video.

Her hatred of our police chief was legendary. And that sentiment was mutual. Straitlaced Nolan, who was nothing but kind and helpful to the rest of us, could barely tolerate her. No one spoke of how this happened or why, but the whole town understood how dangerous it was for the two to be in the same room.

"Sure you can see the target from down there, Dunne?" he taunted, crossing his muscular arms.

Nolan was the size of an oak tree, and Frankie was tiny.

Not that her size had ever stopped her from doing what she wanted.

"Want it lowered to the child height?" he asked.

Frankie tossed the ball up and caught it, smiling sweetly. "Save your pity, Foster. I've been hitting jerks my whole life."

She missed her first shot, earning a chorus of groans.

Nolan chuckled, only fueling Frankie more.

She rolled her shoulders, then shook out her arms. "I forgot to adjust for the size of your ego."

Her next throw hit the mark, and Nolan plunged into the water. The crowd went wild, clapping and cheering as Frankie blew kisses and posed for photos.

Nolan climbed back up, dripping but still smirking, readjusting his sunglasses. "That all you've got? Grandma Olive throws harder."

Olive, who was collecting money for the dunk tank, turned to Frankie. "Soak him, dear. You get an extra throw for free."

She held out two more balls to my friend.

"I'm just getting started." Frankie wound up and hit the target square on. "Consider this community service." As Nolan went down, she yelled, "The badge doesn't make you waterproof."

He stood up and shook his hair out like a guy in a cologne commercial. "Still not afraid of you, Dunne."

"You should be," she hissed. "I've got a pocketful of dollar bills and a heart full of rage."

The second he was settled on the platform, she hit the target again, sending him plunging in for a third time.

While the crowd was laughing and taking photos, the

two of them glared at each other, tension sparking between them. Whatever history they shared, it was a hell of a lot more than just gossip.

Eventually, Jasper and I met up with his family and stuffed ourselves with junk food. I'd been attending town festivals since I moved to Maplewood, since as a citizen, it was required, but I'd never had quite this much fun. And I'd never chatted with so many people or stayed for so long. I'd been content here for two years, but only now did I really feel like I belonged.

Vincent loved the carousel, and I snapped photos of him in Jasper's arms. They were sitting atop a sparkly pink horse, in one of the fancy seats, and my sweet boy was smiling with his cousins.

In the last four months, I'd taken an embarrassing number of photos. I had basically become a paparazzo.

After the carousel, we sat at the back of the audience, watching the pie eating competition while I fed Vincent. He conked out in his stroller immediately after, and we wandered toward the gazebo, where the live music was set up.

As we listened, Jasper tucked an errant strand of hair behind my ear and moved in close.

"He's got your smile," he said. "I've thought it for a while, but these seven hundred photos confirm it."

"Poor kid," I replied.

With a shake of his head, he kissed me, then draped his arm around my shoulder. While we watched the band, I waved to Callie, who was standing with Josh and Jess, scanning the crowd, probably looking for her twins, who very well could have run off and hijacked a parade float by now.

It hit me then, how many of my friends were here. How this place had really become my home.

And I was happy. Ridiculously so. The kind of happy that puts down roots in a person's bones and blossoms.

With Jasper at my side, our baby asleep in his stroller in front of me, and a mild evening summer breeze wafting over us, I was at peace.

My mind wandered, so between that and the noise of the band, I didn't hear the sirens or notice the uniformed officers walking across the green until Chief Nolan Foster strode toward us in a clean, dry uniform, his hand on his gun at his hip and wearing a grim look on his face.

My breath caught and my mind whirled with confusion as he stopped in front of Louisa, who was standing with Marigold Shaw and Bitsy Bramble, a cloth tote bursting at the seams with purchases hanging from her arm.

From here, I couldn't make out his words or see what was printed on the paper he showed her, but the way she stiffened was obvious.

Once I confirmed that Jasper had a hand on Vincent's stroller, I strode toward them, my heart rate picking up.

"Nolan," she said, her tone sharp, "this is an overreach."

As he took her by the elbow, the murmur of the crowd became a buzz, then a roar. People all over had pulled their phones out and were recording the encounter.

With dread growing in my stomach, I moved closer, but quickly, a hand grasped my elbow, stopping me.

I whirled around, finding Jasper, along with the stroller. He pulled me behind him, then stepped in front of Vincent, instinctively protecting us.

Just as I opened my mouth to shout, to demand to know what was going on, Vincent cried out.

Heart lurching, I scooped him up, shushing him. The sirens and crowd noise must have woken him.

When I turned back, Louisa, icy and composed as always, was being led into a waiting police cruiser.

I gasped. "Are they arresting her?"

Josh, who'd suddenly appeared at his brother's side, tapped furiously at his phone's screen. "I'm texting Gabe. What the hell could she have done?"

Chapter 35

JASPER

Once the cruiser pulled out, we loaded Vincent in his stroller and walked to Evie's house as quickly as we could.

She was stunned. Shaken and confused. She didn't speak the whole way home. Inside, I went straight to the bathroom to run water for Vincent's bath.

"They arrested her," she said as I came out to take him from her. Her expression was blank, like she'd drifted elsewhere. "Just walked right up and took her away. A few hours earlier, she was cooing at Vincent and we were talking about fried dough."

"We'll figure this out. I'll call Gabe." My mind raced. I knew nothing about Louisa Meyer other than that she owned the company Evie worked for. And although she wasn't well-liked in town as a citizen, she was respected as a business leader and was generous to our community.

She frowned, her lips trembling. "Do you think it's related to...?"

I shook my head. It couldn't be. Whatever had happened to Will was dark and dangerous. Bad guys and deals gone wrong. I couldn't imagine a forty-something CEO doing that to him.

"If the CEO of the biggest employer in town can be hauled off like that, what does it mean for the rest of us?" she whispered. "For the employees and the farmers and the town?"

I wanted to tell her it would be fine, that it had to be a misunderstanding. That the town wasn't unraveling at the seams. But I didn't make promises I couldn't keep. So instead, I went with the truth. "I don't know. But you're amazing and brilliant. Regardless of what happens, you will land on your feet. And I'm here to help. Always."

She looked up at me, her face so beautiful, her expression earnest. "Is that what you think? That I always land on my feet?" Her lips trembled then, her confidence slipping. Worry and exhaustion were taking over, along with the fierce sense of responsibility she carried for everyone but herself.

I clasped her hand, giving it a squeeze. Then I kissed the inside of her wrist. Damn, I wished I could fix it. Take away all her stress and worries. But Evie didn't need me to step in and solve her problems. She needed me to stand by her side while she handled them herself. "There is nothing you can't do."

Together we bathed Vincent, and while she fed him and rocked him to sleep, I did a load of laundry. As we stood side by side over his crib, watching the rise and fall of his little chest, she grabbed my hand again.

"This town," she whispered. "I really thought it was perfect. My home. But then this happened. I want to raise him somewhere safe. Give him that magical kind of childhood."

That sensation tugged at my chest again. The one that had taken up residence, like a second heartbeat. The constant urge to protect them. My family. I hugged and kissed her forehead.

"Come on. I'll make dinner. Then we can make some calls, see what we can learn."

I had no answers. I had no reassurance. Nothing had been the same since Will's murder. The entire town had changed, and who knew how deep all this ran. All I could do was protect my family. Evie and Vincent. Give them everything I had and hope for the best.

"What if..." She turned and ran her hands up my chest. "What if I want to be distracted for a bit?"

I sighed, considering what kinds of activities would help her manage this anxiety. "Do you want to play Scrabble?" I whispered. "Or watch that Martha Stewart documentary on Netflix?"

She tipped her head and bit her lip, her eyes flashing even in the dark. "Jasper," she teased. "I'm talking about a naked distraction."

It took a minute to register in my brain. I was deep in problem-solving protector mode. So when she turned around, threaded her arms around my neck and pulled me down for a kiss, I was a bit confused.

"I don't want to think right now," she said, her hand resting on the waistband of my pants.

I tilted her chin up, kissing her again. If my girl wanted distraction, I would deliver. Anything. Anytime.

"Tell me," I murmured, my lips brushing her neck. "What does my girl want?"

She whimpered, her body shuddering

I was already rock hard, desperate to feel all of her.

"My tongue?" I teased, gently biting along her jawline. God, I want to taste her. To spread her wide right here on the floor and make a meal of her. "My fingers?" I asked, my hand snaking up the back of her shirt to the clasp of her bra.

"Actually," she breathed. "I had this dream."

I paused, my hand pressed against her spine. "You had a dream?"

With her lip caught between her teeth, she nodded. Then she tugged her shirt over her head.

As her glorious tits came into view, I momentarily lost my train of thought. Fuck it was impossible to keep my hands off them.

"I had a sexy dream," she admitted as I palmed one breast. "A few nights ago."

"You had a sexy dream and didn't tell me immediately?"

"You were at the firehouse."

"You should have called 911." I took one nipple into my mouth. "Had dispatch send me over so I could hear all about it in real time."

She groaned, her head dropped back. "That seems like a poor use of public resources."

I eased her panties down, my fingers trailing over her hips. "Don't care. Now tell me everything."

Kneeling in front of her, I pushed her panties and shorts all the way to the floor and nipped at her inner thighs. "I'm waiting." Brows lifted, I peered up at her.

Her face was pink and her breathing shallow. "I dreamed

you bent me over the couch. It was hard and fast and dirty and I—"

I slipped one finger inside her, and she moaned, the sound low and drawn out. Fuck, she was already soaked.

"You want me to bend you over the couch and fuck you from behind?" I found her clit and rubbed a circle around it.

In answer, she threw her head back.

"What was that?" I teased.

"Yes," she cried. "Please."

Holy. Hell. She was shaking and trembling and detailing a sex dream to me. What had I done to deserve this incredible woman?

"Anything." I scooped her up and carried her to the couch, marveling at how fucking gorgeous she looked naked and in my arms. "I will do anything for you. Anytime. Anywhere."

With an arm looped around my neck, she kissed me.

I was on top of the fucking world. Taking care of Evie, being the man she depended on was the most exhilarating thing I'd ever experienced. And I'd never do anything to hurt her.

Chapter 36

EVIE

I had no idea a family trip to Costmart could be so much fun.

We'd piled into the car, eager to escape the drama of the day before, and headed out of town, despite the rain. My phone had been blowing up nonstop with texts and calls from my coworkers. No one had heard anything more. We didn't even know if Louisa had been arrested or if the encounter had been related to Will's murder.

My stomach had churned all morning.

When Jasper had suggested taking a ride to Costmart to stock up on diapers and pick out a few new outfits for our little meatball of a baby, I jumped at the opportunity.

It had never occurred to me that a mundane task like picking up necessities with the person I loved could be so cozy and fun. Arguing over the playlist on the drive and pushing the cart around the store? More enjoyable than I could have imagined. And that was before we freaked out over all the infant Halloween costumes on display.

I was giddy the whole way home. Jasper's trunk was stuffed full. We'd even picked out a highchair, since we'd started dabbling in solid foods. It felt like a massive new mom milestone.

As we pulled into my driveway, I couldn't help but grin at Jasper.

Dimple popping, he tucked a lock of hair behind my ear.

I was instantly consumed by a wave of peace. Safety and contentment had somehow become my companions, and I hadn't really noticed until now. Was this what I had been missing my entire life? This feeling, the ease that came with knowing that I wasn't in it alone?

He leaned in to kiss me, but I pulled back before he could. We'd been snacking on kettle corn, and I was certain I had a piece stuck between my teeth. Still grinning at him, I flipped down the visor to check myself in the mirror.

As I turned toward it, a dark brown folder slid out, startling me, and landed in my lap. I picked it up to put it back but froze when the words typed on the label at the top registered. *Evangelina Marino and Vincent Marino.*

My stomach dropped and my vision went a little blurry, but I blinked rapidly, clearing it, and opened the folder.

Jasper tensed. "Evie, wait—"

Ignoring him, I pulled out a stack of neatly organized papers.

The first line of the first page caused bile to rise in my throat.

Petition for a Paternity Test?

The next was labeled Sample Parenting Plan.

Then Custody Agreement Draft and Child Support Calculation Guidelines.

Despite the heat outside, the temperature in the car plummeted. The only sound was the pounding of my pulse and the rustling of the papers.

A rush of humiliation flooded me, and my eyes filled with tears. Dropping the documents, I covered my face.

How could I have been so naïve? I thought he loved me. That what we had was real. That we'd bonded and grown. That we were doing life together.

"Evie," he rasped. "Let me explain."

I dropped my hands and turned to him, red crowding my vision. "Was all this part of the plan?" I unbuckled my seat belt and shifted, needing to put distance between myself and this man. "Was all this"—I gestured between us—"just a legal strategy? Make me comfortable so you can catch me off guard and take my son from me?"

Without waiting for him to respond, I threw the door open and climbed out, then I unhooked Vincent's car seat from its base with a violent jerk.

The sharp movement startled him awake, and he wailed.

Dammit. I really was a shit mom.

Jasper had already rounded the car and was standing next to me as I fumbled to put Vincent's binkie in his mouth.

"Nothing has been filed," he said. "Gabe and Brian drafted those for me weeks ago. I forgot they were even there."

I shook my head. A person didn't draw up legal paperwork to litigate the well-being of their infant casually and then forget about it.

I'd foolishly trusted him. And here he was, making choices for me, not with me.

"You know me better than that," he pleaded. "Have I

ever done anything to jeopardize Vincent's well-being? Or yours?"

"It's hard to say when I don't really even know you." My stomach churned. "You slept in my yard for months and have been sleeping in my bed for weeks, but we're still practically strangers. This is a messy situation filled with too many unanswered questions."

He stepped closer and crossed his arms over his chest. "Ask me anything. I'm an open book."

"What are we even doing?" Tears streamed down my face. Shit. Crying was the fastest way to lose an argument, but I couldn't help myself. "This feels temporary."

He reeled back like he had been hit. "Nothing about my feelings for you or Vincent are temporary," he said, his voice a low growl. "You asked to go slow. You kept demanding space. I gave it to you. You were the one with the trust issues."

My stomach twisted. He wasn't wrong. It had been me. I was the problem. Always had been.

"And you can't blame me for exploring my legal rights," he tacked on. "In the early stages, you could barely even stand to let me inside your home."

His sudden anger was unnerving. Jasper was always so calm and easygoing, yet in a matter of seconds, he was close to yelling.

"Custody has always been the elephant in the room," he said, his shoulders deflating. "These are standard things. Look them over if you like. If you do, you'll see that this isn't an ambush. I'm not trying to take Vincent from you."

My hands shook and my heart raced. Those papers, which, admitted, I'd only skimmed, were proof that it was possible for Jasper to take Vincent. And I wouldn't survive it if he did.

"I think you should go back to the farm," I said, willing my tears to stop.

"I'm his dad," he gritted out. "I deserve to be here. But that's not why I stayed. I stayed because I love you both."

Eyes closed, I racked my brain for a way to make him understand my concerns. But the adrenaline flowing through my veins had made rational thought impossible. I needed space. I needed to think. But I couldn't do that with him standing here, looking at me with kindness I wasn't sure I deserved.

My fears were ruining everything. Just like they always had. I wanted to believe him. I wanted to ask him to stay. To sit down and calmly discuss this like rational, mature adults. But that wasn't possible right now.

"Jasper," I said coldly. "We have a lot to discuss. But I'm hurt, and it's hard for me to find the right words. The thought that you could take him from me? I can't explain how badly it terrifies me. And for now, I need to be alone so I can get a handle on all of this."

He dropped his head, lacing his fingers at his nape. "I understand," he murmured. "I'll be back in the morning to stay with Vincent while you go to the office."

My chest tightened. I appreciated those words more than he knew. After the police had showed up for Louisa and had taken her away, I didn't know what to expect. And I had to be at work to talk to the board. I had to check in with several teams and try to figure out this mess.

Jasper spent Mondays with Vincent, which meant I

didn't have to stress about daycare pickup times, allowing me to start the week off strong.

He crouched and kissed Vincent's forehead, then ran his fingers over his cheek. "I'll see you tomorrow, bud," he said. Without looking at me, he popped the trunk and started unloading the things we'd bought.

He set the bags on the porch, all without saying a word, while I remained where I was, frozen in the middle of the driveway.

As he drove away, I couldn't take my eyes off his car, even as my vision blurred and my heart cracked in two.

Hours later, as I cleaned up Vincent's toys and put all his new belongings away, a thought niggled at the back of my brain. I tried to ignore it, even focusing on what I had to do tomorrow, but it wouldn't leave me alone. Because maybe I wasn't scared of losing Vincent. Maybe my real fear was what it would mean if I let Jasper stay.

Chapter 37

JASPER

Sleeping in my room in the farmhouse was the worst kind of torture. I should have been snuggled up with Evie. I should have been prepared to get up to change Vincent's diapers and rock him back to sleep.

Instead, I tossed and turned, cursing myself and the universe. Hours ago, I'd had everything I'd ever wanted, but I'd managed to lose it all in the blink of an eye.

My only solace was knowing how rational Evie was. It gave me hope that once she cooled down, we could talk through this. But between the encounter with her dad and then her boss's arrest, she'd been strung tight lately.

All my life, I'd calmly navigated chaos, making thoughtful choices and avoiding danger. I'd seen enough flames to know when a situation was out of control. I'd been slowly building a foundation with Evie, and somehow, I'd dumped a whole bucket of gasoline on it and struck a match.

But Josh's words echoed in my mind. I was Vincent's

father. I had rights, and sometimes the best thing for a child was establishing clear expectations.

But Evie hadn't let me explain.

The following morning, I drove into town to pick up Vincent, desperately hoping Evie would be willing to talk. But I found her frazzled and rushing, stressed about getting to the office to deal with the fallout of this weekend. So far, we hadn't heard anything about Louisa's arrest, and I could only imagine how messy things were. Evie didn't usually leave this early, but I couldn't blame her today.

She thrust the cooler of breast milk into my chest, barely looking at me as I assured her that Vincent could hang with me for as long as she needed. She didn't look angry anymore, just tired and resigned.

My stomach clenched. I'd rather have her yelling at me than looking so defeated.

My little guy was dressed in a green onesie and matching shorts today, gumming on that damn giraffe. At least he could lift my spirits a little. I'd soak up every minute with him I could.

"We'll be at the farm for a bit," I explained. "Josh has set up a meeting to discuss…" I trailed off. She knew what I meant. The Sugar Moon mess. It was getting more complex every day.

In the car, I adjusted the vents to blow cold air in my face, needing something sharp and real to cut through the noise in my head.

Louisa's arrest had hit Maplewood like a thunderclap. The town Facebook group had been flooded with questions and rumors, and every wannabe TikTok true crime expert had a theory. They varied between corporate embezzlement, contamination, and sabotage. But all I could think about was Evie's face last night, pale and hurt as she held the papers in her shaking hands.

Gabe and Brian had pushed them on me for protection. A safety net. Not a threat or a weapon against Evie. They meant well, but I hadn't even read them. All I wanted was to be with Vincent, this small, astonishing person who had changed my life.

But now Evie regarded me as the enemy.

I had pushed too hard. I'd wanted too much too fast. But I didn't want to be a visitor in my child's life. I wanted to be the kind of father my dad had been. Steady, available, helpful. The kind who showed up and had a secret candy stash specifically for the bad days. The kind who would sit for hours helping me master long division.

I wanted Evie to see me as a partner, not a mistake that kept showing up with good intentions.

Evie. I was in love with her, but now she was doubting that.

Over the past few months, she's slowly revealed parts of herself she kept hidden from the rest of the world. She laughed without censoring herself, and she shared her most vulnerable parts with me. After her encounter with her dad, I had a new appreciation for her strength. She'd built a life for herself and had been surviving alone. But then she'd let me in, and that meant rewriting the story she'd used to keep herself safe.

Every time I looked at the two of them, I felt like a man standing inside a house I hadn't built but wanted to protect anyway. They were my people. Now I needed to find a way to make her understand that.

The driveway was full of vehicles by the time we arrived. Thank God Josh had upgraded the HVAC and installed central air. The humidity was already crushing, and my shirt was already stuck to my chest.

With one arm hooked under the handle of Vincent's bucket seat and his diaper bag slung over my other shoulder, I marched toward the kitchen. With any luck, someone inside had details about what had gone down at the festival. Whatever was happening, it was better to know.

Inside, the low murmur of voices hit me first. Then the sharp smell of coffee. Wayne appeared, tail wagging, and I bent to scratch his ears.

In the kitchen, Josh sat at the head of the table, shoulders squared, jaw clenched. Gabe was seated next to him with a dozen or so documents spread out between them. From here, it looked like delivery logs, order forms, and invoices.

Brian and Jess were on the other side of the table, Brian typing furiously on his laptop.

Jenn hovered by the sink, drying a mug absentmindedly. Her curls were piled on top of her head and she had an apron on, like she'd come here straight from the café.

I eased Vincent's car seat onto the island and freed him from it. With him propped on my hip, I leaned against the counter and took in the scene in front of me.

"We need to steer clear of Sugar Moon," Brian advised. "Their counsel has already called me twice this morning, insisting the arrest of Louisa Meyer was a misunderstanding. He seems convinced that we have evidence of some kind—"

"The feds are sniffing around," Gabe added. "They asked for a meeting at city hall this week. And rumor is that the Department of Agriculture is showing up for farm inspections early."

Josh stiffened, his already hard face going stony. My brother was not a big fan of regulators. They'd given him the runaround when he'd taken over and combined the farms. If they showed up for a surprise inspection? It would not be pretty.

"The feds are looking at anyone with a connection to Will as well as Sugar Moon," Gabe said, his focus fixed on his own laptop. "Anything he handled. Anyone he met with. And the shipments."

Josh's lips thinned. "The shipments were cleared. The dates match, the quantities—"

"It's the signatures." Gabe nodded at Brian. "They're the problem."

As Brian turned his computer toward Josh, I rounded the table so I could see the screen.

"We've been going through all the records. See this one?" Brian asked. "Signed J. Lawrence. And it's not the only one."

Josh shook his head sharply. "That's not my signature."

All eyes turned to me next.

"I don't sign off on anything," I said, "I'm barely around."

"I know." Josh sighed. "That's the damn point. Someone used our name. Or worse. Are these even legitimate invoices?"

Jenn set her mug down too hard, starling everyone. "Did we do something illegal?"

"Not yet," Gabe said.

Brian sighed. "The aggressive emails from Sugar Moon's legal team aren't helping."

Josh grunted. "And those fuckers at Evergreen are sniffing around again."

Pinching the bridge of his nose, Gabe groaned. "They can smell blood in the water."

Over the years, Evergreen, a big ag company in the area, had made several offers for our land. They seemed to be buying up all the mature maple stands in the region. Why, I had no idea. But our trees were not for sale.

And these corporate fuckers did not like hearing the word no.

"So it's fraud?" Jess asked.

Gabe shook his head. "We don't know. Could be simple errors."

"Simple errors happening again and again? No," Josh snapped. "We do not make paperwork errors."

I believed him. My brother was meticulous. A person doesn't make as much money on Wall Street as he did without superhuman-level attention to detail.

He buried his head in his hands. "Are we being set up?"

I pulled up a chair next to Brian and passed Vincent to Jess. Then I leaned in, studying the documents.

They looked like our standard records, the familiar columns consisting of dates, gallons, IDs, and time stamps. Except the tiny handwritten initials. The unfamiliar "J. Lawrence."

It made my stomach clench.

Josh dropped his hands and straightened, looking older and more tired than I'd ever seen him. "I should have triple-checked everything. And I shouldn't have trusted the seasonal help."

"That isn't realistic. This isn't on you," Jenn insisted.

"You've been killing yourself keeping this place running. We know what you do for us."

Josh dipped his chin.

He'd taken all of this on. Continuing the family legacy, caring for our childhood home, integrating Ed and Suzie's farm. And he'd made it profitable. He'd made sure each of us was a shareholder, that we all received a portion of the income, and he worked seven days a week to ensure things never got off track.

"Our name is on every barrel. My signature on every paycheck. This is my fuckup." He admitted.

Outside, a tractor rumbled past, only punctuating the stunned silence in the room.

Vincent fussed in Jess's arms, so I hopped up and dug out a bag of milk so I could make a bottle for him.

Gabe tapped the papers in front of him. "We don't have all the information yet." He took a deep breath. "But keep your mouths shut. No statements, on or off the record. No gossip. We'll gather our intel, cooperate with authorities, and ignore all the noise."

"Easy for you to say, Mr. Mayor," Jenn hissed. "You're not the one making latte art while the people in line whisper about your murderous family."

Bottle ready, I frowned at my oldest sister. "Who is saying that?"

She shook her head.

"The town is turning on itself," Gabe grumbled. "I thought things were improving. The Founder's Festival brought in a decent number of people, and it seemed like a success."

Josh huffed. "Until the CEO of the state's largest maple syrup plant was arrested in the middle of it."

"Now it's open season. Bitsy Bramble is probably texting her Maple Street Mafia counterparts about this. That woman can smell scandal like syrup boiling over."

More than one brief, humorless laugh echoed through the room.

"Let me help." I took Vincent from Jess and cradled him, offering him the bottle. "I'll talk to the guys at the firehouse. There has been so much chatter about unmarked trucks, weird anomalies with farms, and that concentrate—"'"

Gabe stood up. "Stop," he gritted out. "No off the books heroics. We'll cooperate in official investigations only."

"What concentrate?" Jenn asked.

Josh picked up the stack of papers and tapped them against the table, straightening them with a little too much force. "Evergreen's super product. The green fertilizer. We don't use it. I told the sales rep to fuck off when he suggested we could increase our yields with his bullshit."

I'd seen the Evergreen label on a rusted barrel a few weeks ago during a call out to the Jaffrey farm. The product was BGX-9. Not that it mattered, since we didn't use it.

Josh pushed his chair back, the legs scraping against the hardwood. "I'm already behind."

Brian nodded at Gabe, though he didn't stop typing. Luckily, he and Jess and the girls were here for a little longer before school started again. His presence would be helpful during this bullshit, and he had a way of using logic to keep people from getting worked up. He wouldn't lead us astray.

The meeting dissolved. Papers were stacked, chairs scraped across the floor, and half the group took off. Gabe back to the office. Jenn to the café. Josh stomped out toward the barn, whistling for Wayne, who was probably off traumatizing the chickens.

Jess played with Vincent while I drank a cup of coffee, considering the red wooden sign at the end of the drive. The one that had been there all my life.

Lawrence Farm. Established 1948.

And for the first time, I was scared of what that sign might cost us all.

Chapter 38

JASPER

Vincent and I were nearly back to Evie's house after our walk around town, and he was happily snoozing in his stroller when a prickle of awareness rose on my neck.

On instinct, I checked my phone. Nothing.

I sped up, ignoring the way my T-shirt clung to my skin, eager to get my little guy back into the air conditioning. But the strange sensation wouldn't leave me.

Evie wouldn't be home until seven, so Vincent and I had plenty of time to relax first. Maybe I'd make dinner, soften her up a little so she'd be willing to talk.

My hackles rose again, and a heartbeat later, sirens blared distantly. My muscles tensed as the sound got louder. I was not on duty, but my body responded automatically, ready to handle a crisis.

There were three distinct sirens. The ladder and the ambulance and what I assumed was a police car. Shit, this was serious.

I broke into a jog past Evie's neighbor's house and steered the stroller to my car so I could get my radio.

I fumbled with the door, and as I yanked it open, the device squawked. "Dispatch to engine one. What is your ETA to Sugar Moon?"

"Four minutes. What do you know?"

I pushed the stroller onto the lawn and unlatched Vincent's bucket, then pressed the button on the side of my radio.

"Lawrence to dispatch. Please report."

"Dispatch to Lawrence. Structure fire at Sugar Moon Syrup. Heavy smoke reported from the office building."

My heart dropped, and my knees almost gave out.

Evie.

In a matter of seconds, I had Vincent's seat latched into my car and was backing out of the driveway. As I headed toward town, I dialed Josh.

"Fire at Sugar Moon," I blurted as dispatch continued to speak, sending out more units.

Shit. They were sending everything we had. This was no small fire.

"Meet me there," I practically yelled. "You need to take Vincent."

"Done," Josh said. "I'll be there in five."

There was a good chance the fire was nowhere near Evie, since the campus was spread out and consisted of several buildings, but I wasn't going to risk it.

My heart hammered as I maneuvered the country roads, keeping to the speed limit, conscious of my sleeping baby boy in the back seat.

"Two-story corporate office building," Dispatch

explained. "Production facility is separate but attached. High secondary fire risk."

Shit. The sugar in the production facility was extremely combustible. If the fire spread, this could be catastrophic.

I pulled into the parking lot and parked far from the chaos. The engine was positioned near the hydrant, and Walters was already dragging the attack lines into position. The Birch Hollow ambulance was here, along with ours, meaning they'd already called in reinforcements.

With a deep breath in, I pushed my door open and strode to the trunk, where I pulled out my personal turnout gear. I had the basics on me at all times. Every rural first responder did.

I was still getting dressed when Josh jogged over.

"The employees are gathering on the west side," he said, ducking into the car to unlatch Vincent's seat.

"You got him?" I asked, zipping up my turnout coat.

He nodded. "We'll stay back. I'll keep him safe."

With a nod, I plucked my boots out of the trunk. I set them up so I could step in, making a mental note to grab a spare SCBA off the engine.

Gloves and helmet on, flashlight and Halligan tool ready, I slammed my trunk.

"Be careful," Josh warned.

"You know me." I backed away, giving him a grin. "I'm never careful."

Chief, who was already wearing her orange incident commander vest and was barking instructions into the radio, had established a command post. I fixed my own radio to my shoulder and turned it to our channel as I scanned the sea of people, searching for Evie.

"Lawrence," Chief yelled when I approached. "You're off shift. Stand down."

Ignoring her, I headed for the storage compartment on the engine and plucked a SCBA out.

"The interior teams are making a sweep," she said.

I searched the crowd of people on the west side of the building again. Still no Evie. "Are those all the employees?" I asked.

Chief glared at me. "Yes. The manufacturing plant evacuated to the south parking lot. But those are the office employees. All accounted for except one female."

Stomach sinking, I strode toward the crowd, studying every face.

"I told you," Chief called. "Team two is doing a sweep."

I shook my head. I couldn't stop until I laid eyes on her. When I caught sight of Gerry, I headed straight for him. He was annoying at work, according to Evie, but he was a decent poker player.

"Where is she?" I asked as I approached.

Shaking, he blinked at me. "Evie? Not sure. After our team meeting, she left. Said she'd be back. But then the smoke alarms went off."

My brain whirled. She left? To go where? Her car was over by the Birch Hollow ambulance, so I couldn't imagine she'd left the facility completely.

It hit me then. She was pumping. In the windowless closet with the door that sticks.

Fuck.

Heart in my throat, I broke into a sprint toward the main door. Halfway there, I pressed the button on the side of the mic connected to my radio. "Team four entering the west corridor. Possible trapped victim, copy?"

"Stand down, Lawrence," the chief responded.

I ignored her. I was breaking every protocol in the book and I'd probably be suspended, but if Evie had gone to pump, there was a real possibility she was trapped. The heat from the fire would only make the old door swell more, and if the other teams didn't know where to look, it wasn't likely they'd find her in time.

Inside, I had zero visibility. With my supplemental oxygen flowing, the mechanical sound of my breathing grounded me. I focused on the rhythm as I navigated the building.

Crouching low, I brought my right hand to the wall, using it to keep myself going the correct way, then headed toward the marketing department.

"Evie," I shouted. "Call out."

The radio crackled, the sound nearly ear-piercing. "Primary search—first floor clear." Martin's voice was confident and smooth. I'd always been just as levelheaded, focusing on the emergency and tuning out the noise. But knowing there was a good chance Evie was here, I couldn't access my calm.

The exit signs flickered as I crawled toward the back hallway, past the open-plan offices, dodging falling ceiling tiles, my flashlight keeping me steady.

"*Evie,*" I shouted again as I passed the maze of cubicles.

She'd looked so damn pretty a few weeks back when Vincent and I had shown up here to surprise her. Her cheeks had flushed when she saw us, making her glow.

"Primary search," Martin said. "Office side clear."

"Pull back," Chief commanded. "Heavy fire overhead."

Keeping pace, I moved toward the doors lining the back corridor. As I approached each one, I tested the knobs with a gloved hand. The first opened into bathroom. The second was filled with files.

The smoke thickened as I reached the back of the hallway, the air no doubt acrid and full of plastic and insulation fumes. If not for my SCBA, my lungs would be burning. At the last door, I grasped the knob and pushed, but it didn't budge.

Shit, this had to be it.

"*Evie*," I screamed, banging on the door.

A faint cry sounded on the other side.

"Victim located," I radioed. "Southeast corner. Breaching the door now."

Halligan in hand, adrenaline pumping through me, I stood. I used the tool to pop the latch of the door. once, then twice. With a third blow, I had it. The door was still stuck, but I put all my weight into it, ramming it with my shoulder. It was swollen badly, but I wouldn't give up. Eventually it groaned and smoke poured out.

Quickly I dropped low and swept the room with my flashlight.

When the beam passed over a figure, my stomach lurched.

There she was. In the corner on the ground, fallen ceiling tiles piled up between us. She was crumpled against the far wall, one arm overhead, her eyes open but glassy.

She didn't move, as if she couldn't see me or wasn't with it enough to register what was happening. As I crawled to her, she coughed and gasped.

The sound made my already racing heart take off even

faster. It would take time to get out of the building, so I had to be strategic about my exit plan.

"Hey, I've got you." I removed my glove and pressed two fingers to her neck, searching for her pulse. It was thready, but she was okay. For now.

Her lips moved, like she was speaking to me.

"Don't talk," I commanded.

A firefighter should never remove their mask. That was the first rule of the trade. Especially in a structure fire. Because I couldn't save anyone if I couldn't breathe.

But this was not a normal fire. Nor was it a normal rescue. And it gutted me, watching her struggle for air.

So I briefly removed my respirator and fit it over her face. Then I thumbed the purge valve so fresh air hissed into her lungs.

Hot smoke clawed at my throat instantly, making my eyes water, and I was hit with the uncontrollable urge to cough. I quickly reined it in, then showed her how to hold her breath, encouraging her to do the same.

Her eyes widened and her muscles tensed. She was terrified, but at least she was coming back to me.

"Lawrence, this is command. Report."

"With victim. Southeast office area closet," I coughed out. "Request backup for extraction."

"Command copies, en route. Clear a path."

I showed her how to take shallow breaths of the smoky air to minimize coughing, then gestured to the door.

I took another hit from the respirator and had her do the same. Then with it back in place, I crouched low, hooked my arms under her shoulders, and dragged her. Every few feet, I stopped to give her a hit off my respirator, then moved as quickly and safely as I could.

As I slowly headed back the way I came, I kept my attention on her while also reading the fire as best as I could, noting the hisses of air, the pops of the joists, and the screams of the alarms in the distance.

We were about thirty feet from the exit when my teammates found us.

"This is command. Ceiling collapse. South hallway. Get them out now."

"Got her," Polanski shouted, taking Evie from me. He continued dragging her toward the doorway while Olsen pulled me along.

"He's got her," someone yelled from outside. "Move that line."

Finally, we exited, and I tore my helmet and mask off, choking, my eyes streaming with tears as cool air slapped me in the face.

The radio crackled. One of the guys on my crew hauled me up. My vision was blurred, my ability to process hampered by all the coughing.

"Victim recovered. Extraction team is out. EMS, take over."

I was lowered to the asphalt again. On my hands and knees, I coughed, my ribs screaming in pain.

Through the haze, I could see an ambulance. The medics were there. With Evie on a stretcher and an oxygen mask on her face.

Awake. Alive.

Chapter 39

EVIE

The monitors hummed, one beeping steadily as Jasper's chest rose and fell rhythmically. He looked wrong in the hospital bed, too pale against the sheets, too frail with an oxygen cannula taped under his nose and the IV snaking into the back of his hand.

His eyelashes were clumped with soot, his skin streaked black.

I lingered in the doorway in my borrowed hospital scrubs, my hair still smelling like smoke, my heart filled with so much love for this man. But also rage. White-hot rage.

The swollen door had actually helped keep some of the smoke and soot out of my tiny nursing room, so I'd only suffered minor smoke inhalation. Jasper seemed to have taken on more.

Josh sat near his brother's bed, while Jess, who'd shown up shortly after we arrived, rocked Vincent in my hospital room.

"How's he doing?" I asked Josh as he stood and shuffled my way.

"Dangerously high carbon monoxide levels and mild burns in his airway." He shook his head.

"I'm so sorry," I murmured. "He kept giving me the mask."

I'd replayed the moment over and over. The door bursting open. His voice cutting through the fire, the hiss of air when he pressed that mask over my face. He could have died in there.

For me. To save me.

He stirred, coughing gently, snagging our attention. Josh frowned in concern and rushed to his bed.

I followed, and the two of us helped him sit up, adjusting the hospital bed. Then I held a cup of water to his lips.

He looked at me, his eyes bloodshot. "You're okay." It wasn't a question, but a statement.

I blinked back tears. "I should smack you."

Josh flinched, but Jasper only laughed.

My chest pinched as I scanned him. "You took off your mask."

He shrugged, slowly taking another sip of water.

"And you went into a fire against the order of your commander."

He only blinked at me, unapologetic. "I'll talk to the chief," he said, voice like sandpaper. "She's used to me being a pain in her ass." Turning, he frowned at his brother. "Vincent?"

"He's with Jess. We've been here with him the whole time. Should I get him?"

Jasper nodded, coughing again.

"You scared the shit out of me," I said as tears slipped down my cheeks.

Face crumpling, he grasped my hand. "Sorry."

"And you shared your air with me." A sob escaped me. "You could've—" I shook my head, unable to finish the sentence. "Vincent needs his parents."

"I'd do it again," he rasped, bringing my knuckles to his lips.

The words landed heavily, like a weight settling on my shoulders.

I ducked, my throat tightening, and focused on breathing, trying to collect myself. The monitor ticked between us, slow and steady, and the world narrowed to just this room while we silently processed what we'd been through.

Before long, Jasper's hospital room was crowded. Josh returned with Vincent and Jess, and before long, Jenn showed up. Frankie too. She quickly took on the role of bouncer, keeping all the well-meaning townspeople from entering. Jess fussed, Jenn interrogated the hospital staff, and Josh paced, texting furiously.

The love in the room was palpable. It filled every inch of space. This was what family did. They cared and supported. They showed up.

I snuggled Vincent closer, my heart aching in a good way. This was what I wanted for him. Not emotional abuse and fracture. These people stuck together, for better or for worse.

It was ridiculous now, how terrified I'd been to become part of this.

After a shower, several tests, and lots of fussing from the lovely nurses, I was given permission to find the waiting room. Before I even entered, I could smell the sugar cookies over the scent of disinfectant and hear the chatter of several familiar voices. The Maplewood brigade had arrived. In this town, no matter what the emergency, baked goods were delivered within the hour.

After many hugs and kind smiles, I sat in a large chair, cupping a mug of tea. Vincent and Jasper arrived shortly after, my little guy tugging on his dad's hospital gown and giving everyone his signature gummy smile.

I sipped my tea, my throat aching, so grateful to be here surrounded by all this love and support. The room was full. Too full, really. Josh was perched on the windowsill, boots leaving dusty prints on the tile floor. Jess and Jenn were feeding people while Frankie fussed over Brooks, and Ruby and Paul stood with their arms around each other, looking sleep-deprived but happy.

Olive and Bitsy were here too, grilling Gabe about the investigation and the upcoming fall events calendar while Aunt Suzie and Uncle Ed snapped photos of Jasper and Vincent. Even the nurses popped in, snagging scones and cooing at the babies.

Jasper looked handsome in his hospital clothes. How could he not? He looked good in anything. His hair was damp and sticking up in every direction, his voice rough and his eyes bright. Every few minutes, one of our friends would offer him a cookie. He'd put up a hand and half-heartedly protest, only to take one anyway.

Paul and Ruby shuffled closer. "The whole town is buzzing. The fire's out," Paul said. "But the investigators and insurance folks have descended." He scrolled through his phone, no doubt checking the Maplewood group chats. "And a meal train has already been set up for you three."

Jasper laughed and patted his stomach. "Evie, we may need to put a second fridge in the garage."

I stuck my tongue out at him, though I let the sound of that *we* rattle around in my brain for a bit. We had a lot to figure out, but for now, I was content to enjoy this moment. We were safe and the people I cared about were here. I couldn't ask for more.

"I should beat your ass." Frankie lunged at me and wrapped me in a hug that was half threat, half rescue. "When I heard the reports on the scanner, I almost drove my truck into a ditch."

Jasper blinked at her. "You have access to emergency comms channels?"

Without releasing me, she shot him a dirty look. "If I do, you gonna narc on me to Nolan No Balls?"

Jasper opened his mouth, then shut it. "No."

"I was so worried about you." Frankie's voice softened, but her fingers dug into my elbow like she was wound up tight with worry.

"I'm fine. We're fine," I soothed her, deeply touched by her uncharacteristically emotional behavior.

She took a step back, and as she wiped a tear from her cheek with the back of her hand, she blinked, like she was surprised by her own show of emotion. With a single sniff, she straightened up. "You better stay that way. And if Chief No Balls bothers you or causes you more harm"—her features went hard again, her hands balled into fists—"I will make sure terrible things happen to his patrol car."

With that, she stomped away, though she pulled up short

when Marigold Shaw entered holding a basket of muffins taller than she was.

"This is ridiculous." I scoffed. "It's a potluck with IV bags."

Ruby darted over and plucked a muffin from the basket, then another. She held one out for me and sighed. "It's how we process trauma here," she said. "Carbs and gossip."

"And caffeine," Paul added, bouncing happily with Brooks in his arms.

Jasper sidled up next to me and laced his fingers with mine. The comforting gesture was probably second nature to him, but it made my chest ache all the same. Chaos swirled around us, equal parts laughter and chatter about the fire and what could have happened.

I breathed deeply, letting myself enjoy being cared for like this, relishing the solid weight of Jasper's hand in mine, the quiet pulse of support that beat between us.

I never knew this existed. This kind of kindness. The community. The people who showed up.

When I moved to Maplewood, I'd been looking for something new. A way to break free of the patterns I'd been stuck in for far too long.

I hadn't expected to be adopted by this strange place. Never mind have a baby, buy a house and become a card-carrying Vermonter.

Jasper shifted closer. "You okay?"

My throat tightened. "Yeah. Despite everything, I'm okay."

He tucked a strand of hair behind my ear, the rough pads of his fingers making my skin light up with affection for him. "Good."

In the corner of the room, Frankie sighed loudly. "If you guys start making heart eyes at each other, I'm calling the nurses to separate you."

"Hush," Ruby said. "They've earned a moment." She shoved a muffin into her mouth, then turned our way. "You may resume your PDA."

Jasper and I looked at one another and then at the assembled crowd and burst into laughter. Within seconds, though, we were both coughing.

"This town," Jasper wheezed.

A warm feeling spread through me, and it wasn't just the burning of my charred lungs. It was belonging. I belonged not only in my quirky little circle of friends, but also in this town.

And maybe, finally, with Jasper.

Chapter 40

JASPER

Maplewood never remained quiet for long, but for now, I relished the calm. Evie had gone to her own room to feed Vincent, and Josh and Jenn and I sat in the waiting room, the unspoken elephant settling between us.

I could have died today.

That reality sat in my ribs the way the smell of smoke lingered in a person's clothes. Always there, impossible to ignore. I'd done what I always had. I'd run toward the noise, the danger, the risk. It was instinct after the years I'd spent as a firefighter. But this was different. This time the person needing the rescue mattered more to me than anyone, and that changed the calculus of risk.

I'd do it again. I'd do anything to keep Evie and Vincent safe. But I imagined my siblings looked at the situation through a different lens. After the kinds of losses we've had, that fear was always there. Today could have gone in a totally different direction. But it didn't. I clung to that, because the worry on their faces stirred up a whole storm of guilt inside me. It was the kind of look one only gave the people they loved. It was full of pride and fear and resentment all at once. Questions burned in their eyes, but they knew better than to ask. They knew the answer would only worry them more.

After sunset, the chatter settled into a low murmur, but it quieted further when Chief Ashburn appeared in the doorway, still in her gear, her face serious.

I straightened up. "Chief?"

She gave me a nod, then scanned the room, probably hoping for privacy no one here would willingly give us. "I've got an update. Shall we?"

I stood. Josh did too. He put his arm around my shoulder and helped me to Evie's room.

Inside, Evie sat with a sleeping Vincent in her arms while Frankie and Ruby lingered nearby.

"We can talk here," I said firmly.

Chief Ashburn looked around, her expression one of unease.

"They can stay," I told her. "They're family."

Sighing, she shifted on her feet. "If you're sure."

I shuffled over to Evie and rested a hand on her shoulder.

"We've got an update on the fire," Chief finally said, her voice rough. "There's been an arrest."

All the air left the room. Ruby, halfway through folding a blanket, froze, and beside the chief, Josh went rigid.

"Who?" I asked.

Ashburn crossed her arms and bit down on her lower lip, looking from one of us to the next before finally saying, "Caleb Dunne."

The words landed like a grenade.

Frankie's paper coffee cup slipped from her hand, hitting the floor and sending dark liquid splashing everywhere. "No."

Evie passed Vincent to me and darted for her friend.

Frankie shook her head, half-heartedly fighting Evie's hold, her body trembling. "That's not. He's not. He feeds stray cats and shovels snow for all his elderly neighbors. He —" Her voice cracked. "No, he wouldn't."

Ashburn cleared her throat. "I suggest you head over to the police station," she said, keeping her tone professional. "Your brother is going to need you. I can give you a ride—"

"No." Frankie stomped her foot. "No. This is a mistake."

"He admitted to setting the fire," Ashburn told her, sympathy flashing in her eyes. "Investigation is still unfolding, but we found accelerant traces and his fingerprints on the container."

Frankie clung to Evie, shaking.

"We'll figure this out," Evie said into her hair, her face a mask of sadness.

"I've got to go," Frankie said, freeing herself from her friend's hold.

"We'll drive you," Paul declared.

Dread and fear swirled within me. I'd been so focused on finding Evie that I hadn't given any thought to the cause of the fire.

My gut clenched as they headed toward the door.

Caleb Dunne was a good kid. Sure, he'd had a rough few years, but he'd turned things around. It was hard to imagine him doing this.

My instincts told me Caleb wasn't a threat. He was too caring, too compassionate to put lives in danger like that.

I assessed Josh, who was doing his usual pacing. If I knew him, his brain was working on overdrive, puzzling together the facts and sorting out how all of this was related. If anyone could make sense of it all, it would be him. With his steady, practical questions and calm demeanor.

The moment the door closed behind Frankie and Paul and Ruby, Josh stopped and spun to face us.

"Why?" he asked, the silence he was met with deafening. "Why set that fire? Especially in the afternoon when the building was full of people?"

"There's more." The chief tucked her chin, eyeing her boots. "He said he was trying to destroy records and evidence."

"Evidence of what?"

She cleared her throat. "During questioning, he mentioned Will McManus."

The room went still, and my heart thudded heavily.

"What about him?" Josh asked softly. Will's death and the suspicions about our farm had consumed him for months. He wore the guilt like a noose around his neck.

"He confessed to that too," Chief Ashburn said softly.

Evie gasped.

I staggered back. No. I couldn't have heard correctly.

The walls closed in, the sterile hospital lights too bright and the machines too loud. I reached for Evie's hand, needing an anchor.

"He's at the station, but he'll be transferred to the custody of the state police tonight." She shook her head. "I'm just as confused as you all are."

None of this made sense. Caleb and Will had been friends. Caleb had a loving family and a bright future ahead of him, and while he'd certainly struggled with his mental and physical health, he'd never been violent.

When Frankie heard the rest of this, she would be devastated.

"It doesn't make sense," Josh said.

"Violence never does," Ashburn replied. "But the police will investigate. They'll figure it out. But I wanted to tell you." She eyed Evie, giving her a soft smile. "And I wanted to make sure you were all right."

"Yes," Evie said, her eyes welling with tears. "Thank God for Jasper."

The chief wandered my way and clapped me on the shoulder. "Can't wait to write you up for all of this, Lawrence. Your insubordination alone will make for gripping paperwork."

I looked down at Evie's hand, noting how small it was in comparison to mine, and squeezed. "Worth it."

Chapter 41

EVIE

I wiped sweat from my brow as I admired the deep green canopy. As sunlight filtered through the trees, I was hit with the strange sadness that accompanied the end of summer. The feeling that I should grab it all with two hands before the leaves turned. Before fall and winter descended.

The air smelled like pine sap and river mist, a scent I didn't know existed until a couple of years ago. I took a deep breath, willing my lungs to fill. They still didn't work as well as they used to, but day by day, they were becoming better at sending oxygen into my bloodstream.

Hiking was one of my favorite pre-Vincent activities, though what we were doing today was more of a walk.

Jasper had Vincent in a carrier, a giant floppy sun hat shading our little guy's head. While we'd both been discharged from the hospital after a day, neither of us was working for the moment. Jasper was on leave to recover from his smoke inhalation, and I was waiting for information about what the hell was happening at Sugar Moon.

Louisa had been released and was back at work the day after the fire, but she'd then headed to New York to talk to investors. Our offices were closed for now, and the manufacturing plant had paused operations, leaving the future of the company as well as the future of the hundreds of employees in jeopardy.

So Jasper and I were following the doctor's orders. Fresh air, light exercise, and rest.

As Jasper navigated easily up the trail, I admired the flex of his calf muscles. The sound of the falls was faint, though with every step, it grew louder, like a heartbeat in the distance.

For what had to be the hundredth time, he turned around, checking on me.

"Still here," I chirped.

"You're walking too fast for someone recovering from a near death experience."

I shook my head. Despite his injuries, he'd been babying me nonstop. "Says the man who ran into a burning building."

"For the record, I'd do it again."

Vincent squealed and kicked his legs.

Jasper beamed. "See? He agrees with me."

Before long, the trees opened up to the river, and then finally, to the falls.

"We need a family photo," Jasper said, heading to the overlook point.

I complied, and I couldn't help but smile as he stretched his arm out to capture a picture of the three of us with the thundering waterfall in the background. The water was cold and clean, the chill of the mist welcome in the late August humidity.

For months and months, I'd rolled my eyes anytime someone mentioned Cora and Nathaniel, believing the legend was tragic and silly. Believing they were nothing more than two people doomed by stupidity and bad timing. But I saw it differently now. They'd chosen their own destiny when life had tried to push them away from what they truly wanted. That was the true lesson here.

"Maybe they didn't jump because they wanted to die," I admitted to Jasper.

His eyes flashed with amusement, like he was pleasantly surprised by my admission.

"Maybe they wanted to live without fear. On their terms."

Face splitting into a smile, he held a hand out. "Come on. I'm hungry."

He led me down the back way, along a gently sloping path that curved around the granite hills and deposited hikers at the bottom of the falls. By the time we reached the bottom, we were drenched in sweat and starving.

I laid out the blanket we'd packed, and Jasper opened his backpack, procuring a pouch of plum puree for Vincent and a Basil-approved charcuterie assortment for us.

Vincent, who could now sit up on his own, amused himself by scrunching the blanket in his fists and giggling.

"I still dream about the fire." Jasper's tone was serious, though after he popped a piece of Manchego into his mouth, he grinned.

I rearranged my ponytail and chugged my water. It had only

been two weeks since then, so that was natural. Already, I knew that I'd never forget the details of that day. The fear and the panic, then the relief that came when I saw his face. It wasn't just a memory. It was part of me, mapped in my neurons forever.

"I was terrified," he admitted. "And I still am. The thought of losing you. The sight of you slumped in that corner. The feel of your weak pulse beneath my fingers."

Giving him a sympathetic smile, I grasped his hand. "I'm still processing," I told him. "And there's so much we don't know yet."

My career, my town. It was all floating in the abyss. The unknown. Caleb had been arrested for murder and arson and a list of other horrible crimes. My employer was embroiled in scandal, and most of our offices and records had been destroyed.

When I let myself think about all that, the peace I'd worked so hard to achieve felt like it was slipping away. I was beyond fortunate to have Vincent and Jasper. That was more than enough for now. But the guilt ate at me each time I considered all the ruined lives.

"You can't carry all the broken pieces," Jasper said gently. "You didn't make him light the match. But you survived, and that's enough."

I nod, tears stinging my eyes.

"Shh." He scooted closer and put an arm around me. "Listen to the water and breathe. I've got you."

We sat for a long while, watching the rushing water, playing with Vincent and laughing when he made silly faces, and feeding each other.

The day was one of the best days I'd ever had.

"We should get married," Jasper blurted out after a long, satisfying silence.

Heart lurching, I pushed him away. "Are you crazy?"

His face was completely earnest as he met my eye. "I love you. You and Vincent, you're it for me."

"It's not that simple," I said, nerves skittering through me.

With a shrug, he popped a blueberry into his mouth. "It is, actually. The fire, the mess, it's all in the past. Let's build something out of the ashes. Let's take this chance we've been given and do something amazing."

I wanted to laugh it off. Protest. But I couldn't. Because he was right.

Even so, it was too soon.

"We can't get married."

"We don't have to get married yet if you're not ready. Or ever. Just be mine."

"I am yours," I said.

With a slow smile, he pulled me into his lap. "Good. Because I'm all yours, Evie. Be gentle with me," he said, his voice full of tenderness and vulnerability. "I may seem like a big, tough, manly man, but I have a squishy heart."

He took my hand and placed it against his chest.

My stomach flipped at the sweet gesture. For so long, I'd written this man off as unpredictable, wild, and reckless. But that was so far from the truth. He was steady. He was dependable. And he was, above all else, mine.

Arms draped over his shoulders, I kissed him, reveling in the sensation of his warm lips on mine.

"We just have to choose each other. Every day." He

scooped Vincent up and brought him close, his little baby cheeks damp with drool.

He made it sound so simple. So easy. Like we weren't just neuroses stuffed into skin and walking around trying not to mess everything up.

"Don't overthink."

I sighed. "But—"

"Shh." He put a finger to my lips. "Just say yes."

"What am I agreeing to?"

"Everything and anything." He tightened his hold on us.

I shifted, searching for an appropriate response. Or maybe an argument. But before I could formulate the words, my attention was snagged by the falls.

The spray hitting the rocks caught the sunlight, creating two rainbows over the surface of the water.

I gasped, tears once again threatening. It was maybe the most beautiful thing I'd ever seen.

The falls never stopped. No matter the season or the storm. They changed and adapted, but the water kept moving.

Maybe love was the same. Wild, uncertain, constantly evolving. Beautiful in every way.

The three of us clung to one another, in awe of the sight. And for the first time in forever, I didn't think about what was coming next. I just took a breath of fresh air and enjoyed the miracle unfolding in front of me.

Jasper and I didn't need to leap. We'd already fallen. Together.

Epilogue

JASPER

Two weeks later

Evie smiled at me as we walked with Josh through the stand of juvenile trees. Vincent was happily asleep on my chest in his carrier, his little body sweaty against mine. I loved it. This time with my son was one of life's greatest gifts.

Before long, the leaves would turn and we'd begin harvesting. Given all the uncertainty with Sugar Moon, we couldn't afford to slack. I'd been here daily. We'd been in crisis mode, making sure everything was documented and taken care of.

But today, I was here on a special mission.

Wayne, who had been lazily trailing behind Josh, let out a squeak and stopped, his ears perking. When he started to bark, the rest of us stopped too.

"What is it?" Josh frowned down at the dog. Most dogs barked at anything and everything, but not Wayne. He was weirdly calm until he wasn't.

Wayne walked in a circle once, then again, then bolted down the hill toward the equipment barn.

Wiping his brow, Josh followed. "If Betsy Ross got into the feed shed again, I swear I'm gonna shoot her and make a fucking rug."

Evie gasped. I only laughed. Josh talked a big game, but he was a softie. He'd planted a damn blackberry bramble on the north side years ago specifically for her.

We followed him down the hill and through the tree canopy. As the full farm came into view, so did a couple of cars at the guest house.

Wayne was now circling one of our giant tractors. And in the cab of that tractor was an unfamiliar little boy with a mop of dark hair.

He was barefoot, and it looked as though he was planning to take the piece of heavy machinery for a joyride. He wasn't just flipping switches and pulling at the steering wheel. He was studying the panel in front of him, like he was actually contemplating how to drive it. This kid couldn't be more than seven, yet I was pretty sure he was attempting to hot wire a tractor.

"Hey," Josh barked. "Get out of there. That's dangerous."

The boy didn't even look up. He was completely focused on the machinery.

Wayne sat on the ground next to the cab, his tail wagging, delighted by his new friend.

My stomach sank as Josh stormed that way. Shit. My brother wasn't exactly known for his gentle manner with strangers, so this was about to go sideways quick.

"Hey," Josh said. "You can't—"

"Julian," a high, panicked voice called out.

In the next second, a woman was running full speed down the path, wild red hair flying, jean shorts half zipped, and a lacy black bra but no shirt. With a pair of sparkly pink Crocs in her hand, the glitter catching the sunlight like disco balls.

"Holy hell," Evie whispered.

Josh whipped around, his eyes widening when he saw her.

She darted for the tractor, her arms out.

Dutifully, the boy climbed down and jumped into her arms.

She hugged him tight, her eyes closed, then set him on the ground and checked him over for injuries.

"You scared the life out of me." She looked over her shoulder at Josh. "He didn't break anything, did he? Is he hurt?"

Josh blinked, looking thrown by the hurricane that had blown onto his farm. "He's fine. Just curious."

She let out a big breath and closed her eyes again. Then she bent at the waist and kissed the top of his head. "Next time I'll have to put these in sport mode before chasing you." She dropped the Crocs to the ground and wedged her feet into them.

Hands on his hips, Josh scrutinized her, his expression a mix of fear and fascination. "Sport mode?"

She stood, shoulders back, meeting his eyes without a shred of shame. She was small. Barely five foot. She looked like a tiny fairy sprite, but in this moment, she carried herself like a mafia enforcer. "You know, flip the back strap down.

Ready for action." She held out a foot, the glitter catching the light. "Emergency mom gear."

Evie leaned in close, whispering, "I like her."

Josh, on the other hand, looked like he'd swallowed a live wire. "Who are you and why are you trespassing on my farm?"

Brows raised, she pulled her son close. "I'm moving into the cottage up the road."

"You're the new tenant?" My brother scoffed. "You're not set to move in until tomorrow."

The woman lifted her chin, defiant. "We came early."

Josh roughed a hand down his face. He wasn't known for being flexible. "But I haven't given you the keys to unlock the house."

"Was it locked?" she asked, her head tilted. "Didn't notice. Anyway, we're here now."

"But—"

"I signed the lease last week, and you cashed the check I sent. So how about you give me the keys so we can both get on with our days?"

Her expression was sharp, cunning, but as she turned to us, it morphed into the sweetest smile.

She was still standing before us in a bra and shorts, yet she didn't seem the least bit embarrassed by her state of undress.

Her demeanor was at complete odds with my brother's. He was stammering, the parts of his cheek visible above his thick beard flaming.

"I'm Celine LeBlanc." She held out a hand to Josh.

On autopilot, he took it, though he didn't introduce himself.

She turned to Evie next, then me, greeting us the same way.

"I'm Jasper, Josh's brother," I said. "And this is Evie and Vincent."

"Do you run around half dressed often?" Josh growled, disdain dripping from his voice.

Most people would tuck tail and run in response to that tone, but Celine was unflappable.

And I was doing my best not to break into laughter at my brother's expense.

With her arm at her side, she stretched out her fingers, and the little boy slid his palm against hers.

"We've been unloading boxes. I'd planned to change into clean clothes before introducing myself to the landlord." She eyed him up and down. "But Julian ran off, so I didn't quite finish."

"Ma'am," Josh said.

She flinched.

God, he was digging his own grave at this point.

"You can't just let your kid wander around a working farm," he gritted out. "He could get hurt."

Her head snapped up. "You think I just let him?" She gently wrapped an arm around her son and pulled him closer. "This is Julian."

Evie gave him a friendly wave, and Vincent kicked his feet.

"He's autistic," she went on. "You got a problem with that?"

Josh's eyes widened. "No."

"Good." She huffed. "When he gets anxious or overwhelmed, he elopes." She studied Josh, probably noting the confusion on his face. "He runs away. We're working on it, but today has been a big day."

Josh's jaw flexed, tension radiating off him. Wayne, his ever-faithful companion, brushed up against his side and nudged his hand with his nose.

With a long breath out, my brother dropped his gaze. "Sorry. Didn't mean to cause offense. I was just worried."

She crossed her arms, but I looked away, not interested in seeing what the move would do to her bra-clad breasts. "We came a day early," she said, "so we'd have a little more time to settle in."

Julian dropped his mom's hand and shuffled over to Wayne, burying his face in his fur.

"I'm glad you made a friend, Jules," Celine said. "Now we have to get back to the house and put your racecar bed together."

"I can help," Josh said, taking a step forward.

She scoffed, as if the idea of accepting his help was laughable. "I have tools. I'm good."

She turned to Evie and me, that smile returning. "It was nice to meet you. Sorry for the wardrobe malfunction. He's fast."

"Welcome to Maplewood," Evie said, a bright smile spreading across her face. "Are you the new kindergarten teacher?"

Celine smiled. "Yes. School starts on Tuesday. I've got a lot to do between now and then, but I've heard great things about this town."

"We live in town," I explained. "But I'm sure we'll see you around. This is my family farm. Josh runs things and lives in the big white farmhouse."

Celine assessed Josh again, seemingly unimpressed by his scowl. "Reclusive, grumpy farmer, huh? I can see it. You look like a man who yells at clouds."

Julian giggled.

Josh made a sound somewhere between a grunt and a laugh. "You always introduce yourself like that?"

"Only when I'm half dressed and accused of negligence," she shot back. Then, softening a bit, she added. "We'll stay out of your way."

She took Julian's hand again and walked off, sparkly Crocs flashing with every step.

Josh watched her go. And I watched him watch her.

Evie elbowed me, wearing a grin, and I winked at her. What had we just witnessed?

Grumbling about keys and paperwork, Josh took off toward his house.

When it was just the three of us, we resumed our walk.

"What are the odds Josh falls madly in love with Sport Mode Tinkerbell?" Evie asked, uncapping her water bottle.

"Zero," I said. "He's too damn repressed. He'd rather wrestle Betsy Ross than admit he's lonely."

"I'm not sure." She linked her arm through mine, the move causing me to catch a whiff of her sweet scent.

"This is Josh we're talking about," I said as we headed up the east hill. "The man is more comfortable talking to trees than women. Your expectations are too high."

"I think there's a spark there," she murmured as we wandered past the greenhouses. "At the risk of sounding like one of those women so madly in love that they want to pair people up like the animals on Noah's Ark—"

I pulled her to a stop and kissed her, careful not to squish the baby between us. "You're madly in love?"

She huffed a laugh. "You gonna make me say it?"

I rubbed my hands together and bounced on my toes. "Yes. Declare yourself, woman."

Hands on her hips, she shook her head, but she was smiling.

"Jasper Lawrence," she said. "I am madly in love with you. Obsessed, really."

My chest warmed. So did my cheeks. Pulling her close, I kissed her again. "And I think you're okay." I bopped her on the nose, then headed up the grassy hill.

"You asshole," she shrieked behind me.

When we reached the top of the hill, I put my arm around her and breathed in the fresh scent. The air was slightly cooler up here, the valley spread out before us.

"What are we looking at?" she asked, scanning the fields and trees in front of us.

"This is where I'm gonna build our house." I turned to her, nervousness mixing with my excitement. "If you want me to. A spot that's all ours on the farm. Because I plan to love you for the rest of my life. A home for Vincent and any other kids or animals we collect along the way."

"Jasper..."

"I'm not asking for it all today," I told her. "Just showing you my long-term plan. Because I don't just want your today, Evie. I want all your tomorrows too."

Bonus Chapter

JASPER

Want to see more Jasper, Evie and Vincent? Grab the Bonus Chapter HERE:

Scan Me

Acknowledgments

Thank you for visiting Maplewood! I hope you have had as much fun reading this book as I had writing it.

All of my characters have pieces of me inside them. But Evie has more than most. From her PCOS struggles, to her family challenges, to her fierce independence, she and I have a lot in common. And writing her and watching her open up to and accept Jasper's love was healing for me. I hope you can connect with her journey.

Like all my books, it would not have been possible without the support of several talented and dedicated people.

Erica Walsh, this book is for you. Two years ago you came up with this idea. A secret baby that was also a secret from the mother. Your support and love means so much to me. I love you, appreciate you, and can't wait to finally meet you in person this year. From cover design to finding photos and editing blurbs, you are truly in my corner every single day. Your Instagram wizardry is incredible. We have cried and laughed and yelled together over the past four years, and I am a better person and writer because of you. Thank you from the bottom of my hear.

Morgan Leigh, I asked for help, and you jumped in with both feet, quickly becoming the MVP in my life and the person who keeps me organized and on track. I treasure your friendship and your positive attitude. No one is more willing and more capable of learning new things than you are, and I am pinching myself that I get to call you mine.

Beth, thank you for your thorough editing. I am amazed by your patience, professionalism, and kindness. Your careful work has helped bring these characters to life, and I am truly in your debt.

Nina and Summer, thank you for joining me on this wild ride. Your support means so much to me.

To my oldest friend, the indomitable Caroline, thank you for igniting my love of romance by introducing me to Jane Austen (and Colin Firth in a wet shirt) at the tender age of fifteen. My entire romantic worldview has been shaped by our shared love of happy endings and your friendship for these last twenty-eight (!!!) years is a true gift. You push me to grow and evolve and help me edit in airports. You are the best.

Becca, thank you for your professionalism and excitement about this series. You and the Author Agency have been such wonderful partners throughout this process.

To my content and hype teams, thank you from the bottom of my heart for loving these books and this crazy world I've created. Most days, I pinch myself that I'm surrounded by such an amazing group of positive, kickass people.

Thank you to my family for being hilarious, loving, and silly. To my children, G & T, you push me, challenge me, and surprise me every day. Being your mom is my life's greatest adventure. Thank you for never going easy on me. To G, my mini-me, you are my #1 fan and I can't wait to share my author journey with you as you grow. And T, thank you for kicking ass in first grade, so I had the mental and physical energy to write this book.

Thank you to my mother. Who is my best friend, my confidant, and the person responsible for my work ethic. You've taught me how to love, to nurture and to kick ass when necessary.

And finally, I'd like to thank Taylor Alison Swift. For getting me through not only the production of this book, but through all of my life's challenges for the past decade. You have taught me, and countless others, how to harness my creativity and, most importantly, how to invest in my potential. Your work has made me a better mom, writer, entrepreneur, and person. Thank you.

Also by Daphne Elliot

MAPLEWOOD

Sap & Secrets

Maple & Moonlight

LOVEWELL

The Maine Lumberjacks Series

Caught In The Axe

Pain In The Axe

Axe-identally Married

Axe Backwards

Axe-ing for Trouble

The Lovewell Lumberjacks Series

Wood You Be Mine?

Wood You Marry Me?

Wood You Rather

Wood Riddance

Also by Daphne Elliot

THE MOM COMS

Mother Hater

THE DAD COMS

Bonus Daddy

HAVENPORT

The Quinn Brothers Series

Trusting You

Finding You

Keeping You

The Rossi Family Series

Resisting You

Holding You

Embracing You

About the Author

In High School, Daphne Elliot was voted "most likely to become a romance novelist." After spending the last decade as a corporate lawyer, she has finally embraced her destiny. Her small town steamy novels are filled with flirty banter, sexy hijinks, and lots and lots of heart.